Elizabeth Evelyn Allen

Rebel

WARNER BOOKS

A Warner Communications Company

WARNER BOOKS EDITION

Warner Books, Inc.
666 Fifth Avenue
New York, N.Y. 10103

Cover art by Pino Daeni

 A Warner Communications Company

Printed in the United States of America

First Printing: November, 1985

10 9 8 7 6 5 4 3 2 1

JAMIE WAS SITTING UP IN BED
WAITING FOR HER...

He made no move to rise and help Marsh walk those long fifteen feet to the side of his bed. Silently she slipped off her robe and stood for a small breathless moment before she climbed into his bed. He made no move to touch her.

"Are you sure, Marsh?"

"Yes, Jamie."

"Even though there is a big difference between our ages?"

"The only thing between us right now," she whispered tersely, "is that ridiculous night shirt you're wearing."

The laughter rolled from his chest, releasing those taut bonds of tension that had gripped him since he'd held her on the dance floor. Only then did he turn off the light and remove the objectionable garment. Gently he put his arms around her.

"Angus told me you're untouched, Marsh."

"Does it matter, Jamie?"

"No, I'd want you even if I knew you'd worked for a madame. Are you afraid?"

"No, Jamie, not now." Turning toward him she placed her hands on the sides of his face and touched his lips with hers. Then she relaxed and let the warm feeling of being loved take over her consciousness. He felt the stirrings of her body as she pressed against him, but he willed himself to wait. Then he felt his control slipping as the unleashed desire pounded through his body . . .

* * *

"Highest rating, five gold stars! A gifted new author with gifts of insight . . . . Loved that heroine Marsh!"
 —*Barbra Critiques*

Also by Elizabeth Evelyn Allen

THE LADY ANNE

Published by
WARNER BOOKS

PROLOGUE
1786

"Oui, madame, they are all here in the strongbox." The voice of the maid was as colorless and unmemorable as her face. Sitting beside the flustered Lady Wetherall in the swaying carriage, she patiently soothed the fears of her mistress.

"Even my pearls, Lili?"

"Oui, madame."

"Did we remember the key?"

"Oui, madame, it is on the chain you're wearing."

Seeking reassurance, Lady Wetherall fingered the fine gold chain about her neck. "Traveling makes me nervous. So many evil people in the world, Lili," she complained.

"Madame, this is England. We're no longer in dangerous foreign places," Lili reassured her employer.

The Wetheralls were just now returning from a three-year stint on Gibraltar where Lord Wetherall had replaced General Sir George Eliott as commander of the British artillery there. Gibraltar had been a peaceful colony during the Wetherall's stay, in sharp contrast to the earlier five years when Spain had waged a vicious war to regain the fortified tip of its national boundaries. But even so, the unfriendly attitudes of Spain and France had increased Lady Wetherall's nervousness. The years had done little to upset her placid husband, however, except to increase his alcohol consumption. At the moment he was sleeping noisily on the carriage seat opposite his wife and her maid, a rest necessitated by the final shipboard celebration with the six officers who had returned to England with him.

Gazing at her husband with a fond tolerance, Lady Wetherall continued her questioning, "And the money his lordship won at cards, Lili?"

"In the strongbox, madame. You counted it yourself and locked it in."

"So I did, Lili." Irritably now, Lady Wetherall looked out of the tiny window of the rented carriage at the misty English countryside between Portsmouth and Reigate. "I'd forgotten that England was so dreary," she sighed, "and this is such a drafty carriage."

"It was the best the livery stable had, madame."

"I know, Lili, but still I would have preferred one of our own to meet us. It was odd that none of the letters we sent instructing our people to meet us brought any response. You did mail them, Lili, didn't you?"

"Oui, madame, months ago."

Lady Wetherall sighed again. "I guess you were lucky to find this carriage available and a driver. He seems competent enough with the horses. Did we remember to send a rider ahead to make our reservations at the Horsham Inn, Lili?"

"Oui, madame, he left the dock two hours before we did."

"You're a good servant, Lili. Three months ago when my faithful Thelma died so suddenly, I despaired of finding any lady's maid at all on that desolate rock; but you showed up like a miracle and took over. How lucky we were that your previous mistress had departed so unexpectedly and left you behind."

During the last minutes the carriage had slowed down appreciably, and Lord Wetherall awoke and demanded grumpily, "Where the hell are we and where's my bottle?"

Always the flawless servant she had been for three months in their employ, Lili was already pouring him a glass of wine which he readily accepted. "Would madame also care for a glass?" Lili asked politely.

As if making a momentous decision, Lady Wetherall arched her bird-like head to one side. "Why yes, I would, Lili. It might help to ward off the cold." She accepted the offering and sipped daintily.

Ten minutes later the Wetheralls were both dead; and at a signal from the expressionless maid, the driver pulled the four horses to a stop. With unruffled composure, Lili stepped down from the carriage, carrying the bottle and glasses, and spoke to the two dragoons who were riding guard on the footman's perch.

"Monsieurs, Lord Wetherall thought you might like a glass of wine," she said in her usual flat, soft voice. With practiced skill she poured them generous amounts and handed each soldier a glass.

An hour later, four naked bodies had been weighted with stones and shoved unceremoniously into the muddiest waters of the sluggish Arum River, and the trunks stripped of all valuables and thrown into the river with the dead owners. Efficiently, the driver turned the carriage around and raced the horses back toward Portsmouth while the calm woman inside the conveyance repacked the purloined wealth into nondescript suitcases. Ten hours after Lord Wetherall had accepted the glass of poisoned wine, Louise and William Ryder boarded a Portuguese merchant ship bound for Lisbon. Mrs. Ryder's sparse figure was well disguised by four dresses and two cloaks which had once been part of the expensive wardrobe of Lady Wetherall. During the six-day voyage to the capital Iberian city, the drab couple attracted no attention from the Portuguese crewmen since they remained secluded in their cabin the entire time. In the teaming port city of Lisbon, they again avoided any undue interest by disembarking quietly and blending into the teaming multi-lingual crowds of the waterfront.

One entire day elapsed before the three artillery officers and the one dragoon messenger staying at the Horsham Inn thought to notify the authorities about the missing Wetheralls. But by that time a heavy rain had obliterated all signs of unusual activity along the banks of the Arum River. When the constable in charge sought a description of Lady Wetherall's maid, he questioned all four witnesses, whose testimonies agreed on the fact that she was ordinary looking but on nothing else. After months of futile investigation, the case joined thousands of others in the national archives marked "unsolved."

During the year, the Ryders lived in Lisbon in dingy quarters in the oldest part of the city. Louise Ryder produced a wizened son, Joseph; William Ryder scoured the countryside buying fifty of the finest pureblood Arabian horses he could locate. While he was thus employed, his wife cautiously sold most of the Wetherall jewels and three suitcases full of other accumulated valuables, one at a time to the hundreds of no-questions-asked dealers of Lisbon. With fine, housewifely stitches, she sewed the gold coins neatly into the linings of her four dresses. At the end of the year the hard-working couple booked second class passage on an American merchant ship bound for Baltimore, Maryland, and, with their infant son and the fifty horses, endured an uneventful voyage to their new homeland where both of them prospered. William established a horse breeding farm near the nation's capital, and Louise opened a small money lending business in a run-down commercial building in Baltimore. Although William's profits from the sale of horses over his thirty years on the farm were exceptional, Louise's financial success was phenomenal; and she lived long enough to establish her son as one of the respected bankers of that thriving city.

Chapter
1

The white girl worked with the same easy rhythm of the dozen negroes pulling the long golden-red carrots from the rich loamy soil. One efficient pull, a quick shake to dislodge the loose dirt, a twist of the lacy green tops, and the carrot was tossed into one basket and the greens into another. As soon as the baskets were full, other workers carried them to waiting wagons, dumping the carrots into one and shoving the greens into the rabbit hutches piled high on the second. The girl and her fellow gatherers worked steadily without changing the fluid pattern of their labor.

James MacKenzie watched her with much of the same mixed emotions he had held for this particular girl for half a dozen years—part admiration for the willpower that had driven her ever since she had started to work for him, part amusement at her determinedly masculine garb, and part low-key desire for the girl whose beauty had become such an obvious reality after the years of promise. As he gazed at her now, he recalled his dramatic introduction to Pamela Marshall

Creighton six years earlier. Her hair had been redder than the fire-kissed auburn it was today. And her temper had been hotter, too. On his first real tour of the property that had become his on the death of his partner a year earlier, MacKenzie was riding leisurely by the cottage which served as plantation office when his ears were assaulted by a piercing scream. Dismounting quickly, he hurried inside to witness a scene that would remain forever imprinted on his memory. Standing in a position of total defiance was a sproutish girl of thirteen, her hazel-green eyes blazing with hot anger and her still childish lips articulating words of scornful hatred. Clutched in one of her hands and wrapped around her palm was the working end of a slave whip.

"You can't make me cry again, white trash, no matter what you do," she screamed at the other occupant of the room.

James MacKenzie's first impulse was to smile. There was something infinitely appealing about the red-faced defiance of the slim girl child. However, this gentler response changed rapidly to cold anger as his eyes slid down her slender body where thin lines of blood were already seeping through the cotton of the dress plastered against her immature hips. The muscles of his jaw tightened as he gently took the whip from the girl's hand and unwound the several coils of harsh leather, noting as he did that it had been shaped with a cruel, razor sharp cutting edge on one side. As he tried to seat the trembling girl, she cried out in agony. Still without glancing at the man, MacKenzie called over his shoulder to the young black boy standing just outside the open office door on the porch.

"Jeb, ride my horse down to the paddock and tell Dr. Damon and Carina to come here on the double with their whip medicines. And tell them to bring Josh with them." Briefly, he watched as the boy mounted the horse and rode swiftly off before turning back toward the girl. Neither she nor her tormentor had moved. Still ignoring the man, James spoke to the girl, his deep baritone voice with its faint

Scot's burr breaking the tense silence of the room. "What's your name, lass?"

"Marsh."

Quizzically, his eyebrow lifted and a faint smile softened the severity of his handsome face. "Marsh what, lass?"

"Just Marsh."

For the first time the third occupant of the room spoke, his tone belying the accepted idea that a southern gentleman's voice is pleasantly slurred and musical. His voice held a disagreeable, angry rasp which grated on the Scot's ears. "Her name is Pamela Creighton, and this impudent jade is my disgraceful daughter."

Angered still further by this revelation that a father could so callously whip a daughter, MacKenzie turned toward the speaker with contempt. Slowly, his narrowed blue eyes swept the dandily dressed man who stood there, still grasping the stock of the murderous whip. The slender man was short, only an inch or two taller than the girl. His facial coloring was a pallid tan, his small deep-set eyes a pale gray, and his straight hair an ash brown. MacKenzie's eyes were speculative as he looked away from the man toward the vividly colored girl with her bright hair, beautiful large hazel-green eyes and mobile lips now curled into an expression of angry scorn.

"You're Blake Creighton then?" MacKenzie identified the man with a cold assurance and glanced down at the end of the whip he still held in his hand. Raising it slightly, he commented with a deceptive casualness, "When I acquired this property several months ago, I gave orders that there was never to be a whip of any description used on the premises. You were not present during that interview, but I left specific instructions. Would you care to explain your possession of this very interesting weapon, Mr. Creighton?"

With the arrogance of a Southerner for what he considered Yankee ignorance, Creighton snapped, "I've run this place for twenty years, MacKenzie. Nigger slaves understand only one—"

"The blacks of MacKenzie Farm were freed the day Joseph Ryder and I took possession five years ago."

"Freed or not, niggers obey only if you put the fear of punishment into them. You left a hell of a lot of instructions, MacKenzie, when you ordered this plantation changed from cotton to pasture land for horses. You try making niggers who've shuffled along picking cotton for years into fence post diggers. Well, I got the job done for you, but only with the use of these," he indicated the two pistols strapped by his sides, "and this," he raised the butt of the whip.

"And lost me a good twenty workers in the process," the Scot admonished softly. "Now about this beating of your daughter," he prodded.

"She knows why."

"Marsh?" Briefly, the girl's tense features relaxed at MacKenzie's use of her preferred name.

"Mr. Creighton," her voice sharpened as she spat the hated name out, "tried to use this thing on Adah."

"Adah?"

"She's the cook in the big house and my only friend there. She was just trying to protect me from him."

"Your grandfather allows his house servants to be whipped, does he?"

"My grandfather," again her voice reflected the open contempt of an outraged child for an imperfect adult, "is too drunk most of the time to know what goes on anywhere."

Before MacKenzie could question Marsh further, an elegantly tall man entered. Though his skin was a gleaming black, he had the aristocratically sculptured features of an Englishman. His dark eyes flicked with disdain over the short Southerner and came to rest with infinite compassion on the girl.

"Hello, Marsh," he greeted her in the cultured tones of an English gentleman and laid his tapered, capable hand on her hair. Turning to the woman who had entered with him, he nodded briefly. His slim, golden-skinned companion had the carriage of an Egyptian queen as she moved quickly to put her arm around the waist of the now shaking girl. Firmly, she led her toward the rear rooms.

"Are there beds back there, Carina?" MacKenzie asked.

The golden-skinned woman smiled and her glance flickered over the silent Southerner. "Oh yes, Jamie, there are beds," she murmured musically with an educated irony that bespoke her hatred more clearly than a sneer. "Mr. Creighton often requires the services of black women."

Carina moved with a sinuous grace as she opened the door and half-carried the girl into the dimly lit rear quarters; but the silence she left behind deepened until it became a tangible oppression, broken only when the now grim-faced Southerner attempted to leave the office. At his first furtive step toward the open office door, MacKenzie's voice, free from even a tinge of Scot burr and crisply commanding, snapped out, "Not yet, Creighton. You'll remain here until Dr. Damon examines your daughter."

Furiously, the small man sputtered, "I won't let that nigger horse doctor put his hands on my daughter."

"Dr. Damon is an expert in both human and animal medicine." MacKenzie's voice was deceptively calm, but his dark blue eyes glittered as he watched the Southerner's hand move toward the handle of one of his guns. "You touch that gun, Creighton, and you're a dead man. Josh, would you step inside, please?" The black man who entered now had none of the servile characteristics of a slave. He held his rifle with the expertise of a man who enjoyed hunting.

"Josh is one of my men who will take over guard duty in the future," MacKenzie explained lightly. "He has served in that capacity for ten years on the Maryland farm." The Scotsman's smile was cynically controlled as he watched Creighton's hand move swiftly away from his pistol handle. "Damon, I imagine that Carina is ready for you now."

MacKenzie's eyes never left the small man as he waited for

the doctor to leave the room. "Sit down, Creighton, we have several minutes to wait before I accompany you back to the house. Jeb," he called out again to the black boy who was once more standing outside on the porch, his young face alive with curiosity, "run over to the big house and ask the cook to come here."

"What the hell, MacKenzie," Creighton sputtered, "you have nothing to say about anyone there. You don't own a damn thing in that house."

"True, but the house servants were freed at the same time as the field hands."

"You try messing with Sophia Randall's possessions and you'll need a lot more than gunmen like your trained nigger here," the smaller man sneered.

"The cook is no longer a possession and my sister-in-law is no fool. She'll be reasonable when I explain what I have in mind."

Uneasy now to the point of fidgeting, the Southerner drummed his fingers nervously on the desk top with the impatient restlessness of a cornered man. With a desperate energy, he sought to change the focus of conversation. "Would you want to check the books while you're waiting, MacKenzie?"

"No, I'll wait for Angus."

"Angus?"

"My bookkeeper."

"I don't appreciate having a Yankee flunky messing around my books, MacKenzie."

The Scot's smile was frosty. "I'm sure you don't. Incidentally, Angus has been working on the books for the better part of the past week."

"How the hell—" Creighton yanked the drawers of his desk open.

"Jake removed them a week ago. You know Jake, don't you Creighton? The man I assigned to foreman the fence crew?"

"Ignorant nigger. He ran off with the others."

10

"Only as far as the Maryland farm after you forgot to pay the workers their wages two weeks ago."

"Wages, hell, MacKenzie! What does a nigger need wages for? They got their maintenance."

"My orders were for specific wages to be paid. That's why I told the bank officials in Alexandria to impound the money you deposited in your own account last week. Even Virginia bankers take a dim view of embezzlement."

"Embezzlement, hell! I earned that money carrying out the changes you wanted."

"Angus will determine the amount due you." MacKenzie looked up as Dr. Damon reentered the office. "Is the girl all right?"

"She has three very deep cuts. One reopened a wound from an earlier beating. Her hip muscles will require bed rest to heal properly. But even with the best of care, she'll carry the scars the rest of her life, and she'll need someone to take care of her this time until she recovers."

No one had noticed the middle-aged woman standing quietly outside on the porch. "I'm Adah," she announced quietly. "I'll take care of Miss Marsh, suh. I have before all the other times that white trash man done beat her."

"Has he beaten her often?"

"Yes, suh, he done whup her ever since her grandmother died. He even whup Jake onct when Jake tried to stop him."

"My foreman?"

"Jake's my husband, suh. Him and me has done our best to keep her safe, but that trash done whup her anyway."

MacKenzie smiled at the matter-of-fact courage of the woman; he liked the steady, unafraid look of her eyes and her bluntness. "Good, Adah. I've decided to move into the cottage next door for a few months. Would you like to work for me full time?"

"Yes, suh, I surely would 'ceptin' I'll want to stay with Miss Marsh back at the big house."

"She won't be going back there for at least a month. Am I right, Damon?"

A brief smile lighted the doctor's face. "As usual, Jamie, you're right. She can't be moved." His smile deepened as he moved out the door and down the steps without a glance at the white-faced man glaring at him from behind the desk.

Twenty minutes later in the shabbily elegant second parlor of the large Randall mansion, MacKenzie waited with stoic patience for the family to gather. Although he had been an "in-law" since Sophia Ryder Flint had married Clinton Randall five years earlier, he had never visited in their home. In the past hour he had met two of the three family members he had not known before, and now his curiosity extended to only one unknown person—the wife of Blake Creighton and the mother who had produced the extraordinarily colorful child now under James MacKenzie's protection. His sister-in-law Sophia he'd known for fourteen years and disliked almost as much as he had hated her sister Helen, his late, unlamented wife. Sophia's husband he knew almost equally well, the charming fifty-seven-year-old Virginia gentleman whose penchant for gambling had lost him his family estate.

Sophia and Randall were the first of his hosts to arrive. As usual, the affable Clinton was smiling graciously, his hand extended in greeting.

"May I get you a drink, suh?" he asked as he moved to the heirloom liquor cabinet and poured a generous portion of bourbon for himself. MacKenzie's refusal did not daunt the older man's pleasure as he seated himself beside his wife on the velvet covered settee. "'M' dear," he suggested to his unsmiling wife, "perhaps James would prefer tea?"

Sophia, though, had no intention of making this unwanted intrusion into a family social hour. She looked sourly at her brother-in-law and cursed him silently for her sister's untimely death three years earlier. He hasn't aged a day, she thought bitterly as she studied the curly dark hair which still contained no strands of gray. She resented his leanly muscular figure

12

and the strong, good looking face which had made him the target of half the society queens of Baltimore.

"Well, James," she reproved coldly, "what was it you wanted to see me about? Blake told me that you were on some kind of angry rampage."

"Not over you, Sophia, never over you." His Scot's burr was once again pronounced and his smile ironically broad. "I brought the final papers for you to sign regarding the division of this property. You now own this house, the six acres surrounding it, and a twenty-foot right-of-way to the dock."

"Of course I own it, James. I have for five years. And until I read my father's will, I thought I owned the rest of the land, too." She held up her hand as if to ward off his protest. "I won't waste my time arguing with you. However you persuaded my father to divide it, I am assured you were relentlessly legal. You're a canny Scot, James MacKenzie, and I imagine, a very wealthy one by this time. Is this where I sign?" she asked abruptly.

Something about her businesslike aggressiveness amused the Scot; she resembled her dead father intensely at that moment with her protuberant blue eyes and pursed mouth. Without a pause, she continued with her calm, assured questions. "Has the bank's lawyer determined yet what my annual income will be?"

Her brother-in-law's voice became even more burred with irony. "Aye, you'll have a goodly income for life, Sophia; and at your death, the principal and this house will revert to your heirs."

"Heir," she corrected him sharply, "Janet is my only heir."

As if on cue, Janet flounced into the room, and with only the curtest of nods to her uncle, launched into a complaint. "Mother, did you know that Adah was not in the kitchen? And that Uncle James sent for her a while ago?"

MacKenzie, who had risen politely as the petulant young woman entered the room, greeted her. "Hello, Janet. You're right. I did send for Adah and she accepted my offer for another position.''

As the girl spun around in a fury to confront him, he smilingly reseated himself and studied the changes the last five years had made in this twenty-two-year-old whom he had considered as unattractive as all the other Ryder women. Although she was the prettiest of the lot, her features were too heavy for beauty and her light blue eyes too bold for feminine allure. Briefly, he wondered about the aristocratic young Carolinian she had snagged as her fiancé after one of the most expensive coming-out balls in Virginia history. The large dowry that her doting Grandfather Ryder had settled on her probably accounted for some of the conquest, but not all. As far as MacKenzie could determine, Wayne Talbot was not a pauper. Furthermore, he was better connected socially than the Randall family had ever been. Prejudiced by a bitter eleven-year marriage to another Ryder woman, James failed to note that Janet was amply endowed with ripe curves and that she had learned to use them effectively. But at the moment her face had settled into a mulish pattern of anger.

"Mother, will you kindly explain to my uncle''—the contempt in her voice was strident—"that I'm being married in four months and that Adah has already been instructed about her duties for that event.''

"I'm sure you and your mother will find a replacement, Janet,'' MacKenzie said blandly.

Sophia took up the challenge. "Why should we, James? Adah is our cook and will remain so.''

"I think not, Sophia. Her services are needed elsewhere. Marsh met with an—accident today and will be cared for by Adah in the office cottage.'' He turned to see what kind of an effect his announcement had on Clinton Randall. But that amazingly indifferent grandfather was busy pouring his third glass of bourbon. Turning his attention back to Sophia, MacKenzie noted her pursed-up mouth and the knowing glint in her eyes. Sophia, he decided, understood the nature of the girl's injury. However, any comment of hers was delayed by the arrival of Blake Creighton, whose hand clutched the arm of the only beautiful woman in the house.

"Mr. MacKenzie," Creighton intoned the introduction ungraciously, "my wife Melissa."

A devout student of beautiful women, the Scot moved quickly across the room to kiss the lady's hand. As Blake released his wife's arm, MacKenzie noted the angry red marks left on the woman's skin. After he had gallantly seated her close to his own chair, he studied the mother of the flame-tressed girl he had rescued earlier and decided that the girl resembled this parent as little as she did her father. Whereas the girl's face was strong and her coloring vivid, Melissa's features were delicate, with soft brown eyes and silkily curled dark gold hair. At the moment, however, the woman's beauty was marred by an expression of anxious unhappiness.

Now that the group was assembled, MacKenzie wasted no time in idle conversation. Dramatically, he held up the whip for inspection.

"This particular whip is one which is seldom used in America today, except perhaps in the slave pens of Mississippi. Its purpose is to terrorize and cripple. In view of your father's expressed wishes, Sophia, I'm surprised that its use was permitted in your home." He watched their reactions carefully. Janet was bored, Clinton concentrated his attention on his drink, Melissa closed her eyes in agony, and Creighton glared at the speaker. Only Sophia responded verbally.

"I hadn't the faintest notion of its existence, James; I do not allow my servants to be beaten."

"Don't you, Sophia? How about your husband's granddaughter?" Again he watched their reactions with interest, listening with pity to Melissa's choking sobs. "Today I stopped a brutal beating her father was administering. Until she recovers completely, Marsh,"—he stressed the name deliberately—"will be under my protection. For the next three months I will take over the personal management of this farm." Coldly, he concentrated his attention on the former overseer. "Mr. Creighton, as of this moment you no longer have any connection with the MacKenzie Farm. Whether I am in residence or not, you are not to set foot on my property."

In red-faced fury, the small man leaped to his feet. "On what grounds, MacKenzie? On what grounds am I dismissed?"

"On the basis of the protests of twenty of my valued employees. And because I have no intention of being robbed as your father-in-law was for fifteen years and as Joseph Ryder was for five." The Scot watched the Southerner's hand hover over his gun again and sighed, "You're a violent fool, Creighton. I warned you earlier about trying to use that gun. If you'd take the time to glance out the window just opposite you, you'll find that my guard, Josh, has been holding a gun on you since this discussion began."

MacKenzie paused as the smaller man's violent reaction sputtered out before the Scot turned his attention to his host. "Mr. Randall," he was forced by the older man's inattentiveness to repeat the address, "Mr. Randall, your granddaughter has been abused repeatedly in your home. If you ever allow her father to whip her again, the Ryder-MacKenzie Bank will put up for public auction all of your promissory gambling notes; in which case, Sophia will be forced by Virginia law to pay for them."

In the soft, slurred voice of a southern gentleman, Clinton Randall responded, "Suh, my son-in-law is my responsibility. I will vouch for his actions. As for my granddaughter, she is an annoyin' child and always has been. But I give you my word, she'll not be abused again." Only Melissa's muted sobs penetrated the silence in the room as MacKenzie left.

During the months which followed that strained family scene, the Scot was to remember Randall's description of his granddaughter frequently. With a shrewd wisdom that belied her thirteen years, Marsh Creighton latched on to MacKenzie.

Within days the bed had become an untenable prison for her, and the patient Adah had helped her young charge into one of the worn dresses Melissa had brought to the cottage on her first visit. Walking stiffly, Marsh had gone into the office and met the man who was destined to become her most undemanding friend and teacher.

Angus Balfour had lived his life—all sixty-two years of it—in the shadow of the MacKenzie family. As the son of the land agent of the original MacKenzie Farm near Dumbarton in the Highlands of Scotland, he had been trained as a bookkeeper and general business manager from boyhood. He had followed his profession all of his life, just as he had followed Jamie, the younger son of his Highlands employer, Leith MacKenzie. A lifelong bachelor, Angus had immigrated to America with Jamie sixteen years earlier and had worked as loyally for the son as he had for the father.

His first impression of the young girl standing in the doorway watching him was that she was avidly hungry, not for food but for challenge. The old man's sharp blue eyes twinkled at her blunt opening request.

"Can I help you with your work, Mr. Balfour?"

"Ha' you any idea what work I do, lass?"

"Yes, I've listened to you and Mr. MacKenzie talk."

"Can you add and subtract numbers?"

At her eager nod, the man chuckled and handed her a sharpened pencil and a sheet of paper with columns of figures on it. She studied the page with frowning concentration, licked the end of the pencil, and jotted down the answers quickly. Expecting only guesswork, Angus was pleasantly surprised by the degree of accuracy. In the weeks that followed, he found that her desire to learn was an all-consuming ambition.

As soon as her healthy young body was recovered enough for extended walking, Marsh divided her time between the office and the paddock infirmary where Dr. Damon and Carina tended the horses. With sharp eyes that observed both the diagnosis and the cure, she watched Damon treat the animals. As if she recognized the fact that only through her personal mastery of the skills needed to operate this breeding farm could she hope for a continued reprieve from her old life, Marsh dogged the footsteps of anyone and everyone who could teach her. She wheedled her mother into letting her wear the discarded clothes from her father's wardrobe, and clad in those britches and boots, she coaxed the exercise boys to teach her horseback riding. Although she was less aggressive in asking James MacKenzie for help, he too became her teacher. At every opportunity the red-haired girl watched the canny Scot as he sold horses to selective buyers and listened to his expert explanation of the qualities that made MacKenzie horses superior. But mostly she studied the man himself and his commanding authority that made him successful. Secretly, in her room at night, she imitated his determined stride and his technique of looking straight at another man. She memorized the words he used and his crisp way of saying them.

Unaware of her intense interest in him during those first three months, MacKenzie ignored the girl as he concentrated on the job of making this Virginia farm into as lucrative a business as his Maryland farm already was. But sometime during his final month of residency, he began to be annoyed by her ceaseless and sometimes dangerous activities. His annoyance increased when he discovered that he was alone in his disapproval. Most of his employees not only praised her, they actively encouraged her to learn more and more. The foreman, Jake, who had known Marsh most of her life, took her all over the farm with him, to all those remote corners she had been forbidden to visit during her sharply restricted childhood. Finally, after she had gone on an extensive, six-hour patrol with Jake, MacKenzie's patience gave out. This red-haired hoyden was not his permanent responsibility, after all!

Determined to resettle her with her own family, he revisited the big house for the first time since the day he'd fired

Creighton. To his consternation, when he suggested that Marsh be moved back, everyone in the house refused his request. Clinton Randall protested that he'd enjoyed the peace and quiet too much to want her disturbing presence. Sophia and Janet were blunt about their feelings.

"I won't have the creature spoiling my wedding," asserted Janet with a mulish stubbornness.

Her mother was equally determined. "At the present, there is no room for her in this house."

Only Melissa's reasons were unselfish. "She is happier where she is now. Please don't force her to come back here," she begged him in a voice too old and beaten to belong to so young and beautiful a woman.

"Won't her father insist that she return?"

It was her answer to this reasonable question which made the Scot realize that his earlier generosity had now become a permanent commitment.

"Blake Creighton? He hates her, Mr. MacKenzie, and I can do nothing to prevent his cruelty to her."

"Where is he now?"

"He's working in Alexandria, but he'll be back; and I don't want her here when he returns."

Nonplussed at having the care of the turbulent thirteen-year-old shoved onto his shoulders, MacKenzie returned to his own property and went in search of the girl. He found her working sedately with Angus in the office and, momentarily, his irritation was mollified. Privately, he explained to Angus that the girl could continue to live in the cottage with Adah and Jake. The old Scot displayed no surprise or chagrin at the announcement, even when his employer told him that Angus would be responsible for her.

"Aye, Jamie, the lass will be no trouble. Will Damon and Carina be goin' with you?"

"Since most of the future sales will be made at the Maryland farm, they'll be needed there. But I'll make arrangements for them to make regular checks here. Tell the girl good-bye for me, Angus.''

"Dinna worry about her, Jamie, the lass can take care of herself.''

Despite Angus's reassurances, MacKenzie's normal equilibrium was disturbed by nagging doubts as he left his cottage the next day to board the steam-driven tugboat that would take him across the Potomac River to the Maryland farm. Just before he reached the dock, his disturbed thoughts were disturbed still more by the sight of Marsh mounted bareback on a horse too large for her slender weight and galloping at full speed toward him. He waited with trepidation for her to come abreast of him, hoping that he could stop the snorting beast somehow before the pair landed in the river. To his amazement, the girl leaned over the horse's head and spoke into its ear. As if it had been bit-sawed in the mouth, the creature stopped within paces of the waiting man.

In his relief MacKenzie spoke angrily to the girl for the first time during their odd relationship. "I told you, Marsh, that you could ride nothing but mares and only gentle ones at that. How dare you disobey me and mount that stallion?''

Unabashed and unconcerned, she shrugged. "He minds me better than your prancing mares. And,'' she added boastfully, "I'm the only one who can ride this particular stallion.''

My God,'' he exclaimed in awe as he identified the horse as a mixed-breed workhorse stud which had never been broken for riding. "How did you do it, lass? How did you tame that brute enough to ride him?''

"With sugar and carrots. I've been riding him every day for a month.'' Abruptly, she changed the subject. "Mr. MacKenzie, I want to to go with you.''

Taken aback by her directness, he answered curtly, "Out of the question, Marsh, you'll have to remain here.''

"Then will you let me work for you?''

Annoyed by her persistence, he was more negative than he

ordinarily might have been. "There's not really anything you know how to do yet, is there?"

"I can learn Mr. MacKenzie. Besides, how much skill does it take to shovel manure?"

He winced a little at her blunt language, but relented. "All right, tell Jake to let you work around the paddock area."

With the perseverance of a bulldog she pressed her advantage. "For wages, Mr. MacKenzie?"

Amused now, he smiled at her. "For wages, Marsh. Have Angus put you on the books."

"Will you be coming back?"

"Of course I will."

"Tell Damon I'll take care of the horses like he taught me."

"Tell him yourself, he's waiting for me on the barge."

"No, I've already said good-bye to him and Carina." There was something infinitely forlorn about her as she sat astride a giant horse talking about saying good-bye to people who had become her friends. Against his will, MacKenzie felt a sharp pang of pity for the lonely, half-grown girl. Adding his own good-bye heavily, he turned away from her and joined the group standing on the deck of the tug. Carina's welcoming words made him even more aware of the girl's sad lot in life.

"Don't worry about our little rebel, Jamie. It is better that she learn to solve her own problems since life is never going to be easy or placid for that one."

The next two years were busy ones for James MacKenzie as he expanded his holdings, and his visits to his Virginia farm were hurried and infrequent. So rarely did he have any direct communication with the odd young girl that it was a decided shock in the opening months of 1861 when he moved back into his cottage and became reacquainted with her—or, more accurately, found himself at odds with a fifteen-year-old impresario who virtually ran this MacKenzie horse emporium. Jake took orders from her cheerfully; Angus praised her shrewd sense of business; and Damon called her an expert with horses. Even after hearing these enthusiastic recommendations of a girl he had secretly dubbed an unlucky child, MacKenzie was totally unprepared for the changes in her. Her hair had darkened to bright auburn; her nose was dusted by fewer freckles; her figure had matured to a very womanly promise; and she had lost every trace of humility. Clad exclusively now in masculine clothing, additional cast-offs from Blake Creighton's extensive wardrobe, she was mounted on the same stallion she had ridden to the dock two years earlier. While her employer watched, she wheeled the great beast as effortlessly as she would have a dainty mare and drove four targeted geldings from the main group in the pasture toward the paddock show yard. She waved to him as casually as if they had just recently parted, but she did not dismount. Instead, she rode back to the pasture to round up four more horses. Twice more she repeated the foray until sixteen horses stood quietly in the yard and, without a quiver of nervousness, allowed their glossy coats to be groomed.

Impressed by her riding skill even though he was miffed by the lack of an enthusiastic greeting, MacKenzie walked over to talk to Jake, who was supervising the grooming.

"What's the story on these horses, Jake?"

"They belongs to one of the gentry, suh."

"That's nonsense. These are my horses."

"Was yours, suh. Miss Marsh done sold them months ago."

"She sold field horses as riding stock?"

"No suh! These ain't nothin' like field horses. These be battle trained."

"Who the devil gave permission to battle train my horses?"

Uneasily, the huge black man shuffled his feet. "Best you ask Miss Marsh about that, suh."

"I'll ask Miss Marsh about a lot of things." Anger sparked the Scot's voice and glinted his eyes as he strode toward the girl who was bringing the last four horses to the grooms.

MacKenzie almost relented when she glanced down at him and smiled radiantly. But his irritation rekindled quickly when she ignored the hand he extended to help her dismount and leaped nimbly off by herself.

Feet apart and arms akimbo, she greeted him with an impudent challenge. "Well, Mr. MacKenzie, have I learned enough yet to be a good worker?"

"I'm not sure you've learned a damn thing. What the devil do you know about battle training horses?"

At his harsh words her smile faded and the skin around her eyes tightened. Then, in a voice which parodied the honeyed tones of a flirtatious southern belle, she mimicked, "Y'all mean to say that no lil' ol' girl like me could ever learn to do anything so manlike as training horses, Mr. MacKenzie, suh?"

As she finished her taunting question, Marsh swung away from him and remounted her horse in one graceful, fluid movement. Her voice became Yankee flat with her next words. "These sixteen horses and four hundred more like them are rifle trained, cannon trained and fire trained. And, if you have no further objection, I'm on my way to deliver these to their new owners."

Long before she finished with this insolent declaration, MacKenzie was glowering. "You're not going anyplace. Jake, you make the delivery," he ordered.

Marsh glared back at him, her mobile lips curled with contempt. "You been away from the South too long, Yankee, if you think that Jake and the others would be safe on Virginia roads without my protection."

Only Jake's hurried intercession prevented his employer's furious response. "She's right, suh. White folks in Virginy is mighty riled up. Best she go with us."

Several tense seconds passed before MacKenzie finally gave his grudging permission. "All right, but I want to talk to both of you the minute you get back." His harsh look of disapproval did not soften as he watched the precise organization of the next few moments. Marsh wheeled her horse expertly, rode back to the waiting grooms, and took the reins of the two horses which Jake handed her. In smooth, practiced order, Jake and six of the grooms followed her, and the column moved slowly toward the far paddock gates leading to the public road beyond. Once outside, the girl raised her arm in a military signal and all eight riders broke into an easy canter.

Not waiting for their dust to settle, MacKenzie strode angrily into the barn which he had not visited for almost a year. Sourly, he studied the changes which had been made during his absence. Rear doors had been cut into the wall and now led directly to the smithy beyond. Half of the stalls had been removed and replaced with rows of water and feed troughs attached to the walls. In one corner a dozen rifles were neatly stacked next to two army cannons. Without a word to the silent workers engaged in cleanup work, he walked rapidly toward his own waiting horse, mounted up, and rode the quarter-mile distance to the office cottage at a full gallop. Within minutes of leaving the paddock area, he slammed into the office with an explosive force which startled Angus into dropping the armful of wood he was carrying.

"All right, Angus, I want to know everything that has taken place here," he snapped in a tone of voice just slightly less violent than a shout.

Picking up the fallen pieces of wood, the smaller man stuffed them into the potbellied stove before responding to the demand, and then his words were accompanied by a chuckle. "I take it the lassie na' gi' you a straight answer, Jamie."

"That hothead was as impudent as hell. Who made her the boss around here?"

"The customers, Jamie, the customers. They dinna trust me or the blacks, but they sure like that sweet-voiced lassie."

Still stinging from that same sweet voice, MacKenzie blustered, "Were you damn fool enough to actually let that chit do the selling?"

"Aye, Jamie, and a good job she did of it even to the Washington people."

"Nonsense. They've always come to the Maryland farm."

"Not the southern ones of them anymore."

"When did the battle training start?"

"Last August, two Southerners wi' the look of soldiers about them dropped by wi' a proposition. A hundred dollars bonus a head for the battle trainin' of a horse. I'd ha' asked you but you'd already left wi' your brother. Di' you and Ian get what you wanted out west?"

"Aye, we bought ten thousand more acres in Nebraska Territory."

"Di' you get to see your oldest boy while you were there?"

"Aye, Robbie was with us all the time we were buying horses from the Indians. I brought four hundred of those horses back with me. And now I need another five hundred from here."

"We ha' no' that many left, Jamie."

"My God, Angus, how many have you sold to the Southerners?"

"Close to six hundred."

"All battle trained?"

"Most."

"The girl said there were four hundred here."

"More than half of them are already sold."

"Eight hundred horses! That's damn near a whole cavalry battalion."

"Aye. MacKenzie horses will be fightin' on both sides of the comin' war."

"How close do you think it is, Angus?"

"Judgin' by the activity here, I'd say the day after tomorrow. There's trainin' camps on almost every plantation in Virginia."

MacKenzie whistled. "Nothing like that kind of activity in the North. Tell me about the two men you talked to."

"Officers and West Point trained would be my guess. The next day they moved in wi' four soldiers and twenty blacks. After they picked out the eight hundred horses, they brought us a dozen rifles and four cannons."

"I saw only two."

"They took the other two away just before the job was finished."

"Were they army cannons?"

"Aye. I imagine every army post in the South is stripped by this time."

"Who operated the cannons?"

"They left a dozen blacks here and trained some of our workers to fire the rifles."

"We have slave labor working here? I won't permit that, Angus."

"I couldna' free them, Jamie; but there's only four here now."

"Cannon experts?"

"Aye, and those lads are itchin' to get up North."

"Good. I can use them and their cannons in Maryland. How soon can you deliver the other two hundred horses to the South?"

"The lassie can deliver only thirty-two a day."

"I'll deliver the rest myself."

"Jamie, they wouldna' let you get wi'in a mile of their camps. Best you stay out of sight and let the lassie do the work."

"How'd she ever learn so much in such a short time?"

"You've been gone a year, Jamie, and you've not seen her work. She's astride that brute of hers ten hours a day. Ha' you seen her ride yet?"

"Aye, she's good. But it's too big a mount for her."

The old man chuckled. "I wouldna' be tellin' her that, Jamie, or that horse either. She's the only one who can control the beastie."

"Nonsense. Any expert could."

Another dry chuckle greeted this snort of disbelief. "That's what a smart-mouthed Virginia lad thought during a delivery a month ago. Jake told me the lad wound up with two crushed legs when he tried to pull our lassie off."

"Did she actually take part in the battle training?"

"Her horse was the first one trained, and after that she bossed the whole thing. Our workers wouldna' hold still for the southern whites."

"Have you paid for her work?"

"Aye, and every cent of her wages is banked for her."

"Good. Then she'll not be a pauper when I move her back to the big house."

MacKenzie was completely unprepared for the older man's anger. "I'll no' let you do that to the lass, Jamie. You werena' here when her father stormed down and demanded her wages. He's no' a nice mannie. I dinna let him see the lassie and I dinna gi' him her money."

"That fool dared come here?"

"Aye, and often until he left the place to train farm boys at a camp somewhere in the state."

"Well, since he's gone, she'll be safe at the house."

"No, Jamie, I gi' her mother my word that I'd no' return the lass. The puir lady's nought but a servant herself in the house."

"Does the mother ever come to see the girl?"

"Every Sunday."

"And she actually approves of what her daughter is becoming?"

"And what might she be becomin', Jamie?"

"For God's sake, Angus, she's no longer a child."

MacKenzie missed the sudden grin which spread over the old man's face. "I dinna think you'd overlook that development."

If the other man heard the jibe, he gave no indication, but continued on his main theme. "Well, she can't stay here nor on the Maryland farm. Both places will be turned into government training areas for horses within two months."

"This one will no' be easy to defend."

"This farm lies within the defense perimeter of the nation's capital. There'll be soldiers all over the place."

"They wouldna' bother the lassie."

"Maybe not, but she'd just be in their way."

MacKenzie had to retract these cocky words five days of hard work later. While Marsh delivered two hundred horses to the South, he barged the other two hundred over to Maryland. On the first trip he'd taken the four cannoneers and the two cannons to begin the work in Maryland which they'd just completed in Virginia. On the return trips MacKenzie brought back the untrained horses he'd purchased from the Nebraska Indians.

It was on one of the return trips that the near tragedy occurred. One of the twelve federal cavalry soldiers who'd been helping with the transfer went overboard with his horse into the Potomac River just where the current was the swiftest. No one had noticed the girl seated on her stallion watching the crossing. The first MacKenzie and the soldiers saw of her was astride a streak of massive equine power leaping with all four legs extended in a stretched-out entry into the river. Bent low over her stallion's head, the girl seemed a part of her horse. Guiding him with the current, she intercepted the floundering man and horse mid-river. Just how she kept the terrified horse's head above water for the long swim back to the Virginia side, the watchers could not determine. But she did, succeeding in forcing her stallion up the rain-soaked bank some two-hundred feet down from the dock. Once atop the high bank, she backed her horse up until the drenched soldier and half-drowned mount were pulled to safety.

She gave no sign that she heard the cheering that came from the eleven soldiers still aboard, and she certainly never heard the exchange of comments between MacKenzie and a corporal.

"Whoo-ee," the youthful extrovert exclaimed, "ain't she something?"

His jaws clamped shut with an I-told-you-so anger, MacKenzie gritted, "That girl, soldier, is a lady; and you'll watch your mouth around her."

Completely unabashed, the corporal defended himself. "I meant nothin' rude, Mr. MacKenzie, I just never seen horsemanship like that afore. And I ain't never known any woman with that much courage."

Angrily skeptical, MacKenzie kept his eyes on the girl, fully intending to reach her side first. But in the busy confusion of landing, he watched helplessly as two soldiers raced down the levee toward her as she sat, still astride her horse, busily pounding the back of the rescued soldier bent suddenly forward in his own saddle. Within minutes, the angry Scotsman discovered that he had misread the motives of the soldiers. Whipping off their dry ponchos, they had wrapped them around the shivering girl and soldier before leading the river-soaked pair off toward shelter.

It was an hour before MacKenzie could complete the job of pasturing the horses and housing the men. And with each moment his anger toward the reckless girl increased. By the time he reached the stove-warmed office, his temper was just several degrees from its explosion point. Nor did the scene that awaited him inside the office cool his anger. Wrapped in a blanket, the young soldier was huddled in front of the stove nursing a glass of Angus's finest usquebaugh whiskey while Angus himself worked soundlessly at his desk. Both men jerked at the abruptness of MacKenzie's entrance and at his sharp questions.

"Where's the girl and why isn't she drying off, too?"

"The lass changed her clothes, Jamie, and is out back tendin' the horses."

Without another word, MacKenzie swung back to the door and stomped out. He found the girl in the lean-to shed, busily brushing down and talking to the powerful stallion while the other horse contentedly chewed on the oats she had provided for it.

"That was a damn fool stunt you pulled today, Miss Creighton. Not only did you risk your own life, you risked one of my valuable horses, too."

He missed her flare of fury at his use of her hated last name, but there was no missing the contempt in her young voice as she corrected the last part of his accusation.

"You know better than that, Mr. MacKenzie. This horse has too much cob in him to be anything but a stud for other cobs and workhorses. His legs are too short for riding speed and his body too heavy. He may be the most powerful horse you own and the smartest, but he's no Thoroughbred."

"What were you doing by yourself on the levee today? I gave you orders last week that you weren't to wander around alone."

She glared back at him, her anger surpassing his. "Because that batch of horses you delivered yesterday were mares, and your two valuable"—she stressed the word sarcastically—"studs were tearing the barn apart to get at them. Since my horse is the only one that can outpower those brutes, I was just returning from depositing them in their special stalls."

Realizing that her anger was more justified than his, and that his concern had really been for her safety and not over the possible loss of a horse, his tone of voice became conciliatory. "What do you call your horse, Marsh?"

"He doesn't have a name. He knows who he is and he knows who I am. He doesn't need a name."

"But you love him, don't you? Would you like to own him?"

"Not as a gift, Mr. MacKenzie. If he's for sale, I'll buy him."

"All right, Marsh. Get your coat on and let's go back into the office and talk." He had become acutely aware of the January chill in the late afternoon air. He had also noticed the pinched, bluish tinge around the girl's mouth as she put away the grooming equipment. Even when she had finished the cleanup, and joined him at the entrance, she wore no coat. With a contrite look, he removed his own fur-lined jacket and tried to place it around her shaking shoulders.

Stubbornly, she shrugged it off. "I don't need your coat," she mumbled through clenched teeth.

Inside the office, the soldier had finished dressing and was ready to leave, but he was obviously trying to work up the courage to thank his rescuer. He found the necessary reassurance at her flashing smile and friendly words.

"Your horse is all ready for you, Pete. Just keep me posted if you're planning any more swims in the Potomac."

As he went out the door, the youthful trooper blurted out his gratitude, "My buddies and I will never forget what you did for me, Miss Marsh. Never!" At the sincerity of the soldier's respect for her, the remnants of MacKenzie's anger evaporated.

"I have decided," he began magnanimously, "that you do not have to return to the house. You can continue to work—"

He would never forget the look of self-confident determination with which she faced him. At that moment she looked ten years older than her fifteen. "I'll never return to that house, Mr. MacKenzie, whether I work for you or not. But about the horse. Will two months of wages be payment enough if he continues to stud for you?"

"You don't have to buy him, Marsh. He's yours as a gift."

"I won't accept him as a gift. If you want to sell him, I'll buy him. If not—"

MacKenzie looked helplessly at Angus, who had been smiling broadly during the exchange. Irritated by the older man's humor, he shrugged. "All right, if that's the way you feel. But you've earned him as a gift. Angus, will you draw up the papers?"

Angus nodded, but his attention shifted to the girl, who had turned around to go outside again. "You'll no' be goin' outside again, Lassie, not wi'out a coat, and I know that yours is still drippin' wet. I'll make you a wee proposition. If you'll bring mine and Jamie's dinner back, I'll gi' you my old sheepskin.''

MacKenzie watched with some emotion—his middle-aged masculine complacency wouldn't allow him to identify it as jealousy—as the girl kissed Angus's leathery cheek and smilingly accepted the proffered coat, an ancient but durable garment. Not daring to risk her anger or impudence again, MacKenzie watched in silence as she left the room. Just as silently he accepted a glass of Angus's usquebaugh, the pungent Scottish brew now becoming known as Scotch in the Yankee world of hard liquor.

"You'll no' be gettin' the better of that one," the bookkeeper began conversationally.

"Where's she gone now?"

"She puts in an hour stint down at the cook shed. All the workers eat there together. It saves time and money."

"She shouldn't have to do that kind of work. I thought I paid Adah to do the cooking?"

"Aye, you do, but the girl will ha' it no other way than to help out."

"Angus, doesn't she have any clothes?"

"Only her father's cast-offs that her mother sneaks down."

"Can't she buy some out of her wages? Incidentally, Angus, you're not to dock her wages for the horse."

The old man chuckled. "I dinna have any such intention, Jamie. And as for clothes, the lass would no' be so foolish as to waste money on them. The wages she's savin' are the only security she has. According to Adah, nought but the grandmother ever took the time to teach her readin' and numberin'. The lassie's smart though; with her ability to do figurin', she'll no be starvin'—except for love. Di' you know her grandfather re-wed only three months after her grandmother's death?"

"He had no choice, Angus. It was either marrying Sophia or losing his home. What about the girl's mother?"

"She's treated worse than the lassie, both by her father and that pulin' man she married. Her clothes are patched while the two madams dress like royalty. No, Jamie, the lassie's better off in men's clothes right here. And don't be gettin' that look in your eye. She'll no' accept as much as a bonnet from you. She's a bonnie lass wi' a gude head on her shoulders. She'll no lack for interest when the time comes." Once again the old man chuckled. "You wouldna believe it, but I've wished myself thirty years younger on occasion as I've watched her."

Now, four years later, James MacKenzie found himself wishing the same thing. Throughout the four war years he'd found himself more and more intrigued by the girl who had not only survived the hardships, but had profited by them. He smiled as he wondered where she'd banked the money she had made on her own during those years. He knew that her accumulated wages were safe in his Baltimore bank. But three years ago, when the supply of horses had been greatly reduced by the demands of the Union Army, he'd given her permission to turn huge fields into food production and to earn the profits for herself and her fellow workers. As he counted the six wagons full of squealing piglets, squawking chickens, noisy goats, and nervous rabbits, and four more wagons loaded with garden vegetables, he knew that she'd earned a considerable sum of money. He also knew from Angus that she rarely parted with so much as a carrot without receiving good Yankee cash for it. He wondered what she planned to do with her money, and found himself resentful of the fact that she'd no longer be dependent upon him.

Even more intently, he wondered about the other men who must have discovered her appeal by this time. The earlier promise had become a reality. Nothing could disguise the arrogant beauty of her strongly marked face or the feminine curves of her slim body which was inches taller than her petite southern counterparts. Feeling the thirty years difference in their ages to an ego-deflating extent, he turned his horse toward Angus's office and a dram or more of the spirit-reviving usquebaugh.

Chapter
2

James MacKenzie had not been the only man watching Pamela Marshall Creighton. Two others had been observing her with differing emotions so powerful as to make the middle-aged Scot's interest in her seem almost casual. The first was a twenty-six-year-old Union major who had known her less than a month. He watched her with a frustrated woman-hunger so intense he felt damned uncomfortable sitting on a horse. Albeit that Congress had dubbed him an officer and a gentleman three months before the Civil War began, his thoughts at the moment dwelt more with rape than with any alternative, gentler pursuit of a woman's favor. The fact that he'd already tried it once with this particular woman and failed miserably in the effort only added fuel to his growing preoccupation.

Major Stuart MacKenzie had heard of the girl months before he met her from no less a personage than the invincible Phil Sheridan, the military leader Stuart had served under for four years of almost steady fighting. Months before the war had begun in 1861, the then Lieutenant Sheridan had come to the MacKenzie farm in Maryland in search of horses. One of the few experienced combat men in the army, Sheridan knew that battles were won as often by good horseflesh as by reliable guns and men. On that first visit he had urged the youthful Stuart to apply for a commission. The young Scot had never entertained any illusions about the reason Sheridan seemed interested in him. He was an excellent pipeline to the best horses in the North since his father owned not just this breeding farm but an even larger one in Nebraska. Throughout the war years Sheridan had lost five MacKenzie horses in battle, three of them shot from under him. Just last December, after winning the only three major Union victories of 1864 and destroying the entire fertile Shenandoah Valley, General Sheridan had ridden to the Virginia MacKenzie Farm to choose his replacement mounts personally. It was then that he had encountered the girl he called the second-best judge of horseflesh in America; he reserved the title of first for himself.

As Sheridan and his men had been separating the stock they wanted in the show yard, the girl had ridden up and asked Sheridan himself if he were interested in a special horse.

"It'll cost you, General," she warned him.

"It'll cost the Union Army," he responded promptly, "trot it out."

Astride her powerful stallion, she had galloped off and returned twenty minutes later with a thoroughbred which was every bit as good as she'd claimed. Built for endurance and speed, the four-year-old was the most magnificent horse Sheridan had ever ridden, one which had already become famous in the closing months of the Civil War and one which the general now planned to take with him to the Mexican border.

In telling Stuart about the encounter when he returned to camp, Sheridan had asked the young major if the girl were a relative. His curiosity aroused, Stuart had shaken his head; but at his first meeting with Marsh Creighton, he'd been bowled over by her beauty. Still under military orders from Sheridan, he'd left the battleground and the war a week before Appomattox to gather a thousand good mounts for the Mexican expedition. Expecting to turn the assignment over to his father, he'd reported to both the Maryland and Virginia farms only to find his father unaccountably missing and the girl virtually in charge of the sale of horses at both farms. When he introduced himself as Major Stuart MacKenzie and stated the purpose of his mission, she had bestowed a blinding smile on him and asked him irrelevantly if he were related to James MacKenzie.

"Son."

"I didn't realize Mr. MacKenzie was old enough to have a son your age."

Irritated as he always had been when women made flattering comments about his father, Stuart responded tersely, "He's old enough and then some. I have an older brother. Didn't my father ever think to mention us? Or my younger brother?"

Stiffly she replied, "Mr. MacKenzie is my employer. I know very little about his private life." In the silence which followed her prim statement, she studied the man sitting opposite her. Despite his heavy scowl, he was as good-looking as his father with crisp, wavy dark hair, deep blue eyes framed by ridiculously curly black lashes, and lean, predatory features. More to lighten her own emotional reaction toward this attractive man than to insult him, Marsh giggled.

"Now I can see why you look so much like your father. You glower just as he does, and I imagine you have the same temper, Major."

The handsomest of the three younger MacKenzies, Stuart had always resented his resemblance to his father, and her giggling criticism rankled. Determined to impress this impudent girl now grinning at him without a hint of the infatuated look he usually aroused in women, he was goaded into still more foolish words. "Except in appearance, I have nothing in common with my father, Miss—?"

"Marsh. My friends call me Marsh."

"I don't like my father, Marsh, and he obviously doesn't even remember I'm alive." At the soft look of sympathetic understanding that erased all laughter from her face, he found himself telling her his life story, a foolish compulsion he had never yielded to before. He told her about his widowed father selling their home and land in Scotland and bringing his three small sons and fifty Thoroughbred Highland horses to Maryland.

"We moved in with my Uncle Ian on the farm there." His voice had softened considerably at the mention of his uncle's name. "Uncle Ian had come over six years earlier with two hundred and fifty horses and had bought the Ryder Farm. That's how the MacKenzies got mixed up with the Ryders originally. Robbie was lucky, he got to stay with my uncle. But I had to go with my father during that next year when he made his fortune. You know how he did it, Marsh? He married the daughter of the great Joseph Ryder. What a bitch she was, she and her whey-faced daughter! You haven't met Alice yet, have you? No, of course not; Alice would never stoop so low as to know a farm girl. Neither would my younger brother, Craig. I was seven years old when my father finally moved me out from under that woman and her two whelps."

Concentrating with morbid intensity on his own emotional bitterness, Stuart was oblivious to the reaction of the girl now watching him with fascination. During four years of her early girlhood, she too had been shunned by the Ryders. When Sophia's relatives were visiting, Marsh and her parents had been shunted aside to stay in one of the cottages. This man with her now had been one of the boys she'd watched from the distance with such envy.

"What was your stepmother's name?" she asked dully.

"Helen. Helen Ryder Nelson MacKenzie."

"Then she's Sophia Randall's sister."

"You know that lady?"

Again, he missed the irony of her answer. "I've met her."

"Helen died nine years ago, a year before her father did. And my father wound up with half the Ryder fortune. Quite a success story, isn't it?"

"Who raised you, Stuart?" Her use of his given name passed unnoticed as he concentrated on a childhood which still bedeviled him.

"A very pleasant woman named Catherine. Like me, she was one of those unfortunates life played a dirty trick on. Her husband and son were locked away in an institution for the insane and she had to earn her living by taking care of me."

"But she was good to you and gave you a good home?"

"Oh yes, we were very happy together for the first three years until my father spoiled it." He stopped talking abruptly, and Marsh waited for him to continue with a soft prompting.

"How?"

"How old are you, Marsh?"

"I'm nineteen but I don't shock easily."

"He made my moth—Catherine his mistress."

"But she still loved you and cared for you. You almost called her your mother. Why do you hate your father so? If his wife was anything like her sister Sophia, she was what you called her. Maybe Catherine made your father happy, and undoubtedly he made her happy. So why are you so bitter? He supported you and educated you. Where did you go to college, Stuart?"

"Loyola College in Baltimore. But what's the cost of an education to a man who can afford to buy the college?" Aware suddenly of how much he had revealed, Stuart turned his attention back to the girl, whose face reflected a longing and envy which shocked him out of his own self-pity.

"College isn't important for a girl, Marsh."

Her soft answer made him aware of her again as a unique

and perceptive human. "When you're educated, people respect you no matter what your background is." And then, with a flashing smile, she switched from a soft southern accent to a credible imitation of Angus's Scottish burr. "I dinna think you're so unlucky, lad. If it werena' for the MacKenzie name and the education your father gi' you, you'd no' be wearing those pretty gold leaves or such a bonnie uniform." As she uttered this pleasant rebuke, she rose from her seat and moved gracefully toward the door.

Smiling in response, Stuart also rose and intercepted her. Gently, he leaned down and kissed her lightly and responded in like dialect. "For a lassie, you're no' such a dummy. And you ha' the bonniest eyes and lips I've ever—"

Whatever he planned to say about her lips was cut short by the hurried arrival of Angus, who held the door open as the girl fled from the room. His ordinarily warm greeting for Stuart was tempered somewhat by his concern for Marsh.

"It's gude to see you, lad. Di' the lass explain to you about—"

Stuart had not even looked at the old man. His eyes were still fastened on the girl as she swung easily astride her horse and rode off without a backward glance. "Who is she, Angus? Where did she come from?"

With a sigh, Angus seated himself at his desk, opened his drawer and took out a bottle. "Help yourself to a dram, lad, before we get down to business."

But Stuart had a one-track mind. "Damn the business, I want to know about her. What's her background?"

"She's just a local lass who's worked for your father six years."

"Six years? She said she was just nineteen."

"Aye, that she is. But don't you be underestimatin' her or be taken in by that smile she gi' you. You'll find she's no' so soft."

Remembering the warmth of her lips in response to his kiss, Stuart smiled condescendingly. Angus shook his head.

40

"Dinna complain that you werena' warned when she bests you in a deal. She's as canny as any Scot horse trader you'll ever meet. Di' you recall the horse your boss soldier bought from her and paid seven hundred dollars for?"

"General Sheridan paid that much?"

"Aye, and she sold one like it to General Mosby two years ago for a thousand."

"The southern guerrilla dared come here?"

"Aye, right after he'd stolen four thousand Yankee horses and taken a Yankee general captive in Fairfax, he rode over here with ten of his men to buy food. He came up that levee road as bold as brass. Just as bold the lass armed herself and four workers and rode out to meet him. I'd love to ha' seen that meetin'. Jake told me that when Mosby raised his hand to halt his men, she raised hers and then rode over alone and asked their business. That was the first time during the war that horse thief ever paid for anythin'. But that time he paid double for every ham and slab of bacon she let him have. And just before he left, she trotted out that pretty horse and sold it, too."

"And got stolen Yankee money in return. My God, she could have been killed. Mosby gave General Sheridan more trouble than all the other southern generals combined."

"He'd have no' hurt the lass. Wi' that honey sweet voice of hers, she charmed the whole group, and they've been buying food from her ever since."

"Sounds like she made a lot of money for my father."

"Aye, lad, wi' the horses, but no' wi' the food. That money was hers and the workers, and they sold food to both sides."

"She's a Southerner then?"

"Born here, but she never played your father false. As for the workers, she's the best friend they ha'." The old man peered closely at his young friend. "Stuart, dinna let her soft voice fule you. She's a fighter."

Three days later, Angus's description of Marsh was borne

out dramatically for Major MacKenzie. During the routine inspection of a batch of horses by a squad of his men, he heard the girl's voice raised in a parade-ground dressing down that would have done justice to a career sergeant. In this case, however, an army sergeant was the recipient. He had been using his prod in standard army procedure as he inspected the horses.

"What do you think you're doing with that weapon, soldier?" her sharp voice rang out.

Startled, the man held his temper and answered her rude challenge mildly enough. "I never go among strange horses without a weapon, ma'am."

"These are not strange horses, soldier; these are MacKenzie horses. They stand still for inspection."

"Horses are horses, ma'am. They all understand the prod."

"You try that weapon on the horse I'm riding, soldier, and he'll slash you to ribbons. Now get that thing away from MacKenzie stock and keep it away."

Stuart felt sorry for the red-faced man caught in the unenviable position of being tongue-lashed in front of his own squad, and by a woman at that. The major was tempted to intervene, but he wasn't sure he'd fare any better than the sergeant. The look Stuart bent on the girl now was more speculative than it had been previously. She was neither so naive nor so delicate as he'd thought. Imperceptibly, at least he hoped so as far as she was concerned, he stepped up the tempo of his pursuit. Twice during the next twenty-four hours he was able to find her alone, momentarily free from her whirlwind succession of duties.

That night, after dinner in the communal kitchen, he walked her back to the office cottage, and once again he felt her response to his undemanding good night kiss. The following morning, after the first of the many barge trips ferrying the selected horses from the Virginia farm to the Maryland one, he rode ahead with her while his men unloaded the horses. As he helped her dismount, he experienced a moment of triumph at the flush of pleasure that suffused her face. Not a shy man, he pushed his advantage and kissed her more thoroughly than he had the night before. However, when his arms tightened and he pulled her hard against his body, she pushed him away harshly and made the first of what he would soon be calling her barnyard comments.

"You've been at war too long, Major. The women you could use now work right over in Washington." He was so affronted by the bluntness of her words, he ignored the obvious truth of them. He also missed the trembling of her voice and the hurt look in her eyes. Without another word, she strode off in the direction of the barge and waited silently for the return trip.

For the next five days she held him at arm's length if she allowed herself to be near him at all. But on one of the last crossings, this time with the cobs and workhorses purchased for the heavy work of pulling cannons and equipment wagons, their relationship heated up again—more precisely, it exploded. On the forward part of the barge, just in back of the steam tugboat which powered it across the river, the same sergeant who had aroused her anger before used the same cruel prod to keep the large-rumped animals from pressing him into the guardrail. The reaction among the animals developed into panic, and one frightened draft gelding reared up and crashed through the rail. Three other animals followed, pushing a mounted soldier in with them. Instantly, both he and his horse began to flounder while the unsaddled horses drifted in wild-eyed terror.

Because Stuart was closest to the break, he drove his own horse into the water, followed closely by Marsh on hers. While Stuart headed toward the soldier now in senseless panic fighting his horse, she guided hers toward the group of drifting horses. As expertly as it herded horses on land, the stallion forced the creatures back toward the Virginia banks. Only when the first of them were clambering ashore did Marsh turn around to check on Stuart. In horror she saw that

43

he was in trouble. The other man had grabbed onto his leg and was threatening to pull his commanding officer under with him.

Terrified of the river for the first time in her life, Marsh turned her stallion back into the swift currents in the center until she had passed the struggling pair. Abruptly, she swung her horse around and drove him between the riders. The man screamed as he lost his hold on Stuart's leg. Grabbing the reins of the soldier's horse, she gave the beleaguered animal a sideward kick so that the terrified man could not reach her. Looking around for Stuart, she watched him recover control of his mount and begin to turn back toward her.

"Go ashore, Major," she screamed, "we're fine." Indeed, she did feel fine since the terror had left her once she'd seen Stuart safe. But all the long weary way to safety, she cursed the sergeant who had used the prod and vowed he would pay for her earlier fear. As soon as her stallion's hooves reached ground, she leaped off the exhausted animal and allowed him to clamber up the embankment without the encumbrance. But the half drowned soldier was still too unnerved to consider the pathetic condition of his mount.

"Get off your horse, you idiot," she shrieked at him, "or I'll push you back into the river."

"Trooper, you heard the lady. Dismount," came Stuart's sharp command from the top of the levee. Seconds later, Marsh felt Stuart's arm around her, pulling her up the bank. Tiredly, she heard the soldier and his horse clambering up the mud wall, too. When she finally reached safety, she looked for her own stallion which was standing some distance away, wheezing in exhaustion. For a few breathless seconds in time, that powerful animal had kept two other horses and three riders afloat in the swift current of the mighty Potomac—a feat few horses could match. As she started to move toward him, she felt herself restrained by Stuart's strong arm.

"That was a damn fool stunt you pulled, Marsh," he scolded her softly.

Suddenly, she felt that she was back four years in time, listening to his father scold her with almost the same words after she'd pulled another soldier out of the same river. She began to laugh helplessly as the tears of emotional exhaustion ran down her face. Stuart's arm tightened around her as he turned to check on the soldier who was still on his hands and knees in the dust of the levee road.

"Are you all right, trooper?" he asked sharply.

"I think so, sir."

"Then get on your feet, man, and see to your mount," he ordered sharply, "we're going to have to walk the horses. They're in a bad way. Can you walk, Marsh, or should I carry you?"

Angry at her momentary weakness and painfully aware of Stuart's eyes on her breasts, which were outlined graphically under the wet cotton of her shirt, she tried to pull away from him. His face was set with hard-jawed intensity as he raised his eyes to meet hers. Only after he had stroked her half-exposed breasts with his free hand did he release her.

With a blind fury, she rebuttoned her shirt and walked unsteadily over to her stallion and took his reins to begin the long walk back to the office cottage. When she reached the rear stall, she didn't look up as the two men moved toward the similar stalls behind the cottage next door. For an hour she stayed there, silently grooming her horse while her thoughts and emotions churned madly. She jerked violently when she heard Stuart's sharp voice at the entrance.

"Get inside and get those wet clothes off, Marsh. Your horse has more sense than you do."

Stubbornly, she continued brushing the smooth flanks of her stallion, making no attempt to answer the charge. She couldn't; she was too angry to trust herself to speak. But her anger was no match for his. He grabbed her arm and pulled her out of the stall and toward the rear door of the cottage. When she attempted to pull away from him, he picked her up and threw her struggling body over his shoulder and marched into the house.

"Which room is yours?"

Furiously, she fought with him. "It's the one on the left and you get the hell out of here."

"Not until I get those damned boots off of you." Unceremoniously, he dumped her on the bed, stooped down, and yanked first one and then the other water-logged boot before he left her. At the door, he turned around to berate her one more time. "And for God's sake, put a dress on. I'm tired of seeing you look like a field hand. You have ten minutes before I come back." He barely ducked the wet boot she threw at his head. But as soon as the door was closed, she flew into action, peeling off her wet clothes and replacing them with nearly identical trousers, boots and shirt. Pausing only long enough to rake a comb through her half dry hair, she walked rapidly out of her bedroom and through the rear door of the cottage.

He found her before she had time to remove her spare saddle from its stand, and again she was imprisoned in his arms. Only this time, instead of supporting her, they pushed her down unto the pile of hay on the floor of the empty stall next to the stallion's. Whatever shrieks of protest she was attempting, he silenced with a kiss—not a gentle one of exploration, but a plundering, open-mouthed one of conquest. Ignoring her flailing arms, he held her pinned beneath him, one arm keeping her slender body immobile while his free hand caressed her mature breasts and slim, rounded hips. As he felt her nipples harden, his heart pounded with a heavy excitement.

Instantly, she stopped struggling while her hands groped around in search of a weapon, any weapon; and her reaching fingers curled around the most effective one available—the dried manure and loose chaff on the hard packed dirt floor. Slowly sweeping up a handful, she waited momentarily, and then, with a gesture too swift for him to circumvent, she smeared the stinging filth into his eyes, opened at the last split second when he sensed the movement of her hand.

Had she not been too busy extricating herself from beneath him, she might have smiled at his bellow of rage and pain as he scrambled to a sitting position and tried to relieve the smarting agony. But instead of running to safety, Marsh reached down and pulled his hands away from his eyes; then she tugged him to his feet.

"Come on, soldier, I'll wash your eyes out before you damage them." As meekly as a lamb, he allowed her to lead him back into the cottage, seat him before the desk, and bathe his eyes repeatedly with warm water until the red faded and the weeping ceased. Just as efficiently, she hung up the wet towels, threw the water out the door, and returned to the desk. As casually as a barmaid, she unlocked a drawer, took out Angus's bottle of brew, and poured two glasses half full of the amber liquid.

"Now," she announced matter-of-factly, "we'll talk, or more correctly, I'll talk. I admire and respect your father and I wouldn't hurt one of his horses for anything in the world. But you are not a dumb animal. You're an arrogant, conceited man. If you ever try to rape me again, be damned to your father, I'll geld you. And if you think I wouldn't know how, check with Dr. Damon."

Genuinely shocked by the crude frankness of her words, he choked on a mouthful of usquebaugh and sputtered a few seconds before he protested her accusation. "I wasn't trying to rape you."

"Stuart MacKenzie, I've worked with farm animals too long not to know about rape. You were as eager as my stallion."

Smiling ruefully in memory, he agreed, "I guess I was, but you were almost as ready as I was. You're not a passive woman, Marsh—whatever your name is."

She nodded in admission. "I should hope so after what you put me through today, Major. I wouldn't like to think that I was as dried up as some burned-out old mare. But, regardless of my response, I am not a white trash slut who accepts an offer to roll in the hay with a stranger passing through.''

"We're not strangers, Marsh.''

"No, but you're still passing through.''

"What offer would you accept?''

"None that you could afford to make. I may be an ignorant farm girl"—her emphasis was deliberately and bitterly ironic— "but I know enough about your father's wealth to realize that, once you stop playing soldier boy, you'll be the target of every protected little twit in Baltimore.''

He couldn't deny the truth of her words; he knew all too well the future awaiting him. And at the moment he respected the proud young girl sitting across the desk from him too much to insult her with lies. Regretfully, he turned the conversation toward her future.

"What do you plan to do with your life besides rescuing drowning soldiers from watery graves?''

"Angus is going to help me get started in business.''

"Angus Balfour? That old coot?''

"Angus Balfour is one of the only good men I've ever known.''

"Do you live with him?''

Her smile was impish now. "Your father is a more careful man than that. Since the first night he took me in, I've been chaperoned. I live here with Adah and Jake.''

"And do Adah and Jake live together?''

"They've been man and wife for more years than you are old, Major, and the three best workers on this farm are their sons. Come on, Stuart, you'll have to spend another night in Virginia since the barge won't return until morning. We'll be late for dinner if we don't hurry.''

On the return walk that night, she let him kiss her good night once again; but he was careful to note that Jake and Adah had followed closely behind them. All that long night through, he tossed restlessly in bed, all too aware that a girl with beautiful hazel-green eyes and flame highlights in her hair, a girl with a passionate body, had beaten him in a battle of wills. But like a fool with a one-track mind, he'd returned to the attack the next morning and destroyed the fragile truce they'd established. Dead certain that she desired him as much as he did her, he'd burst into the office the next morning where she was working on the Phil Sheridan army account, pulled her to her feet, and kissed her passionately.

"I've decided," he informed her buoyantly, "that instead of Angus, you're going into business with me."

Her smile of welcome faded as she pushed him away. "And what kind of business would that be, Stuart?"

"You'd have pretty dresses and you wouldn't have to do any of this dirty work."

"And I'd be your mistress in some out-of-sight shack."

"It wouldn't be a shack, Marsh, it'd be lovely—"

"It would still be a prison. You don't have much faith in me, do you, Stuart?"

He smiled broadly and foolishly, "I have a lot of faith in you, Marsh. You'd make a man a very happy per—"

In a voice as softly southern as a gentle breeze, she purred, "Y'all mean that if I were all gussied up in some pretty ol' dress, I'd be attractive to men?"

"Only one man, Marsh. I wouldn't share you."

"Well, why not, honey? I'd be sharin y'all."

His eyes narrowed to angry blue slits. "Is that the kind of business Angus is planning to set you up in?"

"Y'all mean as a lady of easy virtue? I know a grand lady in Washington, D.C. who's a very rich and important person. I've delivered food to her house for three whole years, and she's always paid me with the prettiest lil' ol' gold coins. It surely is a temptin' thought to think that a plain, lil' ol' farm girl like me might be able to please men."

"You are a tramp, aren't you? I should have known that no decent woman struts around in men's clothes giving out invitations to every man she meets."

"Well, since I've turned your invitation down, honey, why're y'all still wastin' your time here? Why aren't you up at the big house with your cousin Janet?"

"Janet is still here? I thought she was married."

" 'Course she's married, but that wouldn't stop a sweet lil' ol' lady like Janet. 'Sides, the war did for her husband what I threatened to do for you."

"You've got a foul mouth. I just might take your advice and go see my cousin. At least she wears a dress."

"Y'all do just that. But after she takes that lil' ol' dress off, mind you be careful when you untie her corset strings. Her flab might just smother you." And with a reckless smile that blinded him, Marsh strode to the door and turned back toward Stuart only after the door was opened widely enough to reveal a startled Angus outside.

"Good-bye, Stuart honey, y'all have a good time, hear?"

Usually a mild-tempered man whose philosophical humor dominated his speech, Angus paused to watch Marsh as she strode blindly past him, her smile of a few seconds earlier replaced by angry tears. His opening remarks to Stuart did not add to that young man's self-confidence.

"You're a fule, Stuart. I warned you about the lass but you dinna listen. Di' you think she was a spiritless person like Catherine who'd accept an insultin' relationship wi' you? You hurt her, lad, but you'll no' break her. And just to set the record straight, the lass ha' no' even kissed a man before you came along."

"You were listening outside the door," Stuart accused, his face a thundercloud of embarrassed anger.

"Aye, I was. And I'm thinking the advice she gi' you was good. Janet is more your kind than my proud lassie is."

That was the last time either Marsh or Angus had spoken to him. Sitting now on his horse and watching her work, he felt hopelessly tormented. He'd tried to apologize and to thank her for saving his life, but she had turned and walked away without a word. For days he had ignored his official orders and delayed leaving for the Mexican border, hoping she'd relent enough to smile at him at least. But now his time was up and he could delay no longer. With an impatient frustration he jerked his horse around and started to move off, only to come to an abrupt halt. Forty feet away his father was engaged in the pursuit Stuart had just abandoned—watching a red-haired girl pull carrots. His eyes narrowed with icy fury as he recognized the expression on his father's face. The old lecher wanted her, too! That would account for the girl's arrogance and for Angus's lies. What the great Jamie MacKenzie wanted, he got. To hell with the bitch; if she belonged to his father, she was a real slut—a lying, teasing slut. Without another glance in his father's direction, Stuart prodded his horse and took off at a full gallop toward the waiting barge.

Whenever Stuart MacKenzie's emotions were involved, only time and action could blunt the raw edges of his flaming temper; at no time in his life before had his emotions been as stirred up as they were now. That snit had been the first woman to refuse him; unfortunately she'd also been the only one he'd ever really wanted.

Chapter
3

The passions of the third man who had been watching the girl were more powerful, more entrenched, and more destructive than any emotions the two MacKenzie men had ever experienced singly or collectively. In the case of Blake Creighton they were twenty years in the making—twenty years of seeing his life destroyed and twisted into sour nothingness just because she existed. Looking at her now through his military field glass, he muttered aloud a string of epithets which revealed the foulness of his own mind more than any real attribute of the girl. "Nigger lover, field hand slut, hot-headed termagant, and ungrateful traitor" were the ones he repeated most frequently; and he wondered for the thousandth time how he'd been suckered into fathering her. Only one thought consoled him—he wasn't the bitch's real father. That dubious pleasure belonged to a man whose identity had been a mystery to him until his return three weeks ago after four years of war. Four years of starting as captain and ending as captain.

His return to this house had ended his last faint hope of gleaning any remaining happiness from the debacle of his wasted life. Like every other Confederate soldier, he'd returned in a state of exhaustion, half starved and weakened by the strain and terror of battle. He'd had illusions of reconciling with his wife; he'd thought that, just possibly, she might have grown mature enough to give their marriage a chance. What irony! She hadn't even been there to greet him. His wife—the beautiful, unattainable girl he'd dreamed about as a young man—had finally escaped from her twenty years of bondage. How his gut had twisted when Sophia had told him the details of his wife's escape.

Six months earlier the damned Yankee general, Phil Sheridan, had defeated Confederate General Early in the Shenandoah Valley and sent twenty of the ranking officers from the beaten Confederate Army into detention at the MacKenzie farm in Maryland. Among these gentlemen prisoners was one Colonel Bradford Marshall. Bitterly, the man standing at the window twisted the hated word gentleman around his mouth. Only blooded southern gentlemen ever ranked above captain in the Confederacy; all other poor bastards could fight and die for the proud South, but only cursed bloods were considered aristocratic enough to lead. Well, the incompetent fools had led their South into a miserable defeat with only a devastated land as their reward for four years of bloody fighting.

With her malice and contempt revealed in every lip-smacking word, Sophia had informed him that two months after the defeat of the Confederates in the Shenandoah Valley, a young nigger boy had ridden an old mule to the Randall home and asked to speak to Miss Melissa, not Mrs. Creighton, but Miss Melissa—that southern euphemism used to flatter every blooded female from eight to eighty. He'd seen the note the boy had given his wife, a pleading note from a Mrs. Claire Marshall begging Melissa to intercede with James MacKenzie for the release of her son, Bradford. For twenty years, Creighton's wife had lived only sixty miles away from her lover's home. Sixty miles away on a rich plantation, the scot-free father of that damned girl had lived the life of a gentleman while Creighton had borne the brunt of raising his bastard daughter.

Once again he cursed the girl working in the field. According to Sophia, she'd taken her mother to Maryland, and he could only guess at the details of what must have been a charming reunion of lovers. No one in this house had raised a hand to stop his wife from leaving. Sophia and Janet had been happy to see her go while his father-in-law was too drunk to understand what was happening. That drunken old man had once been the elegant gentleman who'd bribed Creighton to marry his daughter. Creighton's innards writhed even today when he thought of the callous inhumanity of the trap the old man had set for him. He still tasted bitter gall when he remembered the years of hard work he'd spent making this farm productive while Clinton Randall had gambled the profits away. For four years before he married Melissa, Creighton had been the overseer here, a job he'd been grateful for at first. For the third son of a poor landowner in the pre-war South, the job of overseer was an honorable one.

God! How hard he had worked both before and after that magic day when Randall had walked down to the cottage office and offered his beautiful daughter for marriage. At twenty-six, Creighton had been as naive as a virgin, but immediately after the hurried-up wedding he discovered his wife was not. He'd discovered her pregnancy the morning after when Melissa had thrown up all over their marriage bed. But even after the bitter shock had worn off, he'd tried to make a go of the marriage because the old man had promised to leave the farm to the first son he and Melissa would have. It wasn't really the greatest future for an ambitious man, but it was one of the best prospects a poor man could expect in the tradition locked South. He remembered his relief when the bastard child had been a girl; but that relief turned to bile when the only two other children his wife conceived had miscarried. But he'd stayed on even as his hopes faded and even though his wife hated him because he had liked his mother-in-law. Pamela Randall had been a lady, a soft-spoken lady who had treated Creighton with respect. She'd seen to his every comfort and had helped him regulate the slaves. She had always appreciated his hard work and was grateful when he slipped some of the profits into her hands before her husband could lose it over the gaming tables. For those first nine and a half years his life had been bearable enough. Mrs. Randall had taken the trouble to keep her granddaughter away from him for the most part, and she'd forced Melissa to at least be civil to him in front of the family.

Once, in a rare moment of candor, she'd even apologized to him for the failure of his marriage. "Clinton was wrong," she'd said softly, "when he wouldn't let Melissa marry the boy she loved. It isn't your fault, Creighton, that my daughter is so unhappy. Her father's a proud man." Her gentle face had twisted with bitterness on the word proud. But proud Clinton Randall had been. He'd forbidden his daughter and grandchild to leave the plantation, and he had refused to have even one guest invited into his home. These cruel edicts made virtual prisoners out of the other family members. While Randall frequented his gambling clubs with regularity, only Creighton among the others had been free to conduct the necessary business away in the nearby cities and towns, but not free enough to develop any satisfactory social life of his own. The slow-acting poison of isolation had speeded up the decay in the family unity and accentuated the underlying deceit of the marriage of Creighton and Melissa. Unable to break through the resentment of his wife, he had taken his frustration out on the spirited, rebellious little girl who, even as a small child, had fought back. God, how she had fought him when he tried to force her into a spiritless submission. As an infant her piercing screams could drive him out of a room; as a five-year-old her open defiance infuriated him; and as a literate nine-year-old her logic defeated him. And the little hypocrite could mimic her grandmother's soft speech so perfectfully with the other family members, no one but he knew the sharp bite of her fiery temper.

During those years his hatred of her had been a hidden thing. Except for an occasionl slap, administered well away from Pamela Randall's watchful eye, Creighton had been forced into a silent battle of wills with a child who had little of her mother's appealing prettiness and none of her grandmother's gentleness. Restless as a caged bobcat, the cursed brat learned to read with devastating speed, not the charming little fairy tales of childhood but the dusty books of knowledge moldering on the shelves of the unused library. She had learned to cipher with a speed that embarrassed him frequently when she'd blurted out the answers to the questions her grandmother had been asking him about the costs and profits of a business transaction.

However, until the grandmother's death, he had managed to extract some measure of satisfaction from his life because he was essential to the financial survival of the family. But three weeks after Pamela's lonely funeral, the aggressive Baltimore banker, Joseph Ryder, had arrived at the plantation with foreclosure papers and an accurate account of the thousands of dollars of Clinton Randall's gambling debts the bank had purchased from other gentlemen gamblers. Even on that first visit, Ryder had been accompanied by the hard-faced Sophia and her sixteen-year-old, pussy-proud daughter, Janet. Less than three months later the would-be ladies moved into the house as the wife and stepdaughter of Clinton Randall, and Joseph Ryder asked Creighton to stay on as overseer. But an overseer was all he was expected to be, that and a servant. When the socially ambitious Sophia began to entertain the aristocratic neighbors of northern Virginia, the Creighton family was summarily moved into one of the cottages. Sophia did not want the competition Melissa might have given Janet in the beauty department, and Randall clung to his vindictive policy of punishing his wayward daughter.

The first week-long exile in the cottage had finished his marriage and exposed his hatred of the red-haired brat. Away from the repression of the big house, Melissa had lost some of her sullen apathy and had screamed at him when he'd attempted the same half rape he had subjected her to for years. Like an avenging devil, her wild-eyed, ten-year-old daughter had come running in to aid her mother; and for the first time she had used her childish fists to pommel the father she hated and feared. He had beaten her with a whip the next morning.

During that week and the ones that followed throughout the summer, Creighton had begun to use the women slaves for his sexual gratification. One day, when he was half-dragging, half-carrying a terrified thirteen-year-old girl into the quarters behind his office, the damned red-haired brat had tried to come to the girl's rescue with screams and pounding fists. After he had raped the girl, he turned with a savage joy to the punishment of his unholy stepchild. Only Melissa's frantic promise to submit to him had stopped this brutal beating of the ten-year-old Pamela Marsh.

But no temporary truce could stop the continuing deterioration of his life. Six months after he had acquired the farm, Joseph Ryder and his banking partner, James MacKenzie, whom Creighton had never met, freed all the slaves on the farm. And for the first time in dealing with blacks, the overseer experienced a fear of them. As slaves they had no rights, but as free men they might be tempted to do him bodily harm. Prudentially, he armed himself with pistols and a cruel new whip which could cripple a man with one powerful, cutting stroke. Even thus equipped he still felt trepidation whenever he was forced to work with them, because the freedom sickness had spread like an epidemic among them. House servants were rude to him and some of the bolder field hands left the farm to seek jobs elsewhere. As his own tension mounted, Creighton contemplated leaving his job; but since Joseph Ryder had taken over the ownership, the overseer had been able to siphon more and more money away from the profits. He knew that he could not acquire this much money at any other job. So he stayed on, putting up with the unpleasantness in his life and taking the insulting abuse Sophia heaped on him. At the offset of her residency, she made it clear that she considered him an employee whose job it was to do whatever she ordered. By far the most infuriating chore she assigned him was to accompany Clinton Randall on his periodic gambling sprees and to keep the older man from imbibing too much bourbon. At these "gentlemen's" clubs, Creighton was often treated like a servant, and his bitterness grew. Sophia further demeaned his dignity by insisting that he keep his "impudent and willful" daughter under control.

Using the less lethal whip at first, he attempted the requested discipline with a vengeance. He whipped her when he found her playing with a group of black children; he attempted to beat her when he found her watching the nigger doctor deliver a foal. On that occasion the tall aristocratic doctor took the whip away from the short overseer and deliberately cut it into useless pieces with one of his razor sharp medical scalpels. Now, seven years later, Creighton smiled nastily at the memory. He had gotten even with the doctor by using the other whip on the girl, taking care that the wounds were inflicted on the parts of the body least likely to be seen. Oh, she had retaliated all right! She refused to eat at the same table with him, she called him "white trash" in front of the workers, and she enlisted the help of her nigger friends. He'd whipped her often and harshly whenever he could do so without detection, but she still defied him. The last time he'd whipped her, he was just goddamned unlucky. If ever she deserved punishment, it was at that time. When he'd threatened the cook, Pamela Marsh had picked up a pot of hot coffee and thrown it at him.

Creighton still smarted when he remembered the scene in which MacKenzie had fired him and spirited the girl out of his reach. For those insults Creighton had vowed revenge;

and until General Lee had surrendered, he thought he'd been successful. In early April of 1861, he'd stolen twenty blooded horses and the best stallion on the place after coming back to the farm with twenty of the boys he'd been training for war. Holding the farm workers at bay with guns, he'd singled out the horses he wanted and ridden away. He'd tried to take the work stallion the girl rode, but that brute almost killed one of his men. Those stolen horses had paid for his captaincy, and the stallion had been his personal mount throughout four years of bloody battles. And the theft would have succeeded if the South had not been defeated. He still couldn't understand that defeat. Just last June the bungler Yankee, General "Useless" Grant, had been massacred at Cold Harbor, losing seven thousand men to General Lee's fifteen hundred. But only months later Lee had surrendered anyway, and Creighton had no alternative but to ride his tired stallion back to this hell hole. An hour after he'd stabled the animal, it had been quietly removed; and a grinning Angus Balfour had presented him with a bill for eighteen hundred dollars. It might as well have been eighteen million! His carefully hoarded thousands of dollars in the Alexandria bank were in worthless Confederate money. It was this bill he clutched in his hand now, a bill signed by Balfour, but written in his stepdaughter's hand. The amount would have been two thousand had not the bitch carefully deducted the cost of the clothes she'd stolen from his wardrobe.

When he'd first seen the bill, he'd broken out in a cold sweat; MacKenzie was vindictive enough to have him charged with theft. But Creighton had not lived a precarious life for twenty-odd years without developing a strong sense of survival. The next day he'd borrowed Clinton Randall's personal thoroughbred and ridden more than a hundred miles to Richmond. The memory of that seven day trip still rankled. He'd been stopped by no fewer than a dozen victorious Yankee patrols and forced to submit to the indignity of a weapon search. But in Richmond he'd located the man he was after, his cousin, Hiram Creighton. Hiram was a sixty-year-old reprobate lawyer who had profiteered throughout the war by supplying women first to southern officers and more recently to Yankee ones at even higher prices. Creighton had learned from his cousin what he wanted to know; under Virginia law, he was the legal father of Pamela Marshall Creighton and in complete control both of her and the wages she'd squirreled away for her six years of slave work on MacKenzie's farm. As an unmarried woman under twenty-one years of age, she was at the disposition of her legal father. He smiled vindictively at the "disposition" he and Hiram had decided on. The lawyer would marry her and put her to work. He and Creighton would share her future earnings equally, and her current bank account would be used to pay this damned bill for the horses. Until she died a broken-down, diseased hag, she would legally bear the name she'd hated all of her life.

Now the only job he had to do was to get her safely to Alexandria. All the necessary legal papers were neatly folded in his pocket, including a restraint order which would be served by a county sheriff. One hour's ride to fetch the man and one hour back, and the girl would be trapped. And then be damned to MacKenzie and the whole lot of the arrogant Randalls. But first, MacKenzie would have to be off the property. No sheriff in the whole South would be fool enough to face up to the powerful Baltimore banker, so the plans couldn't be carried out until the Scotsman was out of the way.

Impatiently, Creighton checked the clock and sighed; this day was already too far gone. It would be very easy for the girl to slip away in the dark. Hiram would just have to cool his heels for another day in Alexandria. Suddenly, Creighton swung his glass toward the Yankee major who'd been sitting on his horse for the last hour or more. He watched the hated bluecoat gallop off to the dock with satisfaction. At least that one was out of the way. When Creighton returned the first time, he'd seen the same major sniffing around the girl; but she'd evidently given him the shove-off. All to the good since Hiram had sworn that, with careful salesmanship, a virgin could bring five hundred dollars on the first night of her professional life. Strangely enough, Creighton was sure that his stepdaughter was untouched. She was too ambitious and proud to let any man mount her without being married to him, and that horse she rode astride like some savage Indian would have killed anyone who threatened her when she was on its back.

He sighed again and returned to the vigil. In the distance he heard the barge take off, and he knew that MacKenzie would spend the night in the cottage next door to the one the girl slept in. Doggedly, Creighton continued to watch the girl work. Not until the sun was almost down did she straighten up and rub her lower back. With the malice of anticipated revenge, he hoped she would be as tired as hell tomorrow; and he also hoped that she'd saved every cent of her wages. He kept his glass trained on her until she mounted her waiting horse and rode over to join MacKenzie. He felt a curious detachment, an almost impersonal inhumanity as he watched his last tangible asset ride out of range. But damned if she wasn't going to prove more valuable than any illusory prospect he'd ever had. With her vitality and looks she should be good at the trade for twenty years—fifteen at the least.

Chapter
4

All day long she'd felt the prickling of premonition on her neck, and she could have sworn her beloved horse was just as nervous. She knew that the white trash Creighton was back again; not much went on in the big house she didn't know about. But she'd not felt like this when he'd returned the first time three weeks earlier; not that she'd seen him then, either. She hadn't seen his face or spoken to him since the day four years ago when he'd stolen the horses. And at that time their conversation had consisted of insults shouted across the wide show yard. She still remembered his order to one of his men: "Take the slut's horse."

Her response had been a contemptuous challenge. "Why don't you try to take him yourself, white trash, if you have the courage?" Her words had been drowned out by the scream of the horse the young soldier was riding when her stallion reared up and crashed his hooves down on the hopeless creature, knocking both the rider and his horse to the ground. Only her screamed command of "Halt" to her stallion had saved the man's life; his horse was already dying. Had Creighton not hated her with such a blind passion, the second injury would not have occurred. Drawing his pistol and pointing it at her, he had shouted two more orders: "Stand where you are, bitch, or I'll kill you," and to a tall lanky boy near him, "Get a rope on the horse."

The whistling hiss of the expertly thrown rope had terrified both the stallion and its young owner now standing helplessly in the center of the yard. However, as the restraining rope was yanked taut around its neck, the stallion lost its fear and reacted with the aggressive power and fury which had made its distant ancestors the great fighting destriers of the crusades. It charged toward the unlucky man holding the rope, reared once again and brought its hooves down with lethal strength. This time the man's scream mingled with that of his mount. With the released rope trailing behind him, her stallion had raced toward Marsh to stand quiescently between her own body and that of her despised stepfather. For its protective instinct her beautiful horse had received one of Creighton's bullets in its fleshy rump, a bullet Dr. Damon had subsequently removed without leaving any permanent damage to the animal. Damon had also set the arm and the leg of the injured man whom Creighton had callously ordered to be left behind.

That violent scene was the last time she'd seen the little man who'd plagued her life. He'd left with the stolen horses within minutes of firing his gun. Today, four years later, she felt the same fear as she glanced apprehensively toward the big house. Instinctively, she knew that somewhere behind those staring blank windows, he was watching. She was equally disturbed by the sight of Stuart glowering at her from across the field; in a different way his reaction toward her was almost as violently emotional as that of the hidden watcher. In Stuart's case she did not dare relax her vigilance; her own emotions were too treacherously involved with him. Her awareness of James MacKenzie lacked any tension, she was glad to see him; but she dared not stop working long enough to ride over to greet him. Back-strained and bone weary, she continued the endless task of pulling carrots, stripping them, and filling the wagon.

Thank God, this was the last wagon, not just for today but forever on this farm. When the Union soldiers arrived tomorrow morning to convey the final caravan of loaded wagons to Richmond, she would be out of the food production business. During the last three weeks she and her co-workers had stripped the smokehouse, animal pens and fields to fill the empty wagons of eight other relief missions. Once the money was safely banked in her own Washington, D.C. bank account and those of the twenty workers, the bonus years were over; she would become a free agent for the first time in her life. Her freedom papers were the seven thousand dollars she had saved over three years of slaving in vegetable patches, pig pens, rabbit hutches and chicken coops. That modest fortune and the three thousand of wages MacKenzie had paid her for over six years represented her passport to a life far removed from this farm which held so many unhappy memories.

Three years ago, when she was sixteen and as adventuresome as a frisky colt, she had thought raising food would be a lark. It had proved to be a harder and more challenging job than her regular one of working with MacKenzie horses. It had entailed endless planning and division of duties. Adah had proved her worth in the smokehouse, Jake had undertaken the ugly job of slaughtering, while his sons had supervised the constant plowing. Only twenty of the eighty workers on the farm had joined the cooperative enterprise; but the lazier ones who had laughingly refused lived to regret their decision soon afterward. As the sources of food from other farms dried up, those idle workers had been forced to buy their food from their productive mates; and the tensions had mounted between the two groups. Marsh regretted this schism in worker morale, but she'd been delighted when the residents of the big house had been forced to buy their food from her, too. She'd laughed on the day when Sophia tried to insist that Marsh should supply the food free out of family loyalty.

During the first year when production had been limited, sales had been a simple matter. Adventuresome capital dwellers rowed across the Potomac to purchase food directly. But as the river became a dangerous waterway patrolled by Union gunboats and constantly threatened by Rebel snipers, shoppers had ceased to make the hazardous crossing; and the necessity to transport the food to the capital had become almost a daily ritual. At dawn the workers would load the one or two wagons with the available food to be ferried across the river on the MacKenzie barge. On the days when there was only one wagon, she and Jake went alone; but on days when two were required, Jake's oldest boys accompanied them.

Marsh remembered with amusement her first day of doing business in the big city. Although she had already learned to deal expertly with the men who had come to the farm to purchase horses and with soldiers of all ranks, her first encounter with street loiterers and aggressive housewives increased her knowledge of human nature a thousand percent. The men had shouted obscenities at her and made insultingly lewd remarks about her masculine attire. While she was busy selling meat to a carpingly critical housewife, one of the bolder of the degenerate men made the unfortunate mistake of pinching her on one of her rounded buttocks. As fast in her reactions as she was hot tempered, Marsh didn't hesitate. Picking up the leg of lamb she had been showing, she swung it around with all of her farm-hardened strength and sent the startled man staggering over the dock into the river. After that display of self-defense the other street loungers kept their distance. But the housewives were not so easily intimidated, nor were they patient enough to await their turn politely. They shoved each other aside, brawled out orders, argued about prices, and mauled the produce with their busy hands. Being a black man in this frenzied small world of white women, Jake could do little to help a beleaguered and furious Marsh.

She was very thoughtful on the way home with one-third of their food no longer fit for public sale. As Jake drove the wagon onto the barge, she asked one of the dock workers where the other farmers did their selling.

"At the farmer's square," he replied promptly, "there's a policeman there who keeps order. You're pretty new at this game, ain't you?" He grinned at her with open enjoyment.

She smiled back at him. "I was today, but I never will be again," she promised him.

That night, after the unsold food had gone into the communal supper pots, Marsh spoke long and earnestly to the two cooperative members who had done most of the carpentry work for the enterprise. For long hours in the cook shed that night by candlelight, the twenty workers transformed the largest of the wagons into a grocery store on wheels, with boxes that separated the food to be sold into fresh meat, smoked meat, fresh and dried vegetables. When one side of the box was opened, it dropped down to become a working counter for Jake and Marsh to sell from.

"Nobody will be able to ruin our vegetables or steal our meat tomorrow," Marsh announced to the tired crew after the job was finished. Determined to sell every item of food the next day, Marsh ignored the muttered comments made by the farmers and their wives about her attire and her unladylike manners. In a voice that could be heard a city block away, she advertised the products, "Our food is freshest because our farm is closest." When one of the farmers' sons threw a clod of wet mud at her, her voice rang out with earthier comments. "How much do you charge by the pound for that young jackass, farmer?" And in response to a fat farm wife who called her a shameless hussy, Marsh responded cheerfully, "At least I'm a thin one. We fatten our animals, not ourselves."

Whether it was due to the excellence of their products or Marsh's sharp tongue, Jake and she were sold out in two hours; and in the process they acquired their first two regular customers. One was the purchasing agent for a restaurant who asked that they deliver food to the rear of his place of business each morning before they sold anything to the public. For the next twenty-eight months he would buy one-fourth of their total inventory. But it was the second regular who captured the farm girl's imagination. Slender and tall, the woman was elegantly dressed in a gown of cerulean blue which made her glossy hair seem as black as a raven's wing. Piped with black braid, the flounced skirt cascaded out over a framework hoop that made the dress six-feet wide at the hemline. The saucy hat tipped over one eye held two long feathers, dyed the same vibrant color as the dress. Like the restaurant man, this remarkable woman also requested delivery at her place of business and carefully wrote out her name and address. Months later, Marsh was to discover that the finest hams and plumpest chickens were served to senators and congressmen in the company of pretty women whose rosy cheeks came from cosmetic jars. Yvette de Bloom owned and ran the most expensive and discreet brothel on Capitol Hill, and her clients were the men who ran the Union half of the Civil War.

During the first delivery at the rear of the huge, beautiful house, Jake was nervously protective of Marsh, fearing a possible enlistment into the ranks of Washington demimondes. As a black veteran of slavery who had risen far above the ranks of field hand, he was quite knowledgeable about the recreational pursuits of white gentlemen and about the identity of the woman's profession and her place of business. In the company of her two black cooks, Yvette met Jake and Marsh at the back door and smiled broadly when she noticed Jake's expression.

"You don't have to worry, monsieur, about this one. She's pretty enough, but those blazing eyes and that barnyard mouth would scare hell out of my customers." Not for months would Marsh understand the meaning of these words; and when she finally did, she was shocked to hear Yvette casually refer to Mr. MacKenzie as Jamie.

Fortunately in her case, innocence about the facts of life did not last long for Marsh. Wartime Washington, D.C. was a city of busy intrigue, full of disoriented, displaced people who came and went with the tides of war. Because President Lincoln demanded that the city be fortified, there were always Union soldiers in the streets. Curiously, there were also hundreds of Union sympathizers from the South, including Confederate officers who had been captured in battle and then paroled on their word as gentlemen not to attempt escape. Prostitution thrived openly on the crowded back streets, and any ignorance the Virginia farm girl might have had about the nature of their business was rapidly dissipated. These gaudily dressed women were so brazen and obvious, they made Yvette de Bloom's establishment seem like a model of decorum.

As far as Marsh and Jake were concerned, Yvette was a lady and the best friend they had in the capital city. Their sales soon became limited to regular customers, most of whom were the households of Yvette's favored clients. Each day, after their route was finished, Marsh spent a tedious half hour banking the money in her own account and into the twenty accounts of the workers. Because Angus had accompanied her on the day the accounts were opened, the staid banking officials soon accepted the oddly dressed girl as a regular depositor. Intent on conducting her business as efficiently and as swiftly as possible, Marsh was unaware that she had become one of the city's most talked about characters. Except for the occasional jeers she received from street people, she was treated with respect, especially by the customers who now routinely tipped Jake and her for the excellence of their services. While some of the tips were small, others were substantial, although few rivaled the gold coins Yvette pressed into their hands each day. Unlike the rest of the money, Marsh banked these tips into hers and Jake's accounts alone; and they watched with satisfaction as their bank balances grew in volume. Immediately after the banking chore was completed each weekday, she and Jake returned to the farm to take up their assigned duties tending the MacKenzie horses.

Since early 1861 the MacKenzie farm had virtually become an isolated island, its landside boundaries heavily barricaded. After the debacle of the disastrous Union defeat at the first battle of Bull Run, when thousands of demoralized, inexperienced Federal soldiers poured over the farm, terrorizing the workers and stealing whatever was not guarded, MacKenzie had ordered the barricades erected. For weeks the workers had cut down trees and piled them around the perimeter. Every sizable rock on the farm had been added to the barrier, and thousands of holes were dug to discourage any mounted marauders. The public road leading to the paddock gates was dug up and covered with debris, as was the farm boundary on the levee road. Alternating groups of workers were assigned patrol duty to check the outer defenses, and for four years the farm had remained a secure haven. In 1862, when the southern armies had invaded Maryland and Pennsylvania as far north as Antietam Creek, Union soldiers had been posted on the farm to bolster the defenses. But no attack had occurred since the South chose a route far to the west of the capital city. Since that time the occasional inspections by Union soldiers were the only reminders to the farm residents that a brutal war was being waged to the south of them.

Only twice in the last three years of the war were the farm barricades broached, once by John Mosby and again by Phil Sheridan. Both times Marsh had been warned in time to greet them and to wind up with a bad case of hero worship for these leaders. She had laughed when General Mosby—she had no idea what rank he actually held but had decided it would be best to address him as General—paid her in stolen Union money. She felt no qualms about accepting it or about charging him double the going rate for food and for the horse he bought. Charmed by his southern gallantry, she had readily agreed to sell him equal amounts of food in the future. Six more times during the following year, when a small band of his men drove a wagon furtively along the cleared levee road in the predawn hours, more of the stolen Yankee money had changed hands.

For the Phil Sheridan visit in 1864, workers had cleared the main roadway, and Marsh had experienced an almost awesome thrill at the precision of the military parade of horsemen who rode through the paddock gates. The demanding work of filling the order for replacement horses had taken most of the afternoon, but midway through the job Marsh had overcome her temporary shyness to talk to the general informally. She had acted like any besotted girl and actually blushed when he complimented her on her horsemanship. Emboldened by his friendly attitude, she had dared offer him the finest horse on the farm. That moment of sale was the high point of her war years.

The major wartime upheaval of her personal life was also bound up with General Sheridan and his victorious taking of Confederate prisoners. Several weeks after his visit, her mother had entered the office where Marsh was working and demanded that her daughter escort her to Maryland. Annoyed as she always had been by her beautiful, ineffectual mother, Marsh concluded that Melissa had finally reverted completely to childhood.

"Come on, I'll take you back to the house," she coaxed impatiently, all too aware of the hours of work still remaining on her own busy schedule.

"Don't be a fool, Pamela. I want to go to James MacKenzie's farm in Maryland, and I want to go now," Melissa upbraided her daughter in a tone of voice Marsh had never heard her use before.

"Why? there's nothing over—"

"The reason need not concern you, Pamela. Now take me across the river."

Since the entirety of their relationship for the past six years had consisted of a three hour visit every Sunday during which time Melissa had shampooed her daughter's unruly hair and talked primly about the value of ladylike manners, Marsh could not believe that her mother was acting rationally. She had never known her to leave the farm before; and she had never seen her display an iota of the spirit, much less the fire, that lighted her soft brown eyes this day. Nor had she ever seen Melissa so attractively dressed or so glowingly lovely.

Pausing only long enough to wash her own face and rake a comb through her hair, Marsh escorted her impatient mother to the dock where Jake was supervising the loading of horses.

"Have you got room for us, Jake?" Marsh asked.

Even as he was smiling at her mother, Jake scolded Marsh, "Miss Milly cain't ride with the horses, Marsh. I already done tole Sam to take her acrost on the tug. Phoebe done bring your things here already, Miss Milly." Then, without a word of explanation to Marsh, Jake escorted her mother aboard the small tug as if she were a fragile flower, leaving Marsh to scramble on board as best she could.

During the crossing, Marsh waited irritably for her mother to explain the purpose of the trip, but she waited in vain. Except for one charming expression of gratitude for Jake, Melissa didn't say a word the entire journey. She just stood facing the Maryland marshland with a look of shining expectancy on her face. At the dock, one of the Union soldiers gallantly helped the older woman off the tug and sent one of the dockhands to locate James MacKenzie. Marsh, who was generally treated like another soldier by the men, was amazed by the speed with which her mother and she were escorted to a bench on the shady side of the large receiving barn. As they waited, Melissa remained radiantly calm while Marsh became increasingly disturbed. How the devil was she going to explain her mother's sudden flight of sanity to her glowering employer? But she didn't get to say a word, and MacKenzie didn't glower once. In the suddenly imperious voice of a southern lady, her mother did all the talking.

"Mr. MacKenzie, I have information that, among the

Confederate officers who are detained here, there is a Colonel Bradford Marshall.''

Still with a charming smile on his face—he'd never wasted such a smile on her, Marsh reflected wryly—MacKenzie told the sergeant to check; but Melissa insisted with the same arrogance she'd exhibited earlier that MacKenzie take her to the colonel. Confused but still gallant, the Scot offered his arm and escorted the beautiful Virginian lady over the considerable distance to the paddock area. Marsh and the sergeant followed silently behind. Once in the show yard, where several mounted Confederate prisoners were engaged in the training of MacKenzie horses, the Scot called out, "Colonel Marshall, you have a visitor."

When one of the men dismounted and turned around, Marsh heard the sharp gasp of her employer before she saw the face of the man walking toward them. Even in his shabby gray uniform he was the most handsome man she had ever seen, with unruly auburn curls curling crisply around a boyish face. She watched as the man's keen look of inquiry changed first to a tentative smile and then to a blindingly brilliant one.

"Milly? Melissa Randall? My God, it's really you." He didn't even glance at the girl standing with a stunned look next to an equally stunned MacKenzie; he saw only one person.

With a gruff voice Marsh recognized as an angry one, the Scotsman snapped, "Better take the lady into my office, Colonel."

His arm now firmly around Melissa's slender waist, the speechless colonel did not even nod in agreement as he led her off, leaving the angry man and confused girl behind.

"Come on, Marsh, I think you'd better go back home."

"What about my mother?"

"I don't think she plans to return, Marsh. I'll see that she's all right."

"But I don't understand."

"I know you don't. Some people have no sense at all. Why

did your mother have to drag you with her? She could have come alone and spared you."

Marsh looked steadily at the man who now held her arm protectively. "Spared me what, Mr. MacKenzie?"

Bluntly, he told her what he'd realized the moment he'd seen the Southerner's face. "The shock of seeing your real father for the first time. At least she could have warned you."

In a daze, she denied his words. "He couldn't be. He's too young and too handsome."

MacKenzie's face softened. "Haven't you ever looked in a mirror, Marsh?"

"I don't own one," she admitted.

"You look just like him. Except you're a beautiful woman." As if he regretted his praise, he became impatient with her. "For God's sake, Marsh, don't you ever notice the way men look at you?"

More aware now, she focused on his face. "Angus always laughs at the way I look, and you always glower at me the way you're doing now."

"Lord, you're naive."

But her next response caused him to jerk sharply. "Oh, I've seen the expression on the faces of some of the soldiers. They look just like our old boar before it services a sow. But those men would look at any female like that. They've been at war a long time, and not many of them can afford to go to a whorehouse at today's prices."

Shocked, he could only gasp, "For God's sake, Marsh, watch your language. You sound like a guttersnipe. Ladies don't even know words like those."

"You'd be surprised what some ladies talk about in private." She was thinking about Sophia and Janet. "Never in public though; in public they simper and smirk like self-satisfied cats." Remembering her own past hypocrisy, she grinned at him. "It works, too. I sold more than one horse for you in that sweet lil' ol' voice."

Laughing now, he hugged her arm. "I'll bet you have." Then he paused and sobered. "Marsh, about your father—"

"Which one? The one back there," she pointed, "doesn't know I exist and wouldn't give a damn if he did. And the other one has always hated me. But at least I know why now."

"I don't think your mother has had an easy time, either."

"No, she hasn't. But she made the mistake, I didn't. And she probably had fun doing it."

"Marsh!"

"Look, Mr. MacKenzie, my mother just left me without a backward glance, just as she always has. If it hadn't been for my grandmother and for Angus and you, I'd have become a runaway tramp years ago. Now I don't need any parents so let's just forget them."

He looked at the flare of her delicate nostrils and the grim set of her jaw, and was silent. He wanted to put his arms around her, but he didn't dare for his own sake as well as hers.

"I'm crossing over with you," he announced abruptly.

"No. You know good and well that you'll have to help those two back there. I'll bet the laws about runaway wives are worse than those for runaway slaves. If I know you, you'll probably pay to hide them someplace, just as you've paid for me all these years." Then, for the first time, she did a remarkable thing. She stretched up and kissed the startled man on his cheek. "Thank you, Mr. MacKenzie, for everything you've done," she murmured. Pulling away from his restraining hand, she ran lightly down the dock and stepped quickly aboard the waiting tug. She never looked back to see the sudden flush on his face or the hunger in his eyes.

For the first time in years, Adah tucked Marsh into bed that night and then sat calmly down on the edge of the bed.

"Marsh, honey, it's time you know about your mother and real daddy. Now don't you be shakin' that stubborn head of yourn and don't you be askin' fool questions while I tells you about yo' folks, the good ones of them.

"When yo' grandmother wuz jest a little tike, her folks died and she come to live with her aunt and uncle. They 'uz the Bramwells and they 'uz mighty good people. Your grandmother grew up with their own daughter and them two 'uz good friends. They 'uz married at the same time—Miss Pamela to your granddaddy and Miss Claire to the Marshall who bought Miss Pamela's own home. He wasn't no close kin of hers, honey, but he 'uz a good man. He set aside the money for Miss Pamela. She had a whole passel of it when she married your granddaddy, but it didn't take him no time to gamble it all away. That's how come the Marshalls and the Bramwells hated him. Reason I knows all this is 'cause the Bramwells done give me to Miss Pamela as a wedding gift.

"Well, Miss Pamela had a lot of fight in her. Every year she jest told that husband that she 'uz goin' visit her cousin, and she done tuk me and your mother to Miss Claire's house for three months. Your daddy was Miss Claire's only chile, and he and your mother played together 'spite of the fact that he 'uz three years older. When Miss Milly was fifteen, that play done turn into something else, and Miss Claire and Miss Pamela decided that it 'uz time for their young 'uns to git married. So Miss Pamela bring your mother back here 'cause she had to get your granddaddy's permission. She didn't know that you 'uz already on the way.

"Honey, I'm right sorry about this next part. Your granddaddy 'uz mean. No way 'uz he goin' let your mother marry up with a Marshall."

Marsh sat abruptly up in bed and exploded into contemptuous speech. "Why didn't that ninny mother of mine just run away?"

"She tried, honey, but her daddy done cotched her and he whup her good. That 'uz when she tole him about you. Mean 'uz a snake he forced her to marry that white trash overseer, and 'tween them they done broke her spirit. When you turned out to be a girl and a red-headed one instead of the boy your granddaddy wanted, he was meaner than ever to Miss Milly. He done keep her a prisoner in that ol' house and he done tole Miss Pamela to raise you. Don't 'spect your daddy knew anything 'bout you 'til today.''

"And my mother just let that old man ruin both her and my lives?''

"Don't reckon she had any choice. That man she married 'uz a mean one too. I 'spects she done put up with a lot to keep you safe.''

When Marsh remained silent after Adah finished talking, the older woman asked nervously, ''What's you thinkin' about?''

"That I'm damned glad that I'm not related to that scum. And I hope that my mother will be happy.''

"So does I, honey.''

"And I'm glad my mother finally found the gumption to get her revenge on that old drunkard and on that white trash he forced her to marry. Don't worry any more about me, Adah. I've got you and Jake and I don't need any other parents.''

"You jest keeps on rememberin' that Jake and I thinks mighty highly of you, honey. You jest keeps on rememberin'.''

Minutes later, when the black woman climbed into bed beside her husband, she was muttering, ''I hope that white trash man done gets kilt in this war. Effen he don't, he's goin' take his bile out on that chile.''

Half asleep, Jake roused enough to reassure his wife. "Don't fret none, Adah. Mr. MacKenzie won't let nothin' bad happen to her.''

Looking back now on the events of that traumatic day, Marsh reflected that she'd missed her mother very little and that she couldn't even remember what her father looked like. They had no place in her plans anyway. Only Jake, Adah, and Angus were important now; and tomorrow all of them would begin their new life as far from this farm as they could manage. Briefly, she wondered if Mr. MacKenzie would miss her; probably not, she decided, she'd been a worry for him long enough. And as for Stuart, he went tearing out of here as if he couldn't wait to see the last of her. She remembered his kisses with a grim bitterness. Stuart would have to be the one she'd chosen to let kiss her, and all he wanted was to roll her in the hay as if she were only a farm slut. But she'd always known in her heart that no decent man would ever offer to marry her. That kind would demand respectability and background or, she added ruefully, legitimacy at least. And she'd never settle for the kind of arrangement Stuart had suggested; she'd rather join Yvette de Bloom and keep her independence. She laughed when she remembered what Yvette had told her two weeks ago when Marsh had made the final deliveries of food to her Washington customers.

"You're a world beater, Marsh. Jamie told me that you've saved every penny you've ever earned. I wish you were a less ambitious woman. I'd have liked to keep you with me, but I still say you'd scare hell out of my customers."

But not even this heavy humor could stop the dull thudding of her heart as she watched Stuart ride off with that sudden fury of his. I wish he'd been a nobody instead of Jamie MacKenzie's son, she almost said aloud, until her common sense reasserted itself and she shrugged impatiently at her own foul humor.

The sun was setting when she painfully straightened her back, mounted her horse, and rode over to greet her employer, whom she hadn't seen since the day her mother left.

"Is that the last of it, Marsh?"

"The very last. Tomorrow morning when those wagons are driven off, I'm out of business, you'll have your farm back, and we'll be on our way."

"That's what I came to talk to you about."

"What?"

"Your way."

"Who knows where Angus will find us a good farm."

"In Wyoming, Marsh. I've just returned from there. You know my brother has been killed, don't you?"

"Yes, Mr. MacKenzie, and I'm very sorry."

"Thanks, Marsh. You'd have liked him. Before he died, he, my son, Robbie, and I located a great piece of land in a beautiful country which will be ideal for horses. Robert is selling the Nebraska farm and moving to Wyoming. There's room for you, too. Incidentally, I'm giving you a dozen part-Clydesdale mares. They're useless to me on a saddle farm."

"I can't afford them yet, Mr. MacKenzie."

"I'll take my payment in future colts. After all, I'll need some excuse to come and see you."

"I'd think you'd be happy to see the last of me. And don't give me any of your Scot wheedling about my being 'bonnie and braw.' I know what I am."

Unhappy about the heavy pessimism in her voice, he asked sharply, "What's happened, Marsh?"

She shook her head impatiently. "Nothing, I'm just tired. Come on, I'll race you to the office, and maybe Angus will give us a dram of his magic cure-all."

Throughout that evening and all the next morning, both MacKenzie and Angus watched the girl closely, disturbed by her uncharacteristic mood of flippant cynicism. Even when she thanked them both sincerely for all they had done for her, she still could not recapture any of her usual optimism.

"With Angus doing all the business for the new farm and Jake's family most of the work, I'll just be an unnecessary nobody. But then that's all I've ever been, isn't it?"

Angus scowled and silently cursed Stuart MacKenzie. James MacKenzie frowned and almost refused to leave her at the farm long enough to return to Maryland and conclude the sale of the Sheridan horses. But Marsh would have none of his threatened protection. Her smile was pure gamin, but her eyes haunted him.

"I'll be pretty much alone for the rest of my life. I'd better learn to enjoy my own company."

Delaying as long as they could, well after the noon hour, MacKenzie and Angus were finally forced to leave. Only Jake and Adah were at the dock to wave them off. Marsh had said her studiedly casual good-bye at the office, and had taken off on her horse for a final sentimental inspection of the barn and paddock areas. Fragments of memory pricked her consciousness as she wandered from spot to spot—from the barn stall where Damon had let her deliver her first foal, to the table where Carina had showed her how to mix the sedative which could deaden the pain of a wounded horse, and finally back to the office where Angus had taught her the rudiments of record keeping. Most of the good memories of her nineteen years were bound up in this world of utility. She had not one souvenir of youth to tuck into the worn carpetbag which held the entirety of her wardrobe—two extra pairs of boots and trousers, four mended shirts, a worn sheepskin coat, and some hand-me-down pieces of underwear.

By four o'clock, two of the three wagons were packed and ready to go. Marsh smiled when she recalled how she'd acquired those wagons from the argumentative Union colonel who'd rudely demanded all of the farm produce the day after the South had surrendered. In addition to market value in Yankee cash, Marsh had held out stubbornly for the three sturdy wagons. In aggravated frustration, the colonel had finally agreed. She and Angus would drive the first one, Jake and Adah would be in the second, and their three sons would drive the ones which would carry six porcine passengers, one young boar in a heavy crate and five healthy sows. Six work mares would pull the wagons while her stallion and three heavy saddle mares would complete their caravan.

Little remained to be done before the predawn departure the next morning except to clean up their living quarters, a job which Adah and Marsh now tackled with little enthusiasm. Their first awareness of danger was the expression on

Jake's face when he appeared without warning at the open cottage door—a thundercloud expression of hatred mixed with white-eyed terror. He walked woodenly into the room just as Adah's sharp hiss of warning focused Marsh's eyes on the man who followed with his jacket opened wide to expose a large and lethal pistol tucked into his belt. It was Blake Creighton with a smile. of satisfied malice etched deep into his face. The staccato sounds of his polished boots against the wood floor were the only ones to break the emotion charged silence of the room. Twice, when Jake's huge hands tightened into useless fists, Creighton's slender hand moved toward the gun, but the smile did not leave his face.

So intent on watching the man who seemed to threaten their very lives, the three would-be victims almost missed the entrance into the office of a fifth person. Only his pleasantly deep drawl of unmistakable authority lent them the courage to turn their eyes toward the speaker, a tall middle-aged man whose ruddy face bespoke years of outdoor life.

"I'm looking for a Miss Pamela Creighton," he announced in the deceptively soft voice of a Virginian.

Reassured faintly, Marsh gained enough courage to reply. "There's no such person. My name is Marsh."

The man's eyes twinkled slightly as he studied her. "I'm Sheriff Dan Rumford of Alexandria, Miss Marsh, and I have a restraining order for you signed by your father."

Her voice was now sharp and distinct. "If you mean that white trash over there, he is not my father."

Patiently, Rumford tried a second approach. "Was Mr. Blake Creighton married to your mother at the time of your birth?"

Abruptly, Marsh changed the subject. "Sheriff, last week Union soldiers posted notices all over the farm stating that Confederate soldiers could not carry weapons on their persons. This man is armed and has been threatening us. I ask that you disarm him."

"That order is in effect, ma'am, and I'll disarm the gentleman once we reach Alexandria. Now, about my question."

"Yes, he was married to my mother but he is not my father."

"Ma'am, he is your legal father accordin' to Virginia civil law."

"Why am I being restrained, Sheriff?"

"Your father, ma'am, has made an official complaint that you are a rebellious daughter and that he would require official help in making you comply with his wishes."

Her heart was pounding with a deadly fear. "What are his wishes?"

"He has arranged for you to be married to one Hiram Creighton, attorney-at-law. Mr. Hiram Creighton is now waiting at my office in Alexandria."

"Does this man"—her lip curled as she indicated her stepfather—"have the right to force me to marry a man I have never seen or even heard of?"

"Yes, ma'am. According to my records you are an unmarried female of nineteen years. Your father does have the legal right to marry you to a man of his choice."

Jake's rumbling voice reverberated about the room. "Dis man done beat Miss Marsh with a whip, Sheriff. He don't have the right to hurt her more."

"Jake and I are old friends, Sheriff," Creighton interposed silkily, "aren't we, boy?"

"No, suh, I neber was no friend of yourn."

Part of the silk in Creighton's voice was replaced by a rasp. "I'll tend to you later, boy."

Marsh heard the threat and acted to protect Jake. "Sheriff, this man you claim to be my legal father was the overseer on this farm long before my friends were freed from slavery. He was a cruel overseer who used the whip freely on both men and women. The man who owns the farm now fired him for beating me and forbid him to set foot on this property. But Mr. MacKenzie is not here right now to see that his orders are carried out. Can you guarantee the safety of these poeple if I go with you peacefully? I'm afraid that this man whom you called a gentleman a few minutes ago plans to return here to do them harm.''

Slowly, Rumford moved his eyes from the girl, now visibly trembling, to the small man still leaning threateningly against the desk. "Yes, ma'am, I can promise you that this man will not harm your friends.''

"Thank you, Sheriff Rumford,'' she murmured, her speech now soft and southern, "If y'all will excuse me, I'll go saddle my horse.''

Alerted by her changed voice, Creighton snapped, "Don't let her out of your sight, Rumford. She's sneakier than a weasel.''

Ignoring the insult, Marsh turned again toward the lawman. "My horse is stabled in back, Sheriff, if y'all could help me, I'd surely appreciate it.''

"I'll come too,'' Creighton declared. "I don't trust her one damn bit.''

Once again the sheriff studied the man carefully and was still watching him when they reached the lean-to shed. Once again Creighton protested. "Not that damned stallion. Don't let her take that killer.''

Marsh spoke pleadingly to the tall Southerner. "This is the only horse I know how to ride.''

Rumford's eyes were now twinkling merrily. "I've heard about that horse, Miss Marsh. I'd appreciate seeing you ride him.''

As he talked, Marsh cinched on the lightweight work saddle and led the horse out of its stall to the open ground where Creighton was nervously mounting his own horse. Gallantly, the sheriff helped the girl up on her stallion and listened to her next request with amused intent. "Do y'all mind if we go by the levee road? It's so much cooler and I'd admire seein' the river for one last time. This has been my home all my life.''

"Damn it, no," her stepfather barked, "the main road is shorter and I'm in a hurry."

His head cocked to one side as he swung easily into his own saddle, Rumford looked from one to another of the other two riders, and debated the decision orally. "The main road is shorter if there's no traffic, but it's been mighty busy lately. I reckon we'd best take the levee road."

Even before he finished talking, Marsh had turned her horse toward the dock; for the first time that afternoon she permitted herself a slight smile. But like a keyed up contestant at a state fair, Creighton noted the smile and jockeyed his horse close to hers on the path. Deliberately, he raised his crop to a position of instant readiness.

With a sweet smile, Marsh appealed again to the lawman. "Sheriff Rumford, sir, my horse gets mighty nervous around whips. Would y'all mind ridin' between me and that man? I'd feel much more secure if you would. I'd hate to lose control, especially on a levee road alongside this dangerous ol' river."

Smothering a smile, the big man obligingly nudged his horse between the other man and the girl. He'd heard about her earlier river exploits.

"You ride very well for a girl's who's afraid of losing control, Miss Marsh; and I imagine that you and your stallion are a mighty competent pair."

Marsh leaned forward to pat the stallion's head. "He's right intelligent, Sheriff Rumford, and bless his sweet ol' heart, he surely tries to please me."

Without a break in her southern inflection, Marsh gently wheeled her horse toward the river, bent low over its head, and cried, "Go, boy."

Like a released spring, the stallion arched itself into the river, its four legs extended and its head held tautly high. After one mighty splash, it was swimming with powerful strokes toward the far side of the Potomac.

Before she was out of hearing, Marsh heard Rumford's chuckle change abruptly to a sharp command. "You fire that pistol, Creighton, and I'll charge you with murder or attempted murder on the spot.''

The only part of her stepfather's high-pitched scream that she heard was, ''Damn you, Rumford, you let the bitch—''

But Marsh was beyond caring about the dialogue on shore; she was in the middle of a swift river which few horses had the endurance to cross. She prayed that her beloved stallion would prove the exception as she headed him, not toward the dredged-out Washington docks where Creighton might have posted other lawmen to wait for her, but toward the mile-wide marshlands which flanked the Maryland MacKenzie Farm. It was a gamble only a desperate person with nothing to lose would take; and at the moment Marsh was convinced that only her friends could save her.

For two tense days she had felt the threat of unknown danger. But never, even in the moments of deepest gloom, had she thought that the danger would be as great as the one she now faced. Resolutely and soothingly, she murmured encouragement into the ears of her struggling horse.

Chapter
5

The sky was streaked with the dark gold of the spring sunset when the exhausted horse and its rider neared the narrow stretch of land which formed one side of the dock channel leading to the Maryland farm. They had been in the water for over an hour and Marsh knew that her stallion had to reach land or go under. She could hear the heavy pounding of its heart and the tortured straining of its lungs. It's now or never, she prayed and turned the beast's head toward that slender spit of firm ground. She heard its front hooves hit the soft mud of the river shore with a dull swoosh, and felt its rear legs struggle for a land hold. For every two feet gained, the laboring horse lost one; but with hard pull after pull, it lifted itself from the water with muscles strained to the point of collapse. In frantic desperation, Marsh leaped into the water and heaved herself out onto the muddy land. With all her remaining strength she pulled on the reins until her stallion lunged forward one last time and broke out of the treacherous mud which had threatened to suck it down.

She could allow the spent animal to rest for only a few minutes. The sun was setting, and the narrow path in a swampland full of cottonmouths was no place for night travel. Walking ahead, she tested the firmness of the ground before she pulled her horse forward. The mile distance she'd estimated seemed more like ten, and it was almost dark when they finally reached the hard-packed ground of the farm. Unsure of direction now, she paused to listen, and she almost collapsed with joy when she heard the sound of heavy boots approaching. Her joy was replaced instantly with cold fear at the harsh command of "Halt! Who goes there?" She'd forgotten that this farm was an armed camp with patrols. Try as she might, she could not call out her own name. The only sound she could utter was an inarticulate mixture of gurgles and sobs.

"Identify yourself," the sharp voice rang out again. And again she struggled with her leaden tongue until a sodden "Help!" emerged from her trembling mouth. Instantly, the rays of a lantern were beamed into her eyes, and she gasped, "Help!" one last time.

"My God, Sarge, it's Miss Marsh," she heard a twangy Tennessee voice shout, "and she's been in the river." She felt strong arms encircle her and sagged gratefully against the warm, dry body.

"Please help my horse," she panted, "it's just about finished."

"Injun," the Tennessee voice shouted, "git over here and see to the lady's horse."

The stallion moved restlessly as the strange man neared it. "Oh God," she cried, "I'd forgotten. It won't let anyone but me tend it."

Easy laughter greeted her anguished cry of helplessness. "Injun ain't jest any man, Miss Marsh, he's half Cherokee, and there ain't a horse alive that don't understand Cherokee talk."

Anxiously, Marsh twisted around to watch as a dark-skinned man approached the stallion's head, a soft musical string of words issuing from his lips. Lulled by the soothing sounds, the horse quieted, and within seconds the man led the exhausted animal past her. Not once did the flow of strange words cease, and very soon both the soldier and horse had faded into the blackness of night.

Tennessee turned his attention back to the girl who was now shaking with a violent chill. "Chet," the twangy voice rapped out, "git your butt over here and gimmee your coat. We've got to git this girl warm or she's gonna faint."

Dimly, Marsh heard the muffled sounds of disrobing, and then felt the blessed relief of a body-warmed coat wrapped around her shoulders. Slowly, the man holding her walked her over to the three men waiting. It was then that the pecking order of military authority was re-established and a sergeant took over.

"All right, young woman, state your business."

She tried, but she'd begun shaking too badly to get the words of explanation past her clicking teeth. The command was repeated more sternly. And again the uncontrolled clicking of her teeth was her only answer.

At the start of his third order, the sergeant was interrupted by a laconically insolent voice. "You keep her standing here a minute longer, Sarge, and I'm going to shove you in the river. Come on, Tennessee, let's pack her out."

"You're on report, soldier. She doesn't move until I know what she's doing here."

"You planning to shoot us all in the back, Sarge? All right, miss, up you go! Chet, hold that goddamned light on the path and walk ahead of us. You coming, Sarge?"

Held easily on crossed arms between two strong bodies, Marsh felt her blood begin to circulate again and her teeth stop their compulsive chatter. Finally, she calmed down enough to speak. "Sergeant, I forced my horse to swim the river tonight because it is essential that I see Mr. James MacKenzie or Mr. Angus Balfour. Will you take me to them?"

The pinched, uncompromising answer revealed the extent of his anger. "No, I won't, nor will any of my men. We're on patrol."

She felt the chuckle of the man on her right. "Hell, Sarge,—sorry, ma'am—the war's over. And I think we've already caught the one fish that's going to swim ashore tonight. Ma'am, where in hell—sorry, ma'am—did you ever find a horse with that kind of lung power? It must have swum three miles in the current."

Tennessee's voice took over on her left. "What it done tonight was nothing. You should of seen it swim two other horses with riders out of the river after Sarge here started a stampede on the barge."

Oh, God, Marsh thought despairingly, that sergeant! It would be her luck on this unlucky day to run into the one man in the Union Army who had a reason to hate her. Only silence and the sound of marching feet behind her greeted this last disclosure. But once more she felt a chuckle rumble in the chest of the man on her right.

"Heard about that one, Tennessee. Heard too that the major chewed him out for disobeying this girl's orders. Sarge, we've got to travel better than two thousand miles with that major. I'd sure as hell hate to be the one who kept his father from receiving an important message. Tell you what, Tennessee, Chet and I will take her up to the house while you find another patrol."

No answer to this suggestion seemed to be forthcoming. It was Marsh's turn. "Sergeant," she crooned in her dulcet-sweet southern slur, "if y'all will do me this one lil' ol' favor, I'll forget all about mentionin' your name in the letter I was plannin' to send to General Sheridan. You see, I was the one who sold him his favorite horse, and I did promise I'd correspond with him." At that moment she was mad enough to do just that. But she was much more furious five minutes later when they arrived at the parade area in front of the barn, and she heard the sergeant bark an astounding order.

"Lock her up in detention. No one threatens a sergeant in the United States Army."

Quickly, she turned to Tennessee and hissed urgently into his ear, "Get Major MacKenzie."

Instantly, she was on her feet and the lanky soldier was off at a run. Ten minutes later, a red-faced sergeant was on report, Chet had his jacket back, and she was bundled up in one of Stuart's fur-lined coats. However, she faced the dubious pleasure of being escorted the quarter-mile to the house by the very irritated major himself. At first he berated her furiously for her stupidity in swimming the river. When he calmed down to a reasonable level of anger, he demanded to know what the hell her problem was. She made no effort to explain; she just put one tired foot in front of the other and silently cursed all men in general and a few arrogant bastards in particular. When Stuart's frustration with her exploded once more into uncontrollable fury, he grabbed her; what began as a violent shaking wound up as a more violent kiss.

Only one split second later he pushed her away from him. "My God, you're soaking wet and trembling like a sick puppy. When are you ever going to learn that you're just a woman?" Even as her hysterical laughter began, he swept her up into his arms and carried her at an accelerated pace toward the house. On his way up the stairs, he shouted to the two servants lighting the verandah lanterns, "One of you fetch Dr. Damon and his wife and the other open this door for me on the double." Past the three startled men enjoying their after dinner libations in the library, up the wide stairs leading to the second story, through a doorway kicked open with his booted foot, and onto a large bed, Stuart carried the girl. He was stripping off her boots when his father and Angus burst into the room. Marsh didn't even see them; her laughter had changed to a low-keyed weeping punctuated with spasmodic gulps as she tried to steady her breathing.

James MacKenzie took one look at her and bellowed to someone down the stairs. The heavy sounds of running feet added to the increased activity of the household. By now Stuart had her coat off and was attempting to unfasten the belt buckle when two large, capable black hands shoved him away, and a scolding voice admonished him.

"Dis ain't no chore for a man. You jes git out of here and let ol' Maddy undress dis pore chile. She's near froze."

As if in a trance, Stuart stood helplessly and stared at the white face of the sobbing girl. Again the old woman's voice chided him, "Git out of here afore yo' eyes pop out of yo' head, young Stuart; dis ain't no place for a scalawag like you." Reluctantly, he moved over to stand near his father and Angus.

"Do you know what this is all about, Stuart?" MacKenzie demanded.

"I don't know a damn thing except that she and that horse of hers swam all the way over. One of my patrols found her half drowned near the marshlands. She must have gotten herself into some kind of trouble to try a damn fool stunt like that."

For the second time in weeks Stuart was confronted by a defensive, peppery Angus, whose voice shook with the depth of his rage. "Y'are as dim-witted as a booby, Stuart, if you think this lass caused one whit of the trouble she's in. She's been set upon all her life by a pair of devil blackguards who call themselves gentlemen—and I'm thinkin' by a pair of daft Scots too. We should never have left her, Jamie."

"See if she can talk to you, Angus, and tell us what happened. Stuart and I will wait for you downstairs." With a look of deep concern furrowing his brow, James MacKenzie took his son's arm and pulled the reluctant major out of the room as Angus walked hesitantly toward the bed.

"Lass, can you hear me?"

He was greeted by a tired laugh and a voice that held only a shadow of its normal vigor. "I'm not deaf, Angus, just waterlogged."

"Can you tell me what happened, lass? Di' the little man threaten you again?"

"Threaten me, Angus? That slimy little coward sold me." Her remembered terror acted like a blast of hot air on her dampened spirits, arousing her ingrained hatred of her stepfather to a fiery pitch. She told her old friend every grim detail of the ugly confrontation from Creighton's first threat to his last curse. Her voice shook with the intensity of her outrage and with the enormity of her fear.

"He's insane, Angus, insane enough to go back there and kill Jake."

"No, lass, Jake will know where to hide."

"Not from that bast—"

"Aye, he's that and more."

"He knows every inch of that farm. And he won't come alone. He'll bring that cousin of his. I'm afraid for Jake and his family. You didn't see him, Angus. He'd use his gun now. He wanted to use it today; he even smiled when he reached for it."

"We'll send some people over. Dinna fear, lass."

"He'll get even with me this time unless I can get away from here. The sheriff said that he had the right, that he owned me." She struggled to a sitting position and clutched cold hands around her raised knees. "I can't just stay here and let him take me. I'd rather be dead. Angus, can you get me some clothes and some of my money? And will you ask Mr. MacKenzie to lend me a horse? My stallion saved my life, but he's too tired to travel. Oh Angus, our beautiful plans!"

All of the inner strength which had made her an indomitable fighter since infancy seemed to crumble, and she wept in abject hopelessness. No emotion the doughty old Scot had ever experienced could compare with the protectiveness he felt for this girl in her present extremity.

"He'll no' hurt you, Lass. I'll kill him with my own hands first. Now, besides this cousin Hiram, did the villain mention any others?"

Marsh didn't hear the question he'd asked; her attention was riveted on his ferocious declaration of violence—Angus, who rode the slowest horse he could find, who would cross the Potomac only on the tug because he was certain that the barge would be swept out to sea, who used his humor and wit to avoid any semblance of an argument, and who had never hurt another human being. This was the Angus who now promised to do battle for her; no one else had ever given her such a sense of being protected. Her tears vanished along with the paralyzing fear, and she smiled.

"You would really do that for me, wouldn't you, Angus?"

"Aye, I would. You've had more than your share of villainous men. Now, have you told me everything, lass?"

"Yes, there's only the two Creightons. Sheriff Rumford actually helped me get away."

"You rest now and dinna worry. You've a lot of friends to protect you here."

Angus had been quite sincere about his offer of violence. A canny Scot, he knew more about the law than most laymen, and he was convinced that laws victimized innocent people more often than they protected them. When he reentered the library, his face was grim and his words economically terse.

"Jamie, can your boatman navigate the river at night?"

"Back to the Virginia farm? Yes, he can."

"Good. Stuart, you round up some of your men and send a guard over there."

"That I can't do, Angus. We're under orders to leave at dawn tomorrow."

"Then you'll ha' to send Jamie's own guards. Make sure they're armed."

'I'm not going anywhere until you tell me what this is all about."

Angus's voice snapped even more waspishly, "Dinna be a fule. We're dealin' wi' a dangerous man and there's no time to be lost."

Only half convinced, Stuart moved reluctantly, and then

only to the foot of the stairs, where he paused and looked up. Angus rapped out angrily again, "Leave the lass alone and do as you're told, Stuart. This is no' a daft game we're playin' tonight."

Furious about the indignity of being treated like a messenger boy, Stuart glared at the old man before he spun on his heel and strode angrily out the door.

His face still grim with fear for the girl upstairs, Angus turned to the other two men in the room. "It's worse than we thought, Jamie. The lass is in bad trouble."

"Her stepfather?"

"Aye, Jamie, that bastard!"

"What'd he do?"

The quiet, middle-aged man who'd remained seated in the library throughout the entire drama of the last half hour now stood up uncomfortably. "Perhaps I should step outside if this is a private matter."

"Sit down, Bruce," MacKenzie ordered brusquely. "If we ever needed your legal help, we need it now. Get on with it, Angus. What did the bastard do to her?"

With his characteristic economy of words, the old man recounted the details with the accuracy only an accountant could muster. When he had finished, it was the lawyer, Bruce Mac Lachlan who took over.

"I take it this Blake Creighton is her legal father, but not her real one."

"How can he be her legal father when her own father is still alive?"

"That's the way the law's written, Jamie. According to the laws of both Virginia and Maryland, the father listed on the birth certificate is the legal one. And he has the right to marry a daughter under the age of twenty-one to anyone he chooses. And here's another right he has: he can take every cent of her money, if she has any. Does she?"

Heavily Angus sighed. "Aye. All her savings, puir lass."

James MacKenzie had not become a powerful man by

being a coward. "Law or no law, I'm not going to let that degenerate get near her. She's under my protection now and I'll see that she stays there."

Sharply, the lawyer admonished his client. "Don't be a fool, James. You'll be charged with abetting a fugitive to escape. And you're not dealing with the father alone. Hiram Creighton is a much worse problem."

"You know him?"

"Of him. He's a blackguard and a disgrace to my profession. Although other Virginian lawyers have tried, they've never been able to have him disbarred. For twenty years, long before the war, he's been suspected of controlling the prostitution rackets of Richmond, including the crime of blackmail. At one time he was thought to be dying of the pox, but evidently he survived it. He must be in his sixties now, so you know damn well his plans for the girl would be to put her to work for profit. And there's very little the law could do to protect her once she's his wife."

"My God!"

"Jamie, you can be certain that, no later than tomorrow, you'll be served with legal papers demanding that you turn her over to the law officer who come for her. As a lawyer, that old fox will make certain those papers are airtight. There's not one legal action I can take to prevent it without a court order, and I have no way to obtain that court order without an official investigation. By that time, the harm to her would be done."

Angus moved uneasily in his chair and spoke slowly, "I canna' let this happen to her. I have a wee house in Baltimore. I'll hide her there."

"They would find you within two days and charge you the same as they would Jamie."

"Then I'll take her to New York," MacKenzie declared. "She can hide there."

"For two years? If they're determined enough, and I suspect they are, they'll charge you with kidnapping and hunt her down. The law is specific. Until she is twenty-one or married, she is under her father's legal control."

"For God's sake, man," MacKenzie was shouting now. "Do you mean that she can marry without her father's permission?"

"Of course, she's over eighteen. But just where are you going to find a willing bridegroom this time of night? And how do you know if the stranger you choose will not be worse than Hiram Creighton? As I understand it, she isn't a very docile person."

"I can pay someone to marry her with the understanding that the marriage would just be a protective shield. You could arrange for an immediate annulment."

"No, an annulment before she's twenty-one would put her right back in her father's power, and we could be charged with collusion."

It was during the moments of silence following this discouraging announcement that the still irritated Stuart returned. "Your armed guards are outside, Angus, waiting for instructions. And damn it, I'm waiting for an explanation," he reminded the three older men. Angus merely shook his head and went outside to talk to the guards; the lawyer continued to stare into the fire; his father studied the glowering face of his son with a contemplative silence. Stuart exploded with anger. "Then I'll ask the girl. After all, she started this whole hullabaloo." He was halfway toward the stairs when his father rose.

"Just keep right on walking, Stuart. But to the room across the hall. I want to talk to you privately." Unwillingly, Stuart obeyed, swinging on the older man peevishly once they reached the parlor.

"You said you wanted to talk. So talk. I'd like to get some sleep tonight."

"Angus told me that you followed the girl around for a month or more while you were in Virginia."

"So?"

"Why?"

A short explosive laugh greeted this question. "I wanted her. In case you haven't noticed, she has a nice body."

"I've noticed."

"Tell me about it. I watched your face while you drooled over her yesterday. Well, like father, like son. I did a little drooling, too."

"What were your plans for her?"

"Besides a roll in the hay, you mean? Oh, I might have put her up in a hotel for a few months."

"As your mistress?"

"Certainly as a mistress. You're not the only one who enjoys recreation without any responsibility."

"Catherine has never been free to marry me and you know it."

"So you became her 'protector'!"

"I wasn't her first protector, Stuart."

"I don't believe that. Anyway, you ruined the only happy home I ever had, and you ruined her reputation."

"Just like you were planning to ruin this girl's?"

"What reputation? A waif you picked up somewhere in a gutter and used for your own purposes?"

"You're dead wrong about her background, Stuart, and I think you're much more interested in her than you admit."

"Sure, I am. I want her, but she's still a tramp."

"Then why would you want her as your mistress?"

"Why not? What else is there for someone like her?"

"Marriage. She'd make you a good wife."

This time Stuart's laugh was prompted by genuine shock. "Marry her? Your cast-off whore? You must be crazy. Her language is as foul as a New Orleans pimp's. And with those tight pants she wears and her stuck-out breasts, she looks like a strutting advertisement for a bordello. What's your problem, Jamie? Is she already pregnant with another one of your unwanted cubs? Sorry, but I'm not gullible enough to sacrifice myself for the great James MacKenzie's reputation. You'll just have to solve this little mess yourself. I wouldn't marry her if they made me a general for it. When I do decide on a wife, she'll be a lady, not some used harlot, no matter how good a body she has."

During this ugly, rambling catharsis, MacKenzie had watched his son with an expression that mingled disgust and anger with pity. Neither man noticed the girl standing silently in the hallway listening, a girl who bore little resemblance to the half-drowned one who'd been carried upstairs an hour earlier. Even dressed in an odd combination of oversized men's clothing, her eyes blazed green, her hair glinted red, and her lips curled in contempt for the speaker. As if the electricity flowing from her fury shocked both men simultaneously, they whirled around. The son was the first to regain his power of speech, but not with the same fluency he'd just displayed. His apology was mumblingly stammered, "I'm—I'm damned sorry you overheard that, Marsh."

"Why? It was what you were thinking when you first asked me to become your mistress. Only this time you were more honest."

"I didn't really mean all that I—"

"No? Then will you marry me?"

The fumbling look of apology vanished from his blue eyes and was replaced by a suppressed gleam of caution. "If the circumstances were different and if there was more time, I might consider—"

Slashing across his equivocating "ifs" like a razor on a day-old beard, her scorn was a punishing weapon. "You bumbling hypocrite! I'd rather marry the diseased crud my repulsive stepfather chose for me than you. When I marry, I'll want a man, not some sneaky little boy who still thinks that rolling in the hay is adult sport." Slipping his coat from around her shoulders, she held it out at arm's length and dropped it on the floor. "Thanks for your coat, soldier boy. Don't forget to have it deloused before you wear it again." The laughter that floated in her wake as she turned to enter the library sounded like sincere amusement to the two stunned men.

Marsh was still laughing when she strode into the library where another pair of stunned men rose to greet her. With her hand extended, she approached the lawyer first. "You must be Bruce Mac Lachlan. Angus has told me about you. I'm Marsh."

Before the flustered man could do more than take her hand, more of her brittle words rang out. "I understand from what I overheard that I'll have to be married if I'm to escape my stepfather's greedy little hands. I heard everything you said, Mr. Mac Lachlan; your voice carried upstairs beautifully. Well, since there doesn't seem to be any bridegrooms offering for me, I guess I'll have to do my own asking." The harsh, brassy quality faded from her voice as she moved over toward Angus. "Upstairs you promised to protect me by killing the creep. Well, now you don't have to go to that extreme. Marry me instead."

Had the old man's teeth not been his own, they would have tumbled out, so completely did his jaw fall open.

With her head cocked on one side and a gamin smile on her face, Marsh continued. "It wouldn't be so bad, Angus. We could go ahead and buy that ranch with Jake and Adah. And if we could carry enough usquebaugh in the wagon, the Wyoming winters could be fun."

Recovered now with his wit and humor intact, the old man chuckled. "Nay, lassie, I'm too old to put up with your shenanigans." Then he added seriously, "It wouldna' be fair to you, lass. You deserve better in life than to be tied to a doddering old man."

"Are you sure, Angus?"

Sadly, he shook his head. "Aye, lass, I'm sure; but I'll still keep that other promise I gi' you."

She took a deep breath. "Did Mr. MacKenzie say whether or not I could borrow a good horse?"

A heavy voice intercepted Angus's answer. "You won't need a horse, Marsh. If you'll have me, I'll marry you."

The sudden silence in the room was broken by the sound of the front door being violently slammed by the departing Stuart, whose handsome young face was twisted by an angry scorn. Slowly, Marsh turned around to face James MacKenzie. "Mr. MacKenzie, I can't let you make that kind of a sacrifice for—"

"It wouldn't be a sacrifice for me. You'd be the one who'd be miserable. I'm thirty years older than you and I'm not an easy person to get along with. But I can't stand back and let you be destroyed. Will you marry me?"

"I'm not easy to live with either. I'd probably not be a meek wife."

"I know you wouldn't be a meek wife; I know you too well to expect that."

She continued to study his face, searching for the pity she expected to find; but he gazed steadily back at her. "I would be honored to be your wife, Mr. MacKenzie," she said simply.

"That's that then. Bruce, can you get the papers ready during the next hour? Whom do you know who can perform the ceremony on such short notice?"

"There's a judge in Clinton, but he's rural Maryland, and you'll want a signature the Virginia courts will recognize. It'll be better if we go to the capital. There are two judges there who owe me favors, one in particular. Moreover, Charles Beacon is a night owl, but we will have to send a messenger to his home so that he can get to his chambers before we do. Do you have a rider who knows the capital streets well enough to find his way around at night?"

"Angus, which one of our men will be best?"

"None of the workers, Jamie. But the Georgian is still here. His father used to be a senator and I imagine the young lad still knows his way around. I'll go rouse him, Jamie, and order the carriage for you." Angus looked over at Marsh, who still wore a dazed expression on her face. "I dinna suppose any of the people here would have a dress which would fit the lass?"

For the first time since his proposal, MacKenzie smiled. "She's all right the way she is. I wouldn't recognize her in a dress, anyway. And we don't have the time to worry about one now. Get going, Angus. This is going to be a damned long night as it is."

"If you want, I could borrow one of Carina's dresses, Mr. MacKenzie, if you're ashamed of the way I look," Marsh suggested hesitantly.

"Damon and Carina aren't here, Marsh, they left for Wyoming yesterday."

"I wondered why they hadn't come to see me. Stuart sent for them when he carried me in."

At the mention of his son's name, MacKenzie frowned. "I'm sorry about the names Stuart called you, Marsh. He's not very bright when it comes to knowing about people."

"He sure isn't, Mr. MacKenzie. He's a ninny."

The man frowned again in irritation. "Do you suppose you can learn to call me by my given name?"

Marsh wrinkled her nose and grinned at him. "James makes you sound too old and grumpy. But I'll call you Jamie like everyone else does. I've always thought of you as Jamie even when I shook in my boots every time you glowered at me."

His laughter was rich and full. "The only reason you shook when I frowned at you was because of that temper of yours. You were a red-haired spitfire when you were young." The word young reminded him sharply that he was not, and a scowl replaced the pleasant smile. Silent now, he and Marsh listened to the scratching sounds the lawyer's quill pen made as he wrote out the marriage contract and the other necessary papers. Even the fire seemed to lose its cheerful warmth as the minutes ticked by. But at last the lawyer rose, cleared his throat, and left the room. The muffled sounds of MacLachlan's voice explaining directions to someone on the porch could be heard by the tense pair of people remaining in the library. When Mac Lachlan returned, Angus was with him. As MacKenzie looked up from his pensive contemplation of the flickering fire, the other two men nodded in unison, their solemn faces increasing the already pervasive gloom.

It was a silent quartet of people who assembled in the waiting carriage minutes later, each one cocooned in a bulky coat as if to further isolate his thoughts from the others. Twice during the two-hour drive into the nation's capital, Angus passed the bottle around and each occupant took a nervous swallow. Nor did the darkened chambers of Judge Charles Beacon lessen their melancholy withdrawal from each other, nor the long minutes while the judge read the papers Mac Lachlan handed him. To the three watchers who sat mute and forgotten as the legal representatives of client and government conferred with judicial relish over paper after paper, the brief ceremony which followed seemed to be just an unimportant addition to the main event. Certainly it was a sterile service, untouched by a human emotion, except by the unpleasant one of fear on the part of the bride and groom. Since no one had thought to secure a wedding ring, the judge slipped his own from his slender hand and placed it on Marsh's finger. Months later, when she returned it to Charles Beacon, she learned that it was his own wedding ring, a memento of thirty years of happy union with Mrs. Beacon. It was the generous gesture of the lent ring that Marsh would remember as the highlight of her wedding. Actually, she remembered little of the remainder of night because she fell asleep almost as soon as she was reseated in the carriage. She never saw the haggard face of her husband as he sat preoccupied beside her and watched the eastern sky begin its predawn fading from black to gray. Someone carried her to bed, undressed her, and tucked her in; and until Maddy awakened her late the following bright morning, she was oblivious to the world and its problems.

When memory finally flooded back as the huge woman servant helped her bathe and dress in the freshly laundered clothes she'd worn during her swim to freedom yesterday, Marsh experienced little emotion except the comfortable one of security. Unlike her husband, who'd lain sleepless in his own room, she never heard the muffled sounds of Major Stuart MacKenzie moving his fifty men and one thousand horses on the long journey toward the faraway Mexican border. She knew nothing of the dull heartache her husband suffered at the thought of his son's hatred for him. With the buoyancy of untouched youth, she followed Maddy downstairs into the dining room where she devoured a large breakfast. In the rush of last night's planning, no one had remembered to feed her dinner. Only after she had finished eating did she become uneasy about the expected ordeal and long for a familiar face to lend her moral support. Almost timidly, she knocked on the closed library door and was vaguely disturbed when it was Angus who answered her summons and not Jamie. Only the lawyer spoke to her as he escorted her over to his desk in the room which now resembled a court of law.

"Mrs. MacKenzie,"—how strange the title sounded to her—"we have word that your stepfather's group is on its way. Now this is going to be a difficult meeting for you, very difficult, because you are not to say one word while they are here. I am going to do all of the talking for you. Is that understood?"

She nodded mutely, frightened by the sternness of his face and terrified by the thought of having to see her stepfather again. Hesitantly, she looked around, hoping that Jamie could be by her side. Reassuringly, the lawyer patted her hand. "Your husband is instructing his men, Mrs. MacKenzie, two of whom will stand guard here in the library throughout the proceedings. You mustn't be afraid." Marsh noticed the pistol next to the stack of legal papers and was terrified again.

She pointed to it and croaked a shaky, "Why?"

"It seems we underestimated the determination of Hiram Creighton. He has brought his own bodyguards. It was necessary for us to arm some of the workers. Oh, here's Jamie now."

Marsh turned stiffly around to watch her husband enter the room followed by two black men with rifles and expressionless faces. Silently they took their positions to the rear of the lawyer, and Jamie took her arm and escorted her to a chair next to the one occupied by the grim-faced Angus. She almost wept with relief when Jamie took the chair on the other side of hers and briefly squeezed her hand. There was no time for anything else. The hallway was suddenly filled with people, and a half dozen of them filed reluctantly into the library and sat down in the chairs arranged for them. Her heart was pounding so heavily, she didn't dare look up until the familiar voice of Sheriff Dan Rumford broke the uneasy silence. She was shocked by his angry, sad expression.

"It is my duty to deliver this restraining order for Miss Pamela Creighton and to warn all parties that any attempt to prevent her delivery to her legal and rightful father will be considered a criminal offense." With this pronouncement read, Rumford walked the four steps to the desk and handed it to Mac Lachlan. The lawyer adjusted his glasses and reread the document with a thoroughness prolonged enough to make Marsh squirm with impatience. During these moments she looked over at the assembled enemy. Her stepfather was as unattractive to her as he always had been, but she sucked in her breath with raw horror at the appearance of the fat man next to him, the man who was to have been her husband. Not even the opulence of his expensive black suit or the richness of his gold watch chain and diamond stickpin could disguise the repulsive ugliness of his face. Not much taller than his slender cousin, he was three times his girth, and his moon shaped face was unhealthily blotched with broken blood vessels. But it was the eager lewdness of his beady eyes and the looseness of his mouth that made her shudder. Dimly, she was aware of the two men who sat in back of Hiram, white men with hooded, watchful eyes. Even when she was finally able to look away from the trio she could feel Hiram's eyes watching her; she was fancifully convinced that he was licking his fat lips.

Mac Lachlan cleared his throat. "I notice that this order has been signed by a Virginia judge and countersigned by a Maryland one."

Marsh jerked when Hiram Creighton's soft sibilant voice admonished Mac Lachlan with subtle irony, "I don't believe in taking chances with legal trickery."

Mac Lachlan ignored the interruption and continued to focus his attention on the lawman. "Sheriff Rumford, during the course of your investigation, did you have occasion to check the birthdate of Miss Pamela Creighton?"

"Yes, I did."

"What was the date of her birth?"

Ponderously, the sheriff produced another paper from his ample pocket and read the date. "March 20, 1846."

"That would make her—" Mac Lachlan prompted.

"Nineteen years and two months old."

Again, the sibilant voice interrupted. "The accuracy of that record can not be challenged, nor can the validity of Blake Creighton's claim that he is her father since it is his name on the birth certificate. And," the breathy, unpleasant voice continued, "according to the laws of both Virginia and Maryland, any unmarried female under twenty-one years of age is the property and responsibility of her father until such time as she marries, when she becomes the responsibility of her husband."

The slight, inflectionary change on the final words made Marsh shudder with revulsion. But Mac Lachlan seemed unaffected by Hiram's positive confidence as he continued to address the sheriff.

"Sheriff Rumford, are you aware of the Virginia laws concerning the age of consent?"

"Yes, sir, I am. At eighteen a girl may marry without her father's permission."

"The law is the same in Maryland and in the nation's capital city," Mac Lachlan stated, looking at the Creighton cousins for the first time. "Are there any challenges to the existence of these laws?" An oddly charged silence greeted his question. "No? Then we can assume that we're all in agreement that a girl has the right to marry a man of her own choice if she is eighteen or older. Now, Sheriff Rumford, I want you to read the first of the documents I have here." The silence became more oppressive as the man scanned the official paper. "What is the document, Sheriff Rumford?"

"A wedding certificate attesting to the marriage of James MacKenzie and Pamela Creighton." The sharp hiss of shock could be clearly heard.

"And the date?"

"May 23, 1865. Today's date."

"And the time?"

"Two fifteen this morning."

"Roughly eleven hours ago. Sheriff Rumford, are you satisfied that this certificate is legal and that Judge Charles Beacon's signature is valid?"

"Yes, sir." The relief in the sheriff's voice was evident to every straining listener in the room.

"Well, I'm not." The soft sibilant voice had become breathily strident as Hiram Creighton rose from his chair and moved toward the desk with surprising speed for such an obese man. The rings on his plump fingers sparkled as he snatched the document from the sheriff.

"The signature could be easily forged and the whole document a counterfeit," he charged.

Retrieving the challenged certificate from Creighton's hand, Mac Lachlan beckoned to a shadowy figure waiting in the hallway. Instantly, everyone's attention was fixed on the portly, dignified man who walked to the desk with a calm assurance.

"My credentials, gentlemen," he announced as he handed Rumford two impressive parchment scrolls. "These papers state that I am the recorder of vital statistics in the District of Columbia. This morning I was called upon to record the marriage of James MacKenzie and Pamela Creighton. I was asked to come here today by Judge Beacon for the express purpose of attesting to the validity of the marriage and the signature of the judge. I do so attest. Will that be all, gentlemen?"

Self-confident as any entrenched official, the recorder looked briefly at the assembled people and then left the room as efficiently as he had entered. Both Creightons moved with alacrity to follow until Bruce Mac Lachlan's voice rang out, sharply commanding.

"Everyone will please be reseated. These proceedings are not yet complete. I want both Sheriff Rumford and Sheriff Wainwright from Clinton, Maryland, to be witnesses to the next part. I have here an official complaint against Blake Creighton for the theft of eighteen valuable horses stolen from James MacKenzie in 1861. Mr. Blake Creighton now has the choice of paying the bill for eighteen hundred dollars or of being arrested and charged. Can you pay, Mr. Creighton?"

Fear mingled with sullen defiance in Blake's answer. "You Yankees know damn well I can't pay."

"Under the circumstances, Mr. MacKenzie has authorized me to offer you an alternative to payment if you will consent to divorce your wife, Melissa Randall Creighton."

His face flushed with fury, Blake shouted, "The bitch deserted me and ran off—"

Smoothly, the lawyer interrupted. "Since desertion is the only grounds for divorce in Virginia, that fact is admitted. Your wife will be adjudged the guilty partner in a court of law." When Blake hesitated, Mac Lachlan reminded him bluntly, "It is either agreeing to the divorce or being jailed for grand theft. What will it be, Mr. Creighton? If you choose the divorce, you will sign these papers in front of the two sheriffs and the matter will be completely out of your hands. My Virginia colleague will handle your divorce. I believe that both you and your cousin are familiar with his name, Mr. John Mosby.''

Hiram's hiss was more pronounced as he disagreed. "Mosby is still being held by the Union army.''

"Not anymore. He was paroled through the intercession of General Grant on May 13 and has resumed his law practice in Virginia. Mr. Mosby has further agreed to monitor any possible harassment of all parties involved.'' Mac Lachlan's eyes were flinty hard as he addressed Blake Creighton again. "Well, what'll it be for you, divorce or jail?''

"I'll sign the papers and be glad to rid myself of the whining bitch.'' The sound of the quill seemed unduly scratchy as the small man signed paper after paper which the lawyer pushed in front of him. When he had finished, Creighton turned to leave the room; and again Mac Lachlan's sharp voice recalled him.

"There are several other items which must be attended to. Sheriff Rumford, this next document will require your signature. It is a complaint that Mr. Blake Creighton threatened a pair of James MacKenzie's employees on the occasion of the restraining of Mrs. MacKenzie yesterday.''

Rumford's smile was one of enjoyment. "I would like you to add to that complaint, sir, the fact that this man also attempted to shoot Mrs. MacKenzie when her horse took her into the river. Only my knocking the weapon from his hand prevented his firing.'' He waited with patient complacency while the lawyer wrote out the added charge before he signed the paper.

"Now, Sheriff Rumford,'' continued the lawyer, "I want you to file this complaint in your county's criminal records. It will be used as evidence in case Mr. Creighton attempts further violence. One final warning: because of past trouble with this man, Mr. MacKenzie wishes me to inform the law officers here that Mr. Creighton is never to trespass on

MacKenzie properties again. Mr. MacKenzie wishes me to add that in order to protect his wife, he has ordered his guards to shoot on sight if Mr. Creighton does trespass. That, gentlemen, completes the business. Are there any comments?"

The fat Hiram Creighton proved a survivor after all; his voice was soft again as he spoke. "I would like to declare publicly my disassociation with all peoples involved in today's discussion and to affirm my complete willingness to cooperate with the authorities." But the smile he wore as he walked from the room did little to improve his appearance.

In the library, which now seemed hollowly empty, Mac Lachlan gathered up his piles of papers. "Jamie, I'll be leaving for Baltimore now to take care of this work." He smiled tiredly. "And then I think I'm going home to sleep for a week. I'm too old for this kind of nightlife. Mrs. MacKenzie, I want to wish you every happiness."

Marsh reacted to his words with shock; in the drama of the last twelve hours, she'd forgotten the main change in her life—she was now a married woman. Dazedly, she started to move from the room, only to have her new husband, sounding all too unpleasantly like her old employer, bark a question at her. "Where do you think you're going, Marsh?"

She gulped. "I thought I'd go down to the barn and check on my horse."

"You're not to leave this house," he told her abruptly, "until I get word that those people are off of my property. Furthermore, in the future, you're not to wander any place around the farm without the guards I've assigned to watch you. Do you understand, Marsh?"

The rich warmth of fire rekindled in her chilled body at the sound of his autocratic voice. She whirled back to face him with hot words forming on her lips, words which cooled to nothingness when she saw the exhaustion on his face— exhaustion and something very like regret. Her response became a humble acceptance of his authority. "I understand you, Mr. MacKen—Jamie."

Disconsolately, she wandered into the living room and then into the rear of the big house where Maddy was too busy to talk to her. Unhappily, she went upstairs to the bedroom she'd used, sat down on the bed, and stared into nothingness. She never heard the conversation her husband and Angus were having.

"What in God's name am I going to do with her, Angus?"

"You wed her, Jamie."

"I had to. The man was even worse than we'd supposed. But now I feel trapped."

"Jamie, you're lyin' to yourself. You dinna do anything last night you haven't thought about since the lass was fifteen. I've watched the way you've looked at her."

"My son and I both! But what about her? She still thinks of me as Mr. MacKenzie." He paused and looked closely at his old friend. "Angus, how does she really feel about Stuart?"

"I'll no' deny she liked him, but she was too proud to take the insultin' crumbs he offered her, and she dinna let him touch her. I'll take an oath on that."

"That really doesn't bother me."

"What bothers you, Jamie, is that powerful conceit of yours. You've been the spoiled darlin' of too many women and you're afraid this lass will no' worship you."

"That's damn rubbish!"

The old man ignored the protest. "And you've no' ever really been broken to the marriage yoke. You rode roughshod over wee Ellen because she lacked the spirit to fight you. And the second time you wed for money. Dinna deny it to me, Jamie; you couldna' stand the woman until her father offered you a full partnership. That you earned your money, I'll no' deny. She was nought but a scold and a jealous one at that. And the cruel harm she did Stuart as a small lad was enough to turn a man's stomach. I dinna blame you for turnin' from her. And I dinna blame you because the unbalanced woman took her own life. But after her death, Jamie, why dinna you bring Stuart back to live wi' you?''

"Because he was a fifteen-year-old hellion by that time and he hated me almost as much as he hated his damn stepsister.''

"I don't doubt he had cause to hate her. The wee Alice is no' a bonnie lass; she has a nasty, sly way about her. A hot tempered lad like Stuart dinna stand a chance wi' her. As for you, Jamie, Stuart was too much like you no' to fight your overbearin' ways.''

"Funny, isn't it, Angus? Stuart is the one who hates me most, yet I loved him best.''

"Aye, but the lad was unlucky all the same. No mother to love him as a bairn, and a mean and wretched stepmother when he was older! You di' your best, Jamie, but you never took enough time wi' him. Robbie had Ian, and Craig was doted on by his foolish mother, but Stuart was farmed out wi' your Catherine. Will you be tellin' her about the lass now?''

Heavily, the younger man responded, "That I wed a girl thirty years younger in a moment of insanity? How can I tell her about it—or anyone else for that matter?''

"You must, Jamie, you canna' keep the lass hidden forever. She'll no' abide it.''

Restlessly, Jamie began to pace the room, irritably shoving chairs from his path. Then, as if he'd come either to the end of his patience or to a decision, he turned back to his old friend.

"Angus, will you stay with her for the next two months until I decide what to do with her?''

"The lass may decide what to do for herself, Jamie. I'll no' be her jailer, and she'll no' be witless enough to let you get by wi' desertion.''

"I'm not deserting her, damn it! I do have two months of business to attend to, and she is in no shape to meet society yet. I'll stop by in Baltimore and send someone back here to prepare a wardrobe for her. Will you stay, Angus?''

"Aye, you know I will. I'll tell Jake and his family that they'll ha' to wait until you return. I'll put them back on the payroll."

"I'd forgotten about them. Can't they just go on alone?"

"No, Jamie, they'll need me or the lass to do the buyin'. They may ha' been freed, but they'll no' be welcome in many places, I'm thinkin'."

"Do what you think best for them then. Meanwhile, I'll tell Marsh at dinner that I'll be leaving tomorrow." Like all men who substitute action for reason, Jamie was vastly relieved when he left the room. A decision postponed was, with a little luck, one which might never be needed.

But Angus had the last word, only it was more like a chuckle. "He's still a bairn if he thinks this wife will no' change his life."

Chapter
6

Angus was still chuckling two days later at the answer Marsh had given her husband at that dinner when Jamie had told her he had to leave on a business trip. Pompously, after he'd made the announcement, Jamie had risen from the table and walked into the library as if he really needed the after dinner brandy he promised himself. Out of long habit, Angus stood up too, looked closely at Marsh to make sure the news had not upset her overly, and followed his old friend out of the room. Marsh remained seated at the table a minute longer with a look of heavy concentration on her face. She had just been told that, for the next two months, she'd be nothing but a cosseted prisoner on this farm, forbidden to interfere with its management in any way while her control-all husband would go to New York and do what he damned well pleased. As she stood up, the light of battle shone in her green eyes and the smile on her face was the same she'd worn when she'd ridden up to confront General Mosby two years earlier. Jamie MacKenzie might scare hell out of other people with his arrogant look of authority and his powerful bank accounts, but she'd be damned if she was going to let him intimidate her. No soft knock preceded her entrance into the library this time. She strode in, grinned at Angus, poured herself a modest portion of brandy, and turned around to confront her husband of one day.

"Jamie," she asserted boldly, noting the startled look of disapproval on his face, "I hated being Pamela Creighton and I could never be Pamela Marshall, but I am going to enjoy being Marsh MacKenzie. And I plan on being Mrs. James MacKenzie in Virginia, in New York, in Wyoming, and all over the state of Maryland whether you bed me or not."

Angus's chuckle would explode into laughter whenever he remembered Jamie's flinch, and the old Scot leaned back in his seat to enjoy the rest of the lassie's declaration.

"I plan," she continued firmly, "on being your recognized wife wherever you go in public." Her voice softened now and her smile became dazzling. "I know you only married me because I was in trouble, Jamie, and now you don't know what to do with me. Well, you won't have to worry anymore. While you're in New York taking care of all your problems, I am going to become a lady, and you won't have to be ashamed of me. So all of those silly instructions you just gave me are unnecessary. I have never been disloyal to you in the past, and I've no intention of hurting your reputation now. But, whether you like it or not, Jamie MacKenzie, I'm not some frightened little twit who could let any man, even you, tell me what I can or cannot do. Good night, Jamie, I'll see you whenever you decide to return."

As she walked from the room, Angus did not need to look at his friend's face to know that there would be a dazed expression on it. Not even thirty years of experience with other women had prepared this man of the world for the devastating honesty of a girl who lacked even the rudiments of knowledge about the accepted rules for man-trapping. Denying himself the pleasure of saying, I told you so, Angus mumbled his good night and slipped out of the room, leaving a badly rattled Jamie behind—a forty-nine-year-old man who'd compiled a lot of information about women, none of which, unfortunately, applied to this impudent nineteen-year-old girl. To make matters worse, she didn't have the slightest notion that she was so damned beautiful; she made him feel like a lovesick boy. Even New York seemed too close for the objectivity his mind craved at the moment.

Distance, however, could not solve Marsh's myriad of problems in reaching her goal of becoming a lady in two months. How in hell—mentally she corrected herself, but couldn't think of a ladylike substitute—could she learn which fork to use when the only answer she could elicit from Angus was, "The one next to your plate, lass?" He was even more useless as a dance instructor, since he pleaded lumbago as well as total ignorance. Even in the area of language refinement he failed as a coach since his expressions were not only delivered in an unmistakable Scottish burr, they were frequently saltier than her own.

The morning her husband left for New York, Marsh searched through the library books pertaining to deportment, good manners, social dialogue, dancing, or table cutlery usage. The only thing she found was a romanticized drawing of Martha Washington curtsying to George on the flyleaf of an ancient history book. When she tried to emulate the first lady, Marsh fell on her face and skinned her nose.

In disgust she headed for the receiving barn and the ego reviving satisfaction of doing something she knew how to do—taking care of her horse. But all the way there, the sound of her two guards marching stoically behind her irritated her until the hackles actually raised on her neck. From the door of the barn she could hear her stallion's snorting whinny; it was the longest time he'd been separated from her in six years. In her eagerness to get to the stall, she almost missed seeing the posterior end of a human being sticking out from a pile of hay which someone had inadvertently tossed down from the loft above. With characteristic efficiency, Marsh grabbed the man's belt and pulled. Up came a sputtering, half-smothered manboy on whose back she pounded energetically until he coughed out the chaff he'd inhaled. Clinically, she watched him until he seemed recovered, discovering some pertinent facts about him at the same time. He'd been a captain in the Confederate Army and had lost the lower half of his left arm. Other than that, she couldn't determine much since his face and hair were covered with a heavy coating of gray dust.

As soon as his breathing had become fairly normal, she continued on her way to greet the great beast which had recognized her as master since she was thirteen. Joyfully, it nuzzled her as she fed it sugar and rubbed its nose. She was halfway through the job of grooming when she glanced up to see a strange young man watching her. Until she noted the shabby gray uniform, she didn't recognize him as the young man she'd just pulled out of the hay. He had washed the dust out of his dark hair and scrubbed his face and now stood before her as a passably handsome person. As she straightened up to smile at him, he executed an elegant bow and introduced himself in the soft tones of a southern aristocrat.

"Captain Philip Addison at your service, ma'am."

She extended her hand man style, just as she always had at the culmination of a hundred sales of horses and said, "I'm Marsh." As an afterthought she added, "Marsh MacKenzie." When he seemed puzzled by her still extended hand, she withdrew it and apologized quickly. "I'm sorry, Philip, I didn't think about your arm."

His smile was as apologetic as hers. "It wasn't that, ma'am, I've never shaken a lady's hand before."

"Why not?"

Embarrassed by the bluntness of her question, he fumbled for an answer. "Down home, a gentleman just holds a lady's hand. If the lady is important to him, he might kiss it."

"Where is your home, Philip?"

"Pounded into the dust by Sherman's army."

"Then you must be the one who's called the Georgian, the one whose father used to be a senator in Washington?" Having never been reluctant to seize opportunity in the whole of her make-do life, Marsh was already busy formulating plans for this man's immediate future.

"That was a long time ago, before the war."

"Why didn't you go home when the other Confederate officers left?"

"Mr. MacKenzie offered me a job here. Is he your father, ma'am?"

"No, he's not, Philip. What is the job?"

"I'm a laborer."

"I don't think you're very good at it."

He laughed at her bluntness. "No, ma'am, I'm not. But it's a paying job."

"Philip, can you shoot a pistol and can you dance?"

"Yes, ma'am, I still have my right hand and both feet."

"Good. I'm going to change your job."

"Somehow I can't see Mr. MacKenzie paying me for dancing."

"He's not here now, so you're going to be my bodyguard and teach me how to be a lady."

Gallantly, he tried to assure her. "You are a lady, ma'am."

She hooted with laughter. "So's that prancing mare over there—which reminds me, do you know which pasture the work mares are in?"

"Yes, ma'am. Why do you want to know?"

"My boy needs some exercise."

Intimidated and repelled by her gross indelicacy, Philip seemed reluctant to speak; finally, though, he found the courage to admonish her. "Ma'am, if you want to be a lady, you can't talk about such things."

Unabashed, she grinned at him. "I have no intention of being a lady in private, only in public. Tomorrow, we'll put my stallion in the pasture, but right now you're coming back to the house with me and going to work."

At the barn entrance she paused to speak to the two soldier-straight blacks who were her bodyguards. "Gentlemen, what are your regular jobs on the farm?"

"We were dock guards, Mrs. MacKenzie, and cargo checkers."

"Would you rather be back working at your regular jobs?"

As the two looked at each other, their faces mirroring their irritation of having to watch out for this female whirlwind, one of them made a halfhearted effort to lie gracefully. "Mr. MacKenzie ordered us to take care of—"

"Mr. Mackenzie will be gone for two months. In his absence I'll do the ordering. Well, gentlemen, which job do you prefer?"

In unison the two men muttered, "The docks."

"Good. Now take Mr. Addison and me to the gun room."

One of the men protested, "Can't do that, Mrs. MacKenzie, he's a Confederate."

"So am I," she snapped impatiently, "and I'll take full responsibility."

Almost eagerly now, her former bodyguards set off toward the building which housed the office, the tack room, and the armory. Once inside the small enclosure lined with racks of guns, Philip Addison changed instantly from a crippled laborer to a professional soldier, carefully selecting the handgun he favored from the array. Both of the guards and Marsh were impressed to see how expertly he fastened on the gun belt with only one hand, adjusting the position of the gun to the place on his lean hip which was most efficient for a fast draw. Not until he and Marsh had resumed their walk back to the house did his fierce pride at being a soldier again relax enough for him to remember the girl by his side.

"Why didn't you tell me that you were Mrs. MacKenzie?"

"I haven't been her long enough to remember, Philip."

"You're the girl who swam the river the other night?"

"Only because I had to," she declared. "Come on, Philip, we'll go through the kitchen."

Maddy met them at the door with a scowl of disapproval on her face, but Marsh gave her no opportunity to speak. "Maddy, this is Mr. Philip Addison. He is going to be living at the house while Mr. MacKenzie is away." Philip's frown matched Maddy's at this point, but the girl ignored both of them and demanded, "Is the room Mr. Mac Lachlan used clean?"

"Miss Marsh," Maddy began firmly, "Mr. MacKenzie is mighty pertickler who stays here."

"So am I, Maddy, and Mr. Addison stays. Is the room ready?"

"Yes 'um, it's clean."

"Good. Mr. Addison will also take his meals with Mr. Balfour and me. Come on, Philip."

They found Angus at his desk in the library with a smile on his weathered face as he watched them enter. "I see you found the lad."

"Angus Balfour, do you mean to tell me that you let me stew around all morning when you knew about Philip all the time?"

"Lass, I dinna want to spoil your fun. How are you, lad?"

Philip's smile was quizzical. "I'm beginning to wonder."

"Aye, the lass is a wee bit overpowerin' when she has a bee in her bonnet."

"But I'm practical, too, Angus. Not only can Philip teach me dancing and table manners, he can serve as the bodyguard Jamie insisted on."

Cautious about what he knew was important, the old man's puckish humor vanished. "Can you really protect this lass, Philip?"

"I fought for a year after I lost my arm. I can protect her quite well on the farm and even in the city if she does what I tell her to."

"I heard about your war record and about your marksmanship, lad. Well, we'll gi' it a try if you'll gi' me your word to warn us if you find your missin' arm a problem. Guarding the lass is no' just a whim, lad. There's a number of evil men threatenin' her safety.''

"You have my oath, Mr. Balfour, that I'll defend her with my life. Ma'am, you brought me here to work. If Mr. Balfour will act as chaperone we can begin the dancing lessons. But first you'll have to change into a dress, a full-skirted one.''

That order was her first jolt; she hadn't even thought about clothes. A dozen other jolts followed in rapid succession. She was as clumsy on her feet as a three-legged colt and so determined not to be led, Philip finally threatened to tie her arms down if she didn't relax. Discouraged after two miserable hours of failure, Marsh was a good deal humbler when Philip suggested they begin on the proper use of table cutlery. Before he allowed Marsh and Angus to be seated at the dining table, Philip set the table using the glasses, dishes, and silver service stored in the china closet. Angus stared humorously at the four forks, three knives, five spoons, six glasses, and the assortment of plates and bowls. Watching from the doorway, Maddy reacted without any humor whatsoever.

"S'pose y'all tell me, Miss Marsh, what I's gonna cook to put in all dem plates? And jest who d' you s'pose is gonna wash all dem glasses? Dis ain't no hotel and I's got enough work to do as is.''

Angus cleared his throat to calm the angry old cook, but the fire of Marsh's temper exploded first. Lady she might not be, but she'd bossed workers too long to accept this kind of insubordination. While Jamie had been here, Maddy had been as pleasantly cooperative as a puppy dog. With him gone, she'd lost all pretended respect for his young wife.

"Yes, Maddy," Marsh proclaimed with a steely bite in her voice, "I can tell you exactly who is going to be doing both jobs if you're ever rude to me again in front of my guests— your replacement, that's who! Now, if you need extra help, I'll get it for you, but this table is going to be set exactly the way Mr. Addison decides in the future. However, I won't ask you to cook any more courses of food than you normally do.

Tell me, Maddy, who does help you with the work around this house?''

"Jest one no account field nigger Mister MacKenzie hired. But dat yard bird done sleep out to de shed most of de time. He ain't neber around when I needs him.''

"All right, Maddy, when he meanders over for his dinner tonight, you tell him he'll get it only after he finishes every chore you assigned him today. If he gives you any trouble, you call me. Tomorrow we'll get you some decent help.''

"Yes, ma'am, Miz MacKenzie, I hears you.'' The cook was actually chuckling as she shuffled back to her kitchen, and Marsh was already making new plans.

"Tomorrow, Angus, we'll get Sam to take us over to the Virginia farm. There must be at least one couple among the workers there who'd like indoor work for a change. And I can pick up the rest of my clothes.''

"Jamie dinna want you to leave the farm, lass. And I'll no' take the chance of lettin' you go back there where it's no' safe. If you'll promise no' to shake this place up tomorrow, I'll go myself.''

All the next day Marsh remained true to the promise she'd given Angus, with only two slight deviations from the straight and narrow. When one of Philip's worn boots gave out, Marsh gave him a pair of Jamie's finest, and for good measure, presented him with two pairs of her husband's trousers and as many of his shirts. When Philip protested her generosity, Marsh assured him cavalierly, "I'll get to be a lady sooner if my teacher is dressed like a gentleman. Besides, Jamie has closets full of clothes.''

Had Philip been asked at that moment to describe Marsh MacKenzie, he generously would have labeled her a sensitive person who would require only a little polish to become a genteel lady. An hour later he was groaning at the enormity of the job she had hired him to perform. During the absence of the farm owner and his two main subordinates, Dr. Damon and Angus Balfour, a half dozen workers had become drunk and started a roundhouse fight with some of their sober fellow workers. When Marsh was notified by one of the frightened exercise boys, she mounted his horse without a word of explanation to Philip and rode at full gallop toward the paddock area, where the fighting now involved some thirty workers. The workers who knew her promptly disengaged themselves from the melee and stood watching while she rode into the midst of the other men. By the time a breathless Philip arrived on foot, Marsh was bellowing at the men with intimidating authority, using words which embarrassed Philip, but which inspired most of the men to stop fighting almost instantly. Calling out to a dozen of the noncombatants who'd been enjoying the show, she ordered them to lock the drunken men in the strongly built stall used to restrain an occasionally vicious horse and assigned the other fighters harsh work assignments. When one truculent white trainer insolently refused to obey her orders, calling her a loudmouth bitch in the process, Marsh drove her horse straight at the startled man, who turned to flee from her attack. Skillfully, she drove the now terrified man into the arms of two guards who had been watching her actions with knowing amusement. Both of these men had worked on the Virginia farm during the war.

"Royce," she yelled at one of them, "throw this piece of garbage off of the property. Mister," she fumed at the man himself, "if you ever set foot on MacKenzie land again, I'll run you down with my stallion." Within minutes the paddock yard was once again a peaceful work area as the guilty fighters turned to their assigned tasks with diligence.

Watching her with a feeling of helplessness, Philip expected her face to be convulsed with fury when she turned around. Instead, she joked and laughed with many of the workers as she rode back among them. Philip noted something else as well: most of the workers had shown little surprise at her actions. They had, he surmised shrewdly, seen her display this bold courage before. But the Georgian gentleman groaned anyway. How could he ever make a lady out of someone who could outcurse drunken brawlers, ride a horse as well as a cossack, and give orders like a field general? Mounted on a horse the exercise boy brought him, Philip escorted the girl he had sworn to protect with his life back to the house and the interrupted dancing lesson. As far as he was concerned, the only hopeful result of the violent episode was to make her too tired to push him around the library floor; for the first time she was submissive enough to let him do the leading.

When Angus returned with her carpetbag and a pair of excellent workers, both the farm and house were peacefully under control. Even Maddy's ''no account nigger'' was shuffling back and forth from the woodpile with a quicker pace. Later that night, when Philip privately told Angus about her action, the old Scot chuckled. ''Aye, the lass has a brau way of dealin' wi' men.''

''Why in the devil does she need a bodyguard then? I felt like a useless fool today.''

''Lad, I'm thinkin' you'll understand her better if you know what she's gone through.'' Briefly, Angus told the young Southerner about Marsh's background, ending the terse account with a question. ''Can you now see why the lass is a fighter?''

Philip nodded. ''I can also understand why most of the workers admire and respect her.''

''Aye, that they do. And dinna let her rough language fool you, lad. She's also a grand lady.''

Softly, Philip agreed. ''I know she is. Colonel Marshall was my commanding officer during the final battles in the Shenandoah. She's like her father.''

Awake most of the following night in the first comfortable bed he'd had for two years, Philip came to grips with his own lack of courage. Not in battle. Under fire he'd performed well; but later, when he'd received news that his father had been killed at Vicksburg and his mother had died at the beautiful old home, Philip realized that he lacked the courage to return home and fight for what was left of his heritage. Yet here was a girl who had faced up to her problems without flinching. She'd probably teach him more than he would her, but at least now he too had a goal.

Life at the MacKenzie farm was so serene during the next four days that not even the arrival of two live-in seamstresses and a carriage loaded with bolts of fabric caused any inconvenience, except for Marsh. For one hour each morning and another each night, she was stripped, measured, and pin pricked while two efficient Baltimore modistes turned out piles of soft white underwear. It wasn't until they began to select the styles and fabrics for her dresses that Marsh challenged their decisions. Dragging an embarrassed Philip into the sewing room, she forced him to help her choose. After charming the huffy seamstresses, he proved surprisingly adept and cooperative. He agreed with Marsh that she lacked the patience for hoop skirts and that the pastel dimities were too pallid for her vivid coloring. He also helped her veto all dress styles adhering to the current rage for a wasp waist. The first time the head seamstress tried to lace Marsh into a cinch corset, the girl's screams could be heard in the north pasture. But the determined seamstress did not give up without a fight.

"If you don't wear one you'll look like a cow," she sniffed.

Never a diplomat, even when she liked a person, Marsh surveyed herself and the plump woman in the mirror and asked innocently, "Do you wear a corset, Elsie?"

"Certainly I do. Every decent woman does."

Marsh shrugged her shoulders and smiled sarcastically. "Well, you look fatter than I do, so I don't think I need one."

Red-faced with anger, the woman rasped, "I'm not a nineteen-year-old girl. Nineteen-year-old girls are not supposed to have waist lines over twenty inches. Yours is a very ample twenty-three. And just what do you intend to do with those breasts of yours in a ball gown?"

Marsh frowned; ever since her encounter with Stuart in the horse stall weeks earlier, she'd been aware that her unconfined breasts could be a problem, even in an outsized man's shirt. "Can't you make me something that will support them without all those bones about my waist?"

Elsie smiled triumphantly. "Certainly not, madam. It's the corset or nothing," she pronounced with assurance.

Timidly, the second seamstress contradicted the older woman. "I once sewed for an actress lady. If Mrs. MacKenzie will permit it, I can make her the same binders I made for that lady."

Marsh nodded eagerly. "They'll be fine. Now, do you mind finishing with this fitting? I've got some important things to do today."

Three days later, Marsh wore the first of the two dozen dresses Jamie had ordered made for her, the first dress she'd owned in six years of freedom. Even with only three petticoats billowing out the bouffant skirt she felt hopelessly swaddled in useless material. Standing stationary in front of the mirror, she'd been delighted by her altered image. The fitted bodice and puffed sleeves topping the enormously full skirt gave her the illusion of being disembodied, of floating gracefully on air. It was when she attempted to walk down the stairs that she realized the deadly pitfalls of feminine attire. Twice in as many steps she was forced to clutch the railing to keep from falling.

"Philip," she bellowed in frustration to the young man watching her with amusement at the foot of the stairs, "how in hell can I ever get down stairs?" She watched with jealous envy as he ran gracefully up the steps, unhampered by the damn skirts which were now crippling her. Patiently, but with a controlled smugness of expression she thought, Philip escorted her up and down those stairs for an hour, teaching her how to raise the skirts just enough to clear the step, but not enough to expose her lace-trimmed pantaloons. Marsh was grim-faced with disgust by the end of that training, and even more thwarted by the dancing lesson which followed. As ungraceful as she'd felt in boots and trousers, the full skirts were so inhibiting she felt threatened by the constant danger of falling every time she tripped over the hem of her dress. Philip was delighted; her strong arms were kept too busy keeping her skirts off the floor to dominate his efforts to lead her. So victorious did he feel, he was relentless all day, forcing her to walk endlessly across the floor, to sit down and rise from chairs without tipping those treacherous skirts, and to go up and down the steps by herself.

The disagreeable climax of that unendurably long day occurred at dinner time, when Angus made his first contribution to the day's conversation. His faded blue eyes twinkling in his beaming face, he complimented her. "If I dinna know you so well, lass, I'd swear I was suppin' wi' your bonnie mother." Marsh glared at him with an expression of repugnance.

Not for four dreary days did Philip relent enough to let her put on her beloved old clothes for a riding lesson outside the house. He'd tried for two of those days to convince her to attempt riding sidesaddle, but had finally given up the fight.

"My stallion wouldn't let me near him," she declared with a nonnegotiable assurance that brooked no argument.

Grim-jawed himself, Philip selected a slim mare for her to ride, refusing stubbornly all her blandishments that the stallion was the better horse.

"Not for a lady. Furthermore, you're going to ride the way I show you, or we'll go back inside the house for some more dance lessons."

"Blackmail," she muttered as she mounted the mare and followed her teacher out of the barn.

A skilled cavalry man, Philip rode with effortless elegance, ramrod straight in the saddle. When Marsh bent low in hers to instruct her dainty mare to run, Philip's crop landed on her own backside, not the mare's.

"Sit up," he ordered her brusquely, "this isn't a horse

race; it's a lesson in promenade riding. You're not herding horses now."

Marsh grinned at him, straightened up, and copied his style flawlessly. There wasn't much any man, especially a young southern gentleman, could teach her about riding horses. She'd clocked more hours mounted on the back of one than even a Civil War cavalry veteran. Philip grinned back at her in admiration, and their three hours of daily riding became periods of recreation until an incident occurred which turned Marsh's interest toward a whole new magical world.

A young trainer was exercising the prize MacKenzie stallion, a magnificent gray Highland, when the animal took a notion to run. Loping along at a reasonably fast canter, all Philip and Marsh could see was a gray streak as the stallion passed them. Fearful that the runaway might injure himself or his trainer, they galloped ahead to attempt to stop the stallion's mad dash. They found the culprit standing peacefully at the end of the raceway, breathing normally and looking inordinately proud of itself.

"What a great racehorse he'd make," exclaimed an admiring Philip.

"What a lot of beautiful racehorses he'd sire," cried a practical Marsh. Thereafter, lady training took second place to mare selection, an enterprise heartily endorsed by the farm workers who were bored with routine maintenance work. Of the two hundred mares left on the farm, the fifty with the best bloodlines were selected, and what amounted to horse races became a daily event. By twos, the mares were raced and the winners were carefully studied; by the end of two weeks of racing, twenty mares had been chosen. On the last day of the proposed runs, the final racing pair were joined by a strange looking, dark brown mare that had jumped its pasture fence. Not one of the fifty originally selected, this animal surprised the watchers seated along the half mile of fences by passing the other two mares with ease. Saddled and with a rider, the volunteer was raced repeatedly for the next four days and beat all the competition by lengths. Puzzled because they had no records on this horse, the trainers concluded that it must have been the prize mount of some Confederate officer. Philip's explanation made that guess the accepted theory.

"Three of our men died from battle wounds after they were brought here."

On Marsh's order, the choicest pasture was cleared of other horses and the elite mares were placed there with the stallion. She and Philip became daily visitors in the tack room where the trainers congregated. Since none of them had any experience with racehorses, they were overjoyed when Dr. Damon, Carina, and the six most experienced trainers returned from Wyoming. Damon had studied in England, where horse racing had flourished for a century, and knew enough about the techniques to give them suggestions. His laughter at their amateur efforts dimmed the enthusiasm considerably.

"You'd be lucky to get one champion in a thousand colts with that lot. We have no records of their sustained speed or their stress levels. Even the stallion, as good a horse as it is, is no match for English racehorses produced by generations of careful breeding. However, we will get some superior saddle horses from the experiment. I'm surprised Jamie ever agreed to the segregation. He prefers a standard product."

No one spoke, and the once eager experimenters all looked toward Marsh to offer the explanation. For once her voice lacked its usual confidence. "It was my idea. Jamie isn't here."

From his height of six feet, three inches plus, Damon looked down at the girl now standing apologetically apart from the others. "You'll be lucky if he doesn't chew your tail off when he gets back. What are you doing here, Marsh? I thought you and Jake were all set to buy a farm."

"I live here now," she mumbled. Mercifully, Carina came to her rescue; that golden-skinned woman with the magnificently perceptive eyes had been studying the girl.

"I think that Marsh is trying to tell us that she's married to Jamie. When was it, Marsh?"

"Just after you and Damon left for Wyoming."

The silence which greeted her admission stunned Marsh; she had assumed that everyone on the farm knew. Actually, few trainers had been on the farm the morning after the wedding; those who weren't with Damon had accompanied the consignment of the army horses to the railroad. When there was no outpouring of congratulations from the nonplussed group of men, Carina led Marsh from the room with a murmured invitation for woman talk. As they were leaving, Marsh overheard the first derogatory comment about her marriage, whispered sotto voce by a disapproving trainer, "Gawd, he picked a youngun' this time." Her face turned crimson.

While Philip waited on the porch of the neat frame house where the Damons lived whenever they were in Maryland, Marsh discussed her marriage for the first time with a sympathetic friend. To this point she had not admitted, even to herself, her own doubts and fears. As if the floodgates had broken, she poured out to this calm listener all of the confusion she'd experienced during the last six months—the shock of her parentage, the desperate escape from her stepfather, and the clandestine wedding. Oddly, she did not mention Stuart.

"Jamie married me because no one else would, not even Angus."

At this little girl piece of pathos, the older woman smiled cynically. "I've known Jamie for twenty-one years and I've never known him to do anything he didn't want to. I think he married you because you're a beautiful girl and Jamie is a connoisseur of beautiful women."

"Then why did he leave me before he even—" not even to Carina could Marsh articulate the question which had plagued her.

"Made love to you?"

"He never even kissed me good-bye."

"Marsh, Jamie is an egotistical male. He's deathly afraid of remarks like the one we just heard. He's also afraid of that sharp tongue of yours; he's too used to flattery. However, his greatest fear has nothing to do with you personally, only with your age. He never enjoyed being a father, and he'd be terrified of having a child now. Have you met any of his sons?"

"Only Stuart."

"How did you get along with him?"

"Horribly. He treated me as if I were a slut, and he refused to marry me even when Jamie asked him to."

Carina's expressive eyebrow rose. "He was your lover?"

"No. He offered to be very forcefully, but no one—not even someone like Stuart MacKenzie—is going to treat me like white trash."

"Do you love—Jamie?" Carina had started to ask the question about Stuart, but she realized the danger of opening that Pandora's box in front of an already confused girl.

"I've always admired him and now I'm grateful to him, but—"

"Marsh, do you even want to make a real marriage with him?"

"I don't think he expects me to. He acted as if he were ashamed of me when he left."

Carina smothered a smile and studied the girl. "If Jamie returns to you, you can be certain he'll expect bed privileges. There's nothing wrong with his responses; and whether you know it or not, you send out very strong signals. I'm surprised Jamie hired that attractive young man to be your companion during his absence."

"Jamie didn't, I did. And Philip disapproves of me even more than Jamie does. Carina, do you really think he will want me if he returns?"

"Jamie? Yes, but he still won't want children."

"I may be just a dumb farm girl, but I do know you don't

find babies in cabbage patches. How can you not have babies unless you're a ninny like my mother? And even she had me.''

"Damon and I have been married for twenty-two years and we've never had any.''

"Did you want them?''

"No.''

"Then how did you keep from having them?''

"You know that I'm half Carib Indian, don't you? Where my people live, the islands are small, and too many children would cause starvation. My people know how to prevent having them. That's why I've never been pregnant.''

"What do you do?''

"Do you remember all of those roots and leaves you watched me grind up when you were a little girl? Well, the women among my island people grind up leaves which are brought to them by other Caribs who live in the jungles of Venezuela. If they take the powder, they do not conceive. But there is a danger, Marsh. Sometimes, when they do want to have children, they can't. Sometimes the prevention is permanent.''

"You said 'sometimes'.''

"Yes, because there is an antidote, but it doesn't always work.''

"Carina, if Jamie doesn't want children then I'll have to take a chance. Where do I get the leaves and how do I take them?''

"I have a supply, but I won't give them to you yet. You're very young to make such a choice. What if Jamie decides to keep on running from you? You'll have risked a whole lot for nothing. Think about it tonight. You just might want children in spite of your husband. But if you decide not to, come and see me tomorrow. It'll take two weeks of daily doses. Now run along and practice dancing with your young man.''

"Carina, why didn't you have children? They'd have been beautiful.''

"In America, except for the war, they might also have been slaves."

Marsh was thoughtful for the rest of the day. Hers and Jamie's children might be beautiful, and they would never be slaves. But then Jamie would be a miserable husband. The job of transforming Marsh Creighton, untamed farm girl, into Mrs. James MacKenzie, disciplined matron with a difficult husband, had pitfalls she'd never imagined. How does a nineteen-year-old girl keep a skittish husband happy? Especially if he's sensitive about his age and doesn't want children. Suddenly, the thirty years difference in their ages seemed a lot greater than when she'd compared it to the forty-five years between her and Angus. The decisions in her life, she reflected without the self-pity she might have had, always seemed to lie between the bad and the terrible.

At some point halfway through dinner, right after Philip had scolded her for not putting her knife down before she ate a piece of meat, Marsh made her decision. Jamie might not seem an ideal husband for a well-raised, romantic girl, but for Marsh he was better than she had any right to hope for. Determined to learn every damn thing from dancing to dining, she would take Carina's leaves. She hadn't yet come to grips about how to curb her own unbridled tongue.

During the following weeks one more chore was added to the growing list. Each day she dropped by to see Carina and to drink a small glass of an evil tasting brew. Not even Angus's usquebaugh could wash the taste of it from her mouth. But the other distasteful chores of her routine had ceased annoying her. Even though she still missed the solid feeling of boots, she could manage quite gracefully in the dozen pairs of slippers and shoes that had been delivered; and she'd ceased feeling naked without the security of trousers. Even the audible one-two-three count was no longer necessary when she was performing the waltz with Philip, and both hers and Angus's table manners had vastly improved. With

Carina's help, Marsh had learned to discipline her tangled mop of hair and to buff her fingernails.

As the weeks ticked by, she counted up her accomplishments as assiduously as she once had her money. Maddy now ran a well-organized home, the mares were all pregnant, she hoped, and Marsh MacKenzie was a well-dressed lady. Quite a list of accomplishments for eight weeks and six days. Even Philip could find little to criticize, except her occasional lapse into barnyard vernacular; moreover, he'd outgrown his reluctance to return home and had become noticeably restless. Aware as he always was about the emotions of other people, Angus challenged the young man.

"Why dinna you go home, lad?"

"I don't know if I even have any place left."

"Is it money for taxes you're worried about? The lass has already told me to advance you the money to pay them."

Shocked, the young man gasped, "I wouldn't think of accepting—"

"Oh, that lass wouldna' be offerin' you charity, lad, she'll be expecting to buy a bit of your land, and her partners would be Jake and Adah and myself. Would you be objecting to Jake and Adah as neighbors?"

"I wouldn't object to the devil himself if I could retain even a part of my property."

Thus, after the tenth week when the seamstresses finally left the farm, three people began to watch the distant roadway for the telltale cloud of dust which would signal the return of one errant husband. While Angus and Philip waited with a fair degree of assurance about the future, Marsh became more disturbed each passing day. Carina's words came back to haunt her: "What if Jamie keeps on running from you?" What if? She had every damn dance lesson she needed, she had no place to wear the beautiful new dresses, and the Maryland farm had ceased to interest her. Instinctively, she knew that her husband, absentee or not, would not allow her to live on Philip Addison's plantation unless she openly defied him. But, as her sense of rejection increased, her mind roamed far and wide seeking an outlet for her restless energies, stopping just short of employment in an emporium like Yvette de Bloom's in Washington.

It was this last thought which set her laughing as she was dancing the waltz once more with Philip. Still laughing, she glanced up in time to see her partner's face change from the gallant escort's to the stern soldier's as his eyes riveted on the doorway. Quickly Marsh turned to see her husband standing there, glowering as usual. With a bit of acting that would have done justice to a showboat queen, she extended her hand and walked gracefully toward her husband. "Jamie, how wonderful to see you. Welcome home."

With hands of steel he moved her aside so that his vision would not be obscured from its main target of Philip Addison. "I see you found my wife as available as my wardrobe," he rasped angrily.

Chapter
7

More astute about human motives than the startled young wife, Philip recognized the powerful emotion behind James MacKenzie's glower for what it was—jealousy. Steeped in the southern tradition of honor, the Georgian answered the challenge he read in those smoldering blue eyes in a voice which lacked its usual soft overtones.

"Captain Philip Addison at your service, sir."

When the Scot failed to take up the metaphoric gauntlet, Philip continued in the same coldly polite voice. "Sir, Mrs. MacKenzie and Mr. Balfour hired me as both a bodyguard for her person and as a dance instructor. At every lesson she and I have had, Mr. Balfour has acted as a chaperone just as he is doing now. As for the clothing I am wearing, because you insisted that your wife remain on the farm, I have had no opportunity to buy my own replacements. However, since I have not been paid for the six months I have worked here, I am certain that the accumulated amount will cover the cost of these garments." He paused and turned to the white-faced girl now standing apart from her husband with a horrified look on her face; his own reflected his pity for her. Walking over, he picked up her limp hand and kissed it. "Ma'am, it has been my pleasure to serve you."

As Philip passed the MacKenzies on his way to the front door, Angus rose from his place behind his desk. Ignoring Jamie completely, he addressed Marsh, "I'll be takin' care of that little matter we discussed the other day, lass, and I'll be leavin' the wee book in your room. And dinna you be frettin' about the lad."

Still with the angry tension about his eyes, though some of the fire had faded from them, Jamie demanded, "Where do you think you're going, Angus?"

"Since I've no the likin' for the company of fools, I'll be seeing the lad is paid his wages. Then I'll be accompanyin' him to Washington. Dinna fear we'll be takin' your horses, though. It's time my ain two were seeking new pastures. Good-bye, lass, I'm sorry I dinna wed you when you asked and spared you the grief of being yoked up wi' a jackass."

Shaking now with an anger she fought to contain, Marsh felt the added burden of grief burn her eyes as she watched her old friend walk stiffly toward the kitchen and issue an order to Maddy. "Would you be packin' my belongin's Maddy, and puttin' the trunk on the dock tomorrow?"

The shaken "Yas, suh" revealed all too plainly that the cook had missed not a word of the dramatic scene.

Almost involuntarily, Marsh turned to follow Angus out of the house only to have her arm grasped with unyielding fingers.

"You'll stay, madam, no matter how unwillingly," Jamie snapped.

"Why? I'd think you'd be glad to get rid of all the problem people in your life."

"Unfortunately, the news of our marriage has been broadcast all over Baltimore during my absence. I find it necessary to introduce you to my friends there."

"Aren't you afraid I'll prove to be an embarrassing disgrace to your name?"

"Not if you keep your mouth shut and just smile and nod when you're introduced."

Her eyes were flashing fire now. "And just who is going to be your official hostess?"

"I've asked my stepdaughter to perform in that capacity just as she's been doing for several years now."

"Well, you'll just have to unask her. No other woman is going to do my job. I will be your hostess, Mr. Mackenzie, in every capacity or I won't attend your damned party."

He glared at her and shrugged. "Have it your way, but I hardly think that pork and grits are fashionable this season in Baltimore. Anyway, I expect you to be ready to travel within two hours. Have Maddy pack your clothes while I attend to the carriage. And don't entertain any wild ideas of jumping on that horse of yours and reswimming the river."

With the heat of her anger now cooled to an iciness, Marsh responded, "I told you before you left that I intended to be your wife in public. I have no intention of foregoing that pleasure." Arrogantly, she started toward the kitchen only to meet Maddy scurrying toward her.

"Yes 'um, I heered. Zeke and I'll tend to the packin'."

Marsh continued walking with the same deliberate insolence, only toward the library now; she didn't turn around at the sound of her husband's voice as she selected three slim volumes on horse racing. There were always alternative dreams if a person was resourceful.

"Madam," the heavy voice was berating her, "I come home to find my wife, who promised faithfully not to do anything to disgrace me, dancing, madam, not taking a dance lesson, in the arms of another man and laughing like some backstreet coquette in the arms of her lover."

"If you knew what I was really laughing about, Mr. MacKenzie, you'd find a real reason for your low estimation of my character."

"Now that insolent statement, madam, calls for an explanation."

She whirled around to face him. "You were gone three months instead of two, so I was making plans for my own future. Since the blessed state of marriage limits the choice a deserted wife has, I was thinking that if I had no other alternative, I could follow the example of a Washington lady I know. I believe you know her too—Yvette de Bloom? She always spoke very highly of you."

At the sight of his thundercloud expression, she reminded him, "I warned you that I wouldn't be a meek wife. Now, if you'll excuse me, I'll go help Maddy." As she passed him, she neatly avoided his extended arm. "You don't have to use physical restraints on me, Mr. MacKenzie, I'm well aware that you have complete legal power over me."

What her husband subsequently discussed with any of his employees after he strode out of the house or whether he learned anything about her attempts at racehorse breeding, Marsh neither knew nor cared. As she had done all of her life, she faced unpleasant circumstances with the philosophical determination to survive and, if possible, to profit. Although she was hurt about parting from Philip and Angus so bitterly, she was relieved that the long period of waiting was over. Now at least she could begin her new life, and she smiled grimly as she tucked the "wee book" Angus had promised her into her reticule. That wee book was five hundred dollars of her own money she'd asked Angus to withdraw from the bank. It was her freedom money, her traveling money, just in case her husband decided to travel first.

While Maddy packed the two trunks Zeke had dragged into her room, Marsh dressed herself more carefully than she ever had before. Selecting a sea green cotton frock, she surveyed herself critically in the mirror. Since the advent of mirrors in her life, Marsh no longer felt like a faceless nonentity. The dress, with its cool, low cut neckline, perky short sleeves, and cinched belt which made her waistline look smaller than its twenty-three inches, was a beautiful match for her eyes as it billowed over five ruffled petticoats. Adroitly, she arranged her hair and wished she could see Carina to tell her friend how wrong she'd been about Jamie. He wanted his nineteen-year-old wife as much as he wanted a case of measles. Marsh shrugged her shoulders and smiled at herself in the mirror. Want her or not, he was stuck with her, and he had a surprise or two coming.

Exactly two hours after he'd delivered his ultimatum about leaving, Marsh walked gracefully out to the carriage and allowed her husband to help her mount the step as if she'd always been catered to by gentlemen. Even though he maintained his glum silence, she was perfectly aware of the complimentary flicker in his eyes as he joined her on the softly cushioned seat. Marsh watched with interest as two neatly dressed blacks mounted the driving bench. Momentarily, she softened toward her husband; one of the men was undoubtedly a bodyguard hired to protect her even now. But the softening process ended with Jamie's first words once they were underway.

"I trust that your reformation goes beyond the beautiful clothes I provided for you. I would like to think that you've finally settled down enough to become a dutiful wife."

She turned her face swiftly away from him to gain the time to control the flush of anger which coursed through her. He had the barefaced gall to demand obedience and fidelity from her after he'd spent three months with his mistress in New York. Silently, she blessed Angus and his tendency to be talkative when he'd imbibed too much usquebaugh. With a composed face she finally turned back to answer her husband's demand.

"I plan to be just as dutiful as you are, Mr. MacKenzie," she promised reasonably.

For a moment he almost relaxed and believed her until he saw the steady look of defiance in her green eyes. Damn her, he fumed, she looks like a queen, and she's learned all too well that she's beautiful. His eyes narrowed in remembered anger. The Georgian must have done a thorough job of flattery. How in hell does a husband tame a wife with her independent arrogance? Even as a scrawny, freckled, red-haired child she'd been as proud as an aristocrat. He almost smiled when he recalled how angry she'd been able to make him even then. His abortive smile soon changed to a frown; now she was capable of making him act like a fool with her cool insolence. Furtively, he studied her averted profile as she leaned forward to watch the passing scenery with the eagerness of a tourist at the Mardi Gras. Damn her, she wasn't even angry at him anymore; she didn't even remember that he was there.

He was right about her interest in the scenery. This was her first trip away from the narrow little triangle of space which had held her captive, and every country road and small town beckoned to her with the lure of strange adventure. But he was wrong to think that she was unaware of his presence; she knew he was sitting two feet away, still glowering at her.

Three hours after the journey began, it ended abruptly in front of a lovely colonaded hotel on the main street of a sleepy little town. That her husband was a regular guest here became obvious to Marsh when the smiling host greeted him. "Your usual room, Mr. MacKenzie?"

"I think not today, Jules. My wife and I will require two rooms."

Marsh watched with interest the well concealed curiosity on the man's face as he strove not to look at her. An imp of mischief piqued her into flashing a wide smile at the obeisant little man who was paying her husband such lavish attention. Instantly, the hotel owner turned his attention to her, opening the door to her room with a flourish and setting her small suitcase on the bench as if it were packed with diamonds instead of her most modest underclothes.

"Will madame have her dinner served in her room?" he asked respectfully.

Jamie's abrupt "We both will" was ignored when Marsh smiled at the host again and said sweetly, "I think not, Jules, it's such a beautiful hotel, I'd prefer to eat in the public room."

"As madame wishes," Jules assured her as he backed out of the door, leaving a frustrated Jamie alone with his triumphant young wife. She hadn't practiced with forks for three months to have her skills go unnoticed in some second-story hotel room. Nor had she any intention of remaining cloistered in the hotel room without walking down the tree shaded main street and looking in the shop windows. When she announced her intention to Jamie, she listened without expression to his curt refusal to allow her to do so.

"Since you saw fit to involve us in public dining, you will have the courtesy not to display yourself any further."

She waited silently until he left her room to go to his own adjoining one. As soon as his door clicked shut, she smoothed her dress, flicked a comb over her hair, and stepped lightly into the hall. Holding her skirts daintily as she walked down the steps, she blessed Philip and his excellent training. She smiled again at the startled Jules and allowed him to hold the door open for her; and then, as if she'd been doing it all of her life, she promenaded down the main street of Laurel, Maryland. At a genteel shop for ladies she spied a delicately ruffled parasol in the window, walked boldly inside, and purchased it—the first personal item she'd ever bought for herself. The experience was exhilarating; and with the saucy thing tilted at the angle she copied from the other women on the sidewalk, she continued her walk almost in a spirit of jubilation. Not even a stony-faced Jamie, who caught up with her several blocks down the street, could dim her feeling of conquest. She'd been intensely aware of the admiring glances she'd received from passing men, and was thoroughly delighted that Jamie had noted them, too. She even tolerated the steel grip of his fingers on her arm as he escorted her silently back to the hotel.

At dinner in a room full of fashionable diners, she felt an equal to the best looking and most correctly mannered woman there as she deftly manipulated the pieces of tableware for the numerous courses. She even managed to sip her first glass of wine without pursing her lips at the acrid taste. The only element missing from dinner was the polite conversation Philip had forced her to learn. Except for an occasional impersonal remark and a condescending identification of the food they were served, her husband was largely silent until a bluff, hearty-voiced man approached the table and greeted Jamie as an old friend. Minutes later, he returned with his attractive wife to join the MacKenzies for parfait and coffee. The introductions were smoothly accomplished, and not once did Marsh make the wrong response.

The Greg Morrisons were horse breeders too; but unlike Jamie, they worked at the job full time. With the enthusiasm of experts, both husband and wife were eager contributors to the conversation about horses. Marsh watched as her dour Scot husband turned into the charming James MacKenzie she'd heard so much about. He was gallantly complimentary to Arlene Morrison about her gown, her unusual ash blond hair, and her horsemanship.

Having known Jamie for ten years, Arlene accepted his flattery with only a touch of the thrill it used to arouse in her. More than once she had been tempted by this handsome, virile rogue until she remembered his absolute mastery of horse trading and of all other business enterprises as well. His acquisition of a beautiful young wife did not surprise her at all; even without his money, he'd never had any trouble in luring lovely women into his bed. But Arlene was avidly curious about this particular young woman. The girl sat there as aloof as a goddess, saying little but taking everything in with those lovely big eyes. And Jamie was as tense as a coiled spring about this new wife of his. Arlene almost smiled with a delighted malice; the love-them-and-leave-them Scotsman had finally met his match.

With the alert part of his brain which was not occupied with listening to Greg Morrison boast about his new Morgan stud, Jamie was thinking about his wife. Appearing as cool as the green of her very becoming dress, Marsh looked as if she'd dined out at fancy restaurants all of her life. But to his certain knowledge, this evening marked her first time. Her other new accomplishments were irritating him as well—her impudent change of his dinner plans for one. He'd planned on an intimate dinner in their rooms and hopefully for a thaw in their icy relationship. Hell, he'd planned to make love to her. For the last eight hours since he'd first glimpsed her dancing with that damned Southerner, Jamie had been uncomfortably aware of her beautiful face and her vibrant body. And, judging by the reactions of the men on the street today, he wasn't the only one she challenged.

Arlene turned toward Marsh. "Do you ride, Mrs. MacKenzie?"

Instantly, Jamie broke from his conversation with Greg and answered for his wife. "She's an excellent rider, although she prefers a brute stallion to one of my graceful mares." His expansive smile barely faltered when Marsh decided to add to his comment.

With a sweet expression that disguised an extremely bold intention, Marsh murmured, "Jamie, I haven't ridden my stallion since our marriage. I found a mare left by one of the Confederates which I prefer now. I would like it to be my own horse whenever we're in Maryland."

"You can have any horse you want, Marsh. But why don't you choose one of my Highland thoroughbreds?"

"No, this is the horse I want."

"She's yours then."

"Thank you, Jamie. I'll send Damon a message so he'll know my mare is not for sale." And that, she thought in triumph, is that!

Arlene looked at Marsh with increased interest; woman-wise she understood the art of manipulation, and she knew she'd just witnessed a clever example of it. "What have you named your new horse, Mrs. MacKenzie?"

"Marsh Song," the girl responded with a promptness that was surprising even to herself since she'd never considered naming this or any other horse.

When she heard the name, Arlene grinned broadly in understanding. Jamie MacKenzie would never dominate this wife, she thought gleefully. Marsh's thoughts about her husband also dealt with domination. As she watched Jamie's face and his boyish smile, she wondered if she'd enjoy having that charm turned on her. Judiciously, she thought not; a disapproving husband would inhibit the freedom she planned to exercise far less than a charming one. Not that he bothered to waste his charm on her.

Minutes after they'd bid the Morrisons good night and stepped into her room, his gruffness returned. However, he did condescend to talk to her.

"You acted very acceptably tonight."

"I had no idea I was being tested." Polite lies were becoming second nature to her.

"I suppose I owe your Georgian an apology."

"I'm sure Philip doesn't expect or even want one."

"Well, at least I can send him some money in payment. It seems he was teaching you after all."

"That will not be necessary. Angus will have paid him his salary for being a guard, and I made arrangements to pay him for his teaching services."

He frowned at her. "Indeed, madam? And just how did you do that?"

"From my funds in Washington."

"I'd forgotten about those funds. I'll see that you don't have access to them in the future."

"Whatever you decide, Mr. MacKenzie." Neither will you have access to them, she thought maliciously, since Angus has already withdrawn the full amount.

"I will arrange for you to have accounts in the better stores in Baltimore," he continued, "but I won't allow you the independence of spending money as you see fit. You have a remarkable talent for winding up in trouble. If you need money, you will consult me in the future."

"If I'm to arrange for the reception you mentioned, you're going to become awfully tired of being consulted. Did you have a date in mind or do I choose it?"

"This next Saturday night. The invitations are already out, and the cook will choose the menu."

"Am I going to be allowed to arrange the flowers, or is that job also assigned?"

"You're being tiresome, Marsh. Since you won't accept Alice's help, you'll have to memorize the names and particulars of about thirty people. I suppose you'll have to receive with me."

"That's the customary arrangement for a husband and wife. A mistress or lady friend might prove even harder to explain than I'll be," she murmured.

"I'm warning you now, Marsh, not to use that raw tongue on these people. I will not tolerate being publicly embarrassed." Grudgingly, he sought to be fair. "Although I admit that you did very well tonight."

Silently, she agreed with him as she thought about her new horse.

His anger seemed to have dissipated now and he was almost smiling. "And you looked very beautiful."

Back away, she ordered herself in blind panic; two compliments in a row is too swift a pace. Surrender to this man, if any, would be on her terms and only when she'd gained the upper hand. She had no intention of being a sometime wife to a man who had just returned from the arms of his mistress.

"Thank you, Jamie," she smiled coolly, "you're the third person to tell me that today." She watched his face darken with baffled anger again and pressed her advantage. "Was there something else you wanted to discuss with me tonight?" She paused and waited momentarily, noting the sudden narrowing of his eyes. When he didn't answer, she smiled and said softly, "Then good night, Jamie. I had a very nice time at dinner." He looked at her a second more before he turned and left the room without seconding her good night.

She listened to the connecting door close with a vehement snap and breathed easily for the first time in minutes. For an hour, she lay wide awake in the strange bed and contemplated the ways and means of establishing a pleasant, impersonal relationship. This arrogant, high-handed, attractive man was used to having his own way; and she had only one weapon to fend him off—a sharp tongue that could needle him to anger.

During the long, hot drive into Baltimore the next day she certainly didn't need a weapon of any kind to discourage her husband's advances. He didn't even talk to her except to answer her questions with a curt brevity.

"Are the Morrisons neighbors of ours?"

"Yes."

"Where?"

"Northern boundary."

"Will your son be at the party?"

"Craig? Yes."

"And Alice?"

"Naturally."

Marsh finally gave up and retreated into silence herself, little realizing that a stormy battle was being waged within the man her wide skirts brushed against at every curve on the road. Never before had he been refused by a woman, and so subtly he'd been powerless unless he'd resorted to brute force. She had stood there last night and deliberately lashed him into angry responses with her insolent comments. Like a fool, he'd fretted for an hour last night wondering which other two men had told her she was beautiful. Angus and the Georgian probably. When Greg Morrison had congratulated him enviously, Jamie had almost felt lucky, but no longer. His beautiful young wife was flamboyant, disobedient, and unattainable. He was relieved to be free of his own miserable company and of hers when the carriage finally stopped in front of his red brick Baltimore home.

In structure it was similar to fifty others which fronted on the broad, tree lined streets in the most prestigious neighborhood in the city. Marsh studied it with critical eyes. It was a beautiful home, but she'd spent her childhood in a more impressive looking one which had housed only unhappy people. She would reserve judgment until she met the people who lived here. To her surprise, except for servants, Jamie had lived here alone; and it was the most efficiently run place she'd ever been in. Within minutes, her clothing was unpacked and she was being served tea in the library by a maid. A half hour later, Jamie brusquely escorted his housekeeper into the library. Marsh studied the middle-aged, raw-boned woman with great interest as she listened to her husband.

"Mrs. Tucker will introduce you to the staff, Marsh, and help you with the guest list for Saturday's party. See that my wife is comfortably settled, Mrs. Tucker. Since I'll be working late at the bank, Marsh, I won't see you until tomorrow; so I'll bid you good night now."

"Good night, Jamie." She wanted to scream at him, The banks are closed, you fool! But she realized with a dull thud of anger that she was helpless to protest his actions. She wondered if he'd brought his mistress from New York. Probably. Why else would he rush off like a male dog sniffing the scent of a bitch in heat? Marsh's jaw tightened as she watched her husband being driven off in a smaller carriage than the one they'd used today.

"Does he remain downtown for dinner often, Mrs. Tucker?"

"He's been a bachelor for a long time, Mrs. MacKen—"

"Please call me Marsh when we're alone. It's going to be an empty enough house for me. I was hoping his stepdaughter lived with him." Again the easy lie.

The woman snorted in contempt. "That one? No, she lives in her own home closer to town." Good, thought Marsh, she'd met the female relatives of "that one" and was delighted with the housekeeper's scorn.

"And his youngest son?" she prompted.

"Too lonely here for a young man."

Bull's-eye, exulted Marsh; she likes Craig. Now to get the blunt woman to like her.

"Mrs. Tucker," Marsh combined a hesitant voice with a pleading smile, "I know nothing about big houses, so I promise not to interfere with your running this one."

Laconically, the housekeeper asserted, "Mr. MacKenzie already made that clear."

In a second of blinding fury, the uneasiness and uncertainty of three months of waiting for a husband to remember that he had even married her vanished, and Marsh forgot everything she'd learned in her crash course of ladyhood.

"Mr. MacKenzie," she declared succinctly, "is a pea-brained jackass who's asking for a red-hot brand on his rump. And I am going to give it to him. Now, tell me about this thing he's got planned for Saturday night. How does it work?"

"Same as always. Folks come at eight and he and that stepdaughter of his line up in the reception room and greet the guests. Then everyone sets down to dinner for two hours. Afterward, the men go to the library and play cards while the women set in the parlor and chat. About midnight everyone goes home."

"Sounds deadly."

" 'Spect 'tis for some."

"Any young people?"

"His son and four or five others."

"Any of the older people young enough for dancing?"

"Dozen maybe."

"Mrs. Tucker, do you know Craig well enough to ask him to invite six more of his friends?"

"Four of them live next door."

"Let's ask them. Tomorrow, you and I will go downtown

and find out about hiring musicians. Philip said that big parties always need dance music.''

"Reckon so. Plenty of them musicians drifting around town.''

"We'll hire some. Now, how about tables? Do you have enough for six separate tables?''

"Four or five, not six.''

"Then we'll buy two more.''

"Mr. MacKenzie is going to be fit to bust.''

"Good, it'll serve him right.''

The next morning, after finding out that he hadn't even returned home that night, Marsh was more determined than ever to make her first party into a gala one. She and Mrs. Tucker rode downtown in the housekeeper's jaunty little buggy, and Marsh discovered the power of her husband's name on the open market. A beautiful city at anytime, Baltimore seemed particularly exciting to her that day as she and an amused and cooperative Mrs. Tucker rushed from one place to another while Marsh described the kind of party Philip Addison had told her about in glorious detail. A large punch bowl and a small orchestra in the reception hall would be waiting for the people when they arrived. At ten o'clock, everyone would have a sit-down dinner at separate tables, but they'd have to serve themselves from the big buffet. After dinner there would be more drinking and dancing.

"If the old fogies want, they can still sit around and play cards,'' she concluded magnanimously, "but at least this way not everyone will be bored.''

"You planning on talking about this to Mr. MacKenzie first?''

"No. Why should I? He didn't discuss anything with me. And by tomorrow it'll be too late anyway. Now, let's get home and organize everything.''

"You plan on changing the menu cook's planned?''

"No, I wouldn't know what to choose. But I don't want

the punch bowl to run dry. Do we have enough usquebaugh or whatever you put in it?''

''Bourbon. Most folks around here prefer a julep punch. I already took care of that while you was dickering with them music fellows. You're a young 'un to know how to dicker that good.''

''Well, the man in charge of the hiring hall kept insisting that the MacKenzies always hired musicians who played slow music.''

'' 'Spect he was right. The stepdaughter did the hiring and she ain't one to like things lively.''

Marsh grinned. ''She's not going to like the group I hired. People are going to do the waltz at this party.''

''You're right set on that waltz music, ain't you? Don't believe I've ever heard any.''

''Neither have I,'' giggled her companion, ''but I spent three months learning that damn dance and I sure mean to try doing it to music.''

Bound together by the mischief of their conspiracy and by a long day of shopping, they arrived home to be greeted by a tearful maid and an angry cook who'd spent the afternoon being ordered by Miss Alice to ''set the house back in its correct order.''

''She threatened to fire me when I didn't obey her,'' sobbed the maid.

Marsh's eyes narrowed. ''That she won't do, I promise you. And the party will be just like we've planned,'' she stated grimly. ''Miss Alice no longer runs this house. Mrs. Tucker and I do, and we do as we damn please.''

The housekeeper was still smiling late in the evening as she coached Marsh about the guests. Most were prominent businessmen and their wives, and Mrs. Tucker was amazingly knowledgeable about each of them. Marsh was relieved to see the Morrisons' names on the list and the name of the man she'd targeted for special attention—Myles Windom, the manager of her husband's bank. During the process of memorizing the guests' names, Marsh learned something about another person not on the list. When a brief note arrived from Jamie stating that he would not be home until the next day just before the party, Marsh found the courage to ask the housekeeper a question that had been burning her mind for months. "What kind of a woman is Catherine?"

Mrs. Tucker eyed the girl cautiously. "Wasn't sure you knew about her. From all I've heard, she's a nice lady."

"Maybe we should invite her."

"That'd be a mistake, Marsh. Best let sleeping dogs lie."

Marsh agreed wholeheartedly. For the next twenty-four hours she would let that particular pair of "sleeping dogs" lie wherever they wanted; but after that period of time, she'd be damned if they'd lie very peacefully. Either Jamie would become a married man or his wife would become a very unmarried woman. To that end, the ex-farm girl from Virginia laid thorough plans. She chose her ball gown very carefully from the ten in her dressing room, a dress she'd dreamed of wearing ever since she'd seen it finished. It was a dark red silk the color of her hair with a bodice that fit her like a second skin and a neckline cut low enough to be daring. Flaring out from a narrow waist, the skirt was buoyed out widely over supporting petticoats.

Ten minutes before the guests were due to arrive, she walked down the stairs to join a waiting husband whom she hadn't seen for the past two days. For once he wasn't glowering at her as he watched her descend; as usual he was impeccably dressed, this time in an evening suit and a ruffled shirt.

"You've been busy," he commented mildly. "The old house looks very festive. I understand you and Mrs. Tucker rearranged the usual order of things."

Marsh felt a very satisfactory malice as she smiled sweetly and murmured, "The pork and grits will be served a little later tonight, Jamie, and at separate tables."

"And you plan to continue your dancing lessons tonight."

"No, Jamie, tonight I plan to dance." Her eyes met his boldly, but she was the first to look aside; Jamie was being charming to her and she trembled a little at the impact his smile had on her self-assurance. Jerking a little with nervousness at the sound of the musical bells which heralded the arrival of guests, Marsh took her place by her husband's side as the half hour of introductions began smoothly. She was gratified by the number of older couples who drifted onto the dance floor while others hovered quite happily around the punch bowl.

"Now, is it part of the evening's program for me to dance with you?" Jamie asked as the last of the important guests had been checked in.

"I wasn't sure you could," she responded softly with a flash of smiling impudence that brought an answering smile to his face and his arms around her.

Briefly, the dance floor cleared while the host and hostess circled the floor; and Marsh learned that not only could her husband dance expertly, he could make love to her at the same time. His supporting hand caressed her waist as he whispered into her ear, "I never liked corsets anyway, they interfere with a man's pleasure."

Her momentary glow of victory darkened quickly into alarm as she struggled to think of a flippant answer. But he gave her no quarter. "And whatever you're wearing underneath your pretty dress is also very inviting."

"You're holding me too close, Jamie," she protested in panic.

"I know I am and you'd better not let anyone else hold you like this."

Marsh hated the blush that spread over her face and neck, and even more the chuckle that sounded in her ear. "It's nice to know that my hot-headed wife is also very human," he murmured and held her even closer.

It was her turn to chuckle shakily. "So are you, Jamie."

"Did you think I wasn't, Marsh?"

"No," she hesitated, "I guess I've known you weren't for a long time."

Both of them were silent as the music ended and they returned to the entrance hall to greet the last of their guests, seven young people who stared with unabashed curiosity at their hosts. Marsh experienced a moment of guilt as Jamie escorted the five he had not invited into the hall just as the music started up again. She was left alone to endure the open hostility of the young woman she recognized instantly as Alice Nelson and the rather embarrassed stare of the young man who was now her stepson. Because her experience with the female relatives of Jamie's stepdaughter had been unpleasant, she chose to concentrate her attention on Craig MacKenzie.

"Angus has told me so much about you, Craig, I feel that I already know you." When the young man flushed and failed to respond, Marsh gushed on in embarrassment. "I was glad your friends could come on such short notice. I wasn't sure any of the other people would enjoy the music and I like to dance. I'm hoping you do, too." Gulping in relief, he took her outstretched hand and led her toward the other dancers. Remembering the older sister, Marsh turned and extended her other hand; and although the hand was ignored, Alice did follow them into the festive room.

Dancing with Craig was a pleasure Marsh had not anticipated. As if the music had released him from his earlier shyness, he began to talk with a candor that lacked any hint of timidity.

"When I first heard about the marriage, I thought my father was an old fool."

She laughed. "He's not that old, Craig."

"To me he is. He was almost thirty years old when I was born."

"For your information, stepson, he dances the waltz better than you do."

She liked the grin that spread across his face and the

little-boy hug he gave her. "If you think I'm going to call you Mother, you're crazier than my father is."

"My friends call me Marsh."

"Then I will, too. Do you see that girl standing by the table, Marsh?"

"You mean Marilee Windom?"

"That's very good. You did your homework like an obedient wife. Don't look so puzzled. I know my father told you to memorize the names of all the guests. Right?"

"Very right," she smiled.

"That's what he always made me do. Doesn't he scare you when he barks an order at you?"

"If you asked your father, he'd say that I bark right back. But what about Marilee, Craig? She's been watching us."

"Good. Would you mind smiling at me as we dance by her? Since you make her look like a silly twit by comparison, maybe she'll quit acting like God's gift to little men."

"I take it you're one of the little men." Again his grin delighted her.

"Well, you have to admit I'm shorter than my father and not as good-looking."

"You're tall enough, Craig, and you have your father's smile, except that you use yours more often."

"Have you met the handsome MacKenzie son yet?"

"Stuart? Yes, I've met him. But he can't hold a candle to you in the charm department, and I thought you were shy when I first met you."

Craig became serious for the first time during the dance. "I am, Marsh, most of the time. You should see me fumble around at the bank, and Marilee thinks I stutter."

"She wouldn't if you charmed her as you have me."

"Honestly, Marsh?"

"Honestly, Craig. Come on, let's go over and give the silly twit a chance at you." For minutes after Craig and Marilee danced off, Marsh retained her happy glow of pleasure as she walked toward the drawing room to locate her husband. She didn't have to look far; he was standing with a group of men just inside the entrance. Her first impulse was to back away until she remembered that this was show-off-the-new-wife night at the MacKenzie residence. As composed as she could contrive to appear, she approached his side and tucked her hand under his arm, flinching only a little as his hand closed over hers. Although the conversation continued without a break, she knew that several of the men had noticed her gesture and its response. A half hour later her hand was still being held when Jamie announced that the dancing would start again after dinner.

Two of the five guests Marsh had selected for her own table were Arlene Morrison and Myles Windom. Arlene she'd chosen for moral support; but Windom was her target—a middle-aged, balding man whose innocuous face looked more like that of a minister than of a shrewd banker. But Angus had told Marsh that this deceptive looking man knew as much about banking as the Rothchilds of Europe. Tonight, she hoped to convince him to allow her to work part-time at the bank he managed. She'd worry about Jamie's permission later. Just why she wanted a job in a bank, she wasn't entirely sure. She only knew that, sometime between her wedding night and the day her absentee husband returned, she had become increasingly aware of her dependence on men. Her stomach still churned when she remembered her stepfather and his odious cousin with their plans for her future. However, as grateful as she was to Jamie for saving her from that degradation, she wanted to find a way to make herself invulnerable in her relationships with all men—Jamie included. So far, every plan she'd formulated began with money, hence her interest in banks and in this particular banker.

Unfortunately for Marsh's well-laid plans, she'd known too little about the third woman at the table to avoid social disaster. The woman with the unrevealing name of Mrs. Velma Brown was the wife of one of the stock owners of the Baltimore and Ohio Railroad and a nonstop talker, a monologist who allowed no one to interrupt her. In the middle of her third assault on the morality of postwar America, Marsh closed her ears and proceeded to enjoy eating the excellent lobster, turkey, and spiced pork she'd selected from the serving table.

Her return to awareness was barely in time to avoid embarrassment, but even so her inattention did not escape detection. She jerked to alertness when she felt two strong hands on her shoulders and heard her husband's amused voice above her head. Jamie had decided to add to his dimension as host and circulate from table to table to make sure his guests were surviving the novel dining arrangements. Arlene Morrison was the first to reassure him.

"It's a wonderful party, Jamie. When you come across my husband during your travels, tell him that I expect to dance after dinner. He can lose his money at cards some other time."

Myles Windom was next on the complimentary front. "I've enjoyed meeting your lovely wife. If you have no objection, I intend asking her for the first dance after dinner. I'm sure Mrs. Brown will fill in as hostess with the ladies," he added smoothly.

Marsh felt her husband's fingers dig in slightly as he gave his permission. "My wife will be delighted to dance with you. But if she asks you for a job at the bank, your answer had better be 'No'."

Stung by her husband's shrewd perception, Marsh unleashed the imp which was never far below her level of consciousness. In the dulcet sweet southern drawl she could use with devastating effect, she crooned, "Why, Jamie honey, y'all know I wouldn't do anything without asking your permission first. My goodness, where would I ever find the courage?"

She expected to feel those fingers stiffen in an angry reaction to her sarcasm; instead, she heard his chuckle and his light words. "I'll return your dance partner to you in fifteen minutes, Myles; but right now I want to borrow my obedient wife.''

As she rose somewhat unwillingly to accompany her husband on his round of the remaining tables, Marsh heard Arlene's sotto voce comment. ''They're a well-matched couple, don't you think?''

Jamie's only response was a tightening of his hand on Marsh's. At the remaining four tables his conversation to the guests was charming and light, except at the one where his stepdaughter held sway. Her complaint was delivered with the patient suffering of a martyr. ''Jamie, why ever did you permit this terrible table arrangement? It's barbaric.''

''Do you think so, Alice?'' he countered pleasantly. ''I understand it's the acceptable thing among Georgian aristocrats.''

Marsh's face was flushed as Jamie led her on to the next table, and her awareness that she was receiving his full charm treatment became increasingly disconcerting. Suspiciously, she expected him to lash out at her with the stern disapproval he'd displayed throughout their two-day trip from the farm; but he gave no hint of it. By the time he returned her to the waiting Myles Windom, his arm was around her slender waist with an easy familiarity that bordered on intimacy; and Marsh's resolve to maintain an impersonal relationship was shattered.

For the following two hours, her world was centered on the dance floor with one partner after another. Myles proved a delightful contradiction to the accepted conception that bankers were a dull lot. After insisting that she visit the bank, he concentrated on being an entertaining partner, as did Greg Morrison, Craig MacKenzie, and every young man at the party who felt challenged by his radiant young hostess.

Emerging from the dance floor in time to see her husband bid the first of their departing guests good night, Marsh rushed guiltily to join him. When she was still feet away, she stopped to watch Alice Nelson take Jamie's arm and speak to the couple in the process of thanking their host.

"You must excuse my new stepmother," Alice was saying in a soft, almost pleading voice, "she has never had any social training." Her voice became louder as her audience increased in size. "She's just an ignorant farm girl who never even wore a dress until Jamie rescued her when she got herself into trouble." And then, as if suddenly aware that she'd revealed too much of a family secret, she turned appealingly toward her stepfather. "Oh, Jamie, I'm sorry. That just slipped out, but I didn't want our guests to be insulted any more."

Rendered motionless by shock, Marsh felt the icy rage of helplessness as the implication of those words penetrated her consciousness. She trembled visibly when a supportive arm encircled her waist, and the quiet voice of Myles Windom sounded in her ear. "Alice Nelson is a very difficult woman, Mrs. MacKenzie."

Arlene Morrison corrected him sharply. "The word, Myles, is bitch—catty, conniving, old-maid bitch."

But Marsh had lived too long on the outskirts of respectability not to recognize the cold fact that, with one revelation by a jealous woman, her reputation had been compromised beyond redemption. Not even Jamie's furious defense could salvage one shred of it intact.

"My wife," he declared in a strangled voice, "managed my Virginia farm through the war years, and she did it with more intelligence and skill than anyone I know. The trouble my disloyal stepdaughter referred to was not of my wife's making." At his words the frozen tableau in the hallway dissolved, the departing couples left, and Marsh was released from the horror which had gripped her. With a smile which lighted the fire in her eyes, she turned to the woman by her side.

"Thank you for those comforting words, Arlene, she's every bit of what you called her and then some. And as for you, kind sir," she said to Myles, "since I have become a social outcast, one more misdeed can do me no harm. I intend to work in your bank.''

Unexpectedly, Windom began to laugh. "Angus warned me about you, Mrs. MacKenzie. The words he used were 'a brau lassie wi' a fightin' heart'.''

"You know about me then?''

"Since you deposited your first wages. Anyone with your ability to save money belongs in a bank.''

Approaching them in time to hear the last statement, Jamie smiled grimly. "Marsh and I haven't decided yet what our plans will be.'' She could feel the tension in his hand as he wrapped it around her arm and led her away from the pair who had befriended her; but the smile she flashed them over her shoulder was conspiratorially triumphant. She had already decided what her future would be both as a wife and as a worker; and she was free to be herself again. Cheerfully, with the strong fiber of her character restored to health, she removed her husband's gripping fingers and laced her arm through his.

"I wonder how your Alice will explain herself when I don't produce a child in five months,'' she chuckled.

"She's not my Alice, thank God,'' he began testily; but when her laughter continued, his own joined in. During the brief remainder of the party, the older guests polarized into two groups. Solidly flanking the hosts were the Bruce Mac Lachlans, the Greg Morrisons, and Myles Windom. Loosely leading the opposition were the Browns. That talkative lady could not resist continuing her crusade to improve the morals of Baltimorians.

"Miss Nelson informs me, Mrs. MacKenzie, that you swam the Potomac River in order to—uh—convince Jamie that he should marry you,'' she chirped archly.

"As usual, Miss Nelson is inaccurate, Mrs. Brown,'' Marsh answered in kind. "My horse swam the river. I just went along for the ride. As for my stallion's motives, I have no idea, but as you suggested, he may have had a mare or two in mind.''

Turning toward Mr. Brown, whose protuberant gray eyes had been leering at her with the same undisguised desire he habitually had for any good-looking, nubile girl under the age of twenty, Marsh was even more devastating.

"Mr. Brown, you remind me of a lawyer I know named Hiram Creighton. Something about the look in your eyes.'' Her face remained impassive and she paid no attention to Jamie's jerk of tension or to Bruce Mac Lachlan's unwilling smile. She stood defiantly straight as the other guests departed, smiling politely at the ones who seemed uninformed and maliciously at the ones whose eyes revealed their enjoyment of her predicament. A half hour after the last guests had gone, the tired musicians given their wages, and the gas jets extinguished, Jamie escorted her to her room.

"I was proud of you tonight,'' he said gently and kissed her. It was not the passionate kiss she expected, but a lingering kiss of invitation. She understood what the invitation was when he turned from her and walked into his adjoining room, leaving the door open. The choice must be hers, he'd not force her. After undressing slowly, she washed her face, brushed her hair, and stood naked in front of the mirror as if the sight of her unclad body could give her the necessary courage.

"I'd rather swim the damn river again,'' she muttered, "than walk into that room alone. But I guess I have to.'' With shaking hands she put on the white velvet robe which made her look more like an angelic choir singer than a wife about to seduce a cowardly husband. With greater confidence now, she foraged among the boxes in her dressing room and emerged with a bottle of Angus's usquebaugh and two small glasses. Courage from a bottle might not be durable, she reasoned, but at least it would warm the cold, hard knot that was her stomach. Juggling the bottle and glasses in one hand, she turned the gaslights down and walked unsteadily into her husband's bedroom.

Jamie was sitting up in bed waiting for her. He made no move to rise and help her walk those long fifteen feet. Lighted only by one small, shaded lamp on the wall behind his head, the scene resembled a spotlighted stage. Smiling as she had at Sheriff Rumford before she'd turned her horse toward the Potomac, Marsh walked those fifteen feet to the side of his bed. Silently, she handed him the bottle, held the glasses out, and watched as he poured a small amount of the amber liquid into each. With their eyes on each other, they sipped their drinks after he had touched her glass in a silent toast. When they finished, Marsh slipped her robe off and stood for a small breathless moment before she climbed into his bed. He made no move to touch her.

"Are you sure, Marsh?"

"Yes, Jamie."

"Even though there is thirty years difference between our ages?"

"The only thing between us right now," she whispered tersely, "is that ridiculous nightshirt you're wearing."

The laughter rolled from his chest, releasing those taut bonds of tension that had gripped him since he'd held her on the dance floor. Only then did he turn off the light and remove the objectionable garment. Gently, he put his arms around her.

"Angus told me you're untouched, Marsh."

"Does it matter, Jamie?"

"No, I'd want you even if I knew you'd worked for Yvette. Are you afraid?"

"No, Jamie, not now." Turning toward him, she placed her hands on the sides of his face and touched his lips with hers. Softly, he moved his in response and stroked her shoulders with a caress as light as a gossamer butterfly wing. She relaxed and let the warm feeling of being loved take over her consciousness. Languidly, she licked his lips with her tongue, tasting the mellowness of the usquebaugh remaining there; and when he met her tongue with his, he felt the stirrings of her body as she pressed against him. He sucked in his breath and willed himself to wait. Gently, his hands stroked her back as her hips began to move. When he touched her firm breasts, he moved his lips downward to those throbbing nipples and stroked them with his tongue. The tempo of her hips against his increased to a sensual rhythm, and he felt his control slipping as the unleashed desire pounded through his body. But still he resisted her attempts to pull his body over hers, moving his hands further down on her slim thighs to explore gently the moistness within. He could feel the turbulence, the vibrancy of her readiness, and his own body ached with anticipation.

Entering slowly, he stopped against her virgin barrier and waited for his hot pulsing to calm. As her movements continued to build to a wildness, he could sense the intense heat of her awakened passion. At the moment she plunged her sheath over his manhood, he gasped; and his hands which held her hips tingled with the strength of them as he kept her exploding eagerness controlled. Only now did he dare return his lips to hers; instinctively, he knew that the welcoming response would destroy the last remnants of his self-control. He met the warmth of her lips, the writhing of her tongue against his; and his hands moved to her hips to grasp her body to his so tightly, their flesh seemed joined. His own thrusts met and passed hers with a power so intense, Marsh felt the burning sensation of liquid fire. Dimly, he was aware of her legs as they lifted to lock around his hips and the muscles of her arms contracted to hold him against her. He heard her startled cry as her body shuddered and her purr of fulfillment as his hot seed erupted into the velvet of her vibrating womanhood.

Only he could realize the uniqueness of their union; only he knew that he'd never experienced anything so complete as the fiery response of this girl, the response and the soft but passionate aggression. For her it had been the first time, but he knew that she'd bitten too deep into the forbidden fruit of sensuality ever to be satisfied again without it.

Their breathing quieted and once more he wrapped his strong hands around her slim hips and carried her with him as he rolled to one side. Until their passion cooled into sleepy contentment, he continued to hold her close to him.

"Shall I take you back to your own room, Marsh?"

"No, Jamie," she murmured, "from now on I'm going to sleep with you. That way we'll both know where the other one is at night. If one of us is missing, then the other one has the right to roam away, too!"

His chuckle vanquished their sleepiness. "You would, wouldn't you? And I think you'd enjoy the game a lot more than I would." There was a tinge of sadness in his voice when he continued. "Marsh, I told Catherine about us three months ago, and I haven't seen her since."

Still resentful about the hurt she'd sustained by his avoidance of her, she demanded, "Then why did you stay away from me as if I had the pox or something?"

"Because I wanted you so much this would have happened long before you were ready. I spent the time alone in my apartment trying to convince myself that we'd be better off apart."

"Never again, Jamie."

"After tonight? How could I? I'd worry too much about what my independent wife was up to. But I give you fair warning about sleeping with me. I snore."

"I think I do, too. Good night, Jamie."

"Good night, Marsh." And, like two exhausted athletes who had won their laurels, they slept.

Chapter
8

Disciplined by his spartan boyhood on a farm, Jamie awakened at his usual early hour; but on this morning he did not leave the bed. Instead, he looked down at the girl who was now his wife. Even in sleep her face was strong, without a hint of plump-cheeked girlhood to mar the beauty of the fine bone structure that made her look so intensely alive. How long had he loved her? He remembered her as the red-haired vixen spitting defiance at her stepfather even as that sadist threatened to strike her again with the cruel whip. Last night, Jamie had winced when he felt the scars of those lashes on her buttocks and hips. Certainly a part of the desire he'd felt for her at fifteen had also been love. Always, his thoughts had centered on her as he stepped off the boat; and if she was not waiting for him astride that brute stallion of hers, his heart had lurched in disappointment. Only his self-contempt had kept him from reaching for her during the war years when he'd watched her grow into womanhood and develop a spirit that intimidated him with its ferocity. It hadn't been just her youth that had inhibited him—he'd used younger girls at Yvette's and other similar houses and suffered no qualms because of his age—it had been this girl's fierce pride that demanded respect from men.

Remembering the defensive fury he'd felt when Angus had called him a liar the day after his wedding, Jamie could smile now. But he hadn't been able to in Baltimore when he'd selected the fabrics for her dresses and fought the temptation to return to her. Why he wondered, looking at the brilliant highlights of her hair in the early morning light, was a man afraid to admit that he'd fallen in love? It had been Catherine who told him he was.

"No, it's just desire for a young girl," he insisted.

"Jamie, I've listened to you talk about this girl for years and I've always known it would be her. You've never loved before and it's hard for you to accept the ties."

"I've loved you, Catherine."

"No, Jamie, we've been good friends and you were grateful because I loved Stuart. It's been a happy seventeen years. But it's over now. Go back and tell her."

But he hadn't gone, he'd continued to fight the domination of emotion until he was exhausted. The climax to his final surrender came when he'd arrived at the farm full of nervous hope, found her in the arms of another man, and made a damn fool of himself. The impudent minx hadn't let him forget, either. Even at the party last night, her flip tongue had pricked his ego at every turn until Alice had spewed her ugly malice. Alice with her protuberant pale eyes and that pretty mouth which could purse shut with stubborn willfulness whenever she failed to get her way, was as unattractive as her mother had been. Since her mother's death, she'd tried to run his life; and he had tolerated her interference. But never again would he let her hurt this girl—this girl with the courage to walk into his room holding a bottle and two glasses and wearing a smile of pure bravado. He'd never felt desire for any woman as powerful as the hunger he'd felt for her as he fought with every fiber in his being for the strength to let her set the pace. He grinned when he remembered the pace she'd set.

As the sunlight streaked across her face, he rose silently and pulled the heavy drapes shut. Automatically, he began his morning ablutions; but halfway through, his desire for her resurfaced. Still silent he returned to her in time to watch her awaken, not slowly as other women he had known did with mewlings and yawnings and lip smackings and repeated returns to sleep. Marsh opened her eyes, as green as the sea in the morning, and smiled at him with complete awareness and with a full memory of the night before. He watched the smile change from mischief to sensuality as she stretched herself until their bodies met, moving against his arousing manhood with a sinuous rhythm. His hands reached hungrily for her breasts and his lips for her lips. Lazily, languorously, they moved together, content to postpone their joining until their passion roused enough to drive them. And when they fused together, her hands controlled the pace as much as his. But in the last wild moments, they drove at each other and created a wave of emotion that rocked them both. Before he moved aside, he felt compelled to tell her what she'd done for him.

"Did you know you'd be like this?"

"I knew that I would like it. Was I all right, Jamie?"

"More than that, you were wonderful."

"Angus would call me a brazen hussy."

"Don't ever change."

"Don't worry. I wouldn't want it all controlled and dull."

"If we keep this up, we'll produce a child every year."

"Do you want to, Jamie?"

"Lord no! I just want you."

"Then we won't have children."

"With your youth and health, we'll have no choice."

"I've already chosen not to."

Such a casual little statement to cause the violent reaction that sent her husband flying from her to sit on the edge of the bed, drag her from the warm hollow their body weights had made, and demand an explanation.

"Carina," she said cryptically.

"What about Carina?"

"She never had children because she didn't want them."

"How?"

"Her Indian powders. All the woman in her tribes use them."

"I don't give a damn about Indian women. I won't have you endangering yourself."

"I didn't. I took them long before you returned. Long before you were supposed to return," she added.

He groaned. "You planned to be my wife even then?"

She looked at him in amazement. "I was your wife, Jamie."

"I thought you might be shocked by the idea."

She began to laugh as she squirmed deeper into his lap. "I think you're the one who's shocked now. Do we have to get out of bed today?"

His body shook with repressed laughter. "Yes, we do my red-haired temptress. People drop by on Sunday. And any minute now Mrs. Tucker will knock on my door and have my bath water carried in."

"Mrs. Tucker and I are going to have a little talk about a better time for bath water delivery."

However, this was not the day for change in a house run by a punctual woman. Jamie and Marsh barely had time to scramble into their robes before the measured three knocks and the words "Your bath water's ready" sounded.

Without an eyelash flicker of surprise when she saw Marsh, Mrs. Tucker announced, "Yours won't be hot for another hour yet. I didn't know that you got up at the crack of dawn like he does."

"I think that crack of dawn should come an hour later for both of us."

"She's got good sense for a young 'un, Mr. MacKenzie."

Marsh was still in her husband's bedroom a few minutes later, listening to the vigorous splashing coming from the dressing room and watching the housekeeper change the bed linen. Suddenly, she saw the woman straighten up and stare down at the sheets.

"Well, at least, the old tom cat will be staying home at night now," Mrs. Tucker muttered.

Marsh's laughter began pealing out in such uncontrolled merriment even the housekeeper smiled. "Durned fool took his time."

"Sure did," agreed Marsh.

From his tub, Jamie heard the sound of Mrs. Tucker's voice, but not her words, and the full throated glee of his wife's laughter. His curiosity piqued, he hurried out of the tub, wrapped himself in a towel, and reentered the room in time to see the housekeeper disappearing through the door. Marsh moved over to him and began to towel him dry.

"What was that all about?" he demanded.

"What?"

"Your laughter."

"Mrs. Tucker made some comment about the stains on the sheet."

Jamie's eyebrow raised but his eyes held a happy glint. "I've heard some of Mrs. Tucker's remarks." As Marsh continued the job of drying her husband's body, he stopped her hands. "You keep that up and you'll be back in bed."

"Is that an invitation or a complaint?"

He laughed and drew her hand down to place her fingers around the obvious evidence of his reawakened desire. Her hand moved in a caress and he groaned. Carrying her in front of him to the door, he turned the key in the lock, and with their lips together they moved toward the bed. There, in a welter of loose blankets, he claimed her once again; only in this case he wasn't sure who did the claiming.

Afterward, he pulled her up and pushed her toward her

own room. She smiled at him, blew him a kiss, and walked toward the open door. She was halfway there when he picked up her robe and wrapped it around her. "Keep that robe on, you imp, I don't want Mrs. Tucker shocked."

"Mrs. Tucker," she grinned, "wouldn't be shocked if she were in bed with us. I'll race you through our baths to see who gets dressed first."

His only response was a chuckle. To think he'd been worried about her sensitive young feelings. My God, he thought, she'd have made a fortune at Yvette's.

He beat her to the dining room by a good half hour and was on his second cup of coffee when she entered in a dress as green as her eyes and as fluid as the swift currents of the Potomac. Of all the fabrics of her beautiful new dresses this was her favorite because it changed color with the light, from gold to green to·blue; but always it shimmered from the small cap sleeves to the hem of the voluminous skirt. From the sparkle in her husband's blue eyes as he rose to greet her, she knew she looked pretty; but his comment surprised her.

"I liked that piece of silk because it reminded me of the way your eyes change color."

"When did you see it before?" she asked and then gasped in realization. "You picked out the material for my dresses, didn't you, Jamie?"

"And also the styles. I was afraid if I let you choose you'd wind up with a dozen pairs of pants and twenty men's shirts. And I like you better in dresses, except when we're upstairs. There I like you best without them."

"Then I'm glad I didn't let the seamstresses waste their time making me nightgowns."

He chuckled. "Not even one?"

"Not even one. I have to wear so many silly things under my dresses I decided that, at least part of the time, I wasn't going to wear anything at all."

"Not even a wedding ring?"

She held up her hand and looked at the satin gold ring

which banded her finger. "Did you know that Judge Beacon has been married for thirty years, Jamie?"

He looked at the radiant face opposite his and wished that he'd been married to her for thirty years. "I think we should return that one to its owner. I bought you one in New York."

"I hope it's plain like this one."

"It is." He drew out two tiny boxes and pushed one toward her. For a moment, she just held the box and Jamie felt a sudden surge of pity for this beautiful woman who'd received so few gifts during her girlhood. He wished he'd remembered to bring her all kinds when she was growing up. She opened the box and slipped the ring on her finger.

"It's too big, Jamie."

"You're to put that one on my finger. I'll put this one on yours."

"What does mine say? Yours doesn't have anything written on it."

"Read it, Marsh."

She did and leaned over and kissed him on his cheek. "Were you so sure even then?"

"That I love you? Yes, Marsh, I was sure."

"When I'm just as sure, we'll write the same thing on yours."

The momentary hurt which flickered across his eyes changed quickly to amusement when she put her hand on his thigh and dug her fingers in. "If you hadn't been such a ninny three months ago, Jamie MacKenzie, I might know all about love by this time."

They were openly holding hands after breakfast when the entry bell clanged. A dutiful maid rushed to answer it and admitted a hastily dressed young man who rushed past the startled maid and into the dining room.

"My God, Craig, I haven't seen you up this early since you were born, except on Christmas morning."

Ignoring his father, Craig fastened his eyes on Marsh. "My sister," he stammered with a painful earnestness, "my damned sister just spent a half hour talking about you. Finally, she told me what she said last night. Marsh, I had nothing to do with that. I wouldn't hurt you for anything in the world.''

Marsh rose and put her arm through his. "I know you wouldn't, Craig."

"Damn it, son, what did the bitch—what did your sister say now?"

Smoothly, Marsh intercepted any response. "Probably nothing that isn't true, Jamie. And Craig knows that truth as well as Alice does. He should. He spent enough time at my grandfather's place to know everything about me."

"I used to watch you work, Marsh, and I wanted to talk to you, but they wouldn't let me."

"Well, you can now, Craig, any time. How is Marilee's list of little men this morning?"

The grin she liked so much flashed over his features. "It's much shorter this morning, thanks to you."

"Good. I'm at your service. Maybe next time we should try a carriage ride or a promenade past her home. Do you really want that list reduced to one?"

"I've been working toward that goal for a whole year."

"If you two have finished with your nonsense, I'd like to ask a few questions about something important," Jamie interrupted in the stern voice of parental authority. "Craig, have you visited recently in Virginia?"

"Alice dragged me over there while you were in New York and again last week."

"She runs your life pretty thoroughly, doesn't she?"

"Too damned much so."

"I think it's time for you to have your own place. I won't be using my apartment anymore. Why don't you move in there? It's close to the bank and it's—"

"You'll let me use your Baltimore apartment?"

"Yes, on one condition. I want you to get down to serious work at the bank. Myles tells me you rarely study the material he gives you."

"It's hard for me to understand it." Craig's grin reappeared abruptly. "But Marsh has promised to study that stuff with me once she starts working there."

His father frowned in annoyance. "I haven't decided yet whether she's going to work there or not. Meanwhile, I want you moved into that apartment. Just send my clothes and personal effects over here. You can even keep my liquor supply if you promise to hold your entertaining to a dignified level. Marsh and I will come over to see you next week. I'd like to set the record straight about our marriage."

"You don't have to, father. I didn't believe what Creighton said."

"He's still at the Randall place then? I was afraid of that. Well, what are you waiting for, Craig? I want you out of Alice's home today."

"I'm on my way right now. I just wanted Marsh to know that not everyone believed my stupid sister last night."

"We appreciate your support, son. Now get going." Jamie waited until he heard the front door crash shut after Craig raced out before he turned to his wife.

"What was all that nonsense about Marilee?"

"Your son thinks he's in love with her, but she is too much of a silly fool to realize that he's a charming person."

"Craig? He's a dunce, especially at the bank."

"You're wrong, Jamie."

"And I don't want you giving him any ideas. One son in competition with me is all I can take."

Marsh was wise enough not to pretend that she didn't understand his allusion. Even though the golden mood of their early morning happiness had been destroyed, she wanted no more misunderstanding.

"Jamie, you're not in competition with anyone. I just thought Craig needed some help."

"What about Stuart? Are you trying to tell me I'm not in competition with him? He was the one who taught you to kiss like that, wasn't he?'' She shuddered at the bleak severity in his eyes.

"Besides you, Stuart is the only other man I let kiss me. But that's all in the past now.''

"Is it? I wonder. He's more your age. And God knows he acted as if he owned you. Besides kissing, just how much of your remarkable talents in bed did he—'' He didn't finish what he was going to say; a ringing slap on his cheek knocked whatever words were rolling about on the tip of his tongue right back into his throat. Standing now, with her eyes blazing, Marsh was busily trying to twist her new ring off her finger.

"If that's all the faith you have in me,''—the ring was off now and flying toward him, thrown with all the force of her growing fury—"You can stuff our marriage certificate into the nearest slop bucket and I will get the hell out of your house and your life.'' Her last words were shouted back at him over her shoulder as she ran from the room, hampered not at all by her full skirts. She was in her room, already yanking clothes out of her wardrobe, when Jamie caught up with her.

"Where do you think you're going?''

"Where I damn well want to.''

"What will you use for money?''

"I have my own and I can survive on my own. I've been doing it for years.''

"You never were on your own. I paid people to look out for you.''

She glared at him. "That was then. You don't have to pay anyone now.'' As he reached for her, she knocked his hands away. "Don't you dare try to touch me. I'm sorry if my actions last night shocked you, but I've given you no cause to imply what you just did.''

"Marsh, look at it from my point of view,'' he pleaded with her, "my youngest son comes rushing over to defend you when he just met you last night. Philip what's-his-name—''

"Addison."

"Philip damn near challenged me to a duel over you, and Stuart was furious enough to strike me when I offered to marry you. And you say I don't have any reason to worry?"

Understanding flooded through her, obliterating her fury and her blind impulse to escape. She looked at her husband and the hurt helplessness on his face. Her beautiful new clothes were dumped unceremoniously on the floor and her arms were wrapped around him.

"No, you don't have any reason to worry, Jamie." It took a few seconds for the stiffness to leave his body as she pressed against him and for his arms to reach around her. It took even longer for the thunder of his pounding heart to subside. She waited and a giggle began to build in her throat. "Why would I ever risk losing you? You do the waltz better than Craig; and if his taste for women is limited to a twit like Marilee Windom, he sure isn't man enough for me. And your son Stuart was dumb enough to think he could treat me like some white trash camp follower. And you, Jamie MacKenzie, are almost as dumb if you think that I would ever permit any man, even you, to put his hands on me if I didn't want him to."

"I'm jealous of any man who looks at you. And last night every man at the party was looking at you."

"Well, looking was all I let any of them do. May I have my ring back please? I hope I didn't dent it when I threw it at you."

Jamie shook his head. Suddenly, the ridiculousness of the whole argument and the instant switch of his mercurial wife from screaming anger to laughing nonsense was too much for a sensible man who'd developed only one blind spot in a long number of years.

"Your ring is fine, it's my cheek which is permanently dented."

"Poor Jamie. But that should teach you not to make insulting remarks about my manners in bed."

"Just as long as you remember to keep those manners in my bed."

"Since we've agreed to be in bed together every night, when would I have the chance?"

"I think I'm going to keep you with me during the day as well."

An incurable opportunist, Marsh agreed with him readily. "That's exactly what I had in mind. When you work at the bank, I work at the bank. When you go to the farm, I go with you. If it's New York for you, it's certainly going to be New York for me too—especially New York. Since we're not going to have children, and since Mrs. Tucker is a better housekeeper than I'll ever be, and since not one Baltimore lady will ever risk her reputation by being seen with me, there's only one way you can keep me out of trouble."

"I could always lock you in a closet."

"It'd get awfully crowded in there with the two of us, and somehow I think you'd get tired making love to me standing up."

"Would you like to try it?" He was more than half serious as he held her closer. "It might be interesting." Shamelessly, she wiggled against him.

"You'll have to be careful about all these invitations, Jamie, I'm a very susceptible person."

"I'm not sure who does the inviting." He smiled. "But if you move those impudent hips of yours any more, we'll be spending the day in bed, visitors or no." But the moment had passed and both of them knew it. "Come on, hothead, I'll help you hang up your dresses and then we can think about what we want to do today. I don't suppose you're up to riding a horse?" He grinned at her.

"No, Jamie, I'm not; and if you don't wipe that silly smile off your face, I won't be tomorrow, either. Why don't we go for a carriage ride today, and then I can snub all those charming ladies who are waiting to snub me?"

"I'm sorry you were hurt, Marsh."

"Don't be. If you don't mind being a social outcast with me, I think we'll have more fun by ourselves. Come on, Jamie, let's go for that drive. I want to show you off."

The ride, however, was to be delayed. As the arm-in-arm couple reached the bottom of the stairs, they were confronted by an angry Alice.

"I want to talk to you alone, Jamie," she snapped.

He didn't even have time to clear his throat before Marsh asked, "Did you hear the doorbell, Jamie? I didn't."

"Of course you didn't, Mrs. MacKenzie, I have my own key to Jamie's home."

"You won't need it anymore, Miss Nelson, because you no longer have any business in Jamie's and my home."

"I always supervise the servants here; they wouldn't know what to do without me." The smug assurance of Alice's voice matched the mulish complacency on her face.

"That will be my job from now on. May I have the key?"

"No, you may not. You wouldn't know how to manage a pigsty. If you had any consideration for Jamie's reputation, you would go back to the farm where you belong."

The thunder of Jamie's voice drowned her out. "That will do, Alice. You will have the decency to treat my wife with respect or you will get the hell out of here."

Instantly, the woman's pale blue eyes filled with tears. "You've never spoken to me that way before. I came over here to help you and to ask why my brother is threatening to leave my home."

"He's not threatening to leave. He is leaving and he's going to live in my apartment."

The mulish look returned. "I will not permit my brother to—"

"You have nothing to say about anything he does. He's my son and it's time he becomes a man."

"That's not fair. Now I'll have to work twice as hard taking care of his clothes and cleaning up after him."

"You'll not go near there. Since I own the apartment building, I'll see to it that the doorman does not admit you."

Her eyes narrowed craftily. "The Ryder Bank owns the apartment."

"And I own the Ryder-MacKenzie Bank. Now give my wife the key to this house."

"Your wife! Your tramp, you mean. You should have watched her last night. Dancing and flirting with any man who'd put his arms around her—even with the decent men who recognized her for what she is. If you're not careful, Jamie, she'll drag you down into the mud with her. You should have heard what the women were saying about her."

"What were they saying Alice?" His voice held a deadly quality.

"All about her sluttish mother and her birth. How could you marry someone like her and ruin the family reputation?"

"Because I love her and I don't give a damn about your family's reputation."

He didn't notice the radiant smile that flashed across his wife's face; he was too busy glowering at the short woman in front of him. But Alice saw the smile and a nasty one of her own formed in response. With the curious dignity self-righteous people can assume regardless of the circumstances, she fumbled in her large reticule and brought forth the disputed key, handed it to her stepfather, and turned to leave.

"I never stay where I'm not wanted," she announced primly, "but I'd advise you, Mrs. MacKenzie, to enjoy your husband's attention as long as it lasts. He always returns to his mistress after every flirtation." Both Jamie and Marsh were too open-mouthed to speak until the neat little figure had marched out through the door and down the steps.

"That damned bitch is getting to be so much like her mother, she makes me shudder. I need a drink and I think you do, too. Then we'll clear out of here and get some fresh air."

"Too bad we can't have the house fumigated and get rid of the foulness she left behind."

Rumors, however, cannot be fumigated. Circulated freely into a targeted level of society, they quickly become entrenched as a permanent part of the folklore; and the rumors about Marsh had been spread by a vengeful expert. During their next three weeks in Baltimore, as Jamie attacked the piles of work on his desk, Marsh began learning the rudiments of banking procedures. Deadly serious as she always had been when her ambition was involved, she asked Myles Windom endless questions and read the dry chapters he marked for her in the weighty books on finance. Within a week she had graduated to tabulating simple accounts. Out of sight in a tiny office next to Craig's, she was not aware of the occasional slanted comments made to Jamie by the proud wives of some of his depositors. During those weeks, Craig was her main confidante at the bank; he discovered that asking her to check his calculations was less embarrassing than asking Myles. He also learned that she could locate the answers to weightier questions as well.

"Where did you learn all this stuff?" he asked her.

"Some of it from Angus, but most of it from the books right here at the bank."

Only slightly chagrined by her rebuff, he grinned. "I guess I'll finally have to read those dull books."

"You will if you expect to become a banker."

After beginning that chore, Craig visited her office even more frequently for her interpretation of a paragraph or a chart. Lazy by inclination and educated only to the degree of perseverance on the part of his tutors, Craig found it easier to accept her explanation than to formulate his own. He was always charmingly grateful, but Marsh found her patience wearing thin. One day, she sat him down and made him reason through a problem just as Angus had done for her. At the end of this session a beautiful light of understanding flooded his face. It was into this scene of mutual congratulations that Miss Marilee Windom flitted, and Marsh received her first snub.

"What's that woman doing here?" the tinkly voiced girl demanded before she turned around and flitted out, her pert little nose elevated high in the air. Craig flew after her, but returned shortly with a snubbed expression on his own face. Nothing was said about that incident, but Marilee's second snub occurred on the floor of the bank, foolishly in full view and hearing of her dignified father. As the girl passed Marsh, who was talking to one of the clerks, Marilee commented to the girlfriend she was with in a tinkling, bell-like voice which carried admirably to the other customers in the bank, "I don't know why my father allows that woman to work at the bank. He knows as well as I do that, with her reputation, she'll drive important people away."

Marsh had only a glimpse of Myles Windom's suffused red face as he ushered his daughter out the front entrance and sent her away the next day to spend three months with a grandmother on a Pennsylvania farm. Marsh smiled gamely at his flustered apology; she was much more concerned about Craig's possible heartbreak. She needn't have concerned herself; she had failed to take Craig's recuperative powers into consideration, and she didn't remember the male-female imbalance in every American post-Civil War city. Young ladies of all ages and descriptions abounded in Baltimore while eligible men, especially those like the heir to the Ryder-MacKenzie Bank, were rare.

Thus, after a social dearth of five weeks, the invitations began to flow into the James MacKenzie home, soiled stepmother or not. Man-like, Jamie sighed at the necessity of accepting any of them because few of the delicately delivered snubs had penetrated his overwhelming contentment with his present life. He was completely happy not to share his wife with anyone. His relationship with this irrepressible extrovert had become as necessary as food and more so than the brandy he'd once consumed to alleviate his boredom. Except for the hours at the bank, shortened to five for Jamie and his wife, his arms reached for her at even a hint of privacy in the homeward bound carriage or in the downstairs rooms of their home whenever a servant's back was turned. He reveled in her abandon whenever he caught her to him, and actively encouraged her lack of inhibition.

Jamie was in love with the overpowering intensity of a middle-aged man who had never experienced the soul-searing domination of love before. Sex for him was no longer just a physical release with a pleasant woman; it was a driving need. Even on nights when they were too tired or unable to make complete love, he held her and caressed her with an endearing possessiveness. And from the passionate girl who had been starved for affection all her life, his demanding love gained instant response. He had never dressed or undressed before a woman in his life, having preferred the austerity of an orderly dressing room. But, since their first night together, the sight of her naked body had become another obsession; Marsh had merely retaliated and demanded the same privilege. When her acceptance of his still lean, still muscular body was a wild coupling on the covers of their bed, he began to look forward to the freedom and the ease with which they could make love. He also enjoyed the earthy honesty of her impish humor and her impudent grin when the evidence of his arousal become obvious.

So it was with reluctance that he accepted even three of the first batch of invitations. The first two parties were routinely staid affairs in which the triple separation proved dull for all three MacKenzies. At the first one, Craig was pursued by a fifteen-year-old girl who hiccuped in nervousness whenever he looked at her, and Marsh sat through a two hour session with the older woman without being asked to contribute one word to the conversation. At the second affair there was dancing, and Marsh was rescued at the earliest possible moment by an impatient husband who danced her around the floor twice, escorted her back to their host and stated blandly, "John, my wife is not feeling well. I'm taking her home."

Marsh didn't bother to deny a single rumor which floated around town about her pregnancy.

The third party, though, was different, having been skillfully engineered by a twenty-year-old mind of no small ability. The guest list had been carefully pared down to the most tolerant members of Baltimore society. Except for Alice Nelson, whose attendance had been dictated in light of the purpose, there was not a single woman there whose disapproval of Marsh MacKenzie had been any more than tacit. It was several hours before Marsh realized the oddity of the circumstance. She was finishing a dance with Craig when a sober-faced, attractive girl stepped toward the disengaging couple. Marsh recognized her as Phyllis Covington, oldest daughter of the hosts, the Paul Covingtons, whose export business had been devastated by the war. At the critical age of twenty, this incipient spinster had plotted her campaign and was now putting it into execution.

"Mrs. MacKenzie," she began, her intelligent brown eyes concentrated on Marsh, "we met at the reception line. I don't know whether or not you remember me. I'm Phyllis Covington."

Intrigued by the girl's directness, Marsh introduced Craig as her stepson and waited for the next ploy.

"I was busy receiving people when the couples paired off. I was wondering if I might borrow your stepson for a dance."

Equally direct, Marsh returned the girl's challenge. "Craig, I believe you have an admirer."

The girl's bold answer left no doubt about her intentions. "Yes, he does, Mrs. MacKenzie, I've admired him for a long time."

Had Craig been emancipated a few months earlier, he might have been amused by such blatant flattery; but he was still recovering from an extended and overprotected adolescence and from an unrewarding romance with Marilee. Thus, adoring admiration from any girl as attractive as this one met with his uncritical approval and he was more than willing to give her his undivided attention. And undivided it was. For the next two hours, until a sleepy Jamie emerged from the card room to rescue his wife from the attention of an adenoidal young man and an inebriated older one who had competed in claiming her as a dance partner, Marsh watched as Phyllis charmed Craig into a state of dazed infatuation.

On the following Monday morning, when the doorman escorted a decorously dressed Miss Covington into her small office at the bank, Marsh found herself recruited once again as a co-campaigner.

"Mrs. MacKenzie," the girl began with the same lack of reticence she'd displayed at the party, "Craig told me that you often help him with business problems."

Playing the game with interest now, Marsh countered, "Not really with problems, Miss Covington, only with office trivia."

"Would you have any literature that I might study? I believe that I could help Craig with that trivia so that he needn't bother you about it."

The suggestion intrigued Marsh, who had found her own studies too interrupted for good concentration. Graciously, she lent Phyllis some of the books Myles had given her and sat back to await the next step in the carefully planned siege. It came on Friday morning, when Craig brought Phyllis into Marsh's office and exclaimed in a tone of wonder, "I thought you were the only woman in the world interested in learning this stuff, Marsh, but would you believe that Phyllis already knows it and is going to help me study?"

Marsh was impressed. Phyllis must have read the clock around for three days to learn enough of even the basics to have convinced Craig so thoroughly of her knowledge.

"That's marvelous, Craig," she agreed. "I'm certain she is a much better teacher than I am."

Every morning for the next three weeks, Craig escorted Phyllis into his office and Marsh could hear the sound of the girl's serious voice as she explained a problem to Craig. Occasionally, she wondered if Phyllis was smart enough to realize that a MacKenzie male had interests other than banking, and that talented girls are often defeated by the Marilees of the world. She discovered during the fourth week that that part of the campaign had also been successfully executed. Craig came alone into her office and requested a favor. He was flushed with embarrassment and absolutely besotted. At first, his words were nothing more than a fulsome praise of Phyllis's ability. She was brilliant, unselfish, and understanding. Not until the words "at my apartment" slipped into his conversation did Marsh's interest become acute. Carefully, she retained a somber expression on her face, but underneath it was the gleeful realization that Phyllis had braved the guarded entrance of that exclusive bachelor apartment house and visited Craig in his rooms. During one or all of those clandestine meetings, the study of banking had taken a backseat to other pursuits.

Now Craig became almost incoherent in his eagerness to secure his stepmother's help.

"She's everything I want. She's beautiful—you should see her, Marsh; when she smiles at me, I—"

"Do you love her, Craig?"

"I've loved her since the night I met her, but I never thought she'd take anyone like me seriously. But she does. I've asked her to marry me and she said that she would. We want to get married right away. That's where you come in, Marsh."

"Me? How?"

"We want you to get my father's permission. He'll just tell me to grow up, but he won't refuse you anything. Please, Marsh. I know I'm not very bright, but with Phyllis I feel that I could conquer the world."

Objectively, Marsh agreed with him. With Phyllis's help, an idiot could succeed, to say nothing of a charming young man like Craig. And if Phyllis had also proved her ability in the bedroom, she'd make him a good wife. Late that afternoon, Marsh informed Jamie of Craig's wishes.

"Myles says she's a shrewd thinker; but if she's like her mother, she'll be too cold a wife for Craig," he commented without much interest.

"She isn't, Jamie."

"And just how would you know that?"

Marsh grinned at him. "It takes one to know one."

He was chuckling as he reached for her. "There's no way she can match you. But if you think she's right for Craig, maybe marriage will settle him down. At least it will put him out of his sister's reach, that is if what's-her-name—"

"Phyllis."

"Is strong enough to fight Alice—"

"Phyllis is strong enough and smart enough to fight the devil himself, much less a nasty little schemer like Alice. Jamie, how did you know about Mrs. Covington?"

"Until the war, her husband maintained a very expensive mistress here in town."

Marsh stiffened. "Do all husbands feel that they have the right to have mistresses?"

"They do when their wives keep talking while their husbands are trying to make love to them."

"Wives are ninnies if they—"

"Shut up, Marsh," he growled. She giggled and returned his kisses, but she felt her first faint twinge of jealousy.

She felt much more prolonged twinges two weeks later at the engagement party for Craig and Phyllis. Because Phyllis had bluntly asked Marsh not to stand in the official reception line, Marsh had the unusual opportunity of sitting on the sidelines and observing her husband in action at his charming best. She was not reassured by the reasons Phyllis gave for her request either.

"If you're there, Marsh, no one will notice me, and Craig will be comparing the two of us."

When he heard about her exclusion, Jamie almost withdrew his approval for the marriage; but Marsh convinced him that since she wasn't a parent, her presence in the line would be inappropriate. Clad in the same spectacular dress she'd worn at the party she and Jamie had hosted, Marsh was by no means inconspicuous or ignored. Her chair was immediately flanked by two young friends of Craig who kept her glass full of champagne and competed with each other for her attention. Paying these self-appointed escorts only the minimum of response, Marsh focused on the central figures. She hoped that the happy flush on the bride-to-be's face betokened love as well as triumph, and that Craig's look of captive bliss would not be destroyed by a domineering wife. Paul Covington seemed to Marsh to be nothing more than a relieved, middle-aged father who had gotten one of his daughters safely off his hands. Marsh could not believe that he'd ever been a very successful rové. As for Mrs. Covington, Marsh thought her too like the other social leaders of Baltimore whose haughty looks ignored the fact that they were plump, overprotected women who had never earned a bit of the power they wielded.

But Jamie? Jamie was a different matter. From this distance, the faint age lines around his eyes and mouth disappeared, as did the occasional silver in his dark, curly hair. He looked so sure of himself as he smiled at the women of all ages who seemed to pause much longer in front of him than they did the others. Marsh didn't like the feelings that were beginning to boil within her, especially when the reception line disbanded and an attractive blond woman linked her arm through Jamie's and led him toward the refreshment table.

Never a peaceful sideliner, Marsh reviewed her courses of action: she could walk over and reclaim her husband or she could accept the dance invitation from the more aggressive of her two escorts. True to her nature, she made the more defiant choice, maliciously aware of Jamie's eyes on her as she walked beside the tall young man across the room to the dimly lighted dance floor. For the remainder of the party, she danced with one partner after another and smiled recklessly at each one. Whenever she spotted Jamie dancing with an attractive partner, the blond one more often than any others, her conversation became as reckless as her smile.

In the carriage on the way home, she was silent and unhappily moody because she had no one to talk to. Jamie was peacefully sleeping off the excessive alcohol he'd imbibed. Not until the next morning, when he awoke with a heavy head and a surly disposition, did Marsh come to grips about her fiery emotions of the night before. She had fallen in love with her own husband and she had experienced jealousy for the first time in her life. Not particularly elated about the prospect of losing still more of her dwindling independence, Marsh was nevertheless a realist. She had, she decided, been half in love with Jamie MacKenzie during all the years she had worked to earn his praise. Not that he had ever lavished much on her, since he'd glowered more often than he had smiled at her then. But not anymore, she remembered with a glow of impudent happiness, not since their first night together when she'd discovered that he was a passionate, inventive, and skillful lover and that she enjoyed every minute of their lovemaking. Unfortunately, Jamie was in no condition today for any such violent activity.

He was also not in condition for the three sets of guests who dropped by unannounced and uninvited. First was a bubbling Craig and the young man who had been so attentive to her the night before. While Craig talked seriously to his father, the other man attempted to gain possession of Marsh's hand.

"You are so beautiful and so young," he murmured as close to her left ear as he could manage.

"And so happily married," she reminded him bluntly.

"Love can always find a way around such obstacles," he importuned her with an ardor that was rapidly becoming evident to even a casual observer, and Jamie was not by any stretch of her imagination a casual observer. He was glaring at her with hooded eyes that were both angry and heartache-ridden. Taking a belated pity on her husband, Marsh stomped on her admirer's blossoming affection with an undiplomatic finality.

"Love might," she countered, "if it existed. But since it doesn't, there's no problem."

"But last night—" he mumbled.

"I danced with you, that's all," she finished for him and moved over toward Craig and Jamie. Although his expression remained unrelentingly sour, Jamie did accept her arm through his as they ushered the first of their visitors out the door. But right afterward, he bellowed to Mrs. Tucker for another headache powder and snapped at his wife.

"Did you and what's-his-name have a pleasant reunion?"

"What's-his-name," she answered serenely, "is a dumb twit." The Mackenzies had almost reached the truce stage of a reunion when the Covingtons arrived with a grandmother and the blond who had clung to Jamie's arm the night before. She turned out to be Mrs. Covington's youngest sister and a recuperated widow. Marsh performed her duties as hostess and ignored the discussion about wedding plans. She did not, however, ignore the fact that the blond took the chair closest to Jamie; and Marsh seethed with an angry fire when she heard the gentle voice of the departing Mrs. Covington.

"It's too bad, Jamie, that you and Mildred,"—the aggressive blond, Marsh concluded—"were not both free at the same time. You would have made an attractive couple. She's so blond and you're so—"

Jamie had had enough. "During the years of my so-called freedom," he declared, "I was waiting for my wife to grow up enough for me to marry her." Marsh's floundering heart stilled and her joy almost spilled over. During their private dinner, peace returned to the household; and Jamie's head cleared enough to enjoy the after dinner visit of the Morrisons. Only casually interested in the coming nuptials, Greg and Arlene were a welcome relief from the overpowering boredom of a society wedding. Horses were something all four could discuss with enthusiastic abandon over snifters of brandy. By ten o'clock, Arlene was euphoric enough to confuse horses with humans.

"Damon told us that your horse is beautifully pregnant, Marsh. I thought you would be too by this time."

Marsh giggled and ignored her husband's warning hand. "Jamie and I don't plan to have any children," she announced airily, ignoring his pressure on her hand.

Greg Morrison roused enough to mumble, "Very wise decision. Children can play hob with a man's life." Either he or Arlene had proved happily barren for twenty years, and Marsh's bland statement made complete sense to him. It didn't to Arlene, though; having already determined that Marsh should be pregnant, she was equally determined to learn why not. She was still belaboring the question when Mrs. Tucker and a maid put her to bed in a guest room while both the Morrison and MacKenzie drivers wrestled Greg into the bed beside his oblivious wife.

Jamie managed to climb the stairs under his own power, stumbling only twice in the process; but Marsh had to help him undress and, at the same time, avoid his grappling hands. Had the evening's tipple been usquebaugh instead of brandy, she might have been in as sorry a state; but she had not developed a taste for the pungent French spirit. She returned downstairs to check one final time with Mrs. Tucker.

"I don't suppose my husband will feel much like working tomorrow."

"Don't 'spect he'll even come to until late morning. Why'd he take off all of a sudden? Thought you two was getting along."

"I don't think Jamie likes weddings. Anyway, I'll be going to the bank as usual."

"Don't blame you, Marsh. Mr. MacKenzie ain't exactly lovable when his head's bustin' from too much brandy."

He was certainly pleasant though when Marsh slipped his wedding ring off his finger, peacefully snoring at a noise level several times his normal volume. Marsh giggled, tucked his ring into the pocket of the suit she intended wearing tomorrow, and slipped into bed beside him. Tonight she wanted him near her, regardless of his condition.

Providentially, she arrived at the bank early to find Myles Windom doing the work of three men and one woman. Craig and Phyllis were also unaccountably missing. Except for one brief trip to a neighboring jeweler, Marsh remained the entire working day, performing in jobs she had never attempted before. At the end of the long day, Myles walked her to her carriage.

"Angus was right, Marsh. You're a brave woman and a good businessman."

That praise sounded in her inner ear all the way home. It had been the first time she'd felt indispensible since her war years on the farm, and she'd enjoyed the sensation of being important again. She also needed the moral support of that compliment when she found her husband on his hands and knees in the parlor.

"I lost something," he growled.

"What, Jamie?"

"Nothing important. Where have you been until this time of night?"

"Craig and Phyllis weren't there and it was a busy day on the floor."

"I'd fire him if he weren't my son."

"Did the Morrisons get off all right?"

"Not until afternoon. Arlene drinks too damn much."

Marsh smothered a smile and went upstairs to her room, leaving Jamie overturning pieces of furniture in the parlor. Not until they were sipping coffee after dinner did she mention casually, "I found your wedding ring last night."

"Where?"

"In the chair you were using when you entertained your lady friend. I thought maybe you'd removed it deliberately to impress her."

"You know damn well I wouldn't do that. What got into

you Saturday night at the party? You avoided me as if I had
the plague, and you made a spectacle of yourself by getting
half the men there to follow you around like a bitch in heat. I
wanted to shake you.''

''There were far more interesting spectacles there for
anyone to notice my very small one. You put on quite a show,
Jamie.''

''I was drunk. Where is my ring, Marsh?''

''Upstairs. I'll give it back to you before we go to bed.''

''Let's go now. This hasn't been the most pleasant three
days for me.''

''Nor for our marriage, either,'' she murmured as she led
the way to the stairs Jamie had stumbled up the night before.
He followed her into her room persistently.

''My ring, Marsh?''

''Hold your hand out and I'll put it on for you. See that
you don't lose it again.'' She smiled up at him as she slipped
it on his finger and wondered when, if ever, he'd discover the
brief legend she'd had engraved on it: I love you, Jamie—M.

Sitting in front of her dressing table, she was on the
fifty-ninth brush stroke of her hair when she looked up and
met her husband's eyes in the mirror. He was holding his ring
in his hand.

''When did you know, Marsh?''

''Saturday night. I was jealous, and I knew that I wouldn't
be jealous of that blond leech unless I loved you. I think I
always have.''

''And I didn't think you ever could—not really. I thought
that you just—''

''Like sex? I do, Jamie, but I like it just as much afterward
as before.''

''Someday you'll have to explain that remarkable statement
to me. But tomorrow, you and I are going to get away from
here and be alone for a week or two.''

''What about the bank?''

''Let Craig and that manager he's marrying make their own

mistakes. You and I are going to check into the Maryland Horsemen's Club. I own a suite of rooms there, and since most of the women visiting won't be wives, we'll be left completely alone." Marsh stiffened at the implication and she almost spoke the name Catherine aloud. Jamie put his arms around her and shook her gently. "No, Marsh, I have never taken any other woman there. Do you know when I joined that club? Remember the day I discovered you were battle training my horses?"

"You were mad enough to use the cannon on me."

"I also realized that you were better with horses than I was. That's when I joined." He paused and wrapped his arms more tightly around her. "I wanted you then, lass, almost as much as I want you now."

"Shut up, Jamie," she whispered, "you talk too much."

He was still laughing as he carried her to bed; leave it to her to remember his lecture on why men take mistresses.

The laughter and love which united them that night carried over into their stay at the Maryland Horsemen's Club, the most exclusively private club in the state. Except for the grooms who tended the two saddle horses Jamie had stabled at the club, Marsh and her husband saw no one for four days. Each morning they checked items on a list and hung it on the door of their suite: breakfast at eight, and at eight a steaming cart of food was outside their door; bath at ten, and the water was delivered through an outside door and was waiting for them in the bathroom at the appointed hour; riding at one and the MacKenzie horses were saddled and ready; dinner in the room, on the terrace or at the club house, whichever place was marked, the ordered food was exquisitely prepared.

Jamie had been right about their need to be alone. As they sat in front of the fire, he was more relaxed than she'd ever known him to be. He talked about his youth in Scotland, and Marsh had a glimpse of the boy he'd been and an understanding of his driving ambition to break away from the restricted life of a stratified society where a man was locked into the caste level of his father. In other moods he became a playboy, teaching her cards and dice and fighting to win every point when they played.

During those whole glorious four days, Marsh had only one bad moment, the moment when she remembered the design of her riding habit. Made of beautiful, leaf green, hard-worsted wool, the jacket was completely feminine with a nipped-in waist and a hip-length flare. It was the lower half which had caused the seamstresses to stare at her in disbelief when she had forced them to sew a smoothly fitting pair of breeches which tucked snugly into the cordovan leather boots. At the time the outfit had seemed a logical compromise between the dictates of society and her own stubborn refusal to ride sidesaddle. Now she was not so sure. On the first day, when Jamie told her to get ready for riding, she tried evasion. When he persisted, she defiantly dressed in front of him and waited for the expected explosion of anger. As she spun to face him, he walked slowly around her without a hint of a smile.

Finally, in exasperation she cried out, "If you're ashamed of me, just say so and I won't go."

"Marsh, you could ride in your ruffled pantaloons for all I care. I was just taking a sentimental look at the rebellious lass I fell in love with. I never dared stare at you then, but you do have the most beautifully formed bottom I've ever seen, and the most inviting. And my horses will love you in that outfit since sidesaddles throw them off stride and flapping skirts make them skittish. Come on, let's ride those horses before I decide I prefer another form of exercise this afternoon."

The matched pair of geldings were spirited and smooth gaited; mounted on a horse for the first time in months, Marsh felt a wild sense of coming home. For hours, they rode across the gently rolling hills, racing each other on the long flat sweeps of path. When the ride was over, her eyes were shining, her hair was windblown, and her muscles were aching. Jamie smiled as he watched his wife rub her posterior and sent one of the grooms to order a hot bath prepared. By mutual consent they climbed into the steaming tub together and let the hot water soak out their hurts. Clad only in their robes, they ate dinner and sipped wine in front of a blazing fire until sleepiness drove them to seek the soothing comfort of bed. As she shivered in the sharp chill of the crisp autumn air, Jamie rose and dug through his luggage, pulling out a second bright garment. With a serious face he slipped one of his flannel nightshirts over her head and carefully pulled her arms through the sleeves.

"Any disparaging remarks about my nightshirts," he warned her, "and you'll sleep without one." As they curled up together, she had to admit that the ugly things felt heavenly; furthermore, in the morning, she found they impeded love-making very little.

Never had she been so happy. In Baltimore her happiness had been a part-time, stolen thing, sandwiched in between the necessities of maintaining decorum in front of servants, of pretending that the snubs she received didn't hurt, of being a stranger to her husband during working hours, and of becoming involved in the lives of other people. But here at the club, alone with Jamie, her energies were focused on him. She could reach out and touch him while they were eating, make love to him in front of a crackling fire, and talk to him without fear of being overheard. And when he looked at her, she needn't worry that the open invitation in his eyes would be intercepted by unfriendly witnesses. Marsh began to formulate a dream of a life isolated from prying eyes and demands upon their time, a vastly different dream from the one she'd had of her own financial independence just months earlier. But alas for dreams! It was Marsh herself who brought the world crashing into their lives again.

At the completion of their fifth afternoon of riding, they dismounted and handed the reins to the waiting groom. Hand in hand, they began to walk back to their rooms and a hot bath when a committee stepped out of the tack room to intercept them—an official committee, no other words could describe the four men who barred their progress.

"A word with you, MacKenzie," one of the men commanded. Frowning at the intrusion, Jamie halted and stayed Marsh with his hand.

"Wilson," he nodded to the speaker.

"MacKenzie, we've been watching this girl ride for the last three days."

"My wife, gentlemen." Marsh noticed the raised eyebrows of two of the men and the secret smile of disbelief of a third.

"That's even better," the spokesman declared. "As a club member, you can't refuse."

"Refuse what?"

"We want your wife to wear the club colors in the women's race tomorrow."

"Out of the question, gentlemen. My wife has never raced before."

"Maybe not, but she rides like a professional. We'll have to handicap her because she rides astride and the contestants from the other clubs are sidesaddle. But we're all betting she'll win."

"Who's all?"

"The members who've been watching her on the part of the straightaway we can see from the club room. Our regular champion can't perform this year because of an injury. So that leaves Maryland without an entry if you refuse. You know the rules, MacKenzie. All club members must race if they're picked. The same rule applies to wives."

"Damn the rules. I won't let her take the risk."

After listening to this dialogue like an uninvited spectator despite the fact that she was the subject of it, Marsh spoke up. "Do you mean that my husband will be expelled from the club if I do not race?"

"That would be up to a vote by the membership, but it's a strong possibility."

"What is the race?"

"The two-mile path you've been following."

"On the same horse I've been riding?"

"If you like, but you have your choice of any at the club."

"I prefer the one I know. It's a MacKenzie breed."

"Marsh," Jamie chided her, "don't be foolish. Some of the competitors have been riding for years."

"But the horse is what counts; it does the running and your horses are good. Jamie, I'm going to race."

The women's race the next morning made Maryland Horsemen's Club history. During the preceding night Marsh had withstood all of Jamie's angry arguments and even his demand that she be an obedient wife.

"If you love me as you say you do, you'll be ruled by my wishes," he blustered.

"What in the world does love have to do with obedience?" she demanded. "I'm not afraid to race and I've given my word."

Still adamant after a night of stony silence, Jamie escorted her only to the paddock area and left her. Despite her hurt at his lack of support, Marsh supervised the saddling of her horse with businesslike efficiency. Remembering the mobility that shortened stirrups had given her when she was on the back of her stallion, she ordered them shortened on this gelding. In the general excitement of the pre-race scene, she studied the mounts of the other riders; two were thoroughbreds, one an Arabian, and one a breed she couldn't recognize. She paid little attention to the women with their heavy skirts and stiff, plumed hats. Her own hair was tied back simply with a ribbon. She petted her horse's nose and talked to it softly until its ears pricked up at the sound of her voice. When she noticed the heavy crops the other competitors were carrying, she shuddered; she'd never struck a horse with a whip in her life.

At the mount-up order, she swung easily into the saddle and watched as the others used the mounting platforms. Once in her assigned position far behind the other four, she bent low in the saddle and talked quietly into her gelding's ear. As the flag went down, she whispered, "Go," and let her horse reach its own stride. Bred for stamina and endurance, the MacKenzie mixture of Arab and Highland thoroughbred exhibited none of the trembling nervousness of racehorses; instead, they ran easily for long distances without tiring. And this particular horse was one of the best of the MacKenzies, spirited and obedient to its rider's commands. Within sight of the paddock gate, Marsh passed the first competitive rider, and a thousand feet further on, the second. Ahead, she could see the other two riders, one far in the lead. Calmly, she let her horse pace itself, applying only gentle pressure with her knees. On her earlier rides with Jamie, she had sensed the contained power of this animal. Now, as she and the horse adjusted to riding without trail mates, both felt the impetus of freedom, of traveling at their own speed without being constrained by the dictation of others. As she rode, Marsh's exhilaration built until she felt she was flying. Bent low, she offered little resistance to the wind, and shortly after the halfway mark, she passed the leader. From that moment on, there was no race. It was a solo ride for her, the first long one she'd ever had at an undiminished speed. Always at work, her rides had been short, even those she'd enjoyed with Philip Addison. But this was a full-out ride, and she gloried in the feel of the powerful runner beneath her. When she pulled to a stop and saw men running toward her, she dismounted lightly and stood petting her horse. It wasn't winded, and it looked as happy as she was about the freedom of their ride.

Glancing toward the spectator area, she spotted Jamie and flashed a smile at him; then her bright adventuresome mood crashed back to reality. He was still frowning at her as he had for the past eighteen hours and he wasn't walking over toward her. Never far beneath the surface of her consciousness was the independent spirit which had made her shun self-pity since childhood. Nor had she ever worried about her past mistakes. What was, was! Jamie was angry with her, and since she couldn't control his anger, she accepted it. She was miffed, though, when he changed his expression to his charming public one as the Maryland club committeemen escorted her proudly to his side. Fortunately, neither she nor Jamie were called upon to do any talking as the other contestants rode in and dismounted.

Immediately afterward, though, they were forced to join the club members and guests for a traditional after-race drink and good-natured horse talk. Jamie was quickly surrounded by other breeders, and Marsh listened to the frequent mention of racehorses. With Jamie's arm holding her firmly by his side—more with the restraint of discipline than with the bond of love, Marsh did not attempt to join the talk. She tried to avoid attracting any notice at all. But two people in the room were determined to draw attention to her. One was a competitive rider who exhibited a noisy curiosity about the oddity of Marsh's riding costume. Only Jamie's presence kept the comments from passing over into the area of ribaldry. "My wife has ridden astride since she was a child," he explained coldly, "so for her, it is the easier way."

The second person was interested in Marsh for an entirely different reason. In the unmistakable voice of a Virginia gentleman, a pleasant looking man detached himself from the main group and walked toward her. "Ma'am, I watched you ride once before. I was one of General Mosby's men."

The room was now as silent as a tomb as everyone strained to hear the Southerner. "D' you recall the day we rode into your farm to buy food and you sold the general a horse? When you went to fetch that animal, you wheeled your stallion around and we watched you race that brute for a quarter of a mile. I'd never seen riding like that. It was surely a pleasure to watch you again today."

Marsh wanted to groan in despair as she felt Jamie's arm stiffen even more as the club people demanded the details of that long-ago incident. She thought that Jamie would have heard about it from Angus, but his look of consternation revealed that he was hearing about it for the first time. His only comment, spoken to his friends rather than to her, made her feel like a condemned prisoner. "My wife tends to be impulsive."

Not until late afternoon did he make any effort to escape the oppressive revelry of the group, and then only for a brief respite to dress for the celebration dinner at which their presence was mandatory. Rising from the table where they'd been seated for the last several hours, Jamie reclaimed her arm and escorted her out of the clubhouse. Repeatedly, on the way to their rooms, she tried to free her arm, but he held on grimly. Having been forced to be on display while he drank with his friends in order to avoid risking a scene by a precipitous departure of her own, Marsh's temper was nearing its explosion point. She waited until they were inside the room, then yanked her arm away and screamed at him, "Don't you ever treat me like that again!"

"I treated you as you deserved to be treated—like an impulsive, show-off child. Now take your bath." His voice was controlled and calm and icy.

"You go to hell and you go to that damned dinner by yourself."

"I'll drag you there, dressed just as you are now if you don't get busy and change. Now get into that tub."

She glared at him and left the room actually shaking with anger. Had she still been mounted on her horse, she'd have ridden back to Baltimore. As it was, she was tempted to try anyway. For long minutes, she stared at the tub before she finally undressed and climbed in. She washed mechanically, her eyes narrowed and her mind scheming. If she knew exactly where Angus was in Georgia, she could get away from this man whose brooding anger could turn him from a warm lover into a cold tyrant in minutes. By the time the water had cooled, so had her temper—to a resourceful level of practicality. Only a spineless ninny of a wife had to remain a prisoner in a one-way marriage ruled by a self-centered husband. She still had four hundred dollars and a good horse. All she had to do was find her way to the Maryland farm where her stallion was.

Marsh dressed very carefully in her warmest winter outfit, a rust velvet dress with long sleeves and a full skirt. She wished now that the neckline wasn't cut so low. Still, the matching full-length cape was lined with the same velvet and interlined with heavy flannel. With its voluminous hood, she should be warm enough. Frowning in concentration, she transferred her money into the snugly fitted breast binder which retained her natural shape but kept her securely bound, shoved her comb and two handkerchiefs into her cape pocket, and checked to see that her sturdy walking shoes were hidden under her long skirts. Taking her time, she arranged her hair with meticulous care before she reentered the room where her husband was stoically awaiting her.

They arrived well after most other guests had already begun celebrating at the second house party of the day. Inside the fire-warmed hall, Jamie removed her cape and hung it in the cloak room. Marsh carefully noted its location as she stood waiting for him in the lobby. Very impersonally, he escorted her to a small table at one side of the dancing area. "I wish you a good time at your party tonight, madam," he mocked her coldly before he turned away to join his friends at the bar across the wide room. Her face was impassive as she watched him go, but she managed to smile at the Virginian who approached her minutes later and requested the privilege of a dance.

Wilbur Brant was an opportunist, albeit a gentleman one. If it hadn't been for the gold band on her finger, he might have believed what some of the club members were whispering about her. But, in any case, he was more than happy to substitute for an indifferent husband. Sometime after eating the dinner they had served themselves from the bountiful buffet, Brant ventured the first serious conversation with this composed young woman whom he thought one of the most beautiful he'd ever met. Marsh was perfectly willing to talk about her life at the farm and about horses, but about nothing more personal. It was just as well she refrained. Mr. Brant was a journalist with the *Baltimore Herald* who knew that anything to do with James MacKenzie was good copy. Recalling vaguely the rumors about a somewhat hurried marriage for the middle-aged financier, he concluded that his dinner partner was much too self-assured to be anything but a wife, so his questions became more pointed.

"Does your husband approve of your racing style, Mrs. MacKenzie?"

Marsh grinned at him. "Would you if I were your wife?"

Brant laughed and remembered the bold girl she'd been. "Not many men would appreciate your brand of courage."

"Men," she said sweetly, "can be mush-headed boobies when it comes to women." Marsh stood up abruptly and extended her hand. "Good night, Mr. Brant. Tell General Mosby, if you ever see him again, that I thought he was wonderful." Without giving him a chance to reply, she walked quickly to the cloak room, retrieved her cape, and let herself out the entrance door. Drawing a deep breath of the cold, invigorating air, she pulled her hood tight around her head and walked in the direction of the outbuildings where she knew the grooms and carriage drivers were bunked. One of them might be bribable enough to drive her to the farm.

She jerked to a halt and muffled her scream of fright as a shadowy figure stepped out from one of the MacKenzie horse stalls and imprisoned her with strong arms.

"I thought you might be planning something insane, Marsh," Jamie scolded her in a tired voice. Without regard for her sensitivity, he lifted her skirts and rubbed his hand down her pantalooned leg. "I was certain you had your britches on underneath. Were you actually going to ride into Baltimore with your skirts hitched up?"

"I had no intention of stealing your horse, Mr. MacKenzie," she answered huffily.

"Then what were you planning?"

"A very long walk."

"Well, it's been considerably shortened now—just back to our rooms." Marsh didn't resist as he turned her around, took her arm, and started walking. "Did you know that the gentleman you poured your heart out to tonight is a reporter assigned to cover today's race? What were you talking about?"

"My work on the farm, horses, and General Mosby."

"Nothing about a cruel husband who objects to a wife turning their marriage into a public circus?"

"Sorry to disappoint you, but your name was not mentioned."

Without loosening his firm grip on her arm, he unlocked the door to their suite, pushed her before him, closed and relocked the door.

"Now," he announced grimly, "we're going to discuss your unfortunate tendency to seek notoriety."

"I hope you have a pleasant talk with yourself, Mr. MacKenzie, since I have no intention of discussing another damn thing with you. I am going to bed." He followed her to the bedroom, watching uneasily as she removed her clothes— all but her chemise and pantaloons. He waited until she had climbed into bed before he sat down next to her and reopened his attack.

"Are you ready to be reasonable yet?"

"No," she gritted with a glitter in her eye that bespoke of a barely controlled fury. "After thirty hours of your cold, silent treatment and of being dumped like a sack of rotten potatoes at a public ball for your friends to make fun of, I find that I have nothing to say to you." Rolling over on her stomach, she burrowed her head deep into the pillow and closed her eyes. He watched her for a few minutes more before he gave up and joined her in bed. It was a long, uncomfortable, sleepless night for both of them. The next day they packed their clothing and were driven home in the carriage. Their en route conversation was even more divisive than their earlier ones.

"Do you know the date of Craig's wedding?"

"The tenth of December."

"Good, that gives me time to get to New York and back."

"Say hello to Catherine for me."

"Don't be insolent. While I'm gone, you're to remain at the house."

"I won't be there when you return."

"I'm tired of your threats."

"It's no threat."

"And just how do you expect to travel? I'll see to it that neither the carriage nor the horses are available to you."

She shrugged. "The trains are still running."

"To where?"

"If I wanted you to know I'd tell you, wouldn't I?"

After what seemed like ten instead of three hours, they arrived at their Baltimore home, ate a silent supper, and went to bed, each in his separate room.

Chapter
9

By morning, the weather had turned bitterly cold and Baltimore was locked into its first winter chill. But even the inclement weather failed to reduce the activity in the MacKenzie home. Jamie left sometime before eight o'clock without saying anything to Marsh, and she spent the following two hours carefully segregating her clothes in order to fit the most usable into the one suitcase she could conveniently carry. Her morning was interrupted first by the arrival of Phyllis, who spent an hour talking about wedding plans. The only amusing note of the overlong visit was the reporting of an odd incident which had taken place last week at the bank.

"A girl I'd never seen before walks into Craig's office while we were working and demands to know who I was. When Craig introduced me as his fiancé, that odd creature turned around and walked out."

Marsh had to smile. "That was Marilee Windom," she giggled, "what did Craig say after she'd gone?"

"That she was a silly twit."

"She sure was, Phyllis."

The second interruption in her flight planning was Mrs. Tucker bringing her a copy of the *Baltimore Herald* which had been carefully opened to the sporting page.

"Better read the story before your husband gets home, Marsh."

"Mr. MacKenzie won't be coming back."

"Off on one of his black sulks again, is he?"

"Yes."

"Some of them last for weeks. What'd you do wrong?"

"I won a damn horse race."

"That don't sound like him."

"He didn't want me to race."

"That's him. Never could stand anyone to go against him."

"Well, maybe he's not too old to learn. I'm leaving."

"Did you tell him you was?"

"Yes."

"He agree?"

"No. He forbade me to use the carriage or any of his horses. As if his God-almighty orders would keep me any-place I didn't want to be. I can still walk."

"No need for that, Marsh. I'll take you to the train in my trap. Where're you headed fer?"

"To find Angus."

"When d' you want to leave?"

"There's no rush. Tomorrow morning, I guess."

"Sure sorry, Marsh. Thought he was held down too good this time to return to catting around."

"So did I. But according to him a man has a right to cat."

"A lot of them thinks that way. Marsh, since he won't be home, d' you mind if I take the day and night off? Like to visit my sister."

"You go ahead, Mrs. Tucker. Tell the others to go, too. I'm just going to sleep."

Sleep, however, was vanquished from her mind for another

two hours by the best moments she'd had since winning the race. The *Baltimore Herald* article was a wonderful story about her and the MacKenzie horses. She'd expected it to be an exaggerated exposé about a social rebel. Instead, Wilbur Brant described her style of riding with admiration, and he made her wartime meeting with General Mosby seem adventurous rather than commercially sordid. But the best part of the article was his praise for MacKenzie horses. Jamie should be able to sell a hundred more horses easily, she thought with cynical humor. She looked up as Mrs. Tucker handed her a letter.

"Almost forgot, Marsh. This come for you while you was away. Didn't think you'd want him to get it along with the rest of the mail."

For the second time that day, Marsh received good news, this time from Angus; the news was better than good, it was the best she could have hoped for. She, Angus, Jake and Adah now owned three thousand acres along the Oconee River in Georgia; and Philip Addison had been in time to pay off the taxes on his adjoining plantation with the purchase money. She now had a destination and a future with people who had been her best friends. The letter was also full of advice about Jamie; but since he was now past tense, Marsh didn't want the pain of thinking about what might have been.

The house was silent and lonely when she finished her packing and climbed into bed sometime in the mid-afternoon. She shivered a little from the cold of the wintry day and from her own realization of failure. But as sleep took over her consciousness, she counted her assets and found life at least bearable.

Hours later, long after day had faded into late night, she stirred awake, aroused by a familiar sound next to her. She didn't have to turn around to know that Jamie had joined her and was now snoring peacefully, wrapped warmly around her own body. For minutes she lay there, quietly savoring the comfortable feel of him until the pangs of hunger roused her to restlessness and her memory returned in full. As she eased out of bed, she hoped that he would continue to sleep. She still was not ready for that "reasonable" discussion he'd insisted on. She went to the kitchen, which she'd only looked at vaguely before, rustled around the stove, and started a fire to heat the pot of water left standing on the top. Looking around the huge room, lighted only with the candle she'd brought with her, she began to explore the shelves for stored food. She didn't look around when Jamie took the candle from her hand and reached efficiently for the food containers.

"Where are the servants, Marsh?"

"I told them they could have the night off."

"I don't like you being alone."

"I've been worse than alone for three nights."

"So have I."

"I thought you were on your way to New York."

"I never planned to go."

"Then why did you say you were?"

"Because you were trying to leave me, and I noticed that you're all packed to try again."

"I don't stay when I'm not wanted." She giggled nervously, "I think Alice already said that."

"You're wanted, Marsh. I took care of Craig's wedding today. Didn't the bride tell you the plans?"

"So that's how Phyllis knew I was home. I thought the bride's parents took care of a wedding."

"The Covingtons will help, but right now they're hard up."

"Oh."

"They'll live in the apartment."

"Who?"

"Craig and what's-her-name."

"Phyllis."

"They both said to thank you."

"Why?"

"For a lot of things, evidently. Why didn't you tell me about Marilee Windom?"

"It wasn't important. She's just a dumb twit."

"Well, Phyllis and Craig both insist that you be a part of the wedding reception."

"I don't want to be, Jamie."

"Then neither of us will go."

"You have to."

"Not without you."

During the rambling conversation, Jamie had located the food the cook had prepared—fried chicken, apple tarts, and a loaf of fresh bread. Marsh contributed only cheese and shelled walnuts to the tray of food.

"Go light the fire in the library, Marsh, while I make the tea. We'd freeze here in the kitchen."

With her hands already numb from the cold, she was only too glad to be relieved of the chore of waiting for the water to boil. But even when the fire was blazing in the library fireplace, her posterior still felt frostbitten. She dragged two chairs as close to the fire as she dared, and wished she knew where the extra blankets were stored. When he entered the room with the full tray, Jamie took one look at her huddled in front of the fire and set the tray down. Minutes later, he returned with a pile of soft, plaid wool blankets and wrapped one of them around her. Pulling a small table between their chairs, he spread the food out. After two days of missed or half-eaten meals, they were hungry enough to forget both manners and polite conversation as they ate the cold food and washed it down with hot tea liberally laced with brandy. By the time she'd downed two cups of the puckery beverage, Marsh pushed the blanket off and walked the four-foot distance toward her impossible husband, whose glower had turned into a welcoming smile.

"Jamie MacKenzie, you're a coward. You'd have let me sit over there all night."

He stood up and reached for her. "I wasn't the one who got out of bed a while ago."

"I was afraid you'd want to talk."

"No, I didn't want to talk, and if you don't stop doing it now, I'm going to make love to you standing up."

Giggling, she helped him move the table and spread blankets out on the floor in front of the fire, but her lips became too busy to giggle as he pulled her down to him and fumbled with the buttons on her robe. He groaned when she caressed his burning, ready body and guided him into her without any of their usual play. Together, they convulsed within seconds, still half in and half out of their robes.

"I'm sorry I couldn't wait for you that time," he whispered in apology, "but I haven't thought about much else all day."

Impudently, she moved her hips against his. "Stop your boasting, Jamie. I've done a little thinking myself, and I didn't need you to wait for me. Since when have you ever had to?" It was a good thing there was no one else in the house at that moment; his booming laughter might have startled an uninitiated listener. So would the following hour of their uninhibited lovemaking and play on the floor in front of a warm fire. Neither of them noticed when the sky turned to gray or when a wintry sun struggled to send its pale yellow rays through the window. Only the sound of footsteps in the rear of the house ended their beautiful hours of isolated insanity. Like guilty children, they scrambled to toss the blankets behind a sofa and pull on their robes. When Mrs. Tucker poked her head in the door, they were almost decently seated in front of the dying fire.

"Didn't think you'd be durned fool enough to let her go," that worthy housekeeper grunted, closing the door quickly before her employer could retaliate. As an automatic scowl formed on his face, Marsh shoved him vigorously toward the door.

"Don't you dare begin another black sulk, James MacKenzie, at least until we've had a bath and gotten dressed. My

backside is too damned sore for another reunion right now."
He was still smiling two hours later when they descended
from their bedrooms to sit with dignified formality at the
breakfast table. Even their conversation maintained a pleasant
tenor.

"Your southern friend wrote a good story about the race,"
he commented neutrally, "but I wonder where he got the
notion that I raise racehorses?"

"I wouldn't know," she answered blithely.

"That's odd. Damon told me that you'd arranged that
remarkable separation of mares before he returned."

"Oh that," she made a face at him, "all you'll get from even
your fastest mares will be expensive saddle horses—all but
one."

"And that one will be your mare's foal?"

"No, Jamie, the mare's still yours. I tricked you into
giving it to me."

"What makes you think an unknown horse is a racer?"

"You should have seen her. She knew exactly how fast she
had to run to beat her competition. And she never had to
strain once to leave them behind. If her foal inherits her
spirit, we'll have ourselves a racehorse."

"You'd like that, wouldn't you?"

"Yes, Jamie, I would. Besides, it'll help make the MacKenzie
farms pay off again. Right now the only horses in demand are
workhorses, and even my stallion isn't big enough to produce
the massive animals all the farmers are going to want,
especially in the South. Jamie, do you realize that there are
thousands of surplus saddle horses in the country right now?
But if the MacKenzie farms could switch to heavy workhorses
and champion blood racers, we'd make real money."

He looked at her sharply as she gushed out these words;
not for anything would he admit that he'd been worried for
months about the future of both farms. "How would you like
to go to England after the wedding, Marsh?"

"To buy Shires and Clydesdales and some Thoroughbreds? Oh, Jamie, I'd love to."

"For a girl, you've learned a lot about horses."

"As a deserted wife, I had a lot of time to read while I was waiting for you to use some common sense."

"How was I to know you were old enough to be a wife?"

"I was old enough."

"And then some," he grinned. A very dignified conversation!

However, compared to some of the conversations that took place in the frantic three weeks of wedding preparation, Jamie and Marsh's was a model of decorum. Phyllis decided early that only the senior MacKenzies had enough sense to help her. Since her own parents were being spared most of the expense, her mother began with lavish plans for a dozen attendants and two hundred guests. With an eye to future relationships with her in-laws, Phyllis ruthlessly pared the attendants to six and the guests to forty. She elected to wear her mother's wedding dress and decreed that her younger sisters would wear their pink coming out dresses. Only Alice, who was to be the maid of honor, was allowed to choose the style of her dress.

Jamie was amused when Phyllis explained her reason for this leniency. "Alice," she said bluntly, "thinks she is going to run Craig's and my life just as she thought she was going to manage my wedding. I didn't want to get into a fight with her before I married her brother, so I told her that she could help after she got her dress ready. So far she's been too busy with it to have time to bother me. I'll make a prediction that it's going to be blue, and so full of ruffles it'll jiggle when she walks."

At the church, when Alice's dress turned out to be just that, Jamie squeezed his wife's arm and whispered, "You were right. My daughter-in-law can beat the devil. Craig will be a respected banker before he knows how to arrange a mortgage. With that wife he won't ever have to learn a thing.

She'll do the thinking for both of them. She certainly put Alice in her place.''

In this case, unfortunately, Jamie had overestimated Phyllis and underestimated Alice. In deference to Marsh, Craig and Phyllis had decided not to invite his Virginia relatives; Alice had corrected the oversight and extended a blanket invitation to everyone in her aunt's home. Whereas Phyllis had decided on simple sandwiches, Alice had employed her own servants to prepare mounds of shellfish delicacies and trays of spicy tarts. Even as the ceremony was about to begin, the modest cake Phyllis had ordered was being replaced by a seven-tier one from Alice's kitchen.

Marsh was the first member of the wedding party to become aware of Alice's little surprises. While she and Jamie were waiting in the formal entry to the church for the other guests to be seated, she watched as a large showy carriage stopped in front of the church. Out stepped a dapperly dressed Blake Creighton, who turned to help the four occupants descend the two steps to the sidewalk. Sophia Randall was opulently clad in a brown velvet ensemble which must have cost her a month's allowance at least. The cloak was lavishly trimmed with sable fur, and the dress sparkled with a thousand tiny gold beads stitched into the stiff skirt. Like an old-fashioned man-of-war under full sail, she glided past the small Creighton and allowed a fascinated Marsh a glimpse of the full-breasted, petulant-faced woman who followed her mother, gowned in a style of dress Marsh had only seen one other woman wear—Yvette de Bloom. Janet's dress was a bright purplish-pink, with tiers of ruffles edged in black lace. She looked, Marsh thought with contempt, like an overripe plum.

The two women stood dramatically at the foot of the brick stairs as Creighton helped the next passengers out. Marsh, who hadn't seen her grandfather in seven years, was amazed that he was still a handsome man in spite of his look of dissipation. The second man being helped out, she had never met, but she knew that he was Janet's husband, Wayne Talbot. His good looks were marred by a heavy pallor covering the pinched look of pain, and he walked awkwardly with the aid of a pair of canes. It must be agonizingly difficult for a handicapped man to be at the untender mercy of those two self-centered women, Marsh reflected. For the first time in months, she thought of her mother and was fiercely glad Melissa had escaped from them.

Standing with his back to the door, Jamie did not see the new arrivals until his wife's expression alerted him. He swung around and glared at them, his face assuming its darkest, thundercloud expression. Without waiting for the usher, he grabbed Marsh's arm and rushed her unceremoniously to their reserved pew at the front of the church.

"That cursed Alice," he sputtered, calming down enough to speak more gently to his wife. "We don't have to stay if you're upset. I'll explain to Craig."

"Don't worry about them, Jamie, they're Craig's relatives, after all. If my nasty little stepfather acts up, I'll help you stomp on him. Not one of those people can affect us in the least." Had Marsh known that there was a sixth guest coming from the Virginian side of the family, she would have taken Jamie up on his invitation to leave the wedding scene. A week earlier, Stuart MacKenzie had returned from the Mexican border and had accepted Sophia's invitation to attend the wedding. Preferring to remain separate from the others, he'd checked into a Baltimore hotel and was even now walking briskly toward the church, his thoughts a chaotic mixture of anticipation, cynicism, and something vastly more disturbing to him—regret. He hadn't forgotten the blazing green eyes of an auburn-haired girl who had castigated him with such outraged contempt, but who had also once responded to his kiss with an awakening passion that had seared him.

Mercifully unaware that the tenuous serenity of hers and Jamie's current relationship was again threatened, Marsh was enjoying the first real wedding she'd ever attended. The short, expedient service which had made her a wife could hold no comparison to this fulsome ceremony now unfolding like a pageant. Long before she and Jamie had fled to the safety of their seats, the entertainment had begun with the music produced by the brass-piped organ being expertly played by a white-haired man in a flowing black robe. Marsh was enthralled by the magnificence of the haunting sounds that reverberated over the sparsely filled pews. The inside of the church too had awed her with its atmosphere of hushed reverence. To a farm girl whose total religious training was limited to a few Bible stories and several visits to the "spirit" meetings the blacks had held on the farm, this formal church made her aware of another sphere of her own ignorance. However, the wedding itself seemed pretentious to her. Knowing most of the principal participants too well to credit them with much spirituality, she thought that their present expressions of holy solemnity belonged in the theater rather than a church. Alice looked prayerful and Phyllis demure, two very unlikely attributes for these scheming women.

Jamie also was distracted by thoughts other than the ceremony. He was thinking about his wife and depressed for the first time in months about the difference in their ages. She looked as young as the first feathery tendrils of spring grass on the windswept hills of his native Scotland in the soft green silk dress. He knew with the practical part of his mind that there was nothing jeune fille about the cut of the dress or about the firm breasts outlined enticingly by the clinging fabric, but there was a look of unconquered beauty about her that made other women appear jaded to his prejudiced eyes.

Abruptly, their private thoughts and those of every other watcher were terminated by the triumphal organ music which signalled the end of the ceremony. In the rush which followed the bride and groom out of the church, the senior MacKenzies joined the bride's parents in their carriage to make the dash to the Covington home in time to receive the guests. As soon as the youthful contingent of the wedding party scrambled into the warm house, the eleven principals lined up against a holly decorated wall with the oblivious bride and groom in the center flanked by the Covingtons on one side and Marsh and Jamie on the other. Alice chose to stand by Jamie's other side while the bridesmaids and the best man scattered themselves at either end of the line. The three ushers stationed themselves near the entrance of the huge room.

The reception line had no sooner formed than the guests began to arrive. Nothing encourages promptness so well as a chilly, fifty degree temperature lowered still more by a biting wind blowing off the Chesapeake Bay. Marsh listened to the polite murmurings of the guests in the entry hall as maids carried their topcoats, capes, and furs to the remote regions of the house, and wondered if anyone ever calculated the entire cost of a wedding in terms of new outfits, gifts, and general reception costs. The first arrivals to pass in review were old wedding professionals who knew the procedure by heart; first, the introductions, performed when necessary by well-rehearsed ushers; then, the slow perusal of the displayed gifts to make sure their own were prominent enough to be impressive; and finally, the long stop at the refreshment tables where six servants, three from the MacKenzie home, poured the champagne Jamie had insisted on, and served the other delicacies.

When the bride had first seen the altered display of food, her jaw had clamped shut with anger, but that irritation was nothing compared to her fury as the sixtieth guest trooped by. Marsh overheard Craig whisper to his new wife, "I thought we invited only forty."

"Your sister," Phyllis gritted from between smiling lips.

"Oh God, Phil, I'm sorry," Craig whispered back.

Marsh smiled grimly and hoped that Phyllis would be successful in excluding Alice from her and Craig's life in the future. Right now, she wanted to exclude her from Jamie's life. Clinging like a limpet to Jamie's left arm, Alice had managed to turn him away from Marsh, who stood between the groom and his father and was able to talk to neither.

Possibly held up by the agonizing slowness of Wayne Talbot, the Randall party was the last to arrive. First to accost Jamie was the redoubtable Sophia with a smilingly indifferent husband in tow. Only when Sophia nudged his arm, did he recognize his granddaughter. Marsh murmured, "Mr. Randall," as if she were meeting him for the first time.

He looked momentarily puzzled, then smiled again and, like the experienced old womanizer he was, waxed complimentary. "You look very fetching, Pamela," he affirmed gallantly before he moved past the rest of the line with record speed, shrugged off the continued assistance of the usher as he passed the gift table without a glance, and headed for the champagne.

Sophia, though, was in no hurry. She remained firmly planted in front of Jamie. "Well, I see you married her, Jamie, bad blood and all. I understand she's already embarrassed you as a hostess and disgraced you at your club. But at least you got her into a dress for the wedding."

With a grim smile, Jamie dislodged the clinging Alice abruptly and put his arm defensively around Marsh. "As always, Sophia, your good manners are exceeded only by your charm. Did Alice also inform you that my wife and I are going to England this month? I see she didn't, but then Alice didn't know about that, just as she knows little else about Marsh and myself. While we're gone, Sophia, I advise you to forego any further assassination of my wife's character. I still retain the means to reduce your income considerably." Glaring at his former sister-in-law's face, Jamie failed to note the sudden pursing of Alice's lips or the sly look of calculation in her eyes.

Marsh's attention too was directed elsewhere. Wayne Talbot had struggled to pass his mother-in-law in line and now stood before Marsh, so anguished looking that she murmured a hasty "Excuse me, Jamie," and reached out to take

Wayne's trembling arm and escort him slowly over to a secluded corner. Seating him in a comfortable chair, she rushed to the refreshment table and secured a glass of champagne for the exhausted man. From a nearby chair, she watched him anxiously until some color returned to his white face and he was able to breathe more normally. Unwilling to leave him alone, she remained by his side until he recovered his poise; then she stayed on out of pity. Wayne Talbot was more of an outcast than she was.

"You're Pamela," he said with a winsome smile. "I used to watch you work. You looked so alive in a dead world."

"My friends call me Marsh, Mr. Talbot."

"I don't have any friends, Marsh, but I'd like you to call me Wayne."

Marsh grinned at him. "Wayne Talbot, I remember seeing a whole passel of your friends at the house when you and Janet were married."

"That was six years ago. They're gone now."

Marsh remembered the half-dead look in Philip Addison's eyes when she'd first met him, the same hopeless defeat reflected now in this man's. Her mind was busy remembering a line from the one letter Angus had sent her. "I wish we knew someone who could advise us about crops. None of us ha' a grain of knowledge about what to plant, lass." From somewhere or someone Marsh had heard that Wayne's family owned a productive plantation.

"Your home is in South Carolina, isn't it, Wayne?"

"It was."

"Do you know anything about Georgia?"

"Yes, ma'am, I attended school in Georgia and I served with General Johnson there during the war."

"Do you know the Oconee River area?"

"Some, but not all. It used to be rich cotton land."

"Then you know something about crops?"

"I should. I spent three years at college studying to become a planter." He smiled without humor. "That is the most useless education a homeless cripple could have. I'm sorry, Marsh, I didn't mean to burden you with my problems.''

"Wayne Talbot, you're not burdening me with anything. I know how to hoe and harvest vegetables, but I don't know a thing about big money crops. Can you really test soils and tell what grows best?''

"As well as most, I reckon.''

"Would you like to work?''

Never had she seen a smile so hopeful. "Along with every other disfranchised rebel, I'd like a decent job more than anything. But who'd hire me?''

"Some friends of mine would in a minute if you could help them before spring. Wayne, every big landowner in the South is going to replant cotton; and like a bunch of ninnies, they'll flood the market again. There must be crops that don't have so much competition.''

"There are, hundreds of them, but cotton men won't switch. If it were my land on the Oconee River, I'd—'' Before he could finish, Marsh felt her husband's familiar hands on her shoulders and looked up at him with a smile that was tinged with guilt. Talbot struggled to rise, but Jamie restrained him.

"Don't disturb yourself, Mr. Talbot; I just want to borrow my wife for a while. May we bring you something?''

Wayne shook his head and the bright hope faded from his brown eyes. Marsh smiled at him. "Wayne, Jamie and I will be back. I want him to hear what we were talking about. And, if you like, I'll have some refreshments with you later on.'' Marsh suddenly realized that neither Janet nor Sophia had bothered to find out if Wayne were all right, and she seethed with all her old anger at their self-centered cruelty. "Jamie,'' she began, and stopped abruptly at his look of frowning concentration. "Jamie, I'm sorry. I meant to return but Wayne seemed so lonely.'' She sighed.

"It's not that, hinny, it's something else,'' he said distractedly.

She held her breath. That was the first time he'd ever used a term of endearment for her.

"Jamie," she thrilled, "you just called me 'hinny'."

He stopped so abruptly, she almost tripped, and pulled her arm closer to him. "I haven't used that word in years. Do you really want me to call you pet names, Marsh?"

"No, Jamie, but it sounded good when it just slipped out—as if you think of me as someone you love all the time, not just when we—" The words died in her throat and she grinned at him.

"Is that the only time you love me, Marsh?" he asked quietly.

"No, Jamie. If anything, I love you more when you defend me like you just did with Sophia, or when we're in public and we still want to be alone." He just looked at her, but the smile which spread over his face and lighted his eyes made her hug his arm and grin back with happy idiocy.

"I think, Craig, sweetheart," the shrewd-sweet voice of Phyllis sounded somewhere in front of them, "that we're not the only newlyweds here. Welcome to our happy little circle, you two. We don't want to intrude, but we do want to thank you for this wonderful party and for lending us your rooms at the Maryland Club for a week."

Jamie smiled into the pleasant face of his new daughter-in-law. "You'd better stay there for two weeks. You'll need the second one to recover from your first quarrel." He flinched when Marsh's sharp fingers dug into the palms of his hand. "As an old married man, I know it's better," he continued and his smile turned into a grin, "to kiss and make up where you had your fight and not wait until you get home."

Listening to the dialogue with growing interest in the prospect of an extended honeymoon, Craig offered only a perfunctory protest. "Phyllis doesn't think that I should be away from the bank that long."

"Son," Jamie promised, "if you'll trust me, I'll fill in for you an extra week and Marsh will fill in for Phyllis." The smile that accompanied his ironic reassurance was almost professional in its charm; but in this case, his love for the young couple was sincere. "Welcome to the MacKenzie family, Phyllis. I think we'll get along."

Forthright to a fault, Phyllis smiled back. "Craig wasn't sure you'd approve of me. He said that you hate managerial women, but Marsh said you would. She also said that you'd rather be called Jamie than father."

"Craig, why don't you dance with Marsh while I find out from your wife what else has been said about me?"

As if he'd been reminded of a forgotten duty, Craig hastened to obey his father; and Marsh found herself on the dance floor for her first time that afternoon with her husband's son instead of her husband. Despite Craig's friendliness, she felt a pang of jealousy as she watched Jamie move onto the dance floor with the attractive bride. As she smiled at Craig in compensation, she learned that he too was suffering from the same ugly emotion.

"I'm glad my father married you, Marsh."

"That's a very nice compliment, Craig."

He smiled ruefully. "It wasn't a compliment exactly, it was self-preservation. Now the rest of us will stand a chance since you're too beautiful for him to risk." When he realized that Marsh did not understand, he added, "Before he married you, he was—" he gulped and looked embarrassed.

"He was what, Craig?"

"All the women, even the girls liked him; and the rest of us didn't stand a chance if he singled out one to—uh—flatter at a party."

Marsh was silent as she remembered her and Jamie's last "reunion." All he'd done was smile at her and she'd thrown herself into his arms. Catherine, she'd accepted; but how many others had Jamie claimed? The blond Mildred, who was dancing with Paul Covington now? Certainly Mildred had not been shy at the engagement party. Marsh felt young and inexperienced when she remembered those thirty years, but she knew that Craig was even more insecure. "You'll never have to worry about Phyllis, Craig," she assured him.

Eager for sympathy, the young bridegroom asked, "Why not?"

Marsh hesitated only a second. She couldn't say, Because you were her target or She's too ambitious to take chances, so she stretched the truth. "Because she's too much in love with you." Her reward for this small exaggeration was a warm hug and a more attentive partner. But Marsh continued to wonder about her own hold on a man who had proved so elusive to the other women who had possessed him temporarily. Concentrating on Craig and her own problems, she was unprepared for an interruption in the dance or for the man who interrupted it.

"It's about time you shared our stepmother with me, little brother," a familiar voice announced, and before she could protest, she was being held in arms she remembered all too well. Not daring to look at him, she tried to maintain an unemotional pitch to her voice.

"Hello, Stuart; I didn't know you were here."

"No? Then why did you leave the reception line just before I got there?"

His diplomacy had decreased in ratio to the increase of his conceit, she decided, and shrugged. "One of the guests was ill; so even if I had known you were waiting to pay your respects, I still would have been obliged to leave."

"I expected to see you dripping with jewelry by this time. Six months married and not even a diamond necklace? I'm surprised. I thought you'd be able to hold out for top dollar. How is he as a husband, Marsh?"

She sucked in her breath and held her anger back. "As long as he takes his daily tonic, he manages to hobble around."

"So I notice. He's hobbling very nicely with the bride right now. Sorry you didn't take my offer, Marsh?"

Furiously, she lashed back at him, "You conceited jackass!'' Raising her face, she looked at him for the first time; he grinned lazily down at her.

"Now that's the girl I knew. I didn't think that you could forget how to use your tongue completely. But you have learned to make that body of yours look very alluring in a dress—and without girding yourself in a corset, I might add.''

She was acutely aware of the dangerous tension of this man, of his impulsive streak of wildness, and of the remembered possessiveness he'd had for her. She was also aware that he was holding her too closely and that the music was continuing endlessly.

"I bribed the orchestra to make this a long number,'' he taunted her, "a very long number. I want to see if you can resist your natural instincts.''

"Stuart,'' she pleaded, "this is ridiculous. I am happily married to your father. I'm no longer an available target for your insults.'' Despite her calm voice, she knew that her breathing was becoming ragged and that her heart was behaving oddly.

"Your marriage doesn't bother me, Marsh, only you do that.'' He pulled her toward him and stared rudely down at the low neckline of her dress. "You have beautiful breasts. Are you flattered that I remember how beautiful they are, and how responsive? You're not a sweet young thing, Marsh; underneath all that cool independence is a very passionate woman. My offer still stands. Just let me know the next time your husband goes to New York.''

The very blatancy of his proposal and his insulting assumption that her marriage was a sham released her from the attraction that had threatened to dominate her senses. It also released her sense of humor. "Stuart, you always did overrate yourself as a lover. You're not a jackass, you're a fool. Compared to your father, you're an underdeveloped little boy in every department.''

She didn't have to look up again to know that, like his father, he was scowling at her and that his anger was barely leashed. She could feel the strength of his fingers as they gripped her hand and dug into her back. But his voice was soft as he bent his head to taunt her. "Would you care to put that claim to a test? To find out just how underdeveloped I am? Come on, Marsh, you used to have the courage to accept a challenge. Or has a nice, safe marriage made a coward out of you?" His lips were almost against her ear now. "I have a hotel room just blocks away. No one would miss us for an hour or two."

For the past minutes Stuart's dancing had been reduced from a whirling waltz to a slow rhythmic circling, and Marsh became suddenly aware that her back was against one of the doors leading to the verandah. As Stuart's hand reached for the door knob, Marsh raised her knee and took careful aim. She could feel his partially aroused organ bend sharply as her knee hit its target, and she smiled grimly when he uttered a sharp grunt of pain. Extricating herself easily from his arms, which had lost all strength to hold her captive, she turned and smiled broadly at a pair of dancers who'd stopped in alarm and were watching Stuart with concern.

"It's an old war injury," she confided sweetly, "whenever he tries to do too much, it acts up." Leaving the three standing there, she walked away, smiling again as she remembered her old threat to geld him. With a feeling of regret she wondered why a beautiful man like Stuart was such a fool. But such faint sympathy she might have engendered for him dissipated as she felt her arm recaptured and heard his voice drumming once again in her ear.

"I'd forgotten how much you know about gutter fighting," Stuart told her, his face still strained with pain. "After you refused my invitation the last time, you took care of my sore eyes. I'm interested in knowing what form your consolation takes this time."

"This time I'll scream if you threaten me again."

"And ruin your precious new reputation?"

"My reputation was ruined the day I was born, so I have

nothing to lose. But you, Stuart MacKenzie, might find an angry father a permanent price to pay for your insults to me.''

''I'm the one with nothing to lose. I already told my father while you were playing nursemaid to that cripple that I considered my claim on you stronger than his.''

''You have no claim on me and you never have. I'm sorry that you tried to hurt your father, and I'm sorry we can never be friends. Good-bye, Stuart.'' Marsh's mood had gentled into one of genuine sadness for this man she had once almost loved with a girl's romantic intensity, but she knew that his emotions were too involved with his hatred for his father for her to feel safe with him again. Stuart too realized the futility of continuing his pursuit, but his words were still those of a kind of love.

''Someday, Marsh, you'll admit to yourself that we attract each other,'' he said softly, without any of the fierce tension of a moment ago. His face was now relaxed into the boyish smile that made him a handsome, younger edition of his father. Neither one of them seemed to be aware that the dance music had stopped until Janet Talbot approached them and wrapped her arm possessively around Stuart's. Marsh watched the changed expression on his face with fascination as she pulled her own arm free.

''I declare, Stuart honey,'' Janet purred in the worst imitation of a southern drawl Marsh had ever heard, ''that dance was so long, I thought it would never end. I'm just dyin' for some fresh air. Come on, honey, I'm bored. Now that you performed your duty dance with your daddy's wife, we can go back to the hotel.''

Contemptuous fury replaced the regret and pity Marsh had felt a moment ago. Not even Janet would be fool enough to imply such intimacy if it didn't exist, and Stuart's expression of irritated and embarrassed guilt confirmed that it did as clearly as a voiced admission. Marsh had been nothing but a momentary diversion; he already had a full-time mistress.

Her own southern drawl lashed out with deadly accuracy.

"Why, Stuart honey, you old tease. Y'all did take my advice about usin' local talent, after all. It surely must cut down on travel time. Now you just go ahead and get that fresh air and exercise you were talkin' about a minute ago. I'm sure lil' ol' Janet will be most obligin'. Y'all have fun, hear.''

With her blue eyes narrowed into slits and her face suffused with an angry red flush, Janet yanked Stuart away from the slender woman who stood taunting them with a derisive smile on her face. Only after they had moved away did Marsh see the man who had been standing quietly some distance away. Her heart thudded in alarm as she recognized her stepfather and saw the grim determination on his face. Instantly, her defensive mechanisms flashed into action and she whirled around to avoid his outstretched hand. Six hurried steps away she bumped into the solid body of her husband and sagged into his protective arms with relief. She didn't turn around when Jamie addressed her stepfather in a low voice of tightly reined anger.

"Creighton, to my wife's repudiation of you, I'll add my last warning. If you approach her again, I'll have you hounded out of the country by experts.'' Marsh looked up with a happy smile on her face and listened to the retreating footsteps of her stepfather. But her smile faded in shock as Jamie's strong hands gripped her arms with cruel pressure and shoved her away from him.

"That, madam, was the most disgraceful scene I've ever seen on a dance floor.''

"What scene, Jamie?''

"That passionate reunion between my son and you.''

"Is that what you think it was?''

"That's what everyone at this cursed reception knows it was.''

"I didn't even know Stuart was here.''

"Well, it didn't take you long to succumb to him. I expected you to go with him to his hotel. He did ask you, didn't he?''

"What did you think was happening when your nincompoop son tried to push me out of that door?"

"That maybe you'd finally come to your senses."

"I never lost my senses. What I was doing at that door, Mr. MacKenzie, was kneeing your idiot son in the groin. Like you, he has very strong hands, and like you, he thought he had the right to restrain me with them."

Jamie's fingers relaxed and his burning scowl lost its intensity. "We'll discuss this later. Right now, Phyllis wants to see you upstairs."

"We'll discuss it now. You knew what his intentions were because he told you. So you decided that I should be put through another of your tests. And you allowed your son to insult me during that entire dance."

"Marsh, I—"

"This is the fifth time you've called me a slut. It is also the last time. Let go of my arm and don't ever try to touch me again."

Marsh felt no anger as she pulled away from her husband, only the dead cold realization of finality. She had been insulted and used as a cat's-paw by two jealous men, both of whom thought they had the right to claim her as if she were in reality the mindless slut they thought she was. Somber and unsmiling, she entered the room full of four noisy women and one quiet bride who grabbed her arm and whispered tensely, "I want to talk to you."

Marsh was aware of Alice hovering close to her and Phyllis, and she flinched slightly when Alice's voice whipped out from her pursed lips. "What are you doing here, Mrs. MacKenzie? I didn't think you'd be able to pull yourself away from your latest conquest." At Marsh's blank stare, Alice hissed, "My cousin's husband, who else would have you?"

Phyllis slashed across her sister-in-law's insulting tirade. "Get out of here, Alice. Everyone get out of here. I want to talk to Marsh alone." While she was issuing these terse orders, Phyllis did not take her eyes from Alice until even that obstinate woman followed the others out of the room.

"Oh, God, what a bitch she is, Marsh. I want you to take these damned pearls and give them back to Jamie." As she was talking, she shoved a large black velvet jewelry box into Marsh's hand. "Open it and look at them," Phyllis commanded, "those are the famous Ryder pearls that belonged to Craig's great-grandmother." Marsh looked down without much interest at the three-foot rope of large, matched pearls arranged neatly in the box. At the moment, she'd have settled for a hundredth of their value in hard Yankee cash. Phyllis talked relentlessly on. "According to Jamie they're supposed to be given to the wife of the oldest Ryder man in each generation. That's Craig in this one. But when I came up to this room twenty minutes ago, Alice asked me to give them to her. She claims that they belong to her. I don't want them, Marsh, but I don't think she should have them, either. You give them back to Jamie and explain."

"Do it yourself, Phyllis."

"No, he'd just give me that smile of his and insist I keep them. Your Jamie can be very domineering, especially to a woman."

"And also very stupid," Marsh agreed bitterly. "I'll give them to him."

"Now for my real problem, Marsh," Phyllis rushed on, "and you're the only person I can talk to because you know how I persuaded Craig to propose. At first, I didn't realize what was happening. But now I do. He's in and out of me before I can enjoy it. When I tried to tell him, he informed me that decent women weren't supposed to enjoy it."

Marsh shuddered, but not with embarrassment. "Alice again. She's the only woman Craig could have talked to about something like that."

"Well, I want to make my marriage work, but it won't until he learns how to make love to me. Do you have any ideas about how I can make him understand?"

With her own four months of experience limited to one man—one and a half if she counted Stuart—Marsh started to say an automatic denial until she remembered that Craig was her only MacKenzie friend. He at least deserved a chance at happiness. She also remembered something else—the bottle of usquebaugh she'd taken in to Jamie on their first night and his persistent and gentle caresses until she'd been ready. Taking a deep breath to still the sudden pain in her heart, Marsh plunged recklessly into a set of instructions; she had no idea if it would work for Phyllis or not.

"First, have a couple of glasses of champagne to relax you both, then force him to play with you until you're so ready, you can't hold off. Make him—fondle your breasts with his hands and lips, and then your legs and your—'' she gulped and finished lamely, ''insides. Don't you touch him until you're—you'll know when.''

"By that time Craig would have exploded all over the bed.''

Marsh shrugged with a cynical humor. "The MacKenzie men are good studs. Craig will be ready to go again in no time. Just don't be embarrassed. Just be loving to him and then force him to go through the same routine the next time. Once he gets used to your responding, he'll enjoy it more himself. But don't let him get by without your enjoying it, too.''

Marsh's face was flushed and her insides twisted with nervousness, but Phyllis showed no embarrassment whatsoever. "You know a whole lot, Marsh. Do you mind if I ask you a personal question?'' She didn't wait for permission but asked immediately. "Were you a virgin when you married Jamie?''

Marsh stared at the unblushing bride and shrugged. "Not that it matters, but I was.''

Phyllis smiled in triumph. "I knew you were. Craig's relatives are a bunch of nasty cats. Marsh, let's you and I be friends. Except for Jamie, I don't like any of the others. Or trust them, either. But if you and I stand together, even Alice can't go against the two of us."

Marsh smiled faintly, touched in spite of herself by the request. "We're friends, Phyllis. Just don't forget that champagne, and good luck in your husband training." She started toward the door only to be stopped again as Phyllis hugged her and kissed her on the cheek.

"Good-bye, Marsh, and thanks."

The tears were blinding her eyes as Marsh walked into the hall, making no attempt to hide the jewelry box she carried. That had been the first time any woman had kissed her since her grandmother's loving hugs in her early childhood. She could not remember having been kissed by her mother. Marsh felt suddenly more alone than she'd ever been in her life. She didn't notice that Alice was watching her from the balcony or that Jamie was waiting for her at the foot of the stairs. Her thoughts were with an old man on a farm in Georgia—Angus would help make her life whole again. When her eyes finally focused, she saw Jamie's extended hand, and all of her hurt resurfaced. Shoving the jewelry box into that hand, she spoke sharply. "Phyllis doesn't want them and Alice claims that they're hers. Now they're your problem."

"Marsh, let's be friends again."

"Let's not."

"All right, we'll go home."

"I won't go anywhere with you. Just leave me alone, unless you want me to make another exhibition of myself."

"Marsh, I'm sorry I misunderstood about you and—"

"Don't waste your charm on me. Go use it on any of the dozen women here who'd just love to play kitty cat with you. I won't."

His tentative smile vanished and he reached out to grab her arm again. "You're coming with—" Marsh slapped his hand away from her with all of her pent up fury and almost ran all the way to the corner of the hall and to the one man who couldn't hurt her. Wayne Talbot rose to greet her, leaning heavily on his canes.

"Welcome back, Marsh. I've been waiting for you. You look like you could use a glass of champagne."

She smiled at him recklessly. "I just gave the same advice to someone else. And I think you're right. I could use something right now. Sit down, Wayne, I'll go get us some and we'll drink some toasts to our future."

Twice more, she stood up after that first time to bring them more of the bubbly elixir of forgetfulness, then sat companionably with Wayne and watched as the bride and groom departed and the dancing began again. With a caustic smile, she watched as Jamie danced first with the blond widow Mildred and then with the plum-clad Janet. His last partner surprised her. Unless the plumpish Janet could run like a spooked horse, she could never have made it to Stuart's hotel room and back in this length of time. Marsh giggled, maybe now the father and son would fight over another woman.

"Do you want to talk about it, Marsh?" Wayne asked gently.

"No, Wayne, I don't want to talk about it." She grinned at him. "I want to talk about trains. Do they have trains in Georgia?"

"Yes, they have trains in Georgia."

"Will four hundred dollars get us there, Wayne?"

"Are you serious?"

"Yes, I'm serious, but first I have to figure out a way to get my clothes and my money. I can't go to Georgia in this dress." She giggled again. "If only Myles Windom was here, I might even be able to get the rest of my money from the bank."

Wayne put his hand over hers and smiled. "I think we're both a little drunk, Marsh. We'd better eat some food before we do any more planning."

"You're right, Wayne, it wouldn't do to fall on our faces in a train station. I'll go get us some."

"No need, I have our plates right here. I had someone bring them a long time ago and I waited to eat with you." Reaching toward the table, he picked up the two china plates covered with heavily embroidered linen napkins and handed her one. They removed the napkins and looked down at the dozen tempting sandwiches and tiny meat puffs. Smiling in easy comradery, they each reached for one at the same time and began to eat. Marsh's reflexes were swifter than his. Within seconds she felt the violent turbulence of nausea grinding her insides, followed by a dizziness which sent her writhing onto the floor. While one part of her consciousness screamed in terror, the other flashed back to a scene she'd witnessed a dozen times—the sight of Damon shoving his hand down the throat of an animal that had eaten something poisonous. Blindly, she shoved her fingers down her own throat and blacked out briefly as she felt the warm gorge being propelled out of her mouth. In the brief respite from pain, she dimly saw the twisting body next to her own. When her eyes refused to focus, she groped toward Wayne's head and forced his mouth open with her fingers. She plunged them into his throat; using the last of her failing strength, she wiggled her fingers frantically until he too began the horror of vomiting.

Then darkness closed over her, and only vaguely could she sense a strong hand holding her head while strong fingers once again assaulted her throat; again she vomited and vomited until she fainted. Another second of consciousness and the procedure was repeated until she finally gained the strength to whisper, "Poison," to her unseen rescuer, and after a few breaths to push back the dreaded threat of blackness, she panted the words, "Take care of Wayne," before she lost consciousness completely.

When she regained a shadowy degree of consciousness, she was aware of cold air about her face and the sensation of lying in the bed of a moving wagon next to a body much stiller than her own, and somewhere near her head was another body. Mercifully, her consciousness faded repeatedly for the next hours in a place she knew must be a hospital, where her wracked body was subjected to horror after horror. Endlessly, she was forced to vomit, and she felt her whole body involved in the pain of eliminating the poison. Only that one word remained her touchstone to reality through the ordeal: poison. In the untouched core of her brain, she knew with certainty that only poison could have produced this violence. Even when the doctors had finished with their ministrations, all words but the one of poison were meaningless; she was trapped in a suspended state hovering only slightly above oblivion.

The words, "Undoubtedly, Major, your prompt action saved their lives," meant nothing to her. And what took place next, she'd never be able to put a name to; it wasn't sleep, it wasn't awareness, it wasn't unconsciousness. It was a gray area of non-life from which she struggled to escape. Hands held her while her body shook, and soothed her when she sank into nothingness. How many hours or days passed, she had no way of knowing since time had ceased to exist for her. Human shapes were faceless blobs that came and went while human hands did whatever was required to save her life.

Just when her own mind began to respond to her will was unclear, too; but bit by bit, flashes of memory would return only to fade away and then return again until that blessed moment when they stayed, and she became a human person again.

Chapter
10

Unable to lift a hand or move a foot, Marsh lay in the narrow hospital bed savoring each moment of life—each tiny second of freedom from the tyranny of pain and sickness. Even the struggle to raise her eyelids was a challenge of joy; she was alive and her identity was intact. During those first moments, only her old memories returned in full. She could hear the wonderful burr of Angus's accent as she recalled those years of their companionship, and see the warm compassion of Adah's brown eyes and the slender beauty of Damon's hands as he helped a foal being born. She could feel the power of her stallion and remember how his ears pricked up at her command. These old friends seemed so far away now, but so dear, so familiar, so comforting—she wanted to bring them close to her so she could tell them of the beauty of just breathing.

But the sights and sounds around her now she avoided. She hated the strident, relentless cheerfulness of the doctor's voice. "So you've decided to return to the world of the living, Mrs. MacKenzie,'' he boomed into her ear as he held her hand professionally before he tucked it back under the covers. "You'll be fine now, your old self in no time." He flicked her eyelids back and stared into her eyes with concentrated concern. "There's someone outside who's waited a long time to see you."

She wanted to scream, I don't want to see anybody, but she had no strength to say the words. She knew that it would be Jamie even without opening her eyes, and she knew that the anger would be gone from his face and a look of suffering would be there instead. She felt him kneel by the bed and take her hand and heard the doctor's cheery voice again. "Just a few minutes. We mustn't tire our patient." Then Jamie was kissing her hand, first the back and then the palm; but she wanted to be alone, to rediscover her own sensations by herself.

"Thank God, Marsh, thank God you're alive." She didn't stir, and still he held her hand and struggled on to tell her about his terror. "I've never been afraid before. You were white as death when we brought you here." So it had been Jamie with her in the wagon. "All the time the doctors worked, I was in agony for fear they'd fail. I love you so much, Marsh." Sometime during his last words, she simply fell asleep.

How long she slept, she couldn't tell, because she hadn't known whether it was night or day. But now her eyelids responded to her will and she could turn her head to see the gray of an overcast sky through the window. She could also swallow in spite of the stiff soreness of her throat. When the nurse held her head, she could swallow water and, bitter though it tasted, it felt like silk against the dryness of her mouth. The broth which followed dulled the bitterness and warmed the dry hollow spaces. After the feeding was over, she formed her lips around words and talked. "Thank you," she said and rejoiced; not that the scratchy croak sounded like her own voice, but she was jubilant anyway.

"Just whisper, deary," the cheerful nurse said, but somehow her cheerfulness sounded real. "Now you go to sleep and afterward we'll have some more broth." It was a pleasant prospect to look forward to, warm broth in a darkened room after a blissful sleep.

It was the blue which awakened her and triggered another memory, the dark blue of a uniform with dull gold buttons, the uniform and the oddly concerned face above it. The major who had saved her life. She tried to smile as she whispered, "You saved my life."

He did smile. "I only finished the job you'd begun. How did you know what to do?"

"Damon. How did you?"

"Our men were often poisoned by rotten food. We were trained to watch."

"Thank you, Stuart."

"You saved my life once. Now we're even. Are you all right?"

"Yes." She paused and asked the painful question, "What was it?"

"Arsenic."

"Who?"

"The police are trying to find out. They're waiting to talk to you now." He stirred to rise from the chair.

"Don't go yet, Stuart. How is Wayne?"

"Not as well as you are, but still alive." Standing up, he hesitated by her bed. "I'm glad you're alive, Marsh."

"So am I."

"Marsh, I'm—I'm leaving Maryland today for Virginia."

"The army?"

"No, I've resigned my commission. I guess I'm to manage the Virginia farm. I'll miss seeing you there." As if embarrassed by sentiment, he leaned down and kissed her forehead. "Good-bye, Marsh, be happy."

Tears moistened her eyes. "You too, Stuart. Be happy." Her eyes watched him steadily as he backed out the door. For an instant, she didn't see the man who entered, an efficient man who walked with the strong step of authority. But at least he wasn't cheerful.

"Mrs. MacKenzie," he began firmly, opened his small black book, and poised his pencil above it. "I'm John Mason from the Baltimore Central Police. We're looking into this incident." The word incident infuriated her; he should have his insides burned with poison. "Could you tell me if anyone would want you dead?"

How do you answer a dumb question like that? Here's the list and you'll find the reasons in the right hand column? She shook her head. "I don't think I was the intended victim. Someone had brought Mr. Talbot two plates of food. But I don't think anyone knew that I'd be eating with him." She heard the pencil scratching across the paper, and her mind began to function to the rhythm of his writing. Someone had tried to kill Wayne and maybe her if he'd told that someone she was joining him, and that someone had almost succeeded.

"Do you know who that person was?"

She shook her head, but roused to answer when she remembered her grandfather and his long vigil by the champagne bottles. "Mr. Clinton Randall was near the refreshment table most of the time. He might have seen."

"Can you think of any reason anyone would want to kill you?" She shook her head. "Or Mr. Talbot?"

"No. Except that he was injured during the war, badly injured." How do you say he was gelded like some poor dumb horse and his wife is a tramp who is after another man? She had a sudden sharp vision of Janet dancing with Jamie.

"Thank you, Mrs. MacKenzie, that'll be all the questions for now." But at the door he turned around. "One more thing. How many of the pieces of food did you eat?"

"One small sandwich and not all of that."

"Do you know how many Mr. Talbot consumed?"

"Only one."

"Were there others remaining on the plates?"

"Yes, six or seven of them."

He frowned. "Are you certain?"

"Absolutely. We both took one at the same time from our full plates. Why?"

"Your plates were empty by the time we got there."

"Then someone else—"

"It could have been anyone. Thank-you again."

For the next two days, her mind spun in circles as she concentrated on the problem of who would want Wayne dead and maybe her. She refused to think about her own personal problems, even during Jamie's four visits. She also refused to talk much while he was there. During the first three visits, he didn't seem to mind as he discussed his plans for their trip to England. But during the fourth time he asked her what was wrong.

"The doctors tell me that you're talking without much difficulty now. Is there any reason why you're not talking to me? It can't still be the misunderstanding about Stuart. I already told you that I was wrong about that."

She avoided his eyes and fumed in disbelief. Did he really think that she could forget his angry words of accusation?

"Therefore, it's something else," he continued with the calm, reasonable voice that was beginning to irritate her to the point of intense avoidance. "Is it the pearls, Marsh? Do you think they should be yours? I'll buy you some."

She stared at him. "I don't give a damn about pearls, those or any others."

"What is it then?"

"Nothing."

"All right, I'm taking you home as soon as the doctors tell me you're out of danger. You're just becoming moody here. Once you get home, you'll forget all about this."

As she had done during his earlier visits, she smiled faintly, closed her eyes, and went to sleep. But late that night, she rose shakily from her bed and took her green wool cape from the stand. With sad regret, she looked at her beautiful silk dress. It had been cleaned but it was still ruined. For several minutes, she practiced walking around the room, and when the walls stopped spinning, she moved out into the hall and walked directly to her destination: Wayne Talbot's room. The cheerful nurse had liked to talk, and with a little careful prompting she had given very precise directions. Marsh found Wayne only half awake and in much worse condition than she was.

"Who brought you the food, Wayne?"

He blinked at her, trying to focus his eyes and rasped, "Janet's cousin!"

Marsh sucked in her breath. "Alice Nelson?"

He nodded. "Alice wouldn't hurt me," he gasped earnestly, "she's a friend."

"In what way, Wayne?"

"All the time I've been sick, she came to see me."

The idea of Alice as an angel of mercy galled Marsh. And then she remembered the taunt Alice had made to her in the bedroom before Phyllis had told her sister-in-law to leave. Alice knew that Marsh had promised to eat with Wayne!

"Wayne," she said slowly, "I saw you about two weeks after you first came home. You were walking on the verandah and you were using only one cane. Why do you need two now?"

"I've been sick a lot."

"Like you were the other night?"

"Nothing like that. Much milder."

"Throwing up sick?"

He nodded.

"Wayne, did Alice serve you food while she was there?"

His eyes glazed over with a dawning horror and he seemed unable to comprehend. Impatiently, Marsh waited, but he only stared at her.

"Wayne," she commanded him sharply, "listen to me. I think Alice is trying to kill both of us. You just nod while I ask the questions. Do you understand me?"

He nodded.

"Alice did bring you food, didn't she?" Again he nodded.

"Then we have to get away from her. Do you still want that job?" Again the nod. "Will you trust me?" A vigorous nod. "Even if it means a trip to Georgia as soon as the doctors let you out of here?" This time he reached for her hand as he moved his head. "You can't take Janet with you." His answer was a bleary smile.

"Wouldn't want to," he mumbled.

"One more thing, Wayne. Some of my friends who own this property are blacks. Would that matter?"

"Jake and Adah," he rasped hoarsely, "good people."

"They're the best. Good night, Wayne." Her hasty departure was dictated by the sudden wave of dizziness that threatened to send her reeling to the floor. All along that endless corridor she used the wall for support, barely reaching her own room before she collapsed on the floor. Toward morning a nurse found her there, got her into bed, and called the doctor. "Cold," was the only word Marsh muttered during the examination.

"She'd gotten up to put her cape on, poor woman," the nurse told the doctor. Shaking his head, the doctor ordered warming pans, more blankets and another seven days in the hospital. It frightened Marsh to realize that, even after a week, she was still weak and ill, but the extra time in the hospital would at least give her the time to organize and to think. About Alice's guilt she had no doubt, but she could think of no one motive that would apply to both her and Wayne. In her own case it could be simple, unreasoning hatred. Marsh had dared to interfere with Alice's life. But what about Wayne? Gradually, a vague suspicion began to form, and she longed to talk to the policeman again. However, when John Mason finally did come, she was more frustrated than ever.

Ten days after the "incident," the police had reached their verdict, passed it over to a judge who ruled it accidental poisoning by person or persons unknown because neither motive nor means could be determined. Marsh was appalled by this casual conclusion.

"But Mr. Talbot named the woman who brought the food to him, Mr. Mason," she protested.

"We looked into it thoroughly and even searched her house. The food she brought you could not be examined unfortunately."

"Did you talk to Mr. Randall?"

"I'm afraid he'd been drinking too much to remember."

"Who do the police think did it?"

"Probably one of the extra kitchen help hired for the day. Some of them are untrained. One of the women may have mistaken a container of poison and used it accidentally, and then panicked when she heard the ruckus and destroyed the container."

Marsh wasted ten minutes explaining her half-formed theories about Alice. He shook his head politely and declined to comment.

"Mr. Mason, are there private people I can hire to protect myself?"

"Yes, there are. The Pinkertons are the best of the lot."

"Could you choose a good man for me and ask him to come to the hospital?"

"Yes, ma'am, if your husband agrees."

Jamie most emphatically did not agree. In fact, he was irritated with Marsh for suggesting it, although he struggled to keep from frowning at her.

"Be reasonable, Marsh." God, how she hated that word reasonable! "Alice is a wealthy woman, so what possible motive could she have? And why would she even bother with Talbot? I know you dislike her, and so do I. But I've known her for twenty years, and she has always been difficult and even mean—but never criminal. Besides, I plan to keep you very safe in the future."

Marsh turned her face away swiftly and bit her lips to keep

from screaming at him the words, Yes, as a damn prisoner! After a moment, she tried another approach. "I'd like Mrs. Tucker to bring me some things from home."

"There's no need to bother Mrs. Tucker. Just tell me what you want and I'll bring it to you."

As usual in her life, whenever she came up against a barrier in reaching a goal, Marsh switched directions, seeking another path. When the cheerful nurse entered the room, Marsh bribed her to go to the MacKenzie home and tell the housekeeper there to come to the hospital. Since she had no money with her, she gave the nurse the green silk dress and all five petticoats. The woman was delighted, and Mrs. Tucker arrived at ten o'clock the next morning.

"Tried to see you earlier, Marsh, but they wouldn't let me in. What did you want to see me about?"

Marsh blurted out everything—what she knew, what she suspected, and what she planned.

Mrs. Tucker nodded. "They always blame servants," she stated flatly, "whenever one of their own is accused. And that one is as nasty a woman as I've ever known, and as clever. No way is Mr. MacKenzie going to keep her hog-tied. And I 'spect you're right to skedaddle out of here. You might be able to handle him, except he's mighty set in his ways, but the rest of that bunch would need a whole passel of hound dogs to keep them treed. I'll go git your Pinkerton man now."

Within two hours, Mrs. Tucker was back, bringing with her a hard bitten, middle-aged man whose gray eyes were sharp, whose speech was even more succinct than Mrs. Tucker's, and who reached the same conclusion. Seth Hanford wasted no words in describing the case.

"Police rarely pursue cases like this involving important people, especially those with friends in high places. Not on the surface, that is, but you can bet your bottom dollar that they would like to. Their problem is that they can't move without proof, and poisoners on the whole are almost impossible to trap. I think both you and the man are in danger because I don't think this woman will quit until she succeeds.''

His experienced words made Marsh's blood run cold; she had not really believed that her own life was so permanently threatened. But she didn't argue with him; she hired him to take Wayne to the Oconee River property in Georgia. And she hired him to withdraw her own two thousand dollars from the Ryder-Mackenzie Bank: her own money, the wages from six years of labor on the Virginia farm; and Myles Windom would not question her signature.

By the next day, the three conspirators had worked out most of the details and the timetable of operation. Seth Hanford would, by his own methods, spirit Wayne Talbot out of the hospital on Christmas morning, when the staff was reduced in numbers, and leave Baltimore in a Conestoga wagon.

''Always wanted to pilot a covered wagon,'' he chuckled, ''and the assistant I'm taking along is the best trail man in the business. By avoiding towns and cities, we should be able to slip by without being stopped, just in case Talbot's wife should sound the alarm.''

It was decided that Marsh would not leave until the day after Christmas. If she tried to leave with them, Hanford warned her, James MacKenzie would undoubtedly organize a massive search and overtake the wagon.

The two days following this conference were agonizingly slow ones for Marsh because she had nothing to do but wait. Seth Hanford had begun earning his money by explaining the plan to Wayne Talbot and arranging for the wagon and supplies. Beneath her own bed, where the hospital orderlies had not swept in the thirteen days she'd been there, were the same suitcase and clothes she'd packed the first time she had almost left. Although she had avoided analyzing her own motives earlier during her convalescence, she could not suppress her emotion-charged thoughts now. She was not entirely sure how she felt about her husband, but she could no longer live under his temperamental domination. And she would never be satisfied with the limited life he offered her in Baltimore. Even his promise to let her indulge in racehorses lost its appeal when she remembered his accusations and her own misery when he was angry with her. But overriding all these reasons was her fear of Alice, a woman Jamie still defended in spite of what seemed to Marsh to be overwhelming evidence. Phrases flitted through her head—flight back to a more secure girlhood with less demanding companions, flight to avoid having to use trickery to live her own life even to a degree with Jamie, and flight to return to a life of personal independence. Always flight!

During Jamie's visits on these two days, Marsh felt doubly trapped; he was both loving and indulgent, and he remained an endless three hours each day. At his insistence, they played cards, and since she was too restless even to pretend she was sleepy, they talked. He hinted mysteriously about Christmas and talked enthusiastically about their trip; she thought darkly about her own. And he kissed her endlessly on her hands, her cheeks, her throat, and her forehead. He even insisted on brushing her hair which had not yet regained its normal luster. Eventually, he left, apparently satisfied with her physical and emotional recovery. Marsh wept after each visit.

On Christmas morning, her first two gifts were not from Jamie. Her favorite nurse, who had now become a friend, brought her some holiday cookies and informed her that Mr. Talbot's father had come to take him home. Marsh's heart lurched as she prayed that the father was Seth Hanford. Fifteen minutes later, Mrs. Tucker arrived, her face reflecting a smug satisfaction.

"Even the nurses helped get him dressed," she gloated, "they was real happy to see that he'd be with his family for Christmas. Whole thing went slicker than glass, and Mr. Hanford figured they'd be through Virginy before anyone got wise. Not," she added, "that his wife or mother-in-law would give a durn anyway."

The rest of Mrs. Tucker's news, though, was not comforting. "Sure wish you was on your way, Marsh. Your husband's had me packing your clothes for days, and he's acting as mysterious as a cat in a cellar. Two nights ago, Stuart come over from Virginy and them two actually were polite to each other for a change. Used to be they just yelled. Most of what they talked about was the two farms. And yesterday, Craig come over and the three of them was closeted in the library for two hours while that young wife bothered me. Not sure about that one. Thought you was blunt, but she's got you beat by a country mile when it comes to asking questions. That's about all the news, Marsh. Don't reckon I'll see you again. I hope you make it real big whatever you do."

Marsh felt lonely and nervous after Mrs. Tucker had gone, but she was trapped in this bed until tomorrow morning. Not a public conveyance would be moving in Baltimore today, and she did not feel well enough to sit up all night in an unheated train station. Restlessly, she began to pace the floor in increasing agitation. By mid-afternoon the compulsion to escape had become so urgent, she was desperate enough to risk the cold. In a fever of excitement, she began to dress, piling on all the warm clothing she could manage, first her riding breeches and boots over her underwear, then a ruffled white blouse and a green checked gingham skirt, and, finally, her riding jacket and the wool cape she'd worn to the wedding. Exhausted and damp with the sick perspiration of recent illness, she sat on the bed and felt miserable. But the compulsion still drove her. Finally, she could resist it no longer. Checking one final time to see that the complicated train schedule Seth Hanford had prepared for her was in her reticule, along with enough money for her tickets and traveling expenses—the rest was in the lining of her suitcase—Marsh opened the door to her room and looked cautiously down the darkened hospital corridor. Since there were no attendants in evidence for the moment, she simply walked out of the hospital and headed in the direction she'd been told to take.

Twice in the first block, she was forced to rest on the benches which dotted Baltimore's tree-lined streets. Her eyes closed in exhaustion, she didn't look back along the street to see the carriage that stopped whenever she did. Five blocks further on, she didn't even hear the footsteps that were almost upon her. Her eyes could barely focus and her breath was tortured. It's doubtful that she felt the hands that grabbed her as she crumpled to the pavement, or heard the voice of her husband with its ironic message: "Merry Christmas, Marsh, I've been waiting for you."

Consciousness returned slowly, and at first she thought she was back in her hospital bed; only it was rocking with an undulating rhythm that made her stomach increasingly queasy. That queasiness lasted for a full day, just as long as the motion of her bed remained gentle. But when it lurched into hard rolls, she gave up fighting and surrendered to the violent nausea which kept her semiconscious for six miserable days. As she relived her first hours in the hospital, she wanted to die. At one stage, she was back on the river, astride her stallion sinking under the water into a peaceful death. In another moment of blackness, she saw the bloated face of Hiram Creighton and she screamed. And always the pale-skinned image of Alice Nelson drifted across her inner vision with its ugly smile of victory.

Eventually, as it had in the hospital, came the blessed release from agony; she slept peacefully for the fifteen hours it took her racked body to recover. Upon awakening, she focused her eyes slowly, and then wished she hadn't. Jamie's haggard face was not a pretty sight. The suffering she saw there struck her with pangs of guilt which brought helpless tears and the hopeless awareness of her failure—failure to escape, failure to be a good wife, and the most crushing of all, failure to have regained her vigorous health long ago. Her once strong, slender body had become emaciated enough in the hospital; but aboard ship it was so gaunt, her hands looked transparent. For the next week, her most strenuous activity was opening and closing her mouth as the nurse Jamie had hired popped endless spoonfuls of broth and custard in. As her appetite increased, so did the nourishment of the foods she consumed; stew replaced the broth and a variety of other delicacies were added to her diet. On the first glorious day she sat up in bed and fed herself, Marsh felt divinely recovered until she attempted to put her feet over the side of the bunk. Faintly, she echoed Jamie's chuckle as he tucked her back in bed and smoothed her hair away from her perspiring forehead.

"Not quite yet, you're still a sick lassie. Tomorrow will be soon enough to try."

It was his unfailing gentleness which wore down her rebellious will and made her content for the moment to be a docile patient. He read Charles Dickens's books to her by the hour, introducing her to worlds far beyond the confines of their ship's cabin; and the two of them studied the books on horses he'd brought aboard. But Marsh had not forged her independent spirit by flinching from hardship and pain. From the time she'd defied her stepfather, she'd learned to accept aching muscles as the price of accomplishment. Daily now, she forced herself to exercise in the limited space of the stateroom until she felt strong enough to brave walking around the decks of the ship. On the first day she dressed, she was dismayed by the looseness of her dress, but Jamie laughed at her and said she was fat now in comparison to what she had been. By the time they disembarked at South London on the Thames River, Marsh had regained both her weight and her restless energies; so much so that Jamie had to restrain her from wanting to walk through the crowded dockside slums of that part of the ancient city.

"This isn't Baltimore, Marsh, and we've a long ride before us until we reach our destination." While Jamie settled back in the coach he'd hired, Marsh craned her neck endlessly to see both sides of the narrow streets at once. Having little interest in the country and society he'd fled as a young man, Jamie was amused by Marsh's fascination with the antiquity of the buildings they passed and with the packed humanity which bustled in and out of those structures.

"So many people!" she gasped.

"And all of them unhappily stuck in an ugly little country the size of Virginia and Pennsylvania," he told her cynically.

"I think it's a beautiful place."

"The countryside is, and that's where we'll be staying while we're here."

During those three hours of slow, clop-clop travel through the crowded outskirts of London and along the rural roads beyond, Marsh and Jamie maintained the pleasant tone of communication they had established during their final weeks aboard ship while the nurse was still in attendance. But once they had settled into a comfortable suite of rooms in one of the more celebrated country inns in Bexley, they were both acutely aware of the estrangement that had existed between them since Craig's wedding. Jamie's face was somber and strained as he entered the sitting room where Marsh was pacing restlessly. She stopped her agitated movements and stared at him when she noticed the bottle of usquebaugh and the two glasses he held in his hands. Silently, he filled each glass to the halfway level, handed her one, and lifted his in a silent toast. Self-consciously, she returned the gesture. Both were remembering their first night together, Jamie with hope and Marsh with regret.

"Why, Marsh?" he began reasonably. When she shrugged her shoulders, he resisted the impulse to shake her back into some semblance of her fiery old self. "I spend twenty-four terrible hours not knowing whether you'll live or die, and then I'm met by a cold wife who can't wait for me to leave her alone."

Marsh sighed, acting was obviously not one of her talents.

"How did you know when I was leaving the hospital?" she asked curiously.

"I knew when the Pinkerton man withdrew your money from the bank that you were planning another of your flights. After three attempts, I'm beginning to know you pretty well."

"But on Christmas day?"

"I'd checked the train station and cancelled your reservations for the next morning. Were you planning to sleep on a bench that night?"

"I couldn't stand the hospital anymore."

"You could have come home." Again she shrugged. "Do you know, Marsh, that you have not called me by my name since before the incident?"

At that hated word, she glared at him in a sudden rage. "Stop calling attempted murder an incident, James MacKenzie. You may have worried for twenty-four hours, but I fought for my life during that time. And when Wayne told me it was Alice and I told you, you defended your precious stepdaughter as if she weren't as dangerous as a cottonmouth."

"I assume you visited with Mr. Talbot in his hospital room?"

"Yes, and at night. And if you dare accuse me of being an immoral slut, this conversation ends right now and I go back to America, seasickness or not."

"I won't. Talbot told me all about your visit when I talked to him. And about the job offer." She sucked in her breath, she'd forgotten the "gentleman's code" of the South.

"Marsh," her husband scolded her, "you weren't told everything because we thought you were too ill. But the doctors were not stupid. They knew that Talbot was suffering from earlier poisonings as well as from the last one. So did the police. But without evidence, they couldn't prove attempted murder. Incidentally, I talked to your Seth Hanford, and I paid him to do some investigating for me when he gets back from Georgia."

"Did those two tell you where Angus was in Georgia? And have you also told Janet where she can find her missing husband? Maybe now Alice can send Wayne poisoned cookies through the mail—or maybe poisoned apples."

Jamie just looked at her; this much fire he hadn't wanted. "I've known where Angus was months ago. We're old friends, Marsh, he's written to me several times. And I invested some money along with you in the land there. I also replaced your two thousand dollars in the bank. Talbot will pay me back when he's able to."

Marsh felt defeated, her dream of independence had just been destroyed again. "What's the use, Jamie? In the hospital, when I told you that I was afraid of Alice, you said that you planned to keep me safe in the future. How? By locking me in a closet? Well, I wouldn't be any safer there than I was at that wedding. You sure weren't watching out for me there."

"No, I was angry. But Stuart said that you'd had three glasses of champagne. He thought at first that you were just drunk."

"Oh, he did, did he? Since when have you and your son become such good friends that you discuss my faults as if I were a half-wit who needed a keeper?"

"Stuart waited with me the whole time, Marsh, and we talked about a lot of things, including you—but not critically. I understand him better now than I ever have, and I like him. Besides, I was grateful to him for saving your life. He worked with you for an hour while one of the other guests worked with Talbot. He didn't seem like a boy to me that night, he seemed like a very capable man."

"That's not the way you felt about him a couple of hours earlier after he'd danced with me."

"I told you afterward that I was wrong."

"Sure, you told me after you'd already accused me of wanting to go to his hotel room. Just like you accused me with Philip Addison and with Wilbur Brant and with that dumb what's-his-name friend of Craig's.''

"So that's it?"

"Of course, that's it. You get that God-almighty scowl on your face and I'm supposed to cower in fear every time you imagine that I'm advertising myself as an available slut. Yet you dance with that damned, fat-breasted Janet, who is a slut, as if I'm supposed to share you with every man-hungry female there. Don't look so shocked, Jamie; long before Wayne came home, Janet entertained Union officers like it was open house at Yvette de Bloom's. Do you know how often she and some leering Yankee crossed over to Washington for a little recreation? Every damned time she could find one with enough money to pay the bills for a new dress or a new hat, at least. Do you really think that those same men didn't ask me first? I almost let my horse stomp a couple of them. And every time Jake tried to defend me, I had to stop him because even broad-minded Yankees would have shot any black man who dared to strike one of those sacred white jackasses.'' Marsh was laughing now with the bitter, strangled laughter that didn't ease the taut nervousness of her insides. "Poor Jamie MacKenzie, stuck with a loudmouth bastard from a pig farm. No wonder all the real ladies of your life are so shocked and sooo sympathetic. Just think, Jamie, of all those butter-soft women you could have had. Well, you still can. I'm not going to crawl on my belly for you or any other man. And the next time you make a fool of me in public, this scene takes place right there—even if it's in the middle of your Maryland Horse Club."

"Horsemen's Club."

"Or at the homes of your snobby women friends who treat you like visiting royalty and me like the kitchen help."

"Anyplace else? Just so I will know where it'll be safe for me to scold my hotheaded wife."

She glared at him. "It's not funny, Jamie. I'm not the wife for you, and I'll never be able to live your kind of life."

"You're the only wife I have."

"But you don't approve of me and you don't trust me. I've tried, but I can't change. I'll never learn to ride sidesaddle and if I ever get on a racehorse, I'll race. Besides, I've got low taste in people. I think Mrs. Tucker is a lady and that your Mrs. Covington is a stuck-up snob. To me Carina is the most beautiful woman in the world while that blond, Mildred, who cozied up to her charming Jamie every chance she got, looked and acted like an old biddy cat on the prowl. What I'm trying to say, Jamie, is that I'm sure you can pay Mr. MacLachlan to get you a divorce, like he did for my mother, and then I'll go back where I belong."

All trace of humor vanished from Jamie's face as he rose and walked over to her. Reaching down, he unclasped her tense hands and pulled her to her feet.

"Marsh, do you really want me out of your life that much?"

Slowly, she looked up at this man who had been friend, husband, and lover to her. Unwillingly, she remembered the day he'd told her about her real father, and the terrible night he'd offered to marry her when no one else would. His blue eyes now held the same warm, intense look they had the night she returned his wedding ring to him, a look that melted the cold barriers she'd built against him for the past six, miserable weeks. Feeling the hot sting of tears in her eyes, she surrendered.

"No, Jamie," she whispered, "I just want you to trust me."

"Are you well enough to kiss me, lass?"

A smile trembled on her lips even as the tears fell. "I've been well enough for a week, you big boobie, and you know it."

But, cautious Scot that he was, Jamie was taking no chances with a relapse. Picking his still too-slender wife up, he carried her into the bedroom and removed the layers of clothing he'd insisted she put on that morning aboard ship.

He also took the precaution of removing his own and joining her in bed before he risked that kiss.

"That floor in the other room looked awfully hard," he murmured while his hands caressed her breasts. As her nipples hardened and her hips pressed against his, he nodded his head judiciously. "You're right, hinny, you're well enough and then some. Welcome home."

Hours later, after eating dinner together in front of the fireplace and bathing together in the huge tub located in the small necessaries room adjoining their suite, Jamie was ready to continue their earlier discussion.

"Before we talk anymore about our future, Marsh, I think you should open your Christmas gifts. They're in that trunk."

Her eyes glowing with anticipation, she opened the trunk and peeled back the muslin cloth which covered the first garment, and then gasped with pleasure. It was an ivory-white leather cloak with a brown fur collar and wide fur banding around the flaring hemline. The fur muff that went with it had a gold chain and bracelet connected to it, and a deep envelope on the back side for carrying money and other gadgetry a woman might need on an outing.

Jamie nodded his approval as she tried it on. "Robbie sent us the skins as a wedding present. They're antelope skins that his Indian friends bleached white as they do for Indian brides. The fur is Wyoming beaver."

"Oh Jamie, it's the most beautiful thing I've ever seen."

"There's something else that goes with it, Marsh."

That something else was an ivory silk dress with tiny seed pearls stitched into the stomacher that girded the slim waist. Everything about this ball gown was different. The skirt was cut to fit over the hips slimly and was flared only in the back, while the beautiful neckline was a soft crush of the silk fabric draped over the arms to form tiny cap sleeves.

"This is to take the place of the wedding dress you never had," Jamie told her as he wiped the tears from her eyes.

"I'll hang up this finery while you unwrap the rest of your new clothes."

In the bottom of the trunk were another four garments, three of which were made of wool whipcord the warm bay color of a Thoroughbred horse. There was the classic riding jacket and a long wraparound skirt, and there was a pair of slim breeches just like her others; but to offset their masculine look, the white cotton shirt with its ruffles cascading down from the front of the collar was as feminine as a bridal peignoir.

"My tailor thought I was drunk when I ordered that outfit," Jamie teased her, "but I explained that I had an unusual wife. That's why he took special pains with the skirt. He said that if you wore it over your pants and boots, except when you were astride, most people wouldn't guess about your condition. And," he added with a grin, "we won't be run out of England for indecent exposure."

As she curled up in his lap, Jamie spoke softly into her ear. "No more trying to be what we're not, lass. From now on we're going to raise horses and tend to business."

"Just you and me, Jamie, and our friends?"

"Just you and me. I don't need anybody else."

During most of the four months it took to buy a hundred workhorses and twenty-odd racing ones, Marsh and Jamie were virtually alone; although much of the time they ignored business in favor of gentler pursuits. For the first three weeks, they remained in the same inn, leaving their rooms only a few times to do nothing more strenuous than stroll through the sleepy village. They rented horses and rode for miles along country lanes, and they traveled by carriage to visit country fairs. It was at these unique gatherings that the two Americans learned about English workhorses, because such fairs were the main show arenas for farm animals. Attracting as little notice as possible, they crowded around the open-air horse pavilions and listened to shrewd farmers talk about the good and bad points of individual animals. They also ferreted out the names of the four best known breeders of Clydesdales and Shires. From a friendly farmer, they learned that the so-called racehorses at such country fairs were "winders," "spookers," or "enders," third-rate stock that were either broken-down, skittish, or noncompetitive.

"Only good race stock," the farmer confided, "is owned by toffs who never let common folk get an eyeful unless they pays to see the races." After the third round of ale, which Jamie bought, the farmer did give them an excellent tip about the best Shire breeder in the country.

"Old Ridley tends to be a mite sharp about trading. Part Scot he is, so he comes by it natural. Just ask for a groom named Sands who'll show you the stock the old man keeps hidden for his best customers."

Ignoring the slur the farmer had made about Scot horse traders, Jamie nodded his thanks and retrieved Marsh's hand. "Let's find out if you're as good at buying as you were at selling," he smiled at her. "We'll try old Ridley first."

Moving their headquarters to an unpretentious hostelry in Sevenoaks, the village closest to the Ridley Farm, they began the business of buying horses. At the farm, where they'd been invited in response to Jamie's letter of inquiry, they found a number of horses already assembled for their inspection and an impassive-faced man who looked twenty years younger than his reputed eighty.

"Used to be a MacKenzie breeder in the Heelands near Dumbarton," Duncan Ridley began the conversation.

"My father," Jamie admitted briefly. "I own several farms in America now."

"Switching from saddles to works, are you?"

"To Shires and Clydesdales."

"I wouldn't be mixing the two if I were you."

"Mr. Ridley, what I want from you are two proven studs and seventy young mares as I wrote you in my letter."

"Already picked them out for you," the old man pointed to the group in the open yard.

Jamie smiled frostily. "If you don't mind, I'd prefer to have my wife look through your other stock before we decide. Marsh, why don't you go with one of the grooms while Mr. Ridley shows me around?"

Within five minutes, Marsh had located Mr. Sands. An hour's worth of excellent education later, she had chosen two massive stallions and seventy calm young mares. She returned alone to Jamie and the owner.

"You have good horses," she said quietly to the old man. "Have you and my husband settled on prices yet?"

"On which horses, mum?" Ridley asked cautiously.

"Mr. Sands has the list. Will tomorrow be too soon for Jamie and me to learn your estimate?"

"Have you looked over the horses I chose for you?"

"They're good, but they're too old. The mares in that group are already three years or more into breeding and that stallion is a fifteen-year-old."

"They're proven breeders, mum."

"So are the two stallions I picked out, only they are eight years younger than this one. As for your young mares, Mr. Ridley, proven or not, their bloodlines are too good not to be productive. Besides," she grinned at the old man, "you're too careful a man to keep a worthless horse on your property."

Early the next morning, Ridley came to the MacKenzie's inn in Sevenoaks and left two hours later with an order to deliver the seventy young mares and the two stallions Marsh had chosen to Portsmouth Harbor some two months hence. His parting words were pleasant ones.

"Your wife is a canny lass, Mr. MacKenzie, and she knows horses. But you haven't lost your touch. Even after twenty years in America, you're still a good Scot horse trader. If you'll accept my advice, you'll buy your Clydesdales from a man named Parsons in Farmborough. His stock's got more staying power than most of the others."

But Parsons turned out to be the only ungallant man Marsh met in England. He refused adamantly to let her see his stock. "Womenfolk had best stay in the kitchen where they belong. I don't allow my beauties to be spooked by the flighty creatures."

Stung to anger, Marsh responded tartly. "In America women often tend the stock, Mr. Parsons. Your horses sound too damn temperamental to meet our needs." She was in the carriage, waiting impatiently, when Jamie joined her. Two weeks later, they bought a Clydesdale stallion and thirty mares from one of the breeders they'd heard recommended at the fair, a man who graciously helped Marsh select his best stock.

While workhorses in England were plentiful and raised exclusively by men who made their living selling them, pedigree racing Thoroughbreds were an entirely different matter. They were bred by aristocrats who could afford to expend vast sums of money without hope for a break-even monetary return. Contacting such men took exhaustive research at the gentlemen horse clubs around Epsom Downs, where only Jamie was allowed to make discreet inquiries. Of the scores he made, he received only three responses, and these were so shrouded in secrecy, they read like coded messages. On the first of the appointed days, Jamie dressed resplendently in English tweeds and Marsh wore her subdued but elegant gold velvet street dress with its matching cape designed to ward off the chill of the early English spring air. Requested to bring their own rider, they waited impatiently for the one they'd hired to arrive. He finally did, but an hour late and so drunk his bowed legs could hardly support him. Without a word, Marsh returned to her rooms and changed into the riding ensemble Jamie had given her as a Christmas gift. Clad decorously, with the long skirt covering her pants and boots, she rejoined Jamie and said, "Let's go." Jamie's beginning scowl vanished as she stretched up and kissed him. "One word, Jamie, and I go without the skirt." He shook his head and smiled.

At the estate paddocks, which showed signs of disrepair

and general neglect, they were met, not by the lord himself, but by the estate manager and one of the grooms. Americans were, after all, unimportant colonials. When the first of the six mares for sale was trotted out, Marsh removed her skirt and mounted the bay-colored Thoroughbred. At first she walked it sedately around the yard until she knew the animal, then took off down the race path.

"Blimey, she rides like a bloody jockey," the groom exclaimed in awe.

Jamie agreed dryly. "She is a bloody jockey." Six times she repeated her ride and then pointed to the three horses which met her requirements.

At the second appointment, two weeks later and fifty miles away, Jamie did not protest her donning the riding habit. He had become philosophically resigned to the fact that his wife communed with horses. At this estate, Lord Digby Brampton met them personally and offered them tea in his tack room as they read the pedigree charts. He had eight mares for sale and one young stallion. Six of the mares were chosen but the stallion proved too skittish.

"In the market for a champion?" the aristocrat asked.

"Yes," exclaimed Marsh.

"Depends," equivocated Jamie, his knowledge about the cost of champions being roughly a hundred times that of his wife.

"Raikes is cutting his stables in half. Going in for railroads. He has four or five champion stallions and possibly twenty mares too many, but he'll charge you. The Raikes's silks have been in winners' circles for a hundred years. I don't mind asking him if he's interested in selling, providing you're interested in buying. It'll take a few weeks because Raikes is in London right now."

Since breeding-age race mares without a stallion are just expensive saddle horses, James reluctantly agreed; and for three weeks he and Marsh walked the streets of Tunbridge Wells until they knew the age and history of every beautiful old mansion in the town. They also visited the royal wells and walked along the famous tiled Parade, where the feet of royalty had trod for centuries.

At one tiny little silversmith shop with a two-foot display window was the headless velvet form of a woman's throat with the bust neatly buried in black lace. Around the throat rested a strand of evenly matched pearls. Marsh was horrified when Jamie announced that he was buying it.

"Don't you dare," she hissed forgetting the ladylike posture she'd affected in this elegant town.

He grinned at her. "Why not? It's your birthday and I'm tired of watching your bare neck."

"Since when have you ever looked at me that far up?" she demanded in a tone that exceeded a whisper by several yards of listening.

"I was merely checking to see if you've regained all your weight," he answered soberly.

"Jamie, I don't need jewelry and especially not pearls. What I want is a champion stallion. I'll wear a ribbon around my throat." At fifty, Jamie loved his wife even more than he had at forty-nine; her twentieth birthday, he reasoned, had given her the necessary maturity.

However, the day was not completely wasted. At the somber men's tailoring establishment where Jamie was being fitted for a suit, Marsh found a belated Christmas gift for him at the leather counter. It was a man's money holder she'd seen several gentlemen bettors in Epsom using. A gold chain kept the secure leather folder neatly attached to the inside pocket of a man's jacket. The engraved card which advertised the product amused Marsh. To the legend, "With a Hold-Safe, a man won't lose his money to a pickpocket," Marsh impishly instructed the sanctimoniously proper clerk to add the words "or his wife, either."

After paying for the gift, she carefully tucked inside all but a small amount of the money she'd had Seth Hanford draw out of the Baltimore bank, dollars she'd exchanged for

English pounds at a bank in Epsom. In their lovely rooms at the resort hotel, she waited until they were in their robes, ready to go to bed, before she handed Jamie the only gift she'd ever given him.

He read the card first and looked at her steadily. She smiled back at him. "No one can ever take me from you, Jamie," she murmured softly.

His eyes returned to the leather envelope as he studied the bank notes inside silently. "Are you sure you won't need this money, Marsh, for the next time you decide to leave me?" he asked soberly, his voice shaken with emotion.

"No, Jamie, I'm never going to be that foolish again." Her smile became impudent as she continued. "I've decided that the next time you lose your temper at me in public, I'm going to kick you on the shins to remind you to stop being a ninny, and then I'm going to kiss you until you want me again." She giggled as she went to him. "I'll bet we'll be thrown out into the street on moral charges."

Jamie's arms were around her as she proceeded to demonstrate, her body against his, her hips moving sensuously, and her lips meeting his with an abandoned kiss. When he finally released her long enough to pick her up and start toward the bedroom, he chuckled into her ear. "We'd be tarred and feathered, but I'd be the most envied man at the party." He was still chuckling as he slipped their robes off and joined her in bed. "Now I suppose we'll have to buy that champion."

"We were going to anyway, Jamie MacKenzie."

At that moment, had she told him they were going to buy Buckingham Palace, he wouldn't have contradicted her. He suddenly understood the enormity of her gift; for the first time, his hoyden girl-bride had become a woman as far as he was concerned. He kissed her deeply and let their passion take over his consciousness.

Raikes, Lord Albert Leverton Raikes to the uninitiated, came in person to their hotel in Tunbridge Wells. "Digs" —obviously Lord Digby Brampton—"tells me you're converting to racers at your Maryland farm." At least for him, American territories were unprovincial enough to have names. "If you're free right now, you can look my stock over today. Don't worry about a jockey, one of my exercise boys can do the job."

"My wife," Jamie admitted sheepishly, feeling Marsh's shoe caress his ankles, "does the testing for me."

She squirmed a little when the amused gray eyes of Lord Raikes were beamed on her. "I was hoping she would. My wife and I have a friendly little bet. Digs said that Mrs. MacKenzie sits quite a saddle." Marsh didn't hesitate; leaving Jamie and Lord Raikes in the sitting room of their suite, she squirmed out of the pretty cotton-print morning dress and into her riding outfit, feeling the excitement of a happy destiny. One of the Raikes stallions would be hers, and she'd know which one when she saw it.

The celebrated stables were an education in themselves. One room housed nothing but ribands and cups, the spoils of a thousand races; another held the silks, the riding outfits of four generations of gentlemen racers; and a third had the most complete assortment of saddles, bridles, and martingales even Jamie had ever seen. Outside, the racing path was a smoothly graded oval the size of the standard English racetrack.

With a twinkle in his eye, Lord Raikes suggested that Marsh look around while he and Jamie talked price. Followed by a groom who'd been ordered to keep her safe from nervous hooves, she strode past the long row of horses to the six stalls where she'd already spotted her targets. There were six stallions there—six Thoroughbreds of the same bloodlines, all but one of which had champion insignia over their stalls. Carefully, she went from one to another, studying their eyes; then, just as meticulously, she studied their ears. Again, she watched and compared their eyes. Occasionally, she spoke to one and studied its reaction. When she returned to the trophy room, she found her husband and the host happily bending elbows over snifters of brandy.

"Lord Raikes," she announced, "you have two stallions—"

"I have six stallions, young lady."

"You have two stallions I would like to ride."

"Which two?"

"Numbers One and Five."

"That's one bet my wife loses," Raikes laughed. "Why those two, Mrs. MacKenzie?"

"Number One is the sire of at least four of the others; I'm not sure about Number Six. Number Five is the one who inherited the most of his sire's intelligence and spirit."

At Raikes startled look, Jamie hastened to explain. "My wife has talked to her own stallion since she was thirteen. As far as I know, she doesn't have gypsy blood."

"If she can ride as well as she picks horses, MacKenzie, you could make a fortune at the track. All right, let's go saddle Numbers One and Five."

"One first," Marsh insisted.

"One it is. Do you mind a small gallery watching you, Mrs. MacKenzie?"

Jamie scowled fiercely and even Marsh blinked a little until she remembered that she'd once ridden in front of Mosby and his men. "Not if your horses don't," she shrugged.

While she was concentrating on the beauty of the horse which was being led out, she did not notice the group of people congregating at the midway point on the track on the row of bleachers stationed there. Even as she mounted the magnificent animal and walked slowly around the yard, she did not glance at the track. Occasionally, she would bend low over the stallion's neck and talk to it, and her heart leapt in joy as its ears pricked up just as her own stallion's had. Only when she approached the track did she see the spectators; and she petted her horse reassuringly. Then, crouching low over its head, she whispered the word, "Go." Never had any ride been like this one, with the stallion rounding the curves without a break in its even stride. Not once did either she or the horse break concentration, and neither knew when they passed the watching gallery. Only on her own stallion had she felt such response; she had found her sought-after champion.

A white-faced Jamie helped her dismount. "My God, Marsh, I thought you were going to fly through the air."

"Don't be silly. The horse knew I was there."

"How did you like my horse?" Raikes asked as he caught up with them.

"He's magnificent. Will you sell him?"

"I might consider Number Five, but not, I think, Number One. He's a valuable stud, and he still has a few races in him yet."

Marsh was outraged. "Lord Raikes, the only race that stallion would win would be against eight-year-old mares. He's ten years old."

"Then why would you want him?"

"Because he's a fighter and would die trying to win a race. That's the quality he's been able to pass on to his colts, and for another fifteen years he'll be a great sire."

Lord Raikes's laughter filled the trophy room just as a score of people entered. Digs was first with his hand outstretched toward his host.

"Pay up, Bert. Your horse ran today at his old time with this lady up, just as I bet you."

Raikes's answer was lost in the babble of voices that filled the room. Marsh pressed against Jamie and let him do the talking as they acknowledged introductions. Toward the end, one tweedy man asked Jamie, "Would you be the MacKenzie who supplied half the northern cavalry during the recent upset over there?" Jamie nodded, and the informed man carried on. "Your stock is a mixture of Arab and Highland Thorough-bred, isn't it?"

"During the war my farms supplied a lot of western breeds, too."

"I was over there in '63 with a shipload of horses. Small potatoes compared to the numbers you produced. How many all told?"

"How many from Virginia, Marsh?"

"Thirty-eight hundred."

"Then I estimate we sold about twenty thousand."

Lord Raikes cleared his throat, "MacKenzie, this inquisitive man is John Harding, my friend and head trainer. Sorry I didn't recognize your name earlier. Where in the world did you raise that number of horses?"

"I didn't, at least not all of them. My brother brought thousands from the Indians who round up the wild horses on the plains and train them. My people just retrained them for the military."

"You gentlemen can take your mutual admiration elsewhere," rang out the fluty voice of Lady Elvira Raikes. "I want to find out more about this girl who just gave Rake-Star the best ride he's had in years. Mr. MacKenzie, why did you ask your wife about Virginia? I thought that colony was with the Confederacy."

"My farm there was always in Union hands because it's across the river from Washington."

"And your wife stayed on the farm in Virginia?"

"She was born there and during the war she helped manage it."

"Mrs. MacKenzie, what did a girl like you do on a horse farm during the war?"

Marsh flushed a little. People like these English aristocrats would never believe the truth. "I helped keep the books," she admitted reluctantly.

Jamie believed differently about the tolerance of the Raikes. After moving his tender ankles away from his wife's boots, he enlarged on Marsh's feeble admission. "She also battle trained horses, doctored them, and sold them to northern and southern generals alike. That is, when she wasn't raising food for hungry civilians and southern guerrillas."

"And now she wants to raise racehorses?" Lady Raikes asked thoughtfully.

Knowing that Jamie had labeled her accurately with a

devastating honesty, Marsh threw caution to the wind. "I would if your husband would sell us Rake-Star as our stallion," she declared.

"Of course he'll sell you Rake-Star. He's been moaning for a month about getting rid of horses. They're eating us into bankruptcy. Bertie, stop scowling!" Marsh almost smiled. "You know I'm right. And I hope the MacKenzies will take some of those bloody mares off our hands, too. Now, before I forget, John, send two of your sons into town and bring the MacKenzies's luggage back here. I'm not letting them get away from this barren wilderness until they've met all our friends. Any woman who can wear breeches and ride a horse like Mrs. MacKenzie will set the local wig-wags on their tails with envy at the Tunbridge Wells hunt ball tonight. All right, now it's up to the house for everybody and some decent brew. I can't abide Bertie's taste in brandy."

That afternoon and night set the scene that would make Marsh a social lioness for the remainder of her stay in England. At the early dinner served alfresco on the Raikes's terrace, she gained a sense of belonging with these people as she never had with society in Baltimore. Meeting her husband's eyes across the terrace full of relaxed, friendly people, she knew that he belonged, too. As she dressed for the hunt ball in the ivory silk dress Jamie had given her, the sense of destiny she'd felt all day was intensified by a rare mood of sentiment. In the beautifully simple dress, she felt like a bride as she walked down the stairs to her waiting husband, hearing with her inner ear the sound of the organ music of Phyllis and Craig's wedding. Such was her communion with Jamie, she knew he was experiencing the same emotion. His eyes glowed with love as he gently placed the magnificent ivory leather cape about her shoulders. Nor was he the only one to watch her descent down the stairs. Lord Raikes raised his glass in a silent toast to the beautiful American woman whose face held the same unconquerable look of his own ancestors.

Twice more during their stay with the Raikes, Marsh wore

the same breathtaking outfit, once for a reception at the London mansion of a duke who was Lady Raikes's cousin and again at the annual race ball held in the Queen Anne Palace in Epsom. What she and Jamie did not realize was that Rake-Star had become a beloved institution for the English people and that any information about the new owners was national news. Thus, their conquest of the racing segment of the aristocracy and a lavish description of Marsh's ivory cape and gown were duly reported in English newspapers, copies of which were now speeding to America aboard the fast clipper ships.

On the quieter days at the Raikes estate, Marsh wore her riding clothes as if they were the latest fashion instead of merely outrageous. While Jamie tended to the mundane financial and transportation arrangements, Marsh selected twelve mares with the help of John Harding, who had agreed to accompany the MacKenzies to America and establish the Maryland racing farm. Although Jamie was aware that the mare selection process frequently involved races between his wife and one of the several young aristocrats who challenged her, he made no effort to find out who won. But from Lady Raikes smile and Bertie's frown, he gathered only one of them was consistently lucky. Moreover, fragments of a dialogue he overheard held definite clues.

". . . just as soon as my dressmaker can make me a pair."

"You'll never wear pants as long as I'm master here."

"You just lost one bet, Bertie, you can't afford to lose another."

When the MacKenzies finally bid the Raikes farewell, a caravan accompanied them from the estate. In addition to Mr. and Mrs. Harding, six grooms had accepted jobs in America. At Southampton the mares were secured in wood stalls at one end of the ship's hold and the three stallions in padded cells at the other. Separating the two groups were the hundred merino ewes Robbie had requested his father buy to stock one part of the new ranch in Wyoming. As Jamie looked over the cargo, he reflected ruefully that Robbie would probably make a profit from the sheep within two years, and Stuart would have paid off the investment in workhorses in five, whereas he and Marsh might never earn a penny on racehorses. Yet Rake-Star had cost him more than all the other animals combined.

Arriving on schedule in Baltimore, the ship was greeted by a throng of avid racing fans from seven of the seaboard states. For weeks, American newspapers had printed the news of Rake-Star's pending arrival, and his champion status had already made him an international celebrity. Marsh could have hugged the stallion as she led him down the gangplank. He strutted past the awed spectators like a trained circus horse before an audience. She almost expected the beautiful show-off to take a bow as some of the more enthusiastic watchers actually clapped.

Chapter
11

Unloading a hundred and twenty-one mares, three stallions, and as many sheep from the hold of a relatively small cattle boat after twenty-six days at sea was roughly equivalent to opening the sewers of Paris. While aboard, Jamie and Marsh had become accustomed to the stench during their daily work stints in the hold. But in the fresh, windswept air of the Baltimore docks, the smell was overpowering as the horses were led down one by one and the sheep herded down the gangplanks in groups to be caravaned by wagons to recovery pastures on the outskirts of the city. All that day, John Harding and the two MacKenzies directed the careful placement of those animals in separate pastures. The six MacKenzie farm guards who had met the ship were directed to guard the stallions and racing mares while the hardworking English grooms were assigned the lighter task of making sure the animals regained their land legs. In the company of the Hardings, Jamie and Marsh returned to their Baltimore home for the first time in six months.

Elizabeth Evelyn Allen

Mrs. Tucker met them at the front door and announced that four bathtubs were in the process of being filled.

"Thought you might enjoy your dinner in your rooms tonight, you look as tired as all get out."

As the four travelers climbed wearily up the stairs, the practical housekeeper handed each couple a small tray with two glasses and a decanter of brandy.

"Your luggage is already unpacked. If you don't mind my saying so, I'd sleep with the windows open tonight if I was you," she added.

Jamie was tempted to reprimand his outspoken employee, but Mrs. Harding was laughing. "It's a good thing there were no other passengers aboard ship, else we'd have been thrown overboard." The MacKenzies joined in the laughter, bid their guests good night, and headed for their own room. Pausing only long enough to throw their soiled riding clothes into a hamper Mrs. Tucker had left outside the door, Marsh and Jamie headed for their separate tubs and an hour of hard scrubbing. After a small brandy and a light dinner, they climbed wearily into bed, too tired for conversation, other than Jamie's muttered, "Never again. Next time we buy Swiss clocks or French wine."

It was a good thing the Hardings and MacKenzies had their twelve hours of sleep and their second baths the next morning, because by afternoon the house was a beehive of activity. Racing breeders from as far away as Boston were lined up to reserve Rake-Star for stud services. By evening, the list numbered the names of almost a hundred applicants.

"Did you realize that there was this interest in racing here?" Harding asked in awe.

"No, but my wife did." Jamie smiled happily.

"My lord, man, with this kind of demand you'll make the cost of Rake-Star back in a season and a half and get your own colts to boot. Since I only allow seventy-five stud services a year maximum, there'll be no limit on the fees we

272

can charge. But I think my wife and I had better get to the farm and organize.''

"We'll go with you as soon as I notify my son in Virginia to make arrangements for the workhorses and notify my other son that I'm sending his damn sheep by rail. And I think we'd better take Rake-Star with us. The security's better on the farm.''

The security may have been better, but the profit was not. When the Hardings and MacKenzies arrived at the rented pastures the next morning, long lines of people were waiting to pay money for the privilege of seeing the horses, and the English grooms were conducting guided tours. Although Rake-Star was the main attraction, dozens of farmers were gathered around the Clydesdale and Shire pastures.

Embarrassed by the confusion of the scene, Harding introduced the young man who was entertaining the people waiting in lines and collecting their money. "This is my youngest son, Tom,'' he said in disgust. Although Marsh hadn't known he was Harding's son, she knew the young man well. On the Raikes estate in England, he'd dogged her footsteps and revealed an interest in racing that exceeded her own. Never adverse to any profitable business enterprise, Jamie good-naturedly gave Tom permission to carry on the improvised fair, providing that the English grooms did guard duty and that the MacKenzie guards shared in the profits.

Tom grinned happily. "Tomorrow we'll charge more and exercise a few of the racing mares.''

Marsh grinned back at him. "Make sure you time those races, Tom.'' She was remembering her and Philip's excitement at the Maryland farm more than a year earlier. Jamie took one look at his wife, grabbed her arm, and led her back to the carriage.

"I'm taking you home where you'll be safe.''

Home, however, proved not to be the haven of safety Jamie had thought. With the Hardings they arrived in time to hear the high-pitched voice of Alice Nelson issuing from the closed library. While their guests retreated diplomatically to their own room, Jamie preceded Marsh into the library, where Alice was arguing with Craig and Phyllis.

"It belonged to my grandfather and I have as much right as you do in the bank," the furious sister was berating her red-faced brother. Abruptly, she turned to confront the two newcomers and her anger switched to them. "This is family business," she shrilled, "and that woman is not a part of the family."

Jamie put his arm protectively around Marsh and scowled blackly. "What in blazes is this all about?"

Assuming her righteous look of prim dignity, Alice responded, "While you were wasting money in England, I made it my business to inspect your properties in New York and Baltimore. You stole all of them from my grandfather."

Jamie glared at her before he spoke. "Not that my holdings are any of your business, but I'll tell you about them. I acquired the New York assets during the war from the sale of MacKenzie horses. The Baltimore ones are mine as the surviving member of the partnership."

"You cheated your way into a fortune."

"You're wrong again. Yours, your Aunt Sophia's, and Janet's wealth add up to far more than your grandfather's fortune when I joined him. What increases there were, I can take half the credit for. The greater part of my own personal wealth comes from the wartime sale of MacKenzie horses in which your grandfather had no part whatsoever."

"That's a lie. You were nothing but a beggarly foreigner when you first came here."

Marsh could hear Phyllis gasp at this ugly effrontery, but Jamie no longer sounded anything but bored. "Believe what you want to, Alice, but my brother and I owned the MacKenzie farm here free and clear and also the money from the sale of our property in Scotland."

"Well then," the woman persisted, "if that's all you had,

I have the right to inspect the bank's records to find out about all the other assets you now claim."

"You have no such right. According to your grandfather's will, you were left his home and an income for life. Nothing else. When Craig is twenty-one, he will inherit what his grandfather left him—fifty percent of the bank."

From the stunned look on Craig's face, Marsh knew that he had no prior knowledge of his windfall. But her attention quickly reverted to his outraged sister, whose voice was shriller than ever.

"His income will be larger than mine."

"He has to work for his," Jamie said dryly, "you don't. Was there anything else you wanted to know, Alice? If not, I'd like you to leave. I want to talk to my son alone."

If she says she never stays where she isn't wanted, I'm going to throw up, thought Marsh as she watched Alice rise from the chair and face Jamie again. However, Alice was far beyond such polite little disclaimers. "I'll go," she snapped, "in spite of the fact that this is my mother's house, but I won't forget any of your rudeness." For the first time she addressed Marsh directly. "And I won't forget that you're the one who turned Jamie against his own family." As she started to leave, Jamie removed his arm from around Marsh and silently escorted Alice to the front door. No one spoke while he was out of the room, and Marsh moved to the far side where she seated herself in a chair separated from the others. Her heart was thudding heavily with a mixture of fear and anger. The sight of Alice had disturbed her intensely, but Jamie's lack of defense for his wife had destroyed the happy trust she'd developed in him, leaving her once again suspicious and angry. She did not look up at him when he returned.

Craig was the first to break the silence. "She began her demands right after you and Marsh left, and she's been bothering me at the bank ever since. She even demanded those damned pearls."

Preoccupied ever since Alice had gone, Phyllis spoke for the first time. "There's even more unpleasant news both of you should know. After the terrible thing that happened at our wedding, the police searched Alice's home. Since then, no one in town invites her anywhere. And that's not all the bad news. Two months ago, Craig and I went to Virginia to see Stuart, and we were invited to the Randall's for dinner. Alice had been there for a week. Alice said some terrible things about Marsh, and Craig told her to shut up. But Stuart became so angry, he left. After he was gone, Janet said that she was going to start proceedings to have her husband declared dead so that she and Stuart could marry."

Jamie growled, "Stuart's not that stupid."

"I don't know, Jamie," Phyllis insisted, "when we were in Stuart's home, I saw a lot of Janet's things around—personal things."

"He's a damn fool," her father-in-law scowled, then looked over at his wife and smiled ruefully. "He used to have better taste in women."

"Jamie," Phyllis was not to be easily disconcerted from her main topic, "is Wayne Talbot dead?"

"No, he's not, but don't tell Alice."

"Then Janet can't remarry, can she?"

"I don't think so. Only men can get a divorce in Virginia in any case."

"Well, that solves one problem. But what about Alice?"

"Has she been—uh—unpleasant to you personally, Phyllis?"

"No, not to me or Craig. But her attitude about Marsh worries me. I think we should all work to protect Marsh from her."

During the whole discussion, Marsh had been quiet, very quiet for her, but now she spoke sharply. "I can take care of myself. Do you mind if we change the subject? It's not one of my husband's favorites. How was your vacation at the club?"

Phyllis laughed. "Thanks to you, we were celebrities. Did you really wear—uh—a riding costume like that?"

"I wouldn't know how to ride in anything else. Look, Phyllis, we have guests staying with us. Why don't you and Craig join us for dinner?"

Craig accepted the invitation with such enthusiasm, Phyllis made a face at him. "There's just one little problem with our marriage. I can't cook and Craig just hates to eat out all the time. But since I'm at the bank all day, I don't have the time."

As the four left the library, Jamie took his wife's arm and looked down at her; she avoided his eyes but she didn't yank her arm away. At the dinner table with the Hardings, Jamie announced, "I think that perhaps we should get to the farm as quickly as possible. John, tomorrow you and I will make arrangements to ship the horses there by riverboat as soon as your son thinks they've recovered enough, while our wives pack our clothes. Then Marsh and I will stay with you until you've got everything under control before we take off on another trip. She has property in Georgia which she wants to see, and I want to check on things in New York. After that, I'm taking her to see Wyoming. Are these plans all right with you, Marsh?" he asked deliberately.

Flustered, she could only mumble, "I suppose so." But she did lose some of the resentment that had been building. Two days back in Baltimore and their happiness was already threatened by the same damned person whom Jamie still couldn't believe was any more than a quarrelsome woman! Marsh sighed; at least he was getting her away from Alice.

Craig, though, was not happy. "What about the bank?"

"What about it, son? I'll take care of that little problem we just discussed, then you and Phyllis can carry on as you've been doing."

Later, in the privacy of their bedroom, Jamie put an end to his wife's restless evasiveness with two firm hands on her shoulders. "Marsh, I cannot strike another woman just to prove I love you. Did you really think that I was going to let that bitch get near you? You ever doubt me again like you did today and your ankles are going to get kicked. I know she's dangerous, but I didn't want to hurt Craig anymore by accusing her publicly. Tomorrow, I'll see Captain Mason at the police station and tell him to warn her away from the bank and ask him if he's any farther along in the investigation about the poisoning. But don't get your hopes up; Alice is not stupid. She'd have destroyed every scrap of evidence by this time. We're just going to have to stay out of Baltimore in the future. Now get undressed and let's go to bed.''

Marsh rushed to do his bidding, hoping he would not expect an apology for her lack of faith. He waited until she joined him in bed and then chuckled into her ear. "It's not as much fun for you to be wrong, is it, hinny?''

"I don't know yet, Jamie," she whispered back and moved her body close to his. "But I think it's going to be," she added boldly a moment later. He was still chuckling as he kissed her, and again the next morning as he buttoned her dress.

"Some wives would have just said 'I'm sorry,' but I think I like your way better.''

She grinned and shrugged. "Since that's what we're going to do anyway, it's silly to waste time talking.''

Their lighthearted play lasted throughout their riverboat trip to the farm and well into the following month for Marsh. But the minute Jamie walked down the gangplank leading Rake-Star, the weight of converting a casual breeding farm for ordinary horses into a precision one for racehorses crushed his hopes for an immediate departure. First, a breeding pen had to be constructed. Regular stallions make do in the open pasture; champions are monitored in a small enclosure. Then there was the complete reorganization of pastures to make room for the racing oval and the refencing of easily maintained, large areas into securely fenced small ones. But the first and foremost challenge was the problem of taking care of the hundreds of new colts Marsh's unique segregation had produced. Methodically, John Harding ranked every colt as gentleman racer, standard saddle, all-purpose farm, and carriage harness—all but one.

"What about Mrs. MacKenzie's mare?" Harding asked Dr. Damon.

Damon shrugged. "You tell me. I know Marsh had never seen a racehorse in her life. But this mare is different than the others."

Different she was! Harding whistled when he first saw the dark brown mare with the squared off, aquiline nose. "I've only seen drawings of horses like this," he exclaimed. "She's Spanish Arab of three centuries ago with maybe a little modern French Arab, but she's been bred by a professional for racing. Look at her work her colt. Had she ever foaled before?"

"No, this was her first time."

"Then she's had the racing instinct bred in. Where in this country would you find such a breeder?"

"In Louisiana. The French have been there for centuries, and the Spanish part could have come from the wild horses of Texas."

Marsh, who had spent an hour on a pasture fence admiring the colt, was jubilant when she asked Harding what he thought of Marsh Song and her offspring.

Cautiously, Harding temporized, "They're an interesting pair."

"That colt is going to be the first champion stallion produced at this farm," she boasted.

Amused by his wife's confidence, Jamie smiled. "Don't get your hopes too high, Marsh. So far Rake-Star has only produced twenty champions out of five hundred colts, and your colt's sire is no champion."

Harding was less cautious now. "We may not have papers on the mare, but she dominated your stallion's bloodlines, and her colt's lively enough to merit training. My son Tom's an ambitious lad, I'd like him to train—have you given the colt a name yet, Marsh?"

"Not yet."

"What do you think of the name Marsh Wind?" Harding asked her.

Jamie snorted in disgust. "I'm going to get my wife away from here before someone renames the farm Marsh Flats." His disgust was more than a temporary irritation. He was already weary of the cost and care each racehorse required; he was used to dealing with horses in bulk and he could neither understand nor sympathize with the enthusiasm of the Hardings. It was with relief that he finally saw the farm settled down to a semblance of normal commerce, when the last of his own twenty-four racing mares were carefully bred in the new breeding pen and Rake-Star was put to work on the first of the selected mares of other breeders. That one fee alone paid for the three miles of new fencing. When Jamie and Marsh finally began the proposed trip, he vowed never to work again, especially with the kind of mares who couldn't even give birth to their foals without medical assistance. His irritation was especially keen on the morning of their departure when the coastal packet boat was forced to wait at the MacKenzie dock for twenty minutes while an elegantly dressed Marsh bid a farewell to her mare and its colt.

Jamie's vacation from work lasted for the four days of rough passage down coastal waters aboard the buffeted steamship, for the five days in a beautiful old hotel in Savannah, where Yankees like himself were more unpopular than the seasonal hurricanes, and for the two days on a war-scarred train through the devastation of central Georgia. Even Marsh was subdued by the total lack of southern hospitality. "They'd lynch us if they knew that ten thousand MacKenzie horses carried Sherman's men through their state," she whispered.

At the burned-out station in Milledgeville, they were met by the first smiles they'd received in eleven days. Angus Balfour's weather-beaten face beamed at Marsh with approval and at Jamie with joy as he checked the twelve bottles of usquebaugh Jamie had brought along as a goodwill gesture.

Philip Addison greeted Jamie as an old friend and Marsh as a potential field hand. "I hope you still like to work," he smiled at her, "we've saved plenty of it for you." She wondered what had happened to his long list of "don'ts" for a lady.

But the man neither of them recognized at first was Wayne Talbot. Thirty pounds heavier, he was the undisputed leader in charge as he checked the MacKenzie's trunks with the station master, paid a freckle-faced street urchin to pile the lighter pieces of their luggage into the waiting farm wagon, and climbed into the driver's seat with the help of only one cane. His arrival eight months earlier had meant the difference between success and failure for the first year's crops. With an enthusiasm that even Tom Harding couldn't match, he pointed out the acres of Addison land planted with tobacco now within weeks of harvest. Further on, he indicated fields of legume clover which he said was the third crop for the year. "The pigs have already consumed the peanuts, plants and all, and are now fattening on corn. Six hundred of them will be ready for the smoke sheds in two weeks." Jamie groaned.

A half hour after they'd entered the combined estates, they passed the remains of the Addison plantation house. Sitting beside her old dance instructor in the bed of the wagon, Marsh expected to see bitterness and anger reflected on his face. Instead, she saw only wry humor reenforced by cheerful words. "Sherman did me a big favor. That place used to take thirty slaves to maintain, and the plantation lost money every year. If everything goes as we've planned, it'll make the first profit since 1854, and with a work force of only twenty people, including the three of us."

"Aye, it's been no vacation," Angus complained, "but I'm countin' on Marsh and Jamie to spell me off wi' the work." No one contradicted him or insisted that guests were not expected to work, and the accommodation reserved for them was a one-room, bare-wood slave cabin whose two claims to comfort were a bed purchased from another plantation owner who had escaped Sherman's ravages and a new lean-to outhouse with the one basic necessity. Buckets and a basin in the main room supplied the only private bathing equipment.

At dinner that night, served in a three-sided shed with crude cooking facilities at one end, Marsh was reunited with Adah and Jake, and she and Jamie met the rest of the oddly assorted group. The white segment had three other members— Wayne's widowed sister, Philip's dignified uncle and his twenty-eight-year-old spinster daughter. Like Philip's father, Paul Addison had also been in politics. It was through his connections in Atlanta and Savannah that the unharvested tobacco crop and promised yield of smoked pork were already sold. He also served as the procuring agent for the Addison-Balfour enterprise. Marsh noted with interest that the two white women worked without visible prejudice alongside Adah and a large black woman who had been the Addison cook. In addition to Jake's three sons and their wives, there were seven other black men at the table.

After the simple meal was concluded, Marsh rose automatically to help with the cleanup while Jamie joined his hosts in the only sophisticated structure in the compound, a house which had once been the home of the Addison's overseer. He listened to Jake describe the remarkable ability of domestic hogs to produce nine piglets in a litter and to root much of their own food from the soil. But mainly, Jamie listened to Wayne Talbot, who had already planned next year's crops and had begun his second career as soil consultant for other plantation owners. When Jamie inquired about future home building, Philip was adamant. "Jake and I have agreed that all profits will be put into expansion for five years before we waste money on expensive homes."

Jamie hated to inject a note of gloom into the generally happy conviviality of the group, but Wayne had to be warned about his wife's intention to declare him dead. When he suggested a more private setting for the personal conference,

Wayne smiled. "Everyone here knows the story, and I use the name of Addison whenever I leave the farm. If it wouldn't turn my wife loose to make life miserable for some unlucky second husband, I'd divorce her." Jamie breathed a sigh of relief; the unlucky man he was concerned about was his contrary, irritating, and impulsive second son.

"Then you'll have to file affidavits that you're still alive to counter your wife's claims," Jamie warned. "However, my lawyer thought that your whereabouts could remain unknown under the circumstances."

To this proposal, Wayne readily agreed, relieved that his new life need not be interrupted by a potentially dangerous return to the ugly existence he'd left. That this new life was a healthy one, Jamie fully concurred with Wayne and unstintingly did his part in constructing the smokehouses. But that it was not the life he wanted put him in direct opposition to his enthusiastic wife, who was enjoying her daily job of picking tobacco leaves and hanging them in the sheds to dry. Jamie shook his head in humorous resignation and accepted the fact that he had married a farm girl. Two months later, and over the protest of their "partners," Jamie finally succeeded in dislodging Marsh at the completion of the tobacco harvest, but long before the hams and bacon were cured to Adah's satisfaction. By that time, Angus too was willing to return to his more accustomed work as business manager of the Virginia and Maryland farms. Thus, in early November, the three left the Georgia cooperative together and traveled northward by train to Maryland, where Jamie adamantly refused to disembark.

"You and I," he told Marsh, "are going to New York and take that vacation. There are theaters there and magnificent restaurants, and there are luxurious hotels where we won't have to do anything that resembles work."

There were also snowstorms in New York that November, one after another, and crowded hotels full of travelers waiting for passenger ships to resume their scheduled voyages to

Europe. The MacKenzies were lucky to find a vacancy in one of Jamie's own block of furnished flats; and with the help of a part-time maid who would do the cooking and cleaning, they began the leisurely life Jamie craved. Comfortably ensconced before a warm fire with a snifter of brandy and another of Charles Dickens's books, Jamie was content to let the elements rage outside. On the good days between the storms, he took his wife on outings to check on his various properties and to shop in the beautiful stores which made New York the center of the American fashion world. Six times during their first month they went out socially: twice to the large hotels with business acquaintances of Jamie, twice to the music halls which had become postwar favorites, and twice to functions labeled on engraved invitations as balls. The first was at a huge, Hudson River estate which was an overdone imitation of an English manor house containing a ballroom ceiling heavily weighted with European crystal. Marsh wore her ivory silk dress and leather cape to that party and wondered why she'd bothered. Since all the men talked about was the new American craze of horse racing, she'd have felt more at home in her riding costume. The other ball was a routinely dull affair, all too reminiscent of the tradition-stifled ones in Baltimore. None of these social activities were necessary for Jamie's peace of mind. He was more than happy to return to the robe-only nights of their early marriage. But Marsh felt unfulfilled and her bottled up energies sought an outlet. One night, during a four-day storm which had kept them housebound, Marsh was lying on the floor in front of the fireplace listening to the maid rushing through the dinner dishes so that she could return to her own home before the night freeze set in.

"Jamie," Marsh had been worrying about the prospect all day, "are we going to live in New York?"

"Do you like it here, Marsh?"

"I might if we had something important to do with our lives."

"Where would you rather live?"

"I liked it in Georgia because we were busy; but we only helped, it wasn't ours. We may own a piece of the land, but the plan belongs to the others. Maryland is the same way. You and I don't know enough about breeding racehorses to be anything but a nuisance to Mr. Harding until he gets all the real work done. And Craig and Phyllis can do everything that's necessary in the Baltimore bank. So we're left with New York as the only place where other people don't do the work."

"I have a full-time manager here, too, Marsh."

"Then what are we going to do with our lives?"

Jamie watched her troubled face with hooded eyes. How do you tell a girl not yet twenty-one that you'd worked for thirty years to achieve enough success and money to be able to stop working? Especially a girl like Marsh, who thrived on meeting challenges. As his eyes caressed her slim body, beautiful even in the long underwear visible beneath her robe, he knew the challenge which would supply the purpose in her life—a child, perhaps two. The prospect chilled him more than a little; he had not really enjoyed any of his sons when they were young. Only now could he accept Robbie as a friend and look with pride on Craig. The brightest and the best looking of his sons was still an anathema to Jamie, the one he could not reach or understand. Still, his allegiance now was bound up in the happiness of a girl two months younger than his youngest son. Her happiness was of paramount importance.

"Would you like to see your mother while we're in New York?"

"Is New York where you sent her—and her Confederate colonel?"

"He's your father, Marsh."

"Who needs one now, Jamie? Besides, what would I say to him?" She sat up, crossed her knees Indian style and assumed the mocking expression of a child. "Hello, papa. I'm your little girl, Pamela. Mama had me after you went away twenty-one years ago."

"Then how about seeing your mother?"

"About the only things I could say to her would be, 'Yes, I remember to wash my own hair now' and 'Yes, I know I'm a Marshall.' " Her voice rasped a little when she remembered the last time she'd seen her mother. "Jamie, all the time coming over on the tug that day, she didn't tell me one word about my father. And once she'd seen him, she didn't even look back. You were the only one who helped me that day, just like you'd always helped me. I don't need either of them, Jamie. I have you."

Watching the expression of her mercurial face change from cynicism to the smiling impudence which often preceded her uninhibited passion, he was struck by the old-young contrast in his beautiful wife—old in her almost casual acceptance of the hard blows life had dealt her, heartbreakingly young in her intense desire to create a world of her own. As he watched her eyes change from hazel to green, he felt his desire for her quicken and he pulled her toward him. But before passion obscured his sentimental love for her, he knew with an overwhelming certainty that, like Marsh Song, this girl-woman would produce beautiful children stamped with her own fighting spirit. For the first time in his life, Jamie wanted to mate—not just to possess her, but to blend their tempestuous spirits together, to give her a child she would shape into her own. Even knowing that her present immunity made immediate conception impossible, he kissed her with a special purpose that night. And as it always had, his urgency communicated itself to her. Neither partner rushed the other— each wanted to prolong the sweet buildup, to give and receive the gift of love in all its intensity. Even after they were joined, they delayed until the moment of fulfillment stirred them with a power that left them silent, locked in each other's arms. Long afterward, they were still awake, both aware of a new force in their relationship.

"Does Carina's powder have an antidote?" he asked softly.

She nodded and whispered, "Yes." And Marsh, who rarely prayed, prayed that night for the cure to work in her case. The next day, Jamie was suddenly impatient for the child. All morning long, he fussed at Marsh to write the letter to Carina. Using one excuse after another, she dallied until Jamie sat her down at the dining room table and demanded she write the letter without anymore delay. Halfway through a disorganized attempt, she suggested that Jamie write the letter himself.

"The subject," he reprimanded her with a prudishness that triggered a fit of giggling on her part, "is not one a gentleman can discuss with a woman other than his wife. Now stop your nonsense and get it written!"

An hour later, she handed him her finished letter for which the kindest description would be indecipherable. Only the "Dear Carina" and "Marsh" were understandable; the irregular lines in between were ink-blotted and so lacking in verbs and other essentials like correct spelling, the jumbled scrawl had little meaning. That letter was a revelation to Jamie. Because he'd watched her read with impatient speed and add up columns so accurately Angus had seldom checked her totals, he had assumed her education complete. Now, as he remembered that her grandmother had taught her only the rudiments of reading and ciphering, and that only her quick intelligence had made her useful to Angus, Jamie felt a deep pride in her. So fluent was her speech—expressive to the point of pungency—that she projected the image of an educated, cultured woman, but she'd never had a day of formal education. Bitterness twisted his gut when he remembered the expensive tutors he'd hired to teach Alice and Craig, and the costly private schools Robbie and Stuart had attended; yet this girl was swifter than any of them in her speed of comprehension.

He knew better than to offer her false praise or to pretend her letter was other than crude. "You've never written a letter before, have you, Marsh?" he asked gently.

She shook her head. "I tried to teach myself by saying the words out loud, but I talked too fast to get them all down, so what I wrote didn't make sense."

"Would you like to learn?" She looked at him as if trying to measure the degree of his disapproval; she was too proud to apologize or ask for help. Seeing that flare of defiant pride, he reassured her. "I think I could teach you in a few weeks."

"You wouldn't yell at me and glower?"

He laughed. "I'll probably curse a hundred times each lesson, but not at you. I wasn't very good at writing letters in school."

"Then teach me to write now. You write the letter and I'll copy it. I don't want our child to be ashamed of me." The child whose conception was a year away had become a reality to both of them.

The bitter winter of New York that year lasted another ten weeks, but the afternoons were no longer aimless periods. Impatient curses and all, Jamie wrote letter after letter, which she painstakingly copied until she memorized his sequence of words and their correct spelling. By drawing lines across the paper, she learned to place the words evenly. After a few weeks, she could write the letters without his models in front of her. In later years, Angus told her that her letters sounded just like Jamie's. "They should," she admitted with a smile, and told her old friend the story of her "days in school."

During the last two weeks of practice, Marsh was often nauseated and nervous. Eight weeks after the first letter was sent to Carina, a small package arrived in the mail accompanied by instructions written in Carina's graceful style. At the bottom of the page was a personal note: "My people have a saying that a child is a gift which must be shared. Damon and I would like to be friends to yours and Jamie's child." The sweetness of that message almost made the bitter taste and aftereffects of the drug bearable for Marsh, who followed Carina's orders faithfully and was ill every day she swallowed the dose. Before the ordeal was finished, Jamie was almost as worried about her as he'd been after the poisoning. However, when she regained her normal vigorous health, it was Jamie who had to be reassured each month she failed to conceive.

Several days before they left New York, they moved from the flat to a downtown hotel at Jamie's insistence. That first night in the beautiful dining room, Jamie casually informed her that an important guest would join them, and then, just as casually, he excused himself, leaving a puzzled wife sitting in lonely elegance at a table in a secluded corner. Fearing that Jamie might have decided for some quixotic reason to introduce her to a half forgotten Catherine, Marsh was unprepared for the tall man who approached her table. As she recognized him, she sat back in her chair, her face mirroring the agitation of her pounding heart. That he was just as nervous was apparent in his inability to say a word until he was seated opposite her.

Looking at her with a hunger that matched her own, he introduced himself, "I've waited half a lifetime to meet you. I'm your father."

Her first thought was, He doesn't look old enough to be my father. He doesn't look as old as Jamie. But she knew he was anyway, with the unruly, dark red hair still untouched by gray and the same rakish look of self-confidence her own face held. Embarrassed by her emotional response, she fumbled for something to call him. Seeing her hesitation, he came to her aid.

"My name is Bradford and your mother tells me you like to be called Marsh. Ever since I've known you existed, I've wanted to see you. And since you've been in New York, I've asked Jamie to let me visit at your home. But he explained how you felt, so your mother and I didn't insist. I'm sorry we failed you."

For Marsh, emotional shock was never of such duration as to render her mute for long. "How in the world did you fail me? Adah told me what my grandfather had done. You didn't have the slightest notion I existed, just as I knew nothing about you.''

''It's odd that no one in our section of Virginia ever mentioned you, Marsh. I was told about every other pretty girl whenever I was home on leave.''

''I was never away from the farm until the war. Brad—do you really want me to call you Bradford? It sounds so—odd.''

''My friends call me Brad, and I'd like to be a friend to you.''

She shrugged faintly, still oppressed by a feeling of futility about any relationship with a stranger, particularly with a stranger who could have little purpose in her life now. ''Were you in the army before the war? Jamie said you went to West Point.'' She really didn't want to know, but she felt the need to remain impersonal.

''Yes, I was in the national army for eleven years before I joined the Confederacy. I entered West Point after I learned your mother was married. I couldn't stay in Virginia then. Perhaps if I had, you and I wouldn't be strangers today. And maybe your life wouldn't have been so hard. Your husband told me the circumstances of your marriage. I wish I had known.''

''Why? Jamie's taken good care of me.'' There were so many things about Jamie she couldn't talk about to a father she didn't know.

''I'm glad for you.'' He searched for something else to say. ''Your mother and I will be married in another two months when her divorce becomes final.''

''What will you do then?''

''Go to my home in Virginia where your mother and I belong. Did you know that your other grandmother still lives there?''

''No.'' How could another stranger mean anything to her?

''Do you want to see your mother before you leave?''

''No. She has more misery to forget than I have. Why remind her?''

He stood up, discouraged and ill at ease. Her defensiveness and self-sufficiency had crushed the half-formed hopes he'd nurtured. Sensing something of his disappointment, Marsh rose too and slipped her arm through his.

"Brad, let's just be friends and not worry about the rest. I've never been an easy person to get along with, and I'm sorry I can't be the kind of daughter you wanted."

He looked down at her earnest young face. "I think you are, Marsh. You're a lot like I was at your age. I was headstrong and cocksure, too."

"Then I'm glad I'm related to you. Be happy, Brad, you and my mother, and don't worry about me." Stretching up, she kissed him lightly on his cheek. "I imagine Jamie is waiting for you in the lobby. Tell him I'd rather eat dinner in our rooms. Good-bye, Brad, someday maybe we'll get to know each other."

It was his turn to kiss her on her forehead and walk away. She watched his tall military-straight figure disappear among the fronds of palm. He still didn't look old enough to be her father.

In his lonely chair in the hotel lobby, Jamie was thinking miserably about the same thing. As he watched Bradford Marshall approach, he realized with painful honesty that he was ten years older than his wife's father, and he felt doubly the fool about a new fatherhood, twenty-one years after the last one. He was glad the other man didn't want to talk. Solemnly, the two shook hands, spoke briefly about the business affairs they'd already conducted, and bid each other good night. The only allusion either one made to the girl who was so important to both of them was her father's comment about her poise.

"She seems older and more self-assured than I expected."

Jamie only nodded; he could not admit that her independence bothered him intensely. Reluctantly, he headed for their rooms after ordering dinner to be served there, although he would have preferred the impersonality of a public dining room tonight. When he saw her gazing pensively out the window, his heart plummeted; it wasn't like her to brood. Wisely, he didn't interrupt her thoughts except to return her welcoming smile and hand her a glass of wine.

"I would like," she announced after a brief silence, "to meet your other son and see a country that isn't crowded with people."

"Didn't you like your father, Marsh?"

Surprised by his question, she looked at him sharply. "Of course, I liked him. He's a nice person. But our life is ours, Jamie. He's taking my mother back to Virginia, so there's no place for us in their lives. We have to find our own future." She never realized that Jamie's laughter was inspired by relief, not by amusement at her words. Defensively, she explained, "We need our home away from both our families. I feel smothered in Baltimore, and you'd hate having to put up with my father on a daily basis. Jamie, he looked so young, I had a hard time thinking of him as a father."

Reminded once again of age, Jamie sighed heavily. "He's younger than I am."

"That's what makes it ridiculous," she agreed cheerfully. "Our children are going to be confused enough getting used to my temper and your moodiness without having a possessive grandfather around."

He wondered when "a child" had become "children," but he was satisfied not to challenge her. "We can leave New York whenever you want."

"Good. I don't suppose I'll need many dresses there since we'll be on horses most of the time, but I will need some more riding clothes. And what are we going to do about horses?"

Jamie smiled at her practicality. "I've already written the Maryland Club to ship our two horses to Cheyenne, and last month I sent your red outfit to a company in Chicago and ordered three more like it. They'll be ready by the time we get there. Do you feel up to camping on the trail for weeks at a time?''

''You just keep us from getting lost and let me worry about making camp.''

Cheyenne was a bitter disappointment to her. She'd expected a crude village, but it was already a boom town crowded with people; the hotel was civilized enough to have linen table cloths in the private section of the public dining room where she and Jamie were taken to after they'd registered. Within minutes of being seated, she met the four trail mates who would accompany them to the ranch. The oldest man, still clad partially in a United States cavalryman's uniform, was a graying, curly-haired Irishman named Colin Flynn. The younger three were his irrepressible half-Sioux sons with the Irish names of Brian, Lon, and Shannon. As playful as colts as they greeted the MacKenzies, the sons displayed not an iota of self-consciousness about their mixed heritage. Impudently handsome with their broad Irish smiles, they flirted throughout dinner, first with the sedate daughters in the company of a stern father and then with the dance hall girls who passed their table. Colin Flynn watched them with a fond tolerance; the Flynns were already an established and respected family. Just how much their lives were interwoven with the MacKenzies, Marsh would not discover for another month.

Colin and Jamie's friendship went back thirteen years to the time Ian MacKenzie had first pioneered horse breeding in Nebraska. In charge of the procurement of horses there for the United States Army fighting in a series of small Indian wars, the then Sergeant Flynn had soon become a fixture on MacKenzie land. Having been married to a Sioux woman for a dozen years, Colin Flynn moved between the two worlds with a charmed life, as much at home with Sioux, Cheyenne, and Omaha warriors as he was with his army friends. When the Civil War broke out, it was he who had been able to enlist the Indians' help in obtaining horses for the Union Army; and it was he who'd sponsored Ian MacKenzie and Robbie with the Indians. Long before the end of the war, when whole Sioux villages decamped for the less crowded spaces in Wyoming, Ian, Colin, Robbie, and the younger Flynns had moved right along with their Indian friends to continue the roundup of wild horses. Over the war years, Jamie had commuted between these territories and the eastern states, sharing in the MacKenzie immunity from Indian attack.

Only a stroke of bad luck had ended his brother's life at the hands of Confederate irregulars also on a horse procurement mission. In that ill-fated raid on MacKenzie herds, the Confederates had also killed Flynn's two Indian brothers-in-law. Of the people on the ranch at the time, only Flynn and a handful of his Indian crew had escaped unscathed. In the company of a contingent of Union soldiers, Jamie had missed the encounter by two days, arriving only in time to recapture most of the stolen horses. This trip with Marsh was his first return to the West after that earlier tragic time.

Now, as the days in Cheyenne stretched into weeks, Marsh grew impatient with the delayed departure, necessitated because the Flynns were waiting to deliver three hundred Flynn-MacKenzie horses to settlers due to arrive in Cheyenne before forming a wagon train for further travel westward. She'd long since grown weary of listening to her husband and Colin reminisce about shared war experiences and had begun to walk around the thriving town in the company of the young Flynns. One day, the grinning Shannon took her to the end of town where a militant looking woman was haranguing the mixed crowd in front of her. As soon as Marsh heard the strident battle cry of "Give women the right to vote in Wyoming, or we'll leave the territory," she remembered her own fierce desire for financial independence during the months she'd worked at the bank. When Shannon tried to drag her away, she shook her head impatiently and remained to listen. Worried now because he'd thought the show only entertaining, Shannon went to fetch Jamie.

Furious at the crude insults some of the men hurled at the

woman speaker, Marsh held her ground when one roughly dressed man tried to jostle her out of the way. Lifting her foot, she ground the heel of her sturdy walking shoe into his instep and jabbed her elbow accurately into his stomach. "If you don't shut up," she warned him, "I am going to scream out that you put your dirty hands on my person." When she released his foot, he limped to a position far removed from the red-haired woman with flashing green eyes. Jamie caught up with Marsh just as she'd reached the speaker and was offering her help in the campaign for the right to vote.

"Let's go," he said brusquely.

"Not until I find out what I can do to help," Marsh insisted.

Beaming at her new recruit, the speaker—Esther Hobart Morris—announced, "You can come with me for a month of campaigning in other towns."

"Out of the question," growled Jamie.

"Then you can donate money that will pay the expenses for another woman to take your wife's place," Esther Morris promptly told him. "A hundred dollars would be a very suitable donation."

Grudgingly, Jamie removed the leather envelope Marsh had given him in England, extracted the requested amount, and handed it to the smiling woman.

"Jamie and I can also write letters to other women in Wyoming telling them just what you said," Marsh volunteered.

"Good," Esther agreed, "I'll deliver a list of names to the hotel by evening." As Jamie dragged his wife away, his face flushed a deep red, the suffragette leader knew that she'd just met the most liberated woman in America.

Jamie was equally certain that his liberated woman was about to be locked in a closet. "Marsh, what got into you? My God, I thought you'd finally given up wanting to be free from me."

Marsh stopped in amazement and stared at her husband.

"Jamie, I'm not fighting for me. I'm fighting for women who aren't lucky enough to be married to you."

It was his turn to stop. Marsh was the one woman he knew who did not use flattery as a weapon. Smiling now, he relaxed the tight grip he'd retained on her arm and gently caressed the red splotches his gripping fingers had left. "Do you have any idea, my hotheaded freedom fighter, just how long it's going to take us to write those letters?"

She giggled. "You'll just have to help me write the first one. I'll copy it and send the same letter to everyone."

"I won't sign it, Marsh," he warned.

"Of course not. No man in his right mind would." After she told him what Esther Morris advised women with difficult husbands to do, Jamie wondered if he'd be safe in Wyoming if Marsh even signed the letter.

The next day, when the wagon train people finally arrived, Marsh met another breed of pioneer women—women who had left one life of hardship only to begin another in a wilderness they knew nothing about. She envied them the optimistic hope they had in their future homes.

In her own wagon train with four Flynns, six Indians, and her husband, Marsh joined those optimistic pioneer women and found her hoped-for home, too. Eight days out of Cheyenne, after hard driving across the Laramie Mountains and traveling through the Laramie basin, her party camped along the banks of the North Platte River. In the cold crisp air of late spring, she could see snow covered mountains to the east, north, and west, framing a broad green valley just ahead. She knew with a certainty that this wild, untrammeled country was the place where her restless spirit would find both peace and freedom.

Chapter
12

From the morning of their departure from Cheyenne, Marsh had felt her excitement growing. Clad for the first time in the new riding clothes Jamie had ordered for her, she chafed at the restriction of having to wear the long cover-up skirt, especially after she had been reunited with the horse she'd ridden in Maryland. But Jamie was adamant.

"Not until we're a long way out. These settlers are simple folk and might be shocked at the idea of a woman in trousers. Some might even have handy barrels of tar. I don't think the Flynns will mind your outfit providing they don't have to rescue you from some angry Mormons or Redemptionists." Thus, for four interminable hours, she remained sedately between the Indian driver and her husband on the hard wooden seat of a wagon. At the first stop, when Shannon brought up the two MacKenzie horses and stood politely by, wondering how she planned to ride in a man's saddle encumbered by a long skirt, Marsh refused to take refuge for a modest disrobing. Whipping off the offending skirt, she tossed it unceremoniously into the rear of the wagon. Before Shannon could help her mount, she was astride her horse. Amused by the admiration on the boy's face, Jamie mounted his horse and whispered, "Show-off" to her as he reached over and adjusted her bridle.

Just how much time she wasted that day in nonsense riding, Jamie never scolded her about; but she seldom maintained the pace of easy travel. As soon as the other two young Flynns, Lon and Brian, had taken measure of her riding ability, they found frequent excuses to invite her to race. Twice that day she left them far behind, while only once did two of them manage to stay abreast of her. All four of the racers needed to spend extra hours tending their overworked horses in camp that first night. Only once on that trip did Marsh race within sight of Indians other than the six with the wagon train, but that occasion almost ended disastrously.

During one early morning race near the end of their trip, this time against all three Flynns, she was far in the lead when her path was suddenly blocked by a band of befeathered Indians. Instantly, they surrounded her as her horse shied, and she jerked with horror as their brown hands reached for her. She almost prayed aloud that the approaching thunder of horses' hooves were the Flynns and not more Indians. They were Shannon's, and her terror turned to indignation when she heard him laughing with her captors. "Indian men," she thought sourly, "are as intolerant as white ones when it comes to women."

Out of necessity she dismounted, since the Indians had turned their curiosity away from her and toward her horse. Without a by-your-leave, they unsaddled the powerful gelding and tossed its smooth leather saddle carelessly aside. For the next half hour, until the main part of the wagon train arrived, four of the braves took turns riding her horse and talking to the Flynns about it. Familiar with only the smaller wild horses of the West, the Indians seemed fascinated with the larger, taller MacKenzie breed. Ignoring her as any good Indian man would, the warriors addressed all their questions to the Flynns, who could only guess about the horse's lineage. She remained ignominiously on the sidelines, watching them inspect her horse and race it from a standing start, using only the blanket as their anchor. She had never seen their style of riding before, a style in which the rider used only his knees and hands to guide the animal. She had also never seen any horse respond to strange men so readily before, especially men who smelled as oddly as these did.

Her isolation ended abruptly when two of the braves turned their attention back to her, their hands stroking her unbound hair as boldly as they had her horse. Instantly, the Flynns were by her side, explaining with the word "MacKenzie" and pointing to the gold band on her finger. One of the Indians nodded in understanding, but the other continued his perusal of her costume and hair. Twice, she willed herself not to flinch as his hands poked her booted legs, but she had to tolerate his rude curiosity because the Flynns only laughed good-naturedly. By the time Jamie and Colin arrived, driving one wagon at top speed in concern for their missing daredevils, Marsh was resigned to the prospect of an angry husband. Instead, he ignored her completely and addressed himself to her captors by speaking a few of their own words. In turn, the Indians approved of his cavalier treatment of a wayward wife. She was understandably irritated when Shannon informed her that she'd have to help prepare dinner, not just for their own party, but for the twenty braves as well. As Lon and Brian pulled the carcass of the antelope they'd shot and dressed the day before out of the wagon, she shuddered. After they'd placed it on a flat rock, Brian handed her a knife and told her to cut it into chunks while he and his brothers built the fire and hung a huge iron pot filled with water over the flame. An hour later, she was still hacking away at the carcass, her hands bloodied and her arms exhausted from the unaccustomed work. Not once did any of the Flynns offer to help her, although Shannon hovered around sympathetically and explained that the Indians would laugh at Jamie if his wife did not do the squaw work. Wearily, she finished the messy butchery and added the potatoes and onions which Shannon handed her.

When one of the braves wandered over and dipped his fingers into the broth and sucked noisily only to spit it out in disgust, Marsh wanted to hit the man with the hot ladle. Shannon had to restrain her with a pleading smile as the Indian retrieved a handful of something out of a pouch tied to the neck of his pony and threw it into the pot.

"It's just seasoning herbs," Shannon whispered tersely, "they don't taste too bad. I'm afraid that you're going to have to bake the bread now, too. The Indians have been watching you, and they don't permit their squaws to show anger. My brothers have the loaves ready to put in the coals." Not until her hands were reddened from the steaming pot and burned in a dozen places by the hot coals was dinner pronounced ready for consumption. And then it was no formal invitation to dine. The Indians simply converged around the pot with their brown clay bowls ready, grabbed the ladle, and helped themselves to the stew, small groups of them appropriating whole loaves of bread without asking her permission, and retiring to their own campfires to eat with noisy hunger. Callously excluded from joining any group, since Jamie and the Flynns filled their own bowls and rejoined the Indians without speaking to her, Marsh fled from the campsite and headed for the river to cool her burned fingers and flaming temper. Shannon found her there a half hour later and mutely handed her a bowl of the food it had taken her three hours to prepare.

"It's all right for you to eat now," he said. Had he not been smiling with his impudent Irish charm, the hot food might have landed in his face. But, smiling back, she ate her dinner and found the Indian seasonings strange but not unpalatable. Jamie, however, she vowed inwardly, was another matter. He'd pay for treating her like a squaw throughout the long afternoon. Only a quiet walk along the river bank after Shannon had left her revived her growing infatuation with this new land. Indians, she reasoned, would just have to get used to her; this was the one and only time they would ever treat her with masculine contempt.

Long before the campfires were extinguished, she retired to the tent erected each night for her and Jamie's privacy. Exhausted from the strenuous activities of the day, she didn't stir when her errant husband climbed into the bedroll with her. Having shared several jugs of frontier brew with the noble savages, he was in no shape for conversation either. In the morning, when she awakened, the Indians were gone and the camp returned to normal with the young Flynns busily preparing breakfast. Jamie and Colin, however, were nursing heavy heads while her own hands were swollen and raw. It was a subdued group of travelers who continued the trek that day; and it was a scowling Jamie who sat next to his wife on the wagon seat. Correctly assessing the source of her husband's glower, Marsh smiled with malicious satisfaction each time the wagon hit a rut and Jamie groaned. However, even after his head cleared enough for comfort, Jamie continued to frown at her.

"I hope you like this country," he complained peevishly, "your insane demonstration on that horse yesterday cost me a hundred colts, fifty mares, and one of my best stallions. And it cost Lon a long trip back to Cheyenne to telegraph Harding not to saddle break or shoe those colts."

Marsh was not distracted by his grumbling; she knew that he was too canny a Scot to be cheated by anyone, much less by a band of half drunk Indians. "How much Indian land, Jamie MacKenzie, did you buy with those horses?"

Sheepishly, he grinned at her. "Six thousand acres adjoining the Flynn's and Robbie's. But what the devil we're going to do with them is beyond me."

"We're going to build our home and raise our children and whatever else we decide on."

He sighed. "The one winter I was forced to stay here, I almost froze to death. I'll make a deal with you, Marsh. I'll live here with you during the good months, if you'll go back to the Maryland farm with me every winter.''

Her smile was blinding, so was the promise of her kiss. "You try going anyplace without me, and those Indian warriors will seem like tabby cats compared to your red-haired wife," she murmured. His laughter boomed out, almost arousing the Flynns who were already dozing in their bedrolls.

"My red-haired wife," he whispered, "had better not pretend to be asleep when I come to bed tonight."

"Maybe," she whispered back, "Wyoming winters won't seem so hard if the nights are long enough."

Certainly there was little of frontier hardship suggested in the reception they received the next day as they drove into the orderly compound which comprised the MacKenzie-Flynn headquarters. In front of the two stone houses separated by a few hundred feet of tilled vegetable gardens, a man and two women waited. Had Marsh had any lingering doubts about the wisdom of the decision to live here, they would have been dissipated by the trio of human beings who greeted them. She watched as Colin Flynn dismounted and wrapped his arms around the dark-haired woman as if she were a young bride instead of a wife of twenty-four years. Turning her attention to the pair who greeted her and Jamie, Marsh performed a mental somersault. The man must be Robbie; but, except for his blue eyes and proud MacKenzie nose, he resembled his father very little. Sandy-haired and ruddy-skinned, he was not as handsome as his father or Stuart; however, his wide grin and friendly eyes bespoke a sunnier disposition, and his words of welcome, a lively sense of humor.

"In his letter, Marsh, my father described you as needing his protection when he married you. That, my beautiful young stepmother, was the unvarnished truth. I'll bet you do—every time he introduces you to another man." Turning from Marsh, Robbie grinned down at the smiling young woman next to him, a girl who looked very like her father,

Colin Flynn. "I would like you to meet my wife Onawa, which means alert watcher in Sioux. She's the reason my father trusts me enough to bring you here. Besides, I wouldn't risk losing her; it took me a whole two years to get her to marry me as it was."

With his arm comfortably around her, Onawa responded to her husband's jibe in kind. "Hello, Marsh, you mustn't mind Robbie's boastful braying. He often confuses his animal sign. He believes he's a timber wolf when actually he's a stubborn donkey." Onawa reached her hand out to Jamie. "Hello, father-in-law, I'm glad you finally decided to visit. I was afraid that you might resent being related to a Sioux Indian."

"Onawa," Jamie assured her warmly, "you could wear war paint and I still approve of you as Rob's wife. The reason I didn't come to your wedding eighteen months ago was the little matter of a major upheaval in my own life—a red-headed one. Rob, how did those merino sheep I shipped you work out?"

"Fine. They survived the winter and lambed on schedule with only a slight loss. By the time the young rams mature enough for sale to Montana ranchers, we'll be making money on them. Ona, why don't you get Marsh settled in the house while Jamie and I supervise storing the supplies he brought in?" As the two new husbands walked off together, Onawa grinned at Marsh in a friendly conspiracy.

"The secret to handling MacKenzie men is to let them believe they're the pursuers. I met Robbie when I was eight years old and he was seventeen. I decided that day that I was going to marry him. I would have long ago, but my father insisted that I had to get an education first, since Robbie had gone to college. Those two years I kept him 'dangling,' I was away at school back east and very afraid that he would find someone else. So I wrote him a letter every week telling him about all the parties I attended."

"Did you?"

"No, that girls' school was a prison and the only men I saw during those years were two ridiculous teachers."

Marsh smiled knowingly. "But Robbie believed the worst, anyway. He's not as different from his father as I thought."

"He met me at the train in Chicago, dragged me to a minister's house and married me that same day. Marsh, how did you get along with my wild Indian brothers?"

"They didn't seem very wild to me, and they didn't look very Indian either, not compared to the ones we met on the trail. And you don't look Indian at all."

"No, I turned out to look as Irish as a sack of potatoes, so my mother gave me an Indian name. Because my brothers had the good sense to look more Indian, she allowed my father to name them after his sainted Irish ancestors. Wait until you meet my oldest brother Devin. He lives part of the time with my mother's people, and he's the most civilized brother of the lot." Onawa turned toward the woman now walking toward them. The pride in her voice was unmistakable. "Marsh, this is my mother, Winona."

Marsh turned to meet the steady brown eyes which were so like Carina's, she felt an instant sense of relationship with this Indian woman whose words of greeting sounded prophetic. "You belong here. Like the mountain eagle, your spirit will soar."

Long after a boisterous family dinner, when Marsh and Jamie were alone in the small guest room, he told her about Winona. "She always had the gift of insight. Both her people and ours respect her for it, but I didn't really believe in it for years."

"Do you now?"

"Ever since our first night in England." Marsh blushed a little as she remembered her angry words that night and the passionate sweetness of their reunion. Holding his wife now, Jamie told her of Winona's words to him. "During a roundup she told me that I'd be broken to the halter by a filly like the one she was pointing to. It was the color of your hair."

"Are you, Jamie?"

"Broken to the halter? You know I am, even though my filly has turned out to be a racehorse."

"I think I'm going to have to become a workhorse if we're to get our home built by fall."

He groaned. "You would pick a place where the builders still live in wigwams."

While native Sioux Indians might still live in buffalo-hide tepees, the workers on the ranch as well as the owners lived in stone houses or in compartments in the two huge, stone barns. Since the treeless plains of the great valley were dotted with outcroppings of brown-gray granite, stone had been the most available building material for the pioneering Flynns and MacKenzies. Thus, there was no delay in constructing still another home. Under the foremanship of an army corporal who had followed his old sergeant into retirement, Indian stone masons were at work on the foundation within a week. By August, the stone shell with its four fireplaces was complete, lacking only windows and a roof to be winter-proof. From the fir trees growing in the remote, mountainous reaches of the ranches, the massive ceiling beams were hand hewn and dragged by sleds to the site, while wagon trains carted the milled lumber, sheets of glass, and heavy shake shingles from Cheyenne. Such was Jamie's fear of cold weather that one of the wagons carried not only a large kitchen stove, but four smaller potbellied ones as well.

"Every room," he declared, "is going to be warm, just in case we're stuck here some winter." The more experienced residents just smiled—long underwear and sheepskin garments sufficed to keep them active and healthy even during sub-zero blizzards.

During the months of construction, Jamie concentrated his efforts on ranch management, freeing Rob and the Flynns for the necessary inspection trips to the outlying areas of their domain. Left to her own devices to find occupation, Marsh enlisted the aid of Onawa in writing the suffragette letter and found a willing and able confederate. The result stopped a few words short of being a fiery ultimatum to men. That two young women whose husbands were both indulgent and loving could write such an incendiary letter was easily explained by Onawa: "We're the only ones who don't have to take our own advice." When copies of the letter were delivered to the hundred designated homes, the names of Marsh and Ona MacKenzie became household words, although few of the words uttered by husbands, brothers, or fathers could ever have been spoken aloud in church. Two summers later, just before the first territorial legislature met and granted women the right to vote, the MacKenzie letter was published in most of the frontier newspapers in Wyoming, along with one of Esther Hobart Morris's speeches.

By the time the roof of the new home was completed and the windows glazed, Jamie called a halt to construction and told Marsh to pack for the trip back to Cheyenne. Already, in late October, they were risking the grim prospect of being caught on the trail by early winter snows. Sadly, Marsh complied with her husband's insistence and bid farewell to the people who had become her family.

On the last night at Robbie's home, while Jamie visited with his son, Winona and Marsh walked over to the new home, now glinting ruddy-brown in the brilliant red sunset. In her usual abrupt manner, Winona voiced her farewell. "You will be back in spring, Marsh MacKenzie, to bear your son."

Marsh smiled a little sadly and shook her head. Her one disappointment in this new life had been her failure to conceive. The older woman smiled and nodded. "There will be time enough before you return." Marsh was not to understand these words for six months.

Accompanied only by Lon and two trail Indians, Marsh and Jamie left the next morning, already bundled up in their sheepskin jackets. In eight days of hard riding they reached Cheyenne, where Lon lingered only long enough to promise that he and two brothers would be in Maryland by April to help with the horses being delivered to the Indians. Good-naturedly, Lon added that his parents had both insisted on the arrangement. Jamie protested that he could manage until Cheyenne, but Lon smilingly shook his head. "My mother wants us to see the nation's capital."

The first winter storm hit the area when the train from Cheyenne was en route to Chicago. For six stormy days, Marsh and Jamie huddled in the unheated car still dressed in their sheepskins and riding clothes, Marsh's breeches hidden beneath a long leather skirt. With the other passengers, they joined the exhausted railroad crew in shoveling snow from the tracks so that the train could continue at a snail's pace to Chicago. Chilled to the point of numbness, they took the first available train to New York still clad in their western garb. Once they reached their flat, warmed and readied for them through the magic of the telegraph, they remained indoors for a week as they thawed out and bathed repeatedly in warm, scented water. Suffering from a heavy cold, Jamie was the last to recover. At Marsh's stern command, he remained at home for another two weeks while she made the rounds of the MacKenzie buildings with the resident manager and checked the records for accuracy. Only when Jamie was completely recovered did they attempt anything so strenuous as lovemaking. By the time she consented, Jamie was fretful and glowering at her on a daily basis; but once begun, the pursuit quickly regained its power to dominate their thoughts. Here in the warm rooms, visited only by the maid who accomplished her work in a record three hours each afternoon on cold days, the couple luxuriated in a privacy they'd not enjoyed for months. And, sometime during their last weeks in New York, Marsh conceived. Although neither partner was aware of the exact moment, their love for each other had deepened their moments of passion. Once again, Jamie treated her as he had during their early months together in Baltimore, wanting her no farther away than an arm's length in public and much closer in private.

During their cruise to Baltimore aboard a coastal steamer, they rarely left their cabin, where they spent hours relaxing in the luxurious fur-lined robes Jamie had bought them in New York. Later, Marsh was to remember only one serious conversation in the week-long voyage, and that one ended in happy nonsense. Having become resigned to the probability of a childless marriage, Jamie was worried about Marsh's eventual disappointment.

"Would you like to adopt a child?" he asked.

"No," she answered promptly. "I think our own will be much more interesting. Especially the boys," she added with a grin, "with you and my father to choose from, they'll be hellions."

Gazing over at her as she sat cross-legged on the bed, looking more like an impish adolescent than a grown woman, he was struck anew by her vibrant appeal. "I would like a portrait of you just as you are now," he smiled.

Giggling, she looked down at her naked legs and half exposed breasts. "We'd have to hang it in a closet. Not even our Indian friends like nature quite this raw."

"I'd be its only viewer," he promised as he walked over to reach out and fondle one of her tempting breasts. With an honesty he found endearing, she responded without any pretense of modesty or show of reluctance as she invited him to join her on the rumpled bed.

"It's been a bonnie time, lass."

"Wyoming?"

"New York and right here." He smiled and put his arms around her. Marsh smiled back and thought about Winona's promise.

As the steamer was being maneuvered toward the Baltimore docks, they lingered in their stateroom, reluctant to leave the privacy and face the problems of the city they'd left twenty months earlier. Not until the ship's motors stopped did they pick up their remaining pieces of hand luggage and step out on deck. Both of them groaned when they saw the welcoming committee waiting for them. Craig was waving at them, flanked by all the Covingtons except Phyllis. Mrs. Tucker, Mrs. Harding, and the Morrisons stood farther back. Within moments, everyone climbed into waiting carriages which were driven with undue speed, not to the MacKenzie home, but to the larger Covington one. Annoyed by the autocratic treatment, Jamie tried to question his son; but Craig only grinned, looking inanely like a schoolboy whose prank had succeeded. More atuned to youthful humor, Marsh guessed the reason.

She was right. As soon as everyone was seated in the fire-warmed parlor, even the protesting Mrs. Tucker, a proud Phyllis deposited a well-wrapped bundle into Jamie's lap—a baby girl all of six weeks old. "It's your first grandchild, Jamie," Phyllis announced proudly.

To his credit, Jamie bore the surprise well, not once signaling his dismay to his wife; but he held the infant gingerly until he could hand the little girl back to her mother. The christening had been delayed, Phyllis explained, until Jamie and Marsh arrived; it would be held in two weeks with everyone of importance in Baltimore invited. When Jamie started to protest that he and Marsh were due at the farm, Marsh squeezed his arm gently and shook her head. She knew how proud Phyllis was of this child.

Catching up on unwelcome news is always a dull prospect. For what seemed like hours too many, the guests were regaled with accounts of the birth—no problems; of the bank—few problems; of the Covington import business—more progress than problems; and of the deserted apartment—nothing but problems. "There is no room for the baby there," Phyllis complained with an appealing smile at Jamie. "Craig and I will have to find a larger home. We were wondering what your plans were concerning your house here in Baltimore?"

Jamie was reasonably polite as he put down his teacup, reached for his wife's hand, and rose. "Right now our plans are to go there and relax," he smiled. Never had five guests been so efficient in a departure. Within a half hour, Jamie was pouring glasses of brandy for the Morrisons and Mrs. Harding in the library of his own home while Marsh helped Mrs. Tucker with a refreshment tray in the kitchen.

"Where's Alice Nelson?" Marsh asked abruptly.

"Last I heard she went to New York right after Christmas."

Marsh sucked in her breath sharply. Alice had been in New York at the same time she and Jamie were.

"That where you and your husband was, Marsh? I'd say you was lucky to get here in one piece then. You're not planning to stay in Baltimore, are you?"

"We have to now, at least for a while."

"For the christening, you mean? That one's sure no shrinking violet—her asking for this house, cool as you please. You and Mr. MacKenzie going to give it to her?"

Marsh shrugged. "It's up to him. We won't be using it any more, not as long as Alice lives here."

Frowning thoughtfully, Marsh carried the tray of sweet biscuits and cheese into the library in time to hear Jamie conclude, "My wife's colors, dark red and marsh green." At her blank look, he explained, "Those are the MacKenzie racing colors."

"Why the rush, Jamie? I thought we were still a year away from actually racing."

"Apparently not. Young Harding has entered your mare's first colt at the Maryland Sweeps this year."

"Marsh Wind? He can't possibly be ready yet."

It was Greg Morrison who reassured her. "He's tearing up the track surface, raring to begin. I've timed him ten runs and each one has been faster than the last. I'm afraid that in my enthusiasm, I butted in, Jamie, and sponsored him at the club. That's where the race will be this year. We've built an official track there and grandstands. I'm glad your son chose two weekends from now because the race is scheduled on the third. Harding and I have worked hard keeping all information about Marsh Wind a complete secret, that way all the heavy betting is on the two New York favorites. We should be able to clean up. Right now, you two have to stay put in Baltimore. Tom Harding doesn't want Marsh getting any ideas about racing Marsh Wind herself. He sent for one of his pint-sized jockey friends from England who's been training our entry for a month.''

More amused than convinced by this earnest harangue, Jamie asked idly, ''How do you rate his chances?''

He was both surprised and impressed by Morrison's answer. ''Your horse will take any two-year-old in the country. If he continues to develop as he's been doing, in another year he'll be an established champion. My God, Jamie, your stables will have the two best racing studs in America if Marsh Wind produces like I think he will.''

Jamie's amusement had vanished, replaced by the caution of his Scotch ancestry. ''Greg, you and I have knocked heads over too many horse trades in the past for me to accept all your work with my horse as just a friendly gesture. What's your stake in all this?''

Just as canny in his own Yankee way, Morrison hedged. ''For one thing, I'm in on the ground floor for the betting.''

''And the other thing?''

''I want first chance to buy the second stallion colt your wife's mare and Rake-Star produce. I know Marsh won't part with the one Marsh Song foaled three months ago.''

''You'll buy at the going price?''

''You bet I will. I think those combined bloodlines will start a revolution in American racing.''

''Greg, I'd agree if the mare were not my wife's. And right now we have a more urgent problem. Mrs. Harding, did your husband get my telegram about the horses I have to deliver to some Indians?''

''They're all ready to travel. But Mr. Harding wants you to hire more grooms. The ones on the farm are already overworked.''

Remembering the Flynns, Marsh laughed. ''Wait until you

see the ones we've hired." Turning back to the Morrisons, she was more serious. "Greg, the colt will be yours and Arlene's if you'll go on supervising Marsh Wind's racing for the next year. Jamie and I will be busy in Wyoming."

Shocked, Arlene protested. "You'll miss the racing season."

"We have a project there that'll keep us busy." Marsh's fingers had been crossed for the past three weeks, but she had another three to go before she could tell Jamie. This thought was still uppermost in her mind when Jamie's hand on her arm pulled her back to the present, in time to bid her departing guests good-bye and to promise to meet them at the Maryland Horsemen's Club for the race.

"Keep your fingers crossed for good luck," Arlene called out, and Marsh held up both hands with the fingers already crossed for even better luck.

During the next three frantic weeks, Marsh and Jamie quietly concentrated on a private withdrawal from their Baltimore life. Conferring only with Mrs. Tucker, Marsh supervised the packing and railroad shipping of barrels of dishes, silverware, blankets, linens, and cases of imported brandy to Cheyenne, and most of their clothing to the farm. Jamie unobtrusively conferred with Myles Windom and Bruce Mac Lachlan and told Craig that he and Phyllis could move into the house. Had these activities been the only demands on their time, they might have enjoyed their last weeks there. Unfortunately, Baltimore society now considered horse racing the king of sports and the MacKenzies their hometown celebrities. Of the dozens of last minute invitations sent them, Jamie consented to attend only the two most prestigious balls and insisted that Marsh wear her ivory silk dress and leather cape to each. At both events, they were treated as the guests of honor. The *Baltimore Herald* accounts of these parties mentioned the MacKenzie's connection with Lord and Lady Raikes and commented on their ownership of Rake-Star. Jamie's reception of the articles was cynical. "I'm glad we didn't buy that damned horse from Queen Victoria. We'd never get away from here if we had.''

Even the christening, which should have been routinely dull, put Marsh and Jamie on unsolicited display. The infant girl was named Pamela, and Marsh was named godmother, so both she and Jamie were forced to remain standing at the front of the church during the pretentious ceremony and again in the reception line for the elegant dinner party. On that day, and the week which followed when Phyllis and Craig moved into the MacKenzie home, Marsh realized that Phyllis was genuinely fond of her in-laws.

''The four of us,'' she said with genuine enthusiasm, ''will have a wonderful time together.'' Marsh felt guilty about not telling Craig and Phyllis that she and Jamie were moving out permanently.

However, three days before the race, that permanent move was more strongly indicated than ever. During a quiet lull in the busy transitions of moving, the doorbell sounded and a prune-faced Mrs. Tucker escorted a smiling Alice Nelson into the drawing room. Making no pretense at civility, Marsh left Phyllis and the baby to entertain the uninvited guest. She found Jamie in the library, sorting books.

''Your stepdaughter is in the other room disguised as Aunt Alice,'' she exclaimed and finished his glass of usquebaugh without taking a breath.

Calmly, he poured himself another drink and walked across the room to lock the door. ''Then you're staying with me until she leaves. I wonder where the hell she's been?'' Marsh almost answered, Looking for me, but she refrained; in another two months she and Jamie would be safe in the unreachable wilds of Wyoming. At dinner that night, Phyllis told them that Alice had been staying with the Randalls since her return from New York.

''I hope she doesn't intend to drop by here every day. The way she babbled about family unity today, you'd think we were all bosom friends. Do you suppose she has finally come to her senses? She certainly raved enough about the baby, and she seemed delighted when I told her that we'd all be living here together.''

Jamie's dry comment was all that kept Marsh's temper from exploding. "I wouldn't let her take care of the baby, if I were you, Phyllis. Alice tends to be very possessive.''

Craig was very thoughtful as he seconded his father. "Lord no. She took care of me when I was little, and I hated her until I was grown up.''

For the next two days, Jamie kept Marsh by his side, locking both of them in the library during each of Alice's visits. On race day he was lighthearted with relief as he and Marsh boarded the big carriage which was loaded with the last of their boxes and luggage. In a spirit of jubilation, Jamie wore his MacKenzie tartan coat with the red and white plaid on the green background; and Marsh wore her dark red velvet suit with the fitted jacket and full skirt, accented by a soft green silk underblouse. During the three-hour ride, she clutched the largest reticule she owned tightly in her hands. Along with a few small items, it held a slip of official bank paper with Craig MacKenzie's signature at the bottom. Aware of her husband's cautious attitude about money, Marsh had withdrawn a thousand dollars from her own account and asked Craig to bet it on Marsh Wind to win. At first, he had sounded as disapproving as his father, but Marsh's confidence had finally convinced him to admit that he might even wager a dollar or two himself.

During that ride, Marsh was also clutching tight to another special secret, now a six-week certainty. The thought caused her to grip Jamie's arm more tightly. He looked down at her excited face and frowned.

"Marsh," he warned, "I've worked with horses most of my life, and the more I know about them the less I trust them. Don't get your hopes up too high. Your horse may look good to Morrison, but it's still an untried racer.'' His patting hand was almost fatherly.

As owners of an entry, they were allowed inside the paddock area before the two-year-olds' race, mercifully scheduled earlier than the main event of the older, more experienced horses. There, in a circus-like atmosphere, twelve nervous horses pawed the ground while an equal number of small men in gaudily colored costumes fussed with saddles and bridles. Before she and Jamie could reach Marsh Wind, the smallest of these men intercepted them, jumping up and down excitedly like a green grasshopper with a red stripe over its chest.

"Mum," the little man panted, "what in bloody 'ell are you doing 'ere? If me 'orse was to see you, 'e'd forget 'is training and think this was some bloody picnic hinstead of a race. Pardon, mum, me name's 'iggens. I'm the jock Mr. 'arding sent for."

Jamie cleared his throat. "I take it you'd rather my wife stayed away until the race."

"That's hit, sir. Mr. 'arding says she's got a way with 'orses. But this one's got to run me own way today." Nervously, he tapped his crop against his leg.

Marsh wanted to tell Mr. Higgins not to use that bloody whip on her horse, but the club steward gave the mount-up order before she could utter the words. She and Jamie had to run toward the new grandstand if they were to see the race. Breathless and windblown, they reached their seats beside Craig and Phyllis just as the horses lined up. She had no trouble spotting Marsh Wind; like Marsh Song, the young horse was dark in color and had the same aquiline nose.

In later years, Marsh would describe the race in detail, but her recitation would be all hearsay since her eyes were tightly closed the whole time. The first indication that the race was over was Jamie's rueful exclamation: "Morrison was right. Our horse can run." Even more gloomily he added, "I wish I had listened to you, Marsh. I might have risked a small wager."

The second indication was a shriek of shock from Craig as

he leaped to his feet and galloped almost at a one-horse speed down to the gentlemen's compound where money was changing hands at a rate unheard of in civilized banking circles. By the dazed excitement on his face, Marsh was certain that Craig's "dollar or two wager" equalled her own. When the call went out for the owners of Marsh Wind to report to the winner's circle, Marsh shook her head and sat immobile in her seat with a stunned look on her face; Jamie was forced to go alone. Had he realized that his wife's stunned look was due to a rapid calculation of a six thousand dollar profit, he might have lost some of his own stoic composure. Craig was the first to return, bearing himself now more like the dignified banker he was becoming. With the self-important calm of one of his own tellers, he counted out Marsh's seven thousand dollars and handed it to her, ignoring his own wife's eyes, which tended to grow round as saucers whenever she was impressed.

Folding the money neatly into her reticule, Marsh murmured modestly, "I had Craig place a small wager for me."

"I wouldn't have been able to watch the race, either," Phyllis murmured back.

Sitting between the two women, Craig squeezed his stepmother's hand. "I had my eyes closed, too," he whispered out of the side of his mouth, winked at her, and patted his coat pocket. He did not, Marsh noted, mention the windfall to his wife. The three were sitting quietly when Jamie returned to escort them to the clubhouse for a celebration drink. However, Jamie did not look in the mood for a celebration; his scowl was at its darkest.

"Morrison made a bloody fortune on our horse," he growled.

"How much?" Marsh asked.

"He bet a thousand so he made a potful."

"So did we," Marsh admitted smugly, and almost fell when Jamie stopped short and yanked her backward.

"We did what?"

"Bet a thousand."

He stared at her. "Where did *we* get the thousand?"

"From Craig at the bank out of the money you replaced in my account there."

"And what do *we* intend to do with our winnings?"

"We might buy cattle for Wyoming," she said pleasantly, and Jamie resumed walking, looking much more relaxed without his intimidating frown. "Or," she continued sweetly, "we might do something foolish like investing it in our child's future." Silently, she counted his steps—one, two, three, four—and braced herself. This time he'd lost his power of speech as well as locomotion as he stared at her. She just nodded and grinned. When he finally regained his voice, it was more than a little raspy.

"You're sure?"

"Every morning, from seven to nine, I'm damned sure."

"Have you seen a doctor?"

"No, I don't want anyone to know until we get to Wyoming."

"Marsh, we can't go there now. It's too far from a doctor."

"Of course we can go. Winona's there."

"She's just an Indian."

"She's a wonderful Indian."

"I won't risk you, Marsh, not without a doctor."

"All right then, we'll tell Damon, and he and Carina can come there when it's time. But we won't tell anyone else here."

Somehow, they resumed walking, and except for a dazed look, Jamie seemed perfectly normal. However, for the next two hours as the club members gathered around them in the general crush of the crowded room, his answers lacked their usual, accurate decisiveness. Twice, Marsh changed his "no's" to "yes's" and twice the reverse. The next time, she vowed, she had to tell him about an impending child, she'd make sure he was in bed where he could faint quietly out of the public eye. When he started to bid Craig and Phyllis a distracted good-bye, Marsh took over.

"Jamie and I won't be home for a long time. We're going to deliver some horses to Robbie and then probably travel even farther west. The train is supposed to go all the way to California this year."

Jamie apologized to them and explained that he was still shocked about the money Marsh had bet. After that explanation, he managed a warm farewell to his youngest son and Phyllis, reminding them to take good care of his grandchild. Once they were gone, though, he commented on the fact that Craig had acted very oddly.

"He should," Marsh told him, "he hasn't told Phyllis yet about the money he won."

"Craig's a fool. He knows that any banker who is caught gambling can have his bank cleaned out by depositors the next day."

"I imagine he was smart enough to say that he was placing both bets for me." A few minutes later, her surmise was affirmed by Arlene Morrison, who gushed up to them, still charming in spite of several celebration drinks too many.

"Shame on you, Jamie, for not having any faith in your wife's horse. If it weren't for Marsh's two thousand dollar bet, you'd have lost out today." The names of big winners are always public domain in any private club.

"Not entirely," he smiled. "I collected the winner's purse, and I intend to let my reckless wife wonder about the amount. Arlene, we'll see you next week at the farm. Right now, Marsh and I still have three hours of traveling to do before we reach our hotel." Guiding his wife past the crowds still milling around the racetrack, he signalled their alert driver and bundled his silent wife inside before the carriage started to move. Jamie had been frowning heavily ever since his faithful, sober driver of fifteen years had greeted Marsh joyously.

"Bet my whole packet like you said, Mrs. MacKenzie, and cleaned up a bundle. So did the others."

Jamie looked steadily at his errant wife. "Just how many people did you tout for, Marsh?"

"The staff and maybe a few of their friends. I thought it'd be a nice farewell gesture."

"I'm beginning to believe more and more in Wyoming. At least there you won't be able to corrupt the population."

As the next two hectic weeks destroyed the remnants of his patience, Jamie became convinced that Wyoming, even with the certainty of an icy winter, was the only place they would find any peace and quiet. The farm was almost as crowded as the racetrack and even busier than Baltimore had been. Damon and Carina were delivering the second foals of some of the highly bred English mares which could no longer give birth alone. The breeding pens held three guest mares awaiting the supervised services of Rake-Star, and every groom on the place was employed in showing the racing colts marked for sale. Feeling as unnecessary as an overweight jockey, Jamie ordered his driver to take Marsh and him to a hotel in Washington, D.C. where the confusion was more organized.

Unlike the war years, when herds of MacKenzie horses had been welcome on capital streets, new laws now required that they be drayed in expensive wagons. Furthermore, the railroads had added a dozen new fees to the cost of transporting horses. After paying for the complicated arrangements, Jamie had a small pile of bills of lading, paid receipts, and railway tickets to Cheyenne for himself, Marsh, three Flynns and two Indians. On the drive back to the farm, he remarked caustically, "I shipped four thousand head during the war with less trouble than this one hundred and fifty. And the army paid the expenses."

For two more days Jamie was busy. Using the office near the barn as headquarters, he was closeted with Bruce Mac Lachlan for three hours before the lawyer returned to Baltimore. The next day he spent in the company of Stuart, who returned to Virginia without asking to see Marsh, and later on he talked to Damon and Carina, who left the office with smiles on their faces. Having agreed to remain in the house until Jamie was finished, Marsh was delighted when he announced that they would go riding the next day. "Providing," he warned her, "you keep your mare at a slow walk; otherwise I'll warm your backside as I should have done years ago."

"You wouldn't dare," she laughed. "Since there are two of us now, you might not be able to. Jamie, let's visit the old mares and stallions in the rear pastures."

"Why in the world would you want to?"

"They were once your best breeders and no one cares about them now."

"One of those old stallions out there is one of the original Highland Thoroughbreds that Ian brought to America. But it'll take us a couple of days to locate him. Let's take a picnic lunch; while I check fences, you can feed lumps of sugar to old Ben Sim."

The next two days, they picnicked under a picturesque oak tree where Jamie promptly fell asleep and Marsh walked over to pet two venerable stallions which had not lost their taste for sweets. On the third day, they spotted the break in the fence near the tree at the same time.

"Your sugar lumps," her husband scolded her with a smile. "Those ancient stallions weren't used to a pretty girl bringing them treats, and they broke the fence to get more. They won't wander far. Right after lunch we'll circle around until we find them."

But Jamie was no more ready for any activity after lunch this day than he had been on the earlier two. Anchoring his wife with his head on her lap, he closed his eyes.

"Jamie, what are we going to do about furniture in Wyoming?"

He opened one eye. "I was wondering when you'd get around to worrying about a trifle like that. I have no intention of sleeping on a hard floor, so while you were gadding about New York by yourself and I was deserted at home with a cold, I wrote to a Chicago firm and ordered some shipped to the ranch.''

"But I didn't get to choose it," she complained.

"If I can live in a house built by Indians, you can sleep in a bed built by the Humbert brothers.''

"Did you remember to order a baby bed?''

"Since I knew nothing about it then, if it even existed, our child will just have to sleep papoose-style on her mother's back.''

"Or between us in our bed," she teased.

"I won't allow our daughter that broad an education, you minx.''

"Do you really want a daughter?''

"One just like her mother.''

"Wait until the little redhead defies you.''

"Well now, except for horse racing, gambling and inciting Wyoming women to riot, I've tamed you. Besides, I'll love our daughter as I wish you'd been loved.''

"Oh, Jamie, you really want this child!''

"Yes, lass, I do. And I plan to stay home and raise this one.''

"That'll be wonderful. That way I can have six in a row.''

He laughed. "Not if I can get a hold of some of Carina's powder, you won't. Come on, wife, I can see that you're not going to let me sleep today. Let's go round up those gallivanting old studs and pasture them.''

Pushing himself to his feet, he reached down and pulled her up; holding her briefly in his arms, he kissed her. "I'm a lucky man, hinny.''

Only a hundred feet from the oak tree, hidden by a clump of bushes, they found the carcasses of the two horses. Dismounting together, Marsh paused while Jamie strode toward the bodies. Uneasily, she looked across the field at a thick stand of willows, and her heart pounded with a sudden premonition of danger. She was the only one who heard the first rifle shot. Screaming a warning, she reached her husband just as he crumpled to the ground. In blind terror she threw her body over his, but at the moment of contact, she knew. She heard the second shot and felt the burn in her shoulder; but she never heard the third which creased her head and rendered her mercifully unconscious.

Chapter
13

Struggling toward the pale light, she dragged her leaden body slowly out of the black tunnel which had imprisoned her, inching her way past moments of oblivion and pain. As she neared the light, she felt her consciousness return at intervals until the blinding moment she could open her eyes. Exhausted from the effort, she closed them tiredly and slept, only to awaken and struggle again. This time, her eyes stayed open and she could focus them on the source of light, the half draped window of her and Jamie's bedroom at the farm. She could feel the pressure on her hand. Looking down, she caressed the dark, curly head lying there.

"Jamie?" Her whispery voice held wonder.

The head lifted and she could see the misery in the blue eyes of its owner. "No, Marsh, it's Stuart. Jamie's dead."

She sighed and the wonder died. "I know. I was just hoping."

"I'm sorry, Marsh."

"I know you are."

"He died instantly."

"I knew he was dead when I touched him. He never even heard the shot."

"He didn't suffer."

"No, he just died. And I miss him."

"We all do."

"You miss him when you remember. I miss him because I can't forget. I loved him."

"I loved him, too, but I never told him so. I wish now I had."

She left her own emptiness to ease his. "He knew you did and he loved you more than the others. It was hard for Jamie to be loving, but he loved his sons and me deeply."

"What will you do now, Marsh?"

"Go to Wyoming like we planned."

"You can't. You can't go alone to that wilderness."

"I won't be alone."

"I won't let you go. Stay here, Marsh, where you belong."

"No, Stuart. That twisted excuse for a man tried to murder me after he killed Jamie. He won't stop until he succeeds."

"Then you know who it was?"

"I knew when I saw the dead horses. He'd enjoy doing a cruel thing like that."

"He hasn't been caught yet."

"How did anyone else know who it was? I never saw him."

"One of the English grooms said he'd seen a small man near the rear pastures four days before the shooting. He thought your stepfather was one of the new jockies. The sheriff also found a field glass where he'd camped and some boot prints that fit the old pair you used to wear. He'd been watching you and my father from those trees."

"How long before anyone found us?"

"One of the guards heard the shots. It took him a half hour to locate you."

"Then my stepfather had the time to get across the river."

"The authorities are looking for him on both sides."

"They won't find him, Stuart."

"Why did he do it?"

"Revenge. Jamie had always beaten him at his dirty games." But she knew the main part of Creighton's motive was money, just as it always had been. "How long have I been unconscious?"

"You've been in and out for five days. Carina said you wouldn't remember."

"Where did you bury Jamie?"

"Here on the farm."

"I'm glad. He'd have hated it in Baltimore." Her eyes were misted as she looked off to a place beyond the window, toward a distant oak tree where he'd said, "I'm a lucky man, hinny." Hollowly, she returned to the dead present. "Then all I have to do is—survive until—until—"

"Stay here, Marsh. We can protect you. Your stepfather wouldn't dare try again."

She thought with a churning hatred, No, but his partner would and she'd succeed. Aloud she insisted, her voice hardening, "I have to leave in two weeks."

"Why?"

"To finish the home we began in Wyoming."

"By yourself? That's insane."

"No, it's something I have to do alone."

"Will you return here?"

"Yes, in a year when I can—"

"What, Marsh? Can what?"

"Live again," she said lamely, but her words covered a fierce resolve. "And kill the ones who murdered Jamie."

"Would you like me to come with you?"

"No. I have to do this alone."

"If you need me—"

"I'll remember, Stuart."

"Good-bye, Marsh. I won't tell you this time to be happy. Were you the last time?"

"Yes."

"I'm glad." He bent down and kissed her forehead beside the thick bandage, but she'd already drifted away to someplace deep inside herself. Just how long she'd rested she could only judge by the darkened window and by the lamplight which illuminated Damon's look of concern as he bent over her. Silently, he held a glass of water to her lips and then propped her up with pillows and fed her a bowl of vanilla custard.

"Maddy will give you more food in a few minutes. Right now I want to know about this nonsense of your going alone to Wyoming."

"Is my baby still all right, Damon?"

"Of course, it is. You're too strong a brood mare to lose a child over a pair of minor injuries."

"He's the reason, Damon."

"How so?"

She was tired of explaining. "You knew about the poisoning in Baltimore?"

"Yes, I heard."

"It was deliberate."

"For the man, not you."

"No, for me, too. And now it'd be even more for Jamie's child. And then there's my stepfather. Why kill the father when there's still a son?"

"There are three other sons and they're not threatened."

"Robbie doesn't count and Craig is related to her."

"Then what about Stuart?"

"He could be related—through Janet."

"That's nonsense!"

Quietly, like a shadow, Carina had entered the room and listened. Both Marsh and Damon jerked when she spoke. "Marsh is right. She can not take the risk. Now more than ever she'll be their target."

"Why now?"

"I just heard Jamie's will read. Even Alice was there."

Marsh struggled to sit up. "Keep her away from me, Carina."

The Indian woman's smile was not a pretty one. "Don't worry, I already warned her and she knows. Compared to me, she's just a beginner. All the same, the sooner you're with Robbie in that valley, the safer you'll be."

"She can't have her baby there alone." Damon was angry at his wife. Eight days ago, he'd promised Jamie that this child would be safe.

"She won't be alone and you know it. Winona is almost as good a doctor as you are."

This time Marsh succeeded in sitting up. "Do you know her, Carina?"

"Yes, for years. Ever since Jamie's first trip west."

"I thought of you when I met her."

"We're both Indians."

Marsh closed her eyes and murmured, "I'm glad." She felt Carina's hand place a chain about her neck and struggled back to awareness. The tears which had not yet fallen began now as she lifted the object lying on her bandaged chest. It was Jamie's wedding ring, and she remembered his stunned joy on the day she'd had it engraved.

Carina's stern voice recalled her to the present. "It is not for you. It is for the child. He'll want to know that his parents loved each other." But Marsh barely heard the words as she wept the bitter tears of grief. "It is good for you to weep now while we're here to care for you. We loved Jamie, too. But once you leave here, the time for weeping will be past. You must become again what you once were, strong enough to survive alone." She placed her hand over the sobbing woman's nose. "Breathe deep now, Marsh," she said gently.

When he heard his wife's command, Damon moved but too slowly to prevent her action. "What did you give her?"

"Damon, you let your white blood rule you too much when you become so legal a doctor. It was just a whiff of forgetfulness, the same as I have administered to many of your patients. She will awaken in two hours. I couldn't let her grieve so deeply, she is too intense. Besides, I can't let anyone else see her now. Stuart, yes, but not the others yet. Tomorrow is soon enough for her to know that there is another problem. You go down now, Damon, and listen to the terms of the will. I will be with Marsh tonight. Watch Alice, Damon, and listen to her with your black heart. She is evil.''

Damon had heeded his wife's advice for too many years to disagree now; he left her with his sleeping patient knowing that, even as Carina curled up in the chair like a cat, she would remain vigilant and alert. And he knew too that his wife and the young widow were alike in spirit, that their fierce natures would never let them surrender meekly. Jamie would be avenged and the child would be safe. For a brief moment, the primitive part of his own soul joined in the silent communion of the two women, and he cried out voicelessly to his dead friend, All will be well.

The private thoughts and emotions were pushed aside the next morning by necessity. Promptly at eight o'clock, Bruce Mac Lachlan knocked on the door; his was the task of stripping a dead man of his last remaining rights by disposing of the property. With only one young injured woman as his audience, he might have relaxed and been more human. But perhaps, in light of the contents of the will, he had some excuse. He began formally and ended formally.

''Mrs. James MacKenzie, it is my duty to read this will in its entirety. You would make my job easier if you do not interrupt.''

''Before you begin, I want to know if you'll continue as my lawyer?''

His look was speculative. ''I'd be delighted.''

''Then I want you to take two armed guards with you when you return to Baltimore. Next, I want you to contact Seth Hanford at the Pinkerton Agency and have him report to me. And then I want you to send for Angus Balfour.''

''I already have. He'll be here in a few days. Now, may I

read the will, Mrs. MacKenzie?'' At her hesitant nod, he began the reading; long before he finished her face was ashen. Jamie had left twenty thousand dollars and two small Baltimore houses to Angus. He had left ten thousand to Catherine Sanborn and the Ryder pearls to Alice Nelson. The next three legacies pleased Marsh as much as the one to Angus had. Her and Jamie's share of the Georgia property would now be in her name. She would own the racehorses and their colts, but only fifty percent of the Maryland farm. Damon and Carina would own the other half. At the insistence of her father, on the basis on the money lent Bradford Marshall, she now owned half of Marsh Oaks. She was touched by the double legacy. However, the rest of the will horrified her. She owned all the New York properties. In addition, she owned half of the Baltimore bank and half of the Baltimore properties. Craig owned half of the bank, the Baltimore home, and half of the Baltimore properties. Stuart inherited twenty thousand dollars and half of the Virginia farm. Marsh inherited the other half. Robbie inherited twenty thousand dollars and half of the Wyoming ranch. Marsh owned the other half. She owned the second Wyoming ranch recently purchased from the Indians, and she inherited all of Jamie's money not assigned to the other legatees.

Mac Lachlan concluded, ''This will leaves you a very wealthy woman since the money in the bank alone amounts to a fortune. Before you say anything, Mrs. MacKenzie, I think you should read this personal letter from your late husband. I do not know its contents, but he instructed me to give it to you right after the reading of the will.''

Marsh took one look at the familiar writing on the envelope and fought the impulse to cry out in anguish. Disturbed by the violence of her reaction, the lawyer sought to offer sympathy. ''Should I call Dr. Damon for you?''

Taking a deep breath, Marsh shook her head and eased the letter open. It was mercifully short and, like Jamie himself had been, simple and direct. It was dated four days after the Maryland Sweeps.

Dear Lass,

Today I had Bruce Mac Lachlan write out a new will which will protect both you and our promised child. Since I have every intention of being around for a long time to guard you and the child from your own generous impulsiveness, this next warning is probably unnecessary. But just in case, I don't want you to mount up on that high horse of yours and give away what I leave you with all my love. Only in the case of my sons do I give you permission to be generous whenever you think them mature enough. I trust your judgment.

Your loving husband,
Jamie
James A. MacKenzie

Silently, she handed the letter to the lawyer and watched him steadily as he read it and returned her look. "Is there an expected child, Mrs. MacKenzie?"

"Yes, I'm more than two months pregnant."

"And Jamie knew?"

"He knew."

"That explains the will then."

"No one else in Maryland or Virginia must know."

"Why?"

"My stepfather was paid to murder Jamie and me. He wouldn't have done it otherwise; but the person who paid him is far more deadly than he is. She would not hesitate to kill this child."

"You can't hide a child for life."

"No, I plan to return here alone and make sure of his safety."

MacLachlan held up his hand abruptly. "Do not tell me any more of your plans."

"Are you still my lawyer?" At his nod, she rushed on. "Have you sent a copy of the will to Robert MacKenzie yet?"

"No."

"Good. I want you to write out a release for my fifty percent of his property. I'll deliver both the release and the will to him. And you will write out a release for my fifty percent to the bank, but ask Craig not to make that release public."

"And Stuart?"

"Stuart can wait."

"Is there some special reason?"

"Yes. I want him to be safe before I release my half. Mr. Mac Lachlan, you know a lot about me and my marriage to Jamie; but what you may not know is that I loved him and that I plan to work to support myself and my child. I am grateful for Jamie's generosity, but I'd give every cent of it away if he could just be here with me now." This time, as she dissolved in violent weeping, the lawyer didn't hesitate. He called Carina, and once again the merciful opiate eased the wild grief.

Hours later, Craig and Phyllis were allowed separate, brief visits. With Craig, it was Marsh who did the comforting, he seemed crushed and afraid. She held his hand with her one good arm and consoled him as she would have a child. "You're a MacKenzie, Craig, and MacKenzie men are strong and good. Be happy, you and Phyllis, and remember that your father loved you."

With Phyllis, there was no need for sympathy, her eyes may have been flooded with tears, but her common sense and self-preservation were intact.

"Thank you for the release, Marsh; once Craig realizes what it means, that you have confidence in him, he won't feel so afraid without his father to lean on."

"Take care of him and take care of your daughter."

Phyllis didn't pretend to misunderstand. "Alice?"

"Yes, Alice. Has she done anything peculiar since the race?"

"She's been screaming that she's going to break Jamie's will."

"Anything else?"

"When we got back that night, she asked if anything unusual had happened on the way home. It didn't make any sense to me, does it to you?"

"Yes, I told her that Jamie and I were returning to Baltimore. Did you tell her that we had gone to the farm?"

"Yes, I did."

"Then that's how he knew where to find us."

"Oh, my God, Marsh."

"It's not your fault. I just didn't think she wanted Jamie dead, too. Phyllis, I'll be gone for a year. Please be careful."

"Where will you be, Marsh?"

"I don't know yet, but someplace where I can put my life back together again. Be happy, Phyllis." As she watched Craig's wife leave, Marsh's grief was mixed with jealousy and rage. Her husband alone was dead and she alone was the target of a pair of murderers. Carina stayed with her that night and Marsh slept deeply, not knowing that she cried out frequently.

It was Seth Hanford's brief visit three days later that revived her courage and increased her sense of urgency to escape from the oppressiveness of personal loss. With his usual lack of sympathy, Seth agreed to accompany her to Cheyenne and to meet her there again in one year. During that year, he would continue his investigation. With a businesslike lack of emotion, he locked the door to her room and moved into the adjoining one.

"Too many people moving around in this house," he explained laconically, "I don't like to take chances." She slept easier knowing he was there, and her last three visitors were all questioned before he allowed her to see them—even Angus, who arrived the next day.

Marsh was shocked by the grief mirrored in her old friend's eyes, no one but she had loved Jamie as much. She longed to tell Angus about the child, but she didn't dare. For three days, he sat with her and reminisced, telling her about a young Jamie she had never known. In the end, Angus promised to take care of all her inheritance and to advise Craig. His good-bye to her was a touching mixture of love and humor.

"You taught Jamie how to love, lass, when he dinna believe in love. I know it'll be hard for you wi'out him. But you're a MacKenzie now and they're no' so easy to keep down."

By the time the Flynns arrived, Marsh had regained enough mobility to walk around the room, and she had carefully supervised the packing. Both of Jamie's revolvers went into the carpetbag which held her riding clothes; six of his flannel nightshirts were carefully folded into the suitcase with her dresses, the four most practical garments she owned. Only at the last minute did she relent and include the dark red silk which had been one of Jamie's favorites. Mrs. Harding had sewed the outfit Marsh would travel in, a subdued black wool dress which buttoned down the front so that Marsh could manage with her one good arm. The matching cape and hood was lined with the fur from Jamie's robe. Carina was the one who had insisted on that. "Jamie hated the cold, he'd want you and his child to be warm."

On her last day at the farm, she gave Shannon all the papers Jamie had collected for the trip, except her own ticket. Seth Hanford would use Jamie's. The next day, she climbed stiffly into the carriage with Damon and Carina and was driven the twenty miles to the rail station. Two farm guards and Seth rode alongside. She hadn't been allowed to visit Jamie's grave; her only consolation on this grim day was Carina and Damon's promise to be her child's godparents.

On the long trip, pain and grief were her only companions. Seth Hanford preferred to guard her from a distance and the

Flynns stayed with the horses; but on the last long pull into Cheyenne, she felt the first faint fluttering of new life in her womb. She was no longer completely alone.

In Cheyenne, Robbie was waiting for her and his quiet sympathy gave her the strength to complete her business there. First, she made her final arrangements with Seth and was oddly touched by his gruff farewell. Asking Robbie to buy the material she would need to complete the unfinished house she would now live in alone, she went into the general store and handed the clerk the two lists Carina had written for her, one for baby things and one for a year's supply of food staples. Stoically, she hunted among the crude racks of dresses until she located four garments modestly called confinement wrappers. Without attempting to try them on, she carried them to the counter where her purchases were already being stacked. Restless now to get underway, she told the clerk to deliver her purchases to the outskirts of town where the wagons and horses were, paid the bill and left the store. Robbie was waiting for her in the hotel dining room. Silently, she handed him the release paper disavowing her claim on his property, and then, as silently, a copy of his father's will. He looked at her strained, tired face with the disfiguring bandage and ordered dinner. There would be time for talk later. All he told her during that meal was that the lumber and other building needs would be delivered at the ranch in a month.

By the time the two of them joined the others already preparing for three hours of travel before making camp, Marsh was exhausted and throbbing with pain. Uncomplaining, she let herself be lifted into the bed prepared for her on the floorboards of a covered wagon and began her journey into a new life. A life sadly different from the joyous trip of last year on this same trail. Only when the wagon train left the main road to travel toward the Indian village where the horses were being delivered did she take any interest in her surroundings. She told Robbie that she wanted to stand in Jamie's stead to thank the Indians for their land. From that moment on, Marsh began her return to the living. At the Indian village, where she stood stiffly beside Robbie, she watched a tall, graceful Indian approach. Not until he smiled did she recognize him for a Flynn. This was Devin, who had already explained her circumstances to her Indian hosts and who had obtained a legal deed to the property for her. Flanked now by Devin and Robbie, she stood for an hour while the horses were inspected and accepted. Out of respect for her grief, Devin told her that she need not remain for the celebration which normally followed such transactions. Gratefully, Marsh thanked him and followed Robbie back to the restful privacy of her wagon.

Her arrival at the family village three days later was made equally easy for her. Since she had already learned the hard lesson that grief can not be shared, at least not to the same degree of intensity, she moved quietly into her stone shell of a home. There, with only a taciturn Indian squaw named Nakana to cook for her, she lived virtually alone for a month. The first days and nights were difficult, but Marsh forced herself to endure and to walk each day in the uncultivated fields of the ranch. She saw the horses in the distance and longed to be astride one, but she would take no chances with her child. When the lumber Robbie had ordered for her arrived, she hired the ex-corporal to complete her home. Uncomplaining, she lived with sawdust and wood shavings on the floor, exercising until she regained the use of her arm. As one room was finished, she and two of the Indian carpenters moved some of the pieces of furniture Jamie had ordered from Chicago into that room, and her pride in this frontier home grew. With its combination of wood and stone walls, it matched the ruggedness of the land itself. On the day she could no longer wear her regular clothes, she slipped on one of her loose wrappers and walked across the compound to Winona's home. The Indian woman greeted her with warmth and dignity.

"Your heart still hurts, but it is time to join the others. A child suffers if his mother broods too much. Now you must prepare for the birth.'' From that day on, Winona instructed her each day in exercises which had Marsh bending over, squatting down, stretching her muscles, and even running briefly during the frequent walks. Physically, she felt wonderful, and her mental attitude improved each day she spent with Winona. By August, the house was finished and all the furniture moved into place. As she viewed the huge main room with the massive dining table and the long, leather covered sofas flanking the stone fireplace, Marsh wept for the first time in months.

"Oh, Jamie,'' she whispered in the lonely fire-lit room, "you'd have loved it here even in winter.'' And she remembered that long-ago night when they'd made love in front of the fireplace in the library of the Baltimore home.

But life was for the living at her homewarming party. Wearing her red silk dress which Onawa had restyled until it hung loosely from her shoulders, she greeted her arriving guests more warmly than she ever had anyone in Baltimore; and she knew by their faces that she was beautiful again. That night was a happy one as the Indian squaw and her two assistants spread out the platters of beef and venison and the bowls of vegetables from the kitchen garden Marsh had planted in the side yard of her home. After the younger Flynns had left to pursue more youthful activities, Marsh served brandy to the others. Quietly, she told them all about Jamie's death and her own injuries, and about what she knew or suspected of the murderers. When she told them her plans to return to the east in the spring, Winona nodded. "We will keep your child safe here.''

Robbie protested vehemently. "Marsh, you can't go back there. If what you suspect is true, there are two vicious people who want you dead. I don't know your stepfather, but I do know Alice. She's the reason my father moved Stuart out of his home and wouldn't let me visit if he weren't there. She could do cruel things with her hands, and her face would not even change expression.''

"I know, Robbie. But I will not let her go unpunished or remain a threat to my child. Not her or my stepfather." Abruptly, she turned to Onawa. "If something should happen to me, I want you and Robbie to raise this child as your own, telling him only when he is old enough to understand about Jamie and me." She held her breath and her peace of mind rode on their answer. When they assured her in unison that they would, Marsh felt her remaining tension dissolve. This was her home and these people were the family she'd dreamed of finding.

On the arrival of the September supply wagon train from Cheyenne, Robbie brought her three letters whose outer envelopes had been addressed to him. The one postmarked New York was from Angus, and it contained a meticulous accounting of her holdings and the annual profits from them. At the bottom of the third page was a note. "Lassie, it's dull wi' no one to argue wi'. I hope you plan on comin' home."

The second was from Carina, a warning that Blake Creighton was still free. Marsh Wind, though, had won another three races.

Only the third letter disturbed her. Seth Hanford wrote that Alice Nelson had hired detectives to locate her, and he warned Marsh that she wouldn't be too hard to find even in the wilds of Wyoming. He also informed her that he'd traced Blake Creighton to Richmond, Virginia, and to a Hiram Creighton.

This letter Marsh handed to Robbie and explained who and what Hiram Creighton was.

"So that's why you married my father?"

"Yes, but I fell in love with him soon after."

"You're quite a woman, Marsh MacKenzie."

"Your father was quite a man," she smiled sadly.

That night, another fireplace was lighted in her home, and Colin and Winona moved in with her. As the days shortened in length and her time of delivery approached, these two were marvelous companions. Colin had probably been the calmest of fathers, because nothing embarrassed him, not Marsh's awkward stance nor the exercises she performed on the living room floor. He just smiled placidly and went on reading. Her labor pains began in the early afternoon of October 10, 1868, during a pounding rainstorm. In front of a warm fire, Marsh paced endlessly, obeying every one of Winona's instructions. Determined to be a good Indian mother, she bit back her screams each time the agonizing cramps struck. In the end, she squatted on the small sheepskin rug and gave birth, lying down on her back at Winona's signal as the Indian woman knelt to receive the emerging infant. Marsh watched alertly as Colin came out of the bedroom to take the child from Winona and wash it at the table prepared with warm water, towels, amd blankets, while Winona bathed Marsh and cleaned the floor.

"We delivered all five of our own," Colin declared cheerfully, "without a mishap. Your baby is whole—no missing parts and he's all MacKenzie." With a proud look he returned the sleeping baby to Winona, picked Marsh up, and carried her into her bedroom. There, she held her son for the first time; he was as Colin had said—a MacKenzie, another Jamie MacKenzie. That night, the baby slept in his mother's bed, but the next day, Colin moved an infant bed into the room, a crib he had constructed from sturdy pieces of polished wood with heavy belts of leather for the springs. When Marsh tried to thank him, he grinned at her with the same Irish charm he'd passed on to all of his children.

"The MacKenzies and Flynns have been together a long time. We're family, Marsh. Jamie's child and my grandchildren will grow up together on this ranch."

And family they were, a wonderful, uninhibited family. Marsh nursed her son in front of them, refereed squabbles between Shannon and Lon without regard for ladylike language, relieved Robbie of the job of keeping the ranch accounts, and helped Onawa write another batch of letters to the women of Wyoming. On the fourth month of Jamie's life, she hosted her son's christening. Every member of both families, including Devin, arrived bearing bowls of food and bottles of wine. Ceremoniously, Winona unwrapped the package she carried and placed the contents in a row on the floor. Each figure was an animal made of elk leather and hardened to stand as solidly as wood. The wolf was there, the buffalo, the deer, the eagle, and the horse. Jamie was placed on his stomach before them. In ritualistic solemnity, the family watched him as the curious infant contemplated each in turn. When he finally reached out, he chose the horse; Marsh knew that this animal sign would dominate his life. She had lived with blacks in the South too long not to realize that many of the beliefs white people called superstitions influenced men's lives. That horse lived with little Jamie and bore his teeth marks during five years of childhood. Only when he mounted his first real pony did he forsake his leather animal sign.

As the winter months drew to a close, Marsh began to prepare herself to leave this pleasant haven and return to the harsh reality of the outside world. Colin and Shannon became her trainers. Daily, while the snow still covered the ground, they taught her to use her husband's Colt revolvers. Under their vigilant eyes she learned to shoot with accuracy. Colin was professional in his instructions, but Shannon was more understanding of her need. Indian-style, he taught her to kill.

"Visualize your enemy each time you fire the gun. Think of him as something that needs to be destroyed. Do not let thoughts of right or wrong distract you. If you do, you will be killed." Marsh believed him implicitly. She learned to shoot with a deadly accuracy and a deadlier intent. By the end of six weeks of lessons, she was programmed to kill her enemy. On the last day, Shannon made her shoot a tiny, toy-like pistol as well.

"I don't know how to help you with the woman," he admitted, "but this little gun can kill from a few feet away and it's easy to hide. Have you told Robbie what you plan to do yet, Marsh?''

"No, Shannon, only you and your father. But your mother knows just as she knew about my husband last year. Robbie and his brothers would not understand. Does Devin disapprove of me, too?''

"Devin? Lord, no! Devin would go with you if he weren't needed here at the moment. He's meeting us on the trail to provide protection.''

Marsh nodded in understanding. The Indian wars which had been waged for two years against other settlers in Wyoming and Montana had finally come to this peaceful valley, and not even the Flynns and MacKenzies were free from Sioux attack. The farewell dinner was a quiet, apprehensive one at Robbie's house, where five-month-old Jamie was already housed and adjusted to his foster mother, Onawa. Marsh steeled herself to withstand Robbie's arguments and to kiss her son good night without dissolving in tears. Then she left the house and returned to her own, where her three trail mates were already camped on their bedrolls on her living room floor. Only Lon, Shannon, and the best Indian horseman on the ranch would accompany her this trip. Each would ride one saddled horse and lead another; the six pack horses would also be spelled off during this dash to Cheyenne.

There were no delays in the start of the predawn ride the next morning, as all riders took off at a gallop and continued at that speed until Lon signalled for a brief rest and a change of horses. At two-hour intervals, this procedure was followed until darkness forced them to halt for the night. When a saddle sore Marsh dismounted and turned to say something to Lon, Shannon shushed her with a hand over her mouth. Lon silently spread out a cold meal, their first since a hurried breakfast, and the three men ate with efficient dispatch while Marsh nibbled nervously. Abruptly afterward, Lon signalled her to climb into one of the bedrolls. Alarmed by the seriousness of the two young Flynns, who'd been as friendly as puppy dogs around her home all winter, she obeyed mutely and was rewarded with smiles of approval. Exhaustion quickly overcame her apprehension, and she slept so deeply, Shannon had to dump a cup of cold water in her face to awaken her. Breakfast was another dismal meal of cold corn bread and hard-boiled eggs, eaten against the backdrop of a dark sky with only the blood-red streaks of dawn for illumination. Another day and night followed, so like the first ones Marsh no longer needed Lon's signal to pull to a halt and switch horses. On the third day of strenuous trailing, the pattern changed abruptly when two Indians overtook them on the trail and the educated voice of Devin Flynn broke the silence.

Marsh stared at him, not believing her eyes. He lacked only war paint to appear the complete Sioux warrior. His legs were encased in fur boots, his body was covered with a wolf skin garment of some kind, his hair was held down by a leather headband, and his horse was unsaddled. She tried to overhear what he was telling his brothers, but many of his words were Indian and she could only guess at their meanings. When he finally dismounted and walked over to her, she was almost afraid of him, he looked so alien and grim. Only his smile at the last second reassured her, and she accepted his help in getting down stiffly from her own horse.

Not until hot food was being prepared hastily on an open campfire did she learn the odd circumstances that necessitated Devin joining them. The following morning, they would rendezvous with a band of warriors from the Sioux village she'd delivered the horses to the year before. Although the news itself did not alarm her overly, Devin's serious expression did—so did his concluding words. The band was being led, not by the older chief, but by a famous young warrior chief recognized as a hero-leader by all Sioux—Tashunca-Uitco. That name meant nothing to Marsh, but the Anglicized version of it did—Crazy Horse, the brash and brilliant Sioux who'd been the winner in every skirmish he'd had with

American soldiers, including two massacres of large army patrols. His name brought terror to white settlers throughout the plains territories, and she was to meet him tomorrow morning.

"He wants fifty more of your MacKenzie horses, Marsh, and he's offered to race you for them in return for safe passage to Cheyenne."

She stared at Devin in consternation. "How would I get fifty MacKenzie horses out here?"

"You'll have to bring them with you when you return next fall."

"In that case, it isn't necessary to race. I'll just bring them."

"No, Marsh, he's heard about you, and he wants to win those horses. If you lose—"

An earnest and sober-faced Shannon interrupted his older brother, "In the name of God, Devin, she has to lose." Shannon's Irish Christianity often overrode his Indian fatalism, and in this case, even his love for racing.

Devin nodded in agreement. "But she has to give him a good race. That band he's with now all watched her race you two and Brian two years ago when she outran all of you." Lost momentarily in her happy memories of that carefree time, Marsh heard only the last of Devin's next words. ". . . one of her MacKenzies instead of these trail horses."

Swiftly, her mind returned to her immediate problem. For a year she hadn't ridden a horse at more than a canter until this trip, much less raced one, and none of these horses were remotely as good as a MacKenzie. She thought enviously of Rake-Star and smiled at her foolishness. She had to lose this race! Even before the food was cooked, she was on her feet, inspecting the fourteen horses available to her for this most critical race of her life. With Tamca, the trainer from the Flynn ranch, she finally picked his relief horse, a light-skinned western he called a palomino. Of all the horses, its were the only ears which pricked up sharply at the sound of her voice. A calmer horse than most, its eyes showed no fear as she studied it. However, the critical reason she chose the palomino was its gelding status; it would run equally well against stallion or mare—although Marsh seriously doubted that Crazy Horse would be riding a mare. She also chose the trainer's own saddle, an abbreviated one of leather with the merest suggestion of a seat. Carefully, she adjusted the stirrups.

"Why didn't you pick my stallion?" Shannon demanded. "He's faster."

"He's also tired," Marsh answered, forebearing to add, and too temperamental. But no western ranch man can take that kind of criticism about a beloved horse.

Amused by her answer and relaxed now by hot coffee, Devin changed the subject. "Did you know the Indians have a name for you, Marsh? It's 'the red-haired squaw who hunts'." Reminded abruptly of the reason for this insane trek backward into an unhappy past, Marsh felt coldly alone again and realized that she was breaking the taboos of both civilizations. She shrugged in resignation; her son had no one but her to safeguard his future.

Turning back to Devin, she looked at his forehead and asked, "Do you have another of those headbands? If I'm going to ride against an Indian, I'll be Indian." He was not smiling as he removed his own and placed it on her head, but she knew that he was pleased.

All afternoon, with Tamca's help, Marsh practiced on the palomino—racing for short bursts, then walking, then standing—until the horse knew her and her voice commands. By dinner time she relaxed, knowing that the horse would perform its best for her. And by the time the Flynn brothers extinguished the fire, she had lost her nervous awareness of another camp just two miles away that held a man who, at the age of twenty, had already killed hundreds of his hated enemy—the white usurpers of his land. Marsh thought about her own intentions and felt a kinship with the Indian chief.

She recognized him instantly the next morning when the two groups met. He sat gracefully astride the MacKenzie stallion she'd delivered to the Indians, as if he were part of the horse. His eagle feathers were slanted forward at a rakish angle, and his Roman nose was as regal as Marsh Song's. At first, she thought him young looking, until she saw his eyes; they were black and fierce and arrogantly confident. Knowing she was under equal scrutiny, she was determined not to show fear. As a matter of fact, her emotions were the same as the ones which had driven her to leap her horse into the Potomac on three occasions and to ride out to meet General Mosby and his marauders on another—a reckless sense of meeting fate rather than awaiting it. Casually, she looked over the assembled score of Indians as if she gazed at half naked men every day and then looked again into the eyes of Crazy Horse, her own green eyes unflinching as he moved to take his place by her side.

The race would be a mile in length, around a tree located a half mile away from the encampment, and back. At the signal to start, a simple wave of Devin's hand, she bent low in the saddle and ignored the fact that Crazy Horse and his stallion were already underway before she gave her voice signal to the palomino. Keeping far apart from the stallion, she concentrated on racing, crouching low and talking steadily. Once in motion, she maintained the steady pace of maximum speed she could coax out of her horse. Twice, she was almost abreast of the more powerful stallion, and at the end she was only a length and a half behind. Both riders dismounted and turned again to watch each other. Without any change of expression, Crazy Horse removed one of his own feathers and tucked it into her headband, turned, remounted his horse, and led his ponied troop away. Turning once from a hundred feet away, he raised his spear in a salute to her. Marsh raised her arm in response.

She was trembling when Shannon reached her side and hugged her. "That feather is your safety pass when you return with the horses in October," he shouted in her ear, "there won't be an Indian in Wyoming who'd dare touch you now. You're under Crazy Horse's protection."

Devin's praise was more personal. "You're a brave woman. I'm sorry that you'll lose your horses."

"I don't mind," she said, and meant her words. "We're stealing their land and giving little in return. I can understand his hatred. Besides," she grinned, "he earned them. I didn't let him win. I raced all out. He won honestly." When she returned Devin's headband, she proudly stuck the feather in the band of her own leather hat and rode all day with a sense of being part of a destiny.

It was rainy and dreary when they reached the outskirts of Cheyenne and pulled to a stop at the way station maintained by territory ranchers. Normally, there were a dozen cowboys there to help with cattle and horse shipments. But today there was only one, an Indian breed, ex-army scout. His warning to the Flynns and the two Indians was sharp and explicit. Cheyenne was not a safe place even for well-known people like the Flynns. With thousands of whites bottled up in town because of Indian terrorism throughout the territory, the mood was one of ugly hatred for anything remotely Indian. Even as the ex-scout voiced his warning, the new arrivals could see mounted men riding from the town. Marsh dismounted quickly and pulled her two carpetbags from the pack animal. While she fled into the shack, half-dragging her luggage, the ex-scout leaped on her horse and, with the Flynns, rode toward the safety of the trail.

Inside the crude shack, Marsh listened as the sounds of hoofbeats from both groups of horsemen faded before she began her preparation. Following Seth Hanford's detailed instructions, she was to wear concealing female clothing, talk to no one, register at the hotel as Rose Smith, and remain cloistered in her room until he arrived. "Keep your hair covered on the street. The detectives Alice Nelson hired will be looking for a redhead." Removing her dusty riding clothes, she cleaned them as best she could and packed them away before she donned her black wool dress and long, black, fur-lined cape. Carefully, she checked the contents of an inconspicuous reticule which contained, among other things, six thousand dollars and a very efficient derringer. With the hood pulled tight and all but covering her face, she felt reasonably safe from detection as she walked the wet half mile to the hotel.

Once there, though, Seth Hanford's well-laid plans fell apart; the hotel was overflowing with people. Marsh was unceremoniously put into a small room already occupied by two dance hall refugees from Rock Springs, and given an army cot for a bed. Roughly ten levels lower on the social scale of ladies-of-the-evening than Yvette de Bloom, these women were practical, earthy creatures whose language was a basic mixture of profanity, slang and misusage. They made no effort to greet their new roommate, but continued their preparation for a working night. Marsh was fascinated by the procedure. By sitting quietly on her cot jammed into a corner of the room which was strewn with dresses of every hue of gaudy satin, she gained an education about survival on the frontier. Both ladies began by liberally applying another layer of makeup over the unwashed previous ones. Marsh had to admit that, as the skies grew darker, their complexions looked better and better. The younger woman with the dark hair chose a yellow dress with a black lace trim which left nothing to the imagination. On her pulled up, coarse hair she pinned a spray of feathers dyed the same unbelievable yellow as the dress. Such is the competition in this particular profession, she left the room without a backward glance at her co-worker. Older by a decade, the second woman continued her own beautification. Removing a soiled wrapper, she wiggled her overly plump body into a brilliantly green satin dress, smoothed the flounces over well-upholstered hips, and then unwrapped the towel from around her lank, dirty graying hair. Seating herself in front of the mirror, she proceeded to try on each of her three wigs before she settled for the carrot-red one. When she was finally satisfied with her appearance, she looked nothing like the unappetizing creature she had been earlier.

Marsh was very thoughtful as she let herself out of the empty room ten minutes later. Having once stayed at this ugly hotel for weeks, she knew that the hotel workers congregated in a room behind the kitchen. By walking down the back stairs, she reached the room without meeting any other hotel guest and hired the off-duty maid there for three hours of her time. Unlike the other tired and dirty guests, Marsh took her bath in her own room instead of the crowded public one in the hotel's basement. While the maid cleared away the most obvious filth and hung up the clothes strewn around the room, Marsh scrubbed her hair free of the trail dust from eight days of hard riding. As soon as the bath tub had been removed, she sent the maid to bring her clean bedding to replace the musty blankets she had been given earlier. Her final two requests were for three more pitchers of hot water and for dinner to be brought to her room. A half hour later, both assignments had been completed and the maid was richer by a month's wages.

As far as Marsh was concerned, the money was well spent. She had the privacy she needed for uninterrupted contemplation and a virtual emporium at her disposal for costume shopping. Selecting two of the dresses, more by their degree of cleanliness than by color or style, she sponged off the suspicious spots and smears and tried them on. The aqua satin belonged to the heavier woman and looked grotesque on Marsh's slender figure. But the black lace dress with the flesh satin underneath was flattering. Except for the naked look around the shoulders and an inch too much of exposed breast, the dress was obvious without being vulgar, and revealing without being indecent. Standing in front of the mirror, Marsh tried on the remaining two wigs. The brassy gold one made her look like an overblown sunflower, but the pale blond one reduced the strength of her features and contrasted attractively with her suntanned skin. She studied herself intently in the mirror before removing the borrowed finery. Using her own scented soap, she carefully sponged the caked makeup from around the edges of the wig and checked through the layers of blond curls for bugs before she replaced it in the box.

With the first part of the plan she was formulating completed, she donned a garment like those she'd worn every night for a year—one of Jamie's flannel nightshirts. Turning the lamps down to a flicker of amber, she pulled her cot in front of the window and opened the drapes. In spite of the intermittent rain, there were still people milling around on the street below. Most of them were strangers in a town where everyone was a stranger to an extent; Cheyenne had only boomed since the advent of the railroad three years earlier. They were people like herself who wanted to leave the past behind and find a peaceful life somewhere else. For a moment, Marsh wondered what she was doing here. She'd found a peaceful home. She had a child there and good friends. If she had remained there, she would not be involved in an insane project to deliver horses to an Indian who would use those horses to kill some of the same people now walking about on Cheyenne streets. How much of the urgent need she'd felt to seek revenge was really necessary, and how much was due to her own restless nature?

"Let's review the facts," Seth Hanford had written in that letter. Jamie was dead—one year, two weeks and four days dead—and she'd been shot and left for dead. That was a fact, and no amount of wishing had made it into a bad dream. The suspected murderer was still free; another fact. And the woman who had hired him and who had poisoned Wayne Talbot and herself had now hired detectives to find Marsh and complete the job. Alice Nelson was more than just free, she was rich enough and resourceful enough to accomplish her goal. This realization alone justified every violent action Marsh was now planning in order to bring about the destruction of two murderers. Her eyes narrowed as she remembered Shannon's advice: "Think of them as something that needs to be destroyed."

As she idly watched a grizzled man enter the raw-wood building down the street, the building with the red light glaring in its glass container, Marsh's thoughts turned further inward. The Indians were more accurate about her than they suspected when they called her "the red-haired squaw who hunts." Since her son had been three months old, she'd realized that she would never be happy without the physical love she'd known with Jamie. She was too much of a realist to expect the deeper, trusting love she and Jamie had finally exchanged, but the excitement of physical desire she could have. Providing the man she wanted could be persuaded to marry her! She smiled mirthlessly. Stuart MacKenzie was the most marriage-shy man in Virginia. He'd refused her once with a violence that still rankled. And that was before she married a father whom he had resented with a jealous passion! She laughed when she thought of what his reaction would be if he knew that she was a gun-toting, revenge-bound, horse-racing mother of his baby brother. He would probably be so damned horrifed he wouldn't even repeat his earlier offers—offers she would consider even less now than she had at the time. He was a proud, stubborn, contrary Scot who believed implicitly in the double standards for men and women.

The word "contrary" intrigued her. What if she made the offer first? Or what if she were the hard-to-get one? She knew that Stuart still cared, or had a year ago. Perhaps that caring could be turned into tenderness as well as passion. She laughed again, this time with impish humor. Stuart would only be brought to the marriage bed by trickery! And in that ugly little room in Cheyenne, Marsh's fertile imagination devised the ways and means of that trickery and established her priorities: first Stuart, then her stepfather, then Alice, and finally Crazy Horse—all in the space of six months. It was an ambitious schedule even for a Marsh MacKenzie.

She was still awake when her roommates returned; she had expected them to be gone all night. But Cheyenne was already supplied with their brand of entertainment, and the older one had been forced to buy her own drinks in a saloon. When their conversation turned to their scarcity of money, Marsh entered the dialogue. The wig and dress cost her a hundred and fifty dollars, but the lesson about makeup was free; so was the name and occupation they invented for her: Blanche La Tour, dance specialist.

Two days later, when the Union Pacific train rolled in from Chicago, Blanche La Tour was prepared for a triumphant entry into the staid scene of backwater Virginia. Seth Hanford recognized her only when she spoke to him at the station, but he considered her disguise so good that he actually sat with her throughout the eight days of train travel. During the two-day stopover in Chicago, he helped her buy two more La Tour-type dresses, as well as three slightly subdued Marsh MacKenzie ones. In the spirit of the masquerade, he spruced up his own drab working clothes with a gambler's black frock coat and a dapper western hat.

"You may be in that disguise for a long time," he told her, "the developments in the case are not good." Her heart sank as he enumerated these developments. Hiram Creighton had established an alibi for Blake Creighton during the time of Jamie's murder. Five people—one a prominent politician— swore in court that Blake Creighton had been with them throughout a two-day card game in Richmond. Official attention was now turned toward some disappointed racehorse owner. Her stepfather had been cleared of all charges and was seen frequently in the company of Alice Nelson. Nor had Alice been inactive. She had hired a lawyer to recover the property she claimed was stolen from the Ryder estate.

"What's the reaction to her charges in Baltimore?" Marsh asked numbly.

"About what you'd expect. A lot of people there think that you were overpaid for three years of marriage to an older man."

She sucked in her breath. "And you, Mr. Hanford?"

"They don't know about the child. I do. Dr. Damon told me so that I could watch out for you. What did you have?"

"A son. Do you still think the people I'm after are guilty?"

"They're as guilty as hell, Marsh. But it's going to be harder to prove it now. Before we make any final plans, I've got to have some blunt answers from you. Will you go along with my circulating a rumor that you're returning to accuse both of them with murder, even if you have to perjure yourself?"

"I'm returning to do more than that."

"Are you really prepared for that kind of action?"

"Well prepared. It's the only way I can keep my son safe."

"All right, as long as you understand that it'll probably come to that." He smiled at her ruefully. "I was sure you'd say what you did. I did a little investigation into your background and found out you were a lot different from the sick woman I met in the hospital. Do you own a gun?"

"Three of them, and I've been taught to use them."

"Good. It'll take me a month to bait the traps. Meanwhile, you'd better keep on as Blanche La Tour. It's a damn good disguise, but one that may get you into as much trouble as you would have as Marsh MacKenzie. You'd have been a lot safer as a middle-aged schoolmarm."

Marsh smiled recklessly. Her timetable was now set. She had exactly a month to rope and tie a very elusive thirty-year-old Scot, and Blanche La Tour was just the bait needed for that trap. With Seth Hanford's help, she registered in one of the very expensive, very discreet hotels that flourished in Washington, D.C., where men of importance could safely go in the company of women who were not their wives. With the detective's additional help in delivering a carefully worded invitation, it should take Stuart MacKenzie about three hours to arrive here in a state of furious agitation.

During those hours of waiting, she turned herself back into Marsh MacKenzie, and then back into a red-haired Blanche La Tour. Her disguise was not as alien to her own personality as the Pinkerton man had thought. The more daring of her Chicago La Tour dresses, an ivory velvet with the beaded stomacher and hip-fitted skirt suited her adventurous, daredevil mood. Even in daylight, it was hard to see the skin-colored net that covered her arms and shoulders and held up the low cut, velvet bodice. With her own hair expertly groomed by the maid whose services came with the expensive room, she checked the quality of the brandy she'd ordered, and sat down to wait in the elegant sitting room of her suite.

When his heavy knock sounded at the door, she rose to answer it, knowing that Stuart's first words would be angry ones about her peremptory summons. They were, and his scowl was endearingly familiar.

"Who the hell do you think you are ordering me to get over here to answer your damn questions?" His eyes focused on her when she smilingly handed him a snifter of brandy, which he swallowed and almost choked on. When the violent red had faded from his handsome face, he exploded again. "What the devil have you done to yourself? Do you have any idea what kind of a hotel this is?"

"You do get around, Stuart," she murmured. "I had no idea you knew that much about Washington. This is a very pleasant hotel and very private. I thought we might dine here while we discuss your activities on our farm." She smiled again and awaited his predictable response. Now would come his personal accusations. He would help himself to another brandy, sit back, and study her. She watched as he poured the drink and smiled as he sat back, then broke into his concentration. "Would you pour me a glass, Stuart?"

He frowned at her. "It didn't take you long."

"To do what?"

"Revert to type. The last time I saw you, I thought you'd finally lost your damned compulsion to act like a man. But you're just another rich widow on the prowl."

She shrugged. "I am a rich widow, but I don't need to prowl."

"Did my brother prove too down to earth for you?"

"Robbie? No, he's very happily married."

"So now you're hunting in greener pastures."

"If you mean the greener pastures you and I own jointly, yes. Angus wrote me that you were having trouble with profits."

"Angus is a bloody liar," Stuart sputtered. "He knows that I've sunk all the profits into improvements. If you're so damned greedy, why don't you come back to the farm and do some of the work yourself, partner?" The last word sounded like gall in his mouth. "Like you used to. But you don't have to work anymore, do you? You've got the MacKenzie brothers to do it for you. How did Robbie take the new partnership?"

"He was very gracious about it. So was Craig."

"So that leaves me as the only honest bastard in the family."

"Something like that. You don't approve of your father's will, do you?"

"Why the hell should I? What did you ever do to earn all that fortune except marry a man thirty years older than yourself and fool him into thinking that you loved him?"

"As usual, your opinion of me is not very flattering." Marsh turned away and breathed slowly. If she didn't, the fiery temper building in her would explode and she'd claw the skin off the face of this monumental egotist. She stood up and forced a stiff smile to her lips. "I'm sorry I sent for you. I foolishly thought that we might become friends. Whatever happened to the Stuart who offered to go to Wyoming with me?"

"That was when I thought you were helpless. But you're about as helpless as a barracuda."

Her control broke. "And you're the same jackass you always have been without the brains of a ninny. Now get the hell out of here."

Stuart was smiling broadly as he rose to face her. "Well, well. At last we're back to normal. I'm not going anyplace and I doubt that the management of this hotel would dare throw me out." His face sobered. "We still have things to talk about, Marsh, beginning with you. You look like you've had a rough year." His hand reached out and cupped her chin. "How have things really gone for you?"

For a moment, the tenderness in his voice shook her anger, and she was tempted to tell him about the loneliness and the heartbreak, until she remembered her child and a twenty-year-old Indian named Crazy Horse. Then she shrugged her shoulders and lied. "I've learned to live alone."

"No men in your life yet?"

"Friends, but no men."

"Is that invitation for dinner still open?"

"I don't think you'll approve of the way I look in public."

"Try me." His hands had moved to her shoulders and his eyes bore their old intent emotion as he looked at her. "You're more beautiful than you were, and your eyes look—" She pulled away from him sharply, in another minute she'd have been in his arms all too willingly.

"I won't be a minute," she called over her shoulder and fled into the safety of her bedroom. But that minute lengthened into five as she put the wig on and stared at her unfamiliar face in the mirror. She didn't think that she was a good enough actress to continue the charade with a man who could turn her insides to jelly. Her opening challenge, when she rejoined him, was more to bolster her own sagging courage than to ease his shock.

"Meet the new me, Stuart."

After a moment, his stunned look receded. "It's a disguise, isn't it? You're still afraid of your stepfather." Like Jamie had been, Stuart was a canny Scot.

She nodded. "I'm registered here as Blanche La Tour."

"That's why you chose this kind of hotel."

"They wouldn't have let me in a hotel like the Clairmont."

"It's a good disguise." His eyes glinted and his voice softened. "But a very dangerous one. You just may attract more attention than you can handle in the dining room downstairs."

Typical of establishments like this one, which catered to an exclusive clientele, everything was geared toward maintaining the aura of luxurious privacy. The red velvet chairs in the dimly lit dining salon were tucked into cozy alcoves, and the orchestra was discreetly screened behind palms. Couples dancing in the middle of the room were indistinguishable under the soft, low lights. As Marsh sipped her wine while Stuart ordered dinner, she had to remind herself that she was playing a role and that this glamorously romantic atmosphere was contrived and not real. She was certain Stuart was having a similar problem as he pulled her up to join the dancers. After the second dance, neither his voice nor his hands were steady.

"I don't think it'd be very wise for you to dance with me again unless you're willing to take the consequences," he challenged her in a harsh whisper.

She didn't pretend to misunderstand. "Are you repeating the offer you once made me?"

"You refused it both times, very violently."

"I was young then and I believed that marriage was safer and more permanent. But in my case, it didn't turn out to be true."

"You'd consider it now?"

She shrugged lightly. "Now I'd own the building the apartment was in."

"Why in hell would you settle for that kind of life? You could marry any one of the most eligible men in the country. You'd be a fool!" His voice had changed rapidly from whispered seduction to loud argument.

She took a deep breath and baited the hook she'd prepared. "I don't think I want the restrictions of marriage again. I like the independence of being Marsh MacKenzie."

Dinner was a silent and unfriendly meal. As he escorted her stonily to her room, she smiled shakily and asked, "Stuart, would you do me one last favor?"

Suspiciously, he looked down at her. "That depends on how much it's going to cost me."

"Oh, it won't cost you a penny. I need someone to help me inspect another piece of property I own jointly."

"I remember now. Marsh Oaks, isn't it? Another of your fifty percenters. Another partner who does the work. And this one even named his farm for you."

"I take it you're refusing."

"No. I'd like to meet one of my fellow slaves. How many days will this inspection take?"

"About two weeks there and two days on the road each way."

"You know damn well what will happen if we're together that long."

"Only if I permit it," she murmured.

"Let's find out right now just how much you do permit."

"Not tonight, Stuart. I don't think you like me much at the moment."

"I just think you're trying to be something you're not."

"At one time that was all you thought I was good enough for."

"That was different."

"Why? Because I was a nameless nobody? And now you're just worried about the MacKenzie name and money. You're a hypocrite, Stuart."

He glared at her. "What time tomorrow do you want to leave?"

Rapidly, she calculated the distance Seth Hanford said lay between here and her father's estate and hoped that the inn he'd made reservations in was as old-fashioned and strict as he'd claimed.

"I'll have a buggy waiting here at the hotel at eight. Good night, Stuart." She smiled with relief as he strode angrily away from her, down the private hallway. She might not be any great shakes as an actress, but she was proving to be a better than average fisherman.

Chapter
14

Few places on earth are more beautiful than the countryside of Virginia on a flawless spring day. Blossoming trees scent the air with subtle fragrances, long sweeps of green sward delight the eye, and the gentle sun warms the flesh. None of this beauty, however, penetrated the wintry chill which kept the two occupants in the speeding buggy wrapped in a cold silence. Stuart's greeting had been two ungracious comments: "Well, at least you had sense enough to rent a two-horse buggy," and "I hope to hell you know where we're going."

Marsh, who had picked the horses out herself, didn't bother to nod, she just handed him the map Seth Hanford had drawn. During the first three hours, she was buried deep in her own thoughts. She was a good deal more shaken than she'd expected to be by the prospect of visiting her parents in a home that might have been her girlhood one had she been luckier. She learned what Stuart was thinking only after a hurried lunch in a dusty roadside inn when he had again resumed driving.

"How did my father get control of this man's place? The usual carpetbagger route?"

"I don't think it would be wise to call your father a carpetbagger in front of this particular man. You might lose some of your pretty teeth."

"Have you met him?"

"Just once."

"Why in hell did you need me to go along then?"

"I wanted your opinion. Besides, as my stepson, you're a good chaperone." She smothered a smile as she watched his jaw tighten.

"Just how old is this man?"

"Very young, actually, for all he's done. He's a West Point graduate who served as a colonel in the Confederate Army."

"You're taking me to meet some hotheaded Confederate colonel?"

"He's a Virginia farmer, just like you. Do you mind changing the subject?"

"What subject would you like to talk about? Us?"

"There isn't any us."

His expression didn't change as he guided the buggy to the side of the road, secured the reins, put his arms around her and kissed her long and intimately. He was smiling as he released her and straightened her wig. "There's an us, Marsh, there always has been." She was the one who maintained a tight silence for the next hour, even after she regained control of her breathing.

The New George Inn proved to be even more proper and staid than Seth Hanford had said it was. Marsh swallowed her laughter as Blanche La Tour was led upstairs by a disapproving host to the maiden-lady wing, where the rooms were about as accessible as the vaults of a United States mint. Stuart noted her expression and smiled broadly as he ordered the private dining room and charged the expense to her account. He was still smiling an hour later when she descended the stairs in the black lace number she'd purchased from the brunette in Cheyenne. It was the most daring dress he'd ever seen, and it was being worn by a very daring woman, he thought, particularly since he'd made no secret of his feelings for her. Almost in a parody of southern chivalry, he offered his arm as they walked behind the haughty waiter, past the roomful of shocked guests, and into the fire-lit, private dining room. As soon as the man had poured their wine and gone, shutting the door with a vigorous click, Stuart moved toward her.

"About us now, Marsh," he began and then stopped his own words to kiss her again, slowly this time, while his hands moved downward to caress her hips. She struggled to free herself, cursing the stupid impulse which had led her to wear this damned dance hall dress. She'd meant to taunt him with it; she certainly hadn't known about this deadly private room.

"What about that interesting proposition you made me last night, Marsh? Just what did you have in mind?" She was spared the ignominy of trying to evade the answer by the return of the waiter, whose face above the steaming tray of soup was more contemptuous than it had been before. Stuart smiled broadly and winked at the man. "This lady is my stepmother, and we haven't seen each other in some time."

He released her long enough to steady the tray the waiter almost dropped and to allow Marsh to escape to the safety of a chair. Still laughing, Stuart took the one opposite and proceeded to pay her ridiculous and lavish compliments throughout that long meal—he'd ordered the twelve-course specialty.

"With your money," he taunted her at one point, "we could afford several hideaways and travel from one to another. Naturally, we'd have to hire a manager for our farm. But then we'd be together most of the time, except during those intervals each year when we might want to try a little variety. Variety does spark up any relationship, especially for an independent woman like you." At this effrontery, her frustrated indignation almost slipped out of control.

When she rose to leave the table after the interminable meal, he also stood up and reached for her arm. "After that indulgence, we'll walk for a while. I certainly don't want a fat mistress."

She almost shouted, You mean another fat mistress, but she gritted her teeth as he led her outside to the torch-lighted paths of the garden. Only when he kissed her in a darkened corner did she feel his strain. "One way or another, Marsh, we're together this time." It sounded very like a threat.

Both of them were tense the next day as they resumed driving. Marsh was dressed in one of her own pretty, soft green silk dresses, and her face was devoid of makeup. Stuart seemed as preoccupied as she was, except that he pulled her over on the seat until their bodies touched and put his free arm casually around her shoulders. That he'd studied the map was evident; he made the turns at Brooke and Fairmouth without changing the pace of the horses. As he turned the buggy into the private lane with the locked metal gates under the graceful wrought iron sign of "Marsh Oaks," he withdrew his arm abruptly.

"I'll say this much for the owner. He knows how to flatter a woman. Your name looks very impressive up there."

With relief, Marsh saw an attendant and called out, "I'm Miss La Tour, the owner is expecting me." They drove in silence for ten minutes until the great colonnaded mansion appeared behind a stand of magnificent, century-old oak trees. Her face alight with awe, Marsh stared at the breathtaking beauty of the home where three people were waiting for them. Only at the last minute did she remember to remove the wig and run a comb through her own disordered hair. Stuart watched the tall man who approached the buggy. "Your southern colonel is also damned good-looking," he muttered.

But Marsh was paying no attention to him; her eyes were on the man whose arms were stretched toward her. Without hesitation, she let those arms enfold her as he lifted her down and kissed her on the forehead. Her eyes were moist as she turned back to her glowering escort of two days.

"Stuart, this is my father, Bradford Marshall. Brad, this is Jamie's son, Stuart." As the two men shook hands, disciplined training alone forced the scowl from Stuart's face; Marsh smiled spitefully as she walked over to greet the women. She hugged her mother, who looked beautiful and so young Marsh momentarily felt the older, and then turned to the other woman whose eyes were filled with tears.

"You look so like your father. What I've missed in not knowing you, Pamela."

Marsh laughed unsteadily. "I'm a lot easier to know now. I was a pretty wild little girl." For the next half hour, Brad and Stuart remained apart from the three women, who sat on the verandah chairs and talked, or rather, Melissa talked while the other two listened on and off. Melissa fairly bubbled about Canada, New York, Marsh Oaks and Bradford. Her two personal comments to her daughter were "Oh dear, your hair is still so unruly," and "I'm glad you were gracious to your father; you used to be difficult about social manners." Marsh and her grandmother exchanged glances. Several times, Marsh deliberately avoided Stuart's accusing eyes and allowed a faint smile to soften the graceful shrug of her shoulders. When Brad thought the arrangement had continued long enough, he brought Stuart over and introduced him.

"Milly, Mother, entertain this young man while I have a talk with my daughter." But before Marsh accepted his proffered arm, she kissed both her mother and grandmother on their cheeks. In the study, her father poured her a glass of wine before he began to talk.

"Your mother and I were in Canada when your husband was killed; that's why we weren't there to help you. By the time we returned, you were gone. Since then—thanks to your Mr. Hanford—I've learned about all those things that happened to you. My God, why didn't you tell me about the poisoning when I saw you in New York?''

"I thought it was all over.''

"Hanford says it's not.''

"I guess it isn't.''

"You'll be safe here. I have a dozen of my old troopers who work for me and guard the place. I'd like you to make this your home now, Marsh.''

"No, Brad, my home is in Wyoming. I'll be going back there in October.''

"You can't. It's too dangerous. The Indians are massacring the settlers.''

"I'll be safe.''

"No, you won't. I've fought Indians on the warpath and they're a formidable enemy. Most white people underestimate them.''

"I'd never do that.''

"Well, it's impossible for you to get into that basin now. It's in Indian hands.''

"Why shouldn't it be in their hands? They own it.''

"Marsh, for God's sake, I don't want you killed. This is your home now.''

"Brad, why is it my home? Why did you deed half of it to me? You and my mother could have other children.''

"No, your mother can't. I deeded half to you because, without your husband's financial aid, I wouldn't have anything. I liked him, Marsh. I liked your husband very much.''

"I loved him.'' He looked at her closely and she rephrased her answer. "I loved him in every way.''

"I didn't know, Marsh. When I first saw him in New York, he told me that your marriage was in name only.''

Marsh grinned at her father. "It was until he got back, and I convinced him that I had no intention of being a virgin wife.''

"I just thought he was a little old for you.''

"Well, he wasn't.''

Diplomatically, Brad changed the subject. "Now that he's gone, why would you want to live alone in Wyoming?"

"I'm not alone. I had Jamie's baby there last October. Brad, except for my lawyer and Damon and Carina, no one on the east coast knows about my baby. Promise me you won't tell anyone."

"Your mother has a right to know."

How can you tell a man that the woman he loves is a ninny? That in a half hour's conversation she didn't once ask her newly widowed daughter how she was?

"My mother talks too much," she said bluntly and met the flashing anger of her father's eyes.

"You're too hard on her. She was sixteen years old when she had you, and she had two damnable men who brutalized her. If it weren't for her and her happiness, I'd kill that scum who murdered your husband."

"No, you won't, Brad. His death wouldn't be enough to keep me or my son safe. Did Seth tell you about Alice Nelson? She's the real danger."

"You can't kill them both."

"I will if I have to."

"I'll help you then."

"No, Brad. You're right about my mother. It would kill her if something should happen to you. I told you about my baby so you could look after him. Oh, he's in good hands now. Jamie's oldest son, Robbie, will raise him if I can't return. But thanks for your offer, Brad. I won't forget it. Now, let's talk about something cheerful."

"All right. Next Saturday night you're going to meet an old friend of yours, John Mosby. Your mother and I are giving a party for you."

"Why in the hell did you do that? I don't want anyone to know I'm back."

"Then why did you tell Stuart?"

"He and I are old friends. I knew him before I married his father."

"So he told me. Did you love him first, Marsh?"

"Not really."

"Do you love him now?"

"Yes. I plan to marry him."

"Has he asked you?"

"Not to marry him."

"Then he's not eager for marriage?"

"No, he's not. He once turned me down flat."

"But you still want him?"

"Yes."

Brad grinned at her. "And I'm supposed to help you change his mind?"

She grinned back. "That's the idea. Between the two of us and John Mosby, we should be able to convince him that he'd be a hell of a lot safer with me as a wife than a mistress. That is, as long as we don't tell him about his baby brother."

Brad looked over at his beautiful daughter, who faced life with reckless courage rather than self-pity, and became her confederate. "All right," he smiled, "let's make a gentleman out of that Yankee rogue of yours."

In retrospect, the campaign waged during the next five days was a skillful one, but in the end it was Stuart's jealous temper that made it successful. The morning after their arrival, Stuart finally cornered an evasive Marsh and demanded to know why she hadn't told him about her father years ago.

"Had I known," he scolded her, "I would never have acted the way I did."

She smiled at him with contempt and wondered why she wanted him. "I hadn't even met him then. Don't get any illusions about me, Stuart, I never saw this place until yesterday, and that sign you admired is a hundred years old."

"Your father told me."

"And when I leave here," she continued hotly, "I'll live my life exactly the way I want to, and I'll never be completely respectable."

"So we're back to that again."

"Yes."

Marsh may not have been respectable, but she was the unchallenged belle of her father's party. The day before, Brad had given her two gifts, a dress and a necklace. "My father's mother was a redhead just like you, and this was hers." It was a necklace of rubies and amber, intricately bound together with gold. "The dress," he told her, "I had made for you in Canada. It's a little daring, but not too much for a girl like you." Not since the ivory silk gown Jamie had given her in England had Marsh seen one as beautiful. It was made of an iridescent silk, a burnt orange color that changed with each movement, glowing like hot coals one moment and a blazing sunset the next. The bodice fit like a second skin and the draped skirt flared into a dramatic fullness in back. She felt as if she had been transformed into a flame herself as she tried it on.

Introduced as Pamela Marshall, with no mention of her married name or status to some thirty of the bluest bloods of northern Virginia, Marsh was an instant success even before the still dashing John Mosby described her as a Confederate heroine who'd fed his men during the war. From that moment on, she danced—six times with Mosby, four times with the hot-eyed son of a neighboring plantation owner, twice with her father, who warned her that her Yankee major was about to start another Civil War, and only once with that Yankee major. Even as the last carriage was being driven off, a scowling Stuart almost dragged her into a dark corner of the verandah.

"You've ignored me all night and I want to know why," he demanded.

"I thought I'd take your advice about variety adding spice," she quipped.

"And did it?"

"Of course, it did."

"All right," he sputtered, "let's find out how I compare with my competition." His arms and lips were hard and brutal as he crushed her to him. And, with a gambler's daring, she responded and added a passionate promise of her own. It's now or never, she figured, with the small part of her brain that still could think sanely.

Stuart was shaking as he released her lips. "I wish to hell we were back at your hotel room in Washington," he muttered thickly. She pulled sharply away, her passion replaced by ice water. He still wanted her, but only in the same old way. He was too thickheaded, too egotistical, too damned immature for marriage; and she wanted to hurt him as he had her.

"Well, we're not. And if you plan to indulge in those grownup games of playing house, you'd better learn not to treat every woman you invite into bed like the tramps you're used to." He was still in shock when she left him with her pride intact, but her dreams of happiness in tatters. By dawn, she had regained some of her resilience and all of her will to survive. Donning her boots and breeches and the leather jacket Shannon had given her with the stiffened holster pockets, she hiked to the far edge of her father's estate. There, in the trunk of a dead oak, she buried all twelve bullets from both pistols within a four-inch target area. Twice, Stuart's face blotted out that of her hated stepfather. Back in her room, she cleaned and reloaded her pistols, hung her jacket up, and joined her grandmother at breakfast. Claire Marshall smiled at her.

"You look pretty even in those things, Pamela." Marsh felt better about life then. She was still in her riding clothes when one of the servants told her that she was wanted in the library. Striding impatiently into the dignified room, she confronted a startled Brad and a tense Stuart. When both of them scowled at her choice of apparel, her temper flared again and she glared back at them.

"Stuart," her father began, "has just asked for your hand in marriage."

"How quaintly old-fashioned," she snapped. "He should have asked me."

"But," Brad continued, ignoring her interruption, "he seems to think that you want something other than marriage."

"The 'other than' was his idea, not mine. Will that be all?" She turned to leave, her face set in anger.

Stuart was on his feet, shouting at her. "You're going to marry me if I have to tape that big mouth of yours shut and cut those damned clothes off you. You're going to wear dresses and act like a female or you're going to get the spankings you've needed since you first started to flaunt that body of yours like a red flag in front of a bull."

Marsh was laughing long before he finished talking. In the first place, it was the most ridiculous proposal she'd ever heard of; in the second place, Stuart had looked like his father when Jamie had been angry at her. Finally, she was laughing with relief. She stopped only when her father echoed Stuart's accusation.

"Stuart's right, Pamela Marshall, you've acted the tomboy long enough. Now kindly give him your answer."

"Of course I'm going to marry him. I decided weeks ago when I was in Cheyenne." Neither man could top that declaration, but both entertained serious doubts about any future domestication.

Although no one made any comment during the next three busy days of preparation for the wedding at Marsh Oaks, Marsh became outrageously feminine—wearing dresses as if she had invented them, riding a horse sidesaddle at a mincing walk, and acting the shy virgin until Brad wanted to shake her. At the wedding itself, she wore the dress and necklace her father had given her and a lacy veil her grandmother had dyed the same color. Clinging to her father's arm as they walked down the broad, curved stairway leading to the drawing room where a few friends were gathered, her eyes were modestly lowered. Suppressing a smile, Brad whispered to her, "You'd better watch your impudence, young lady, this man isn't an indulgent Jamie. He's angry enough to do exactly what he promised." Quite gently really, she pinched her father's arm, and promised in a clear voice to obey her new husband.

During the lovely champagne buffet which followed, Marsh had three private conversations. Quietly, she told her grandmother about her infant son and accepted the uncritical love the aristocratic old woman offered her. She had her first complete conversation with her mother, who wished her daughter the same happiness with Stuart as Melissa had with Brad. "I'm glad, Pamela, that you didn't grow up to be the coward I was. But be sweet to your new husband, dear; he's not as strong as you are." Marsh kissed her mother without the condescension she usually felt and wondered if Melissa might not be right. Watching her husband covertly from across the room, she was dismayed to realize how little she knew about him. And several times, when she caught his brooding eyes on her, she shivered at the coldness in them.

Her father was equally concerned about Stuart. "I'll keep in close touch with you through Hanford. If you need me for anything, including protection from Stuart, I'll come immediately. He's a very moody man, Marsh, and you certainly don't need anymore problems right now."

That night, in the bridal suite of the New George Inn, she remembered her father's words. It was one thing for her to sound outrageously independent when she accepted his proposal in the safety of her father's library; it was another to face Stuart's gloomy look from ten feet away in the privacy of a hotel suite. After the smiling landlord had escorted them in and wished them happiness, Stuart had moved away from her and opened the bottle of Scotch Brad had given him. Without a word, he held it up, mutely asking if she wanted to join him. She did, but she was too unsure of herself in this cold and angry moment to say so. Nervously, she went into the bedroom and carefully removed the dress she'd treasure for years, but she couldn't don the frothy bridal gown and peignoir her mother had given her. Instead, she put on the fur-lined robe Jamie had bought for her and huddled in front of the window until she fell asleep. Hours later, she awoke and gazed morosely at the empty bed. So much for her second unconsumated wedding night!

In the other room, she found Stuart asleep and snoring on a chair in front of the dead fire, the half empty bottle carefully corked on the hearth. She dragged a blanket from the bed and covered him up. She knew that she'd underestimated him badly and felt a cold foreboding. She had counted heavily on the blind, consuming passion that had always flared between them to unite them until they could build the trust in each other that she and Jamie had had. But, whereas Jamie had always wanted to talk, Stuart brooded in silence. She slept finally in the lonely bed and awakened in the morning to emptiness. Stuart was gone. Out of habit and a disciplined sense of survival, she bathed and ate breakfast. After dressing carefully in her green travel outfit, she applied makeup and put on her wig. Carrying only her carpetbag with her precious pistols and riding clothes, she went downstairs to the desk and rang the tinkling little bell. The landlord himself ran to answer her summons and stopped short when he saw the wig. The beautiful bride last night had had dark red hair and had sounded very unlike this commanding woman.

"I want my buggy out in front in five minutes and the luggage in my room put aboard. Now give me my bill and I will pay it."

He looked at her with contempt. "Your husband left instructions that you were not to leave the hotel, Mrs. MacKenzie. You are to await his return from Baltimore. He left you this letter."

She didn't touch the envelope he pushed toward her. "How long ago did my husband take the boat from Quantico?"

Surprised by her knowledge of local transportation facilities, the landlord admitted that one of the hotel grooms had just returned from driving her husband there. "Now, Mrs. MacKenzie," he added with ill-concealed irritation, "please do as your husband suggests and return to your suite."

Marsh smiled pleasantly and spoke in a soft, reasonable tone. "Mr. Greer, you have a nice, quiet hotel here. But if my buggy, with my luggage aboard, is not standing by your front door in fifteen minutes, I am going to scream this whole damned place down around your head."

Mr. Greer took one last comprehensive look at this green-eyed termagant and sent two hotel employees scurrying. "And now my bill, Mr. Greer," she prompted. He hurried to prepare it.

"Do you want to leave a letter for your husband?" he asked with subtle insolence.

"No, but I want you to send a note to my father, Mr. Bradford Marshall." She watched in amusement at the landlord's change of expression from shocked disapproval to unctious concern. "When my husband returns, tell him that I'll be at Marsh Oaks," she ordered. Her note to her father contained only thirteen words: "When Stuart comes calling, tell him I've gone to New York. Love, Marsh."

All the way from the New George Inn to Quantico, an hour's distance away, she drove the horses at a fast pace, her mind churning with calculations and plans. It would take Stuart another six hours to reach Baltimore by boat; her telegram would arrive in a third of the time. Leaving the buggy at a livery stable after ordering that the horses be rested and tended, she carried her carpetbag and walked down the main street of town. At the first office with the title "Attorney-at-Law" written in gold lettering beneath the name C. R. Williams, she entered and requested the help of the young man sitting idly behind his desk.

"I want you to attest to the contents of some telegrams I wish to send and to countersign all of them." Silently, she blessed Jamie's memory. By this procedure he had bought and sold property without leaving his own desk at the bank. Eager for business, the young lawyer accepted her credentials with alacrity: the letter from Angus about the extent of her holdings, a bank book issued by the Ryder-MacKenzie Bank, and the letter Jamie had written her prior to his death.

The first telegram was sent to the Greg Morrisons telling them that the Rake-Star colt was theirs in return for their quartering all of the remaining MacKenzie breed horses until October 1, 1869. The attorney was impressed. The second telegram, to the Hardings, was the request that they move the designated horses to the Morrisons and withhold the information from any interested parties. C. R. Williams was even more impressed by his client.

On the third telegram, the lawyer began to earn his fee. It was a four part request addressed to Mr. Angus Balfour in Baltimore to rearrange her money in the Ryder-MacKenzie Bank there: fifty thousand dollars was to be credited to the account of Mr. Robert MacKenzie in the territorial bank of Cheyenne, Wyoming; one hundred and fifty thousand was to be transferred to the account of Marsh MacKenzie in that bank; twenty-five thousand dollars was to be left in her account at the Ryder-MacKenzie Bank; and all other funds transferred to the account of Angus Balfour at the same bank. Her demand for secrecy was a personal note: "Not a word of this to anyone and not a drop of usquebaugh for three days. Love, Marsh."

In the fourth long, complicated message, Marsh divested herself of three-quarters of the fortune Jamie had left her. It contained proxy releases for pieces of property owned wholly or jointly: to Stuart MacKenzie the Virginia farm and the New York properties; to Damon and Carina the Maryland farm; to Craig MacKenzie the Baltimore properties; to Bradford Marshall sole ownership of Marsh Oaks; and to Jake and Adah, Marsh's share of the Georgia farm. This last bequest held the proviso that Angus Balfour conduct the actual transfer. Once again, the recipient of this telegram, Bruce Mac Lachlan, attorney-at-law, was cautioned not to make these releases public.

For another hour, the young lawyer scratched away with his

pen flying over sheets of paper until all the details were carefully recorded in lengthy legal language. As Marsh signed the final paper, she felt curiously relieved. She now owned a ranch in Wyoming, some racehorses, and the leftover MacKenzie horses, while the money in the Cheyenne bank was the inheritance of Jamie MacKenzie's fourth son—a small boy he hadn't lived to know.

It was late afternoon by the time all the business was conducted and the legal papers filed in the Hall of Records. Marsh dreaded the lonely hours she would spend this night in still another hotel whose owner disapproved of single women guests. On impulse, she turned to the young lawyer.

"Mr. Williams, are you married?"

Startled, he flubbed the answer slightly. "I think not," he said and laughed. "No, Mrs. MacKenzie, I'm not. Not on my earnings."

"Good. Then I'd like to hire you for another few hours to be my guest at dinner."

"Mrs. MacKenzie," he assured her gallantly, "you could hire me anytime."

Four brandies later, after a pleasant dinner in the unpretentious hotel he had recommended, his assurance had increased to a fervent, "Mrs. MacKenzie, you could hire me for life." Marsh paid him his fee and retired to her room with mixed feelings. C. R. Williams had been attractive, educated, and completely available; and she hadn't the slightest interest in him as a man. She wondered if an unlucky and capricious fate had destined her to love only MacKenzie men; more precisely, only Jamie and Stuart MacKenzie. But her unhappy thoughts were of short duration this night; the brandy she had consumed proved an excellent soporific. She slept soundly, rose the next morning with a reasonably clear head, and drove back to Washington, D.C.

Out of the necessity, to remain where Seth Hanford could contact her, Marsh moved back into her rooms at the same hotel in the capital city where she had been prior to her ill-starred second marriage. During the next week, Blanche La Tour became a familiar figure at the railroad station and the draying company, arranging for the shipment of more than two hundred MacKenzie horses to Cheyenne. By prepaying all costs, including the wages of the men whom the railroad would hire to handle the horses in transit, Marsh was assured that her debt of honor would be paid to Crazy Horse. Now she was free to concentrate on the remaining goals she had set for herself in this civilized eastern part of the United States— the destruction of two people whom the courts had declared innocent.

She knew instantly that her truant husband was in residence when she unlocked the door to her room and saw the half finished snifter of brandy on the table. She tensed in anger as his tall figure emerged from the bedroom and approached her. "Welcome back, Mrs. MacKenzie, you've led me quite a chase. But now you're going to settle down and become an obedient wife. If you don't want your wig and costume ruined, I suggest you remove them. Incidentally, my father's lawyer was delighted about our marriage."

She tensed instantly. "Was Mr. Mac Lachlan also cooperative about your taking control of your father's fortune?"

"Is that what you thought I went there to do?"

She shrugged and waited.

"Marsh, did you really think I was going to play lapdog to you as my father had done? He was a fool to give you the power to control my brothers's and my lives. I went to the lawyer to equalize the distribution of his estate."

"And did you?"

"To all practical purposes, yes. Your signature will be necessary, of course, before the actual division can be made."

Marsh let her breath out slowly. Shrewd, clever Bruce Mac Lachlan had not betrayed her. "And what division did you have in mind, Stuart?"

"Four equal shares, Marsh. Had you bothered to read the letter I left for you at the New George, you'd have known my intentions. And if you'd been the obedient wife you promised to be, you'd have remained there. The landlord told me about the threat you made.''

"I am not your wife, Stuart, obedient or otherwise. I have already consulted a lawyer about annulment proceedings.''

"They won't be valid after today. Did you really think I'd let you go this time? In ten minutes, our marriage starts whether you're willing or not.''

Marsh rose unsteadily to her feet, her heart pounding with a confusion of emotions of which anger was no longer the main part. But she had by no means surrendered completely yet. With the bravado that was her automatic escape from domination, she smiled at her husband.

"All right, Stuart, I'll be your mistress for a few months.'' She was through the bedroom door before he could splutter a reply. He never heard the words she muttered to herself: "And if I'm lucky, I'll conceive another child and Jamie will have his brother.''

Knowing that Stuart's temper was barely under control, she removed her wig and dress carefully and, in a spirit of contempt, donned one of Jamie's old nightshirts and her fur-lined robe. Before she settled down at her dressing table to clean the makeup from her face, she rummaged through her husband's luggage and dragged out the bottle of Scotch she knew would be there. She didn't intend to be the only sober partner in bed that day. She was standing in front of the window, sipping from her half emptied glass, when she heard Stuart disrobing in the other part of the room. She didn't turn around when she felt one of his hands on her shoulder while the other one reached down and took the glass from her hand.

"Why, Marsh? Why did you make a fool of me in front of your father?''

"Because I was angry. Until you met my father, you still thought of me in the same way that you had when you called me a foulmouthed gutter waif, a cast-off whore and a used harlot. I was just paying you back.''

"Why in God's name did you marry me then?"

She twisted out from under his hands and turned to face him, her eyes burning into his. "Because I wanted you and I didn't want to become any of those things you called me." Reaching her arms around his neck, she pulled his face down to hers and silenced him with a kiss. Reluctantly, she thought, his arms went around her and he began returning her caress. She could feel his desire build even before his hands dropped downward to cup her buttocks and pull her toward him. Then the electric attraction which had always existed between them became a powerful, driving force, until neither knew how they reached the bed or wound up naked beneath the covers. She wasn't aware when her robe was removed or the night-shirt she'd worn in defiance. Every part of her consciousness was concentrated on the fire which blazed inside of her and on the man who drove into her blindly, with a frenzy of passion which built until she felt consumed. When he exploded within her, her body was ready with a response that rolled over her like a wave, and she was transported into a floating world of sensation so throbbing with ecstasy, she felt spasm after spasm before her body quieted.

They had no easy words to say to each other afterward; their passion had been too raw, too primitive for sophisticated comment. Nor could they sleep, the experience had shattered the peace of mind necessary for simple slumber. On her part, Marsh missed the consolation of love which had accompanied her and Jamie's unions; while Stuart, who had never known a love like that, felt oddly disturbed by his own violence with this woman. He wanted the safety of separation from her until he could regain the detachment he'd always had after making love with other women, and he wasn't sure he liked being sucked under by the power of her magnetism.

Feeling the need for the impersonality of a more public atmosphere, they dressed wordlessly in their formal dining clothes. But even the ivory velvet Blanche La Tour dress and the pale blond wig failed this time to add the necessary hardness to be a good disguise for Marsh. Her eyes were too wide and luminous with shock to look like the eyes of an experienced courtesan. Gravely, Stuart bent and kissed her lightly before he escorted her to the discreet dining room they'd visited once before.

Silently, they sipped their wine, still unable to talk to each other; and not until they finished eating did they trust themselves enough to dance together. Once on the floor though, the soft music and the rhythm of their synchronized movement bound them both up again in the strange new world of sensual domination. In the end it was exhaustion which broke the spell and dissolved their tension. On the way back to their rooms, they relaxed enough to smile at each other tentatively, and Marsh regained a small measure of her normal humor, although she was still a long way from feeling like the raucous imp she'd been with Jamie.

In the softly lit bedroom designed to stimulate human senses far more jaded than theirs, they undressed again, but before she could slip on her concealing robe, Stuart pulled her toward the light and traced his fingers over the scar on her shoulder and the lash marks on her thighs. His eyes were gentle as he wrapped her trembling body in the robe and held her close to him.

"When did that little bastard beat you like that?"

"Until I was thirteen and your father rescued me."

"I didn't know. I didn't even know you belonged up at the big house when I first met you."

"I didn't. I hated that house."

"What really happened on that night I made a fool of myself?"

Touched by his tenderness, she told him about both Creightons, the hasty wedding, and the trial-like scene the next morning.

"No wonder you loved my father and hated me."

"I didn't hate you, Stuart. I loved you both times you came to help me when I needed you." When he continued to hold her somberly, she wanted to break his moody concentration on her past. "We're tired now, Stuart, let's go to bed."

Even more than the physical release of their violent lovemaking in the afternoon, the simple joy of having a man's warm body curled around her without passion once again gave Marsh the feeling of coming home. Snuggling close to his relaxing strength, she closed her eyes and slept. In the morning, the first glimmer of redeeming humor entered into their embryonic relationship. She opened her eyes to find him smiling down at her.

"You snore," he teased her.

"I know," she chuckled and wiggled against him, "so do you." He had the grace to grin back at her and to follow her other lead as well.

"Do you always wake up like this?" Since his growing response assured her of his approval, Marsh answered honestly.

"When I'm happy."

"Half of our children are going to be born in the morning then," he whispered, and proceeded with his hands to demonstrate why. What began as play soon became passionate sensuousness and, finally, the irresistible need to belong to each other. As he held her pulsating body, Stuart's hands were possessively strong; he lifted her hips so that they seemed a part of him when he entered her. Tender with her this time, he prolonged his thrusts until their bodies fused together with the urgent need for completion. The moment when it came was sweeter than the earlier one had been, and neither partner felt the need to separate. Even when they did, Stuart did not release her as his hands smoothed her tumbled hair and his lips caressed her cheek. "I think, my independent mistress," he murmured in between kisses, "you have just become my wife." She smiled at him without comment, but with a tinge of sadness; the time for testing was still in the future.

Because he didn't want the confusion of a Blanche La Tour

interrupting his concentration on the redheaded sylph now dominating his thoughts and emotions, Stuart arranged to have their meals served in their rooms. For three more days of isolation, they explored their limited areas of unity. Lacking the bold self-confidence of his father, Stuart was defensive, so Marsh did not pry; nor did she invite him to question her too closely. Her own secrets were as inhibiting as his. But in the limited area of their tentative love—since the fire between them was a form of love—they soon lost any self-consciousness about each other's responses to overtures, and luxuriated in more relaxed unions. Marsh rarely dressed in anything other than her robe, and frequently not even in that after the one time she wore the frothy bridal peignoir set her mother had given her. Digging his hands through yards of the filmy white material, Stuart removed it impatiently.

"You don't need all that stuff to make you look desirable. I always knew you had a beautiful body."

The closest they came to an argument during those days was a reminder of their wedding night at the New George Inn. Marsh asked him how he'd known where to find her. "I wrote my father to tell you I'd gone to New York."

"I didn't even see your father. I just asked the landlord which direction you'd driven off in. Why didn't you read my letter, Marsh?"

"Why did you ignore me the night before?" she countered.

"No man likes to feel trapped."

"Neither do I."

"Do you feel trapped now?" Marsh looked at the taut line of his jaw and ended the conversation with a giggle.

"No, Stuart MacKenzie, I always knew you'd have a beautiful body, too."

After that tiff, Stuart reached for her even more often with possessive arms. "My God," he complained, but he was smiling sheepishly when he did, "we'll never get any work done if this keeps up." Seated comfortably on his lap at the time, she grinned at him.

"I could always wear a corset," she quipped; his instant frown told her she'd struck a sore point. She changed the subject and stretched around to kiss him.

"Better still, I'll just wear my riding clothes."

"No, you won't. I'm going to make sure that your impudent rear end is well covered in public." He shut up then because the disputed part of her anatomy had just wiggled him into a state of acute arousal. Laughing a little, he pushed her off his lap and into bed. His comment afterward was the first time he came close to an admission of love. "You're mine, Marsh, don't ever try to leave me again."

"I won't," she whispered, but she knew she would probably have to. Sadness mingled with her growing sense of urgency that night as her thoughts reverted to the ugly realities of her life. By morning, she was restless and impatient for action; her allotted time had been reduced to four and a half months. Dressed in her La Tour street ensemble, a flashily elegant, honey-blond dress with a black striped, billowing skirt and a matching parasol, she dragged a nonplussed husband out of the suite and the hotel. Walking beside him with a brisk step and a determined expression, she insisted, "We need to see the world and let the world see us."

Had she known that she had just been observed by an unsavory character in the hotel lobby, a man who had already followed her on one of her earlier business trips, she would not have used those precise words. Kerry Daniels was a procurer of the type which abounded in Washington. Womanizers themselves, they had built-in instincts about the emotional temperatures of potential additions to their supply of high priced women. Even in this peculiarly feminine world of employment, the men in charge resented independent operators who managed alone. Daniels had been puzzled the first time he'd noticed this particular woman because she had not followed the usual pattern, but this morning, when she'd come downstairs with a man, he knew he'd been right.

Walking over to the desk, he handed the cooperative clerk a dollar and received the information he wanted. With a cynical expression, he took a sheet of the expensive hotel paper, scrawled a very explicit note to Miss Blanche La Tour, and handed it to the clerk. Then he returned to his usual chair in the lobby.

Thus, when Marsh and Stuart returned a half hour later, she was handed not just the letter she expected, but another one as well. Sighing, she knew from experience that no eye was keener than a MacKenzie male's and no temper more explosive if he thought his wife was attempting to conceal something from him. And, if anything, Stuart was more possessive than his father had been. She could feel the electricity of his demanding curiosity as she attempted a futile concealment of the offending letters in her reticule. Withstanding the silent pressure until they were seated in the dining room, she surrendered one unopened letter to him, the one not addressed to her in Seth Hanford's familiar writing. Alarmed, she watched Stuart's dark brows descend over eyes, which were now a fiercely predatory blue. Without telling her a word about the contents, he reached out his hand and snapped his fingers for the other one. Reluctantly, she gave it to him, realizing that the contents of Seth's letter would end the honeymoon more surely than the other letter, whatever its contents had been.

"It would seem," Stuart accused her after he'd finished reading, "that my wife has many hidden talents and more than a few admirers. Would you care to explain who these men are?"

"I only know one, Stuart, and he's an old friend."

"And my father allowed you to rendezvous with an 'old friend' whenever you wanted?"

Marsh remembered Jamie's part in keeping Seth a willing employee. "Your father appreciated this man's talents very much," she answered.

Not a whit mollified, Stuart snapped at her, "Since it is my appreciation you must be concerned with now, you will forego the pleasure of keeping this appointment.''

"May I see the letter please?'' she asked in a level tone.

"No, dear wife, you may not. When an 'old friend' can tell my wife to meet him at some agreed upon place, I think I have a right to interfere.'' Marsh shrugged in compliance to his arbitrary decision and smothered a smile which threatened to destroy her sober expression. Stuart had told her most of what she needed to know. Her problem now was the relatively simple one of getting to that agreed upon place without arousing any more suspicion. She was still debating ways and means when his voice sounded once again, even more peremptorily. "Since you claim you don't know this other man, I think you should read his letter.''

As Marsh read the insidious, half-threat, half-invitation to join the author in the mutually profitable fleecing of governmental officials, her face and fury flamed. Clutching the letter and her reticule in one hand and her parasol in the other, she stood up and charged back to the desk, followed by an embarrassed Stuart. "Kindly tell me,'' she demanded of the clerk in a voice that would have made even Crazy Horse sit a little straighter, "just when this letter was delivered and by whom?''

Mortified by the strident command of a woman in a hotel which prided itself on quiet discretion, the man reprimanded her in subdued tones. "Shortly after you and your gentleman friend left the hotel this morning, Mr. Daniels inquired about your identity. He's sitting across from us in the lobby.''

Marsh did not deign to turn around. Mr. Daniels would keep for a few minutes more. "Now tell this gentleman,'' she jerked Stuart's arm, "about the man who helped me register here several weeks ago.''

More conciliatory now, the man studied the records. "It was a Mr. Seth Hanford, a Pinkerton detective.''

"Now tell this gentleman,'' again the jerk on Stuart's arm

as she bore down relentlessly on the perspiring clerk, "just how many visitors I have had during my two stays here."

Again, the clerk perused the records and gestured toward Stuart, "Just this one gentleman, Miss La Tour."

"You're sure I couldn't have sneaked a dozen others up the back stairs?"

The man's face was openly scandalized. "Such a thing would be impossible here. We pride ourselves on protecting our guests."

"Except," she spat at him, "your women guests from vermin like that parasite across the room. Now, get my bill prepared and have it ready by the time I return from delousing your lobby. This gentleman, who happens to be my husband, and I are leaving to return to his home." She spun around before Stuart could stop her and strode across the room where a florid man with gold caps on two side teeth was smiling at her in unctious welcome. Jabbing the sharp metal point of her parasol into his ample stomach, she hissed, "Get up and start walking toward that door before I lean on this thing and puncture your fat gut." Stuart arrived in time to prevent her from taking the threatened action while Kerry Daniels fled for the safety of Washington streets.

Back in their suite, where she packed with efficient speed, her anger cooled, and she chuckled as she realized that her other problem was also solved. She and Stuart should be at the farm in less than two hours. Her humor increased when she realized that Stuart was deliberately dawdling over his own more meager packing.

"Marsh," he temporized, "I don't have a home prepared for you yet."

"Don't worry about it," she assured him airily, "anyplace will do for the time being. I want to see those improvements you've made."

All the way down the stairs and through the lobby to the waiting taxi, she ignored his apologetic suggestion that they stay in another hotel or at the Maryland farm. As they neared the Virginia side of the Potomac, her glee became even more malicious as she remembered his arrogant treatment of her at the breakfast table. Well, now the shoe was on the other foot! Let's see, she smirked silently, how Mr. High and Mighty explains Janet's things in his bedroom and maybe Janet herself.

The first of Stuart's improvements was the new dock and the warning bell which clanged as the ferry eased alongside of it. Within minutes of landing, the luggage was being piled into the wagon which had responded to the summons. Not until the driver reached the office cabin did Marsh relent and ease her husband's obvious perturbation.

"I'll wait for you in the office, Stuart. I don't think Janet's and my perfume will blend very well."

He spoke before he realized the completeness of her understanding. "You don't wear perfume."

She smiled. "I didn't think that your nose was educated enough to know the difference."

Embarrassed, he floundered, "Marsh, I'm—"

"Don't say it, Stuart. I've known about Janet for years." She leaned over and kissed him on the cheek. "We're even now." She was off the wagon and into the old familiar office before he could respond again, but she didn't remain in the building. As soon as the wagon moved on, she hurried out the back door and along the path to an old tool shed which had been a guard outpost during the war. From the small openings on each of the four sides, one watcher could survey the dock, the cottages, the road, and the big house. Inside, she found an impatient and uncomfortable Seth Hanford.

"I expected you yesterday," he greeted her.

"The damned hotel neglected to give me your letter until today."

"I've been worried that our suspects would leave before you got here."

"He's here now?"

"They all are, including the fat lawyer. They've been waiting for MacKenzie to return."

"Stuart? Why would they want him in such a hurry?"

"Hiram Creighton pulled a slick move off in a Virginia courtroom. He produced a body which Janet Talbot swore was her husband's. So did her mother and your grandfather. Neither Mosby nor Mac Lachlan had ever seen Talbot, so they couldn't testify, and I arrived after the hearing was concluded."

Marsh's heart was pounding. "It wasn't Wayne's, was it?"

"No, he's on his way here now, but he may not arrive in time to save MacKenzie some damned unpleasant involvement. According to the house servants, he's going to be greeted with a shotgun reception to make an honest woman out of that—"

"Fat slut," Marsh finished tersely. "Stuart's not in any trouble. He's already married."

It was Hanford's turn to look amazed, a facial expression normally impossible for his impassive features. "Since when?"

"Twelve days ago at my father's home."

"That'll put you doubly on the spot, Marsh."

"Good, maybe we can get the thing over quickly then."

"You're sure you want to take the risk?",

"I have to and you know it."

"I know it, but what about your new husband?"

Her face hardened. "If I have to put up with his mistress, he'll have to put up with my actions. How have you planned to do it?"

"First, we have to let them know you're hiding on the farm, and then wait for Creighton to make his move. He'll probably try to lure you away to a remote part of the farm. Do you still know your way around?"

"Not as well as he does, but well enough, I guess. How are we going to—" Her words were cut short by his warning hand on her arm as he pointed toward the road. Walking at a pace unbecoming to overweight people were a set-faced Janet

Talbot and a perspiring Hiram Creighton. Marsh's insides knotted with revulsion; like two fat homing pigeons, they were headed straight for Stuart's cottage.

Hanford's whispered question was thoughtful. "Would either of those two recognize you in that getup?"

"Janet might not, but that monster inventoried me down to my toenails four years ago. He'd recognize me if my skin were dyed as brown as an Indian's."

"Are you brave enough to face him right now?"

"If I have to."

"Do you have your derringer handy?"

She patted her reticule. "Always. But why do I meet them now?"

"Because it's a good way to let your presence be known. Let those two get inside and then you go in and act like Blanche La Tour to the hilt. I think the lawyer will be slick enough not to challenge you. He'll be smart enough to let you think the disguise worked. While you're there, if your husband hasn't told them yet, you can spill the beans about your marriage. I'll stay here and watch the house for any sign of your stepfather. Incidentally, I have four good men on the farm to help me. Are you sure you can handle it?"

Marsh wasn't at all sure; her heart was beating unpleasantly loud and she was frightened, but she nodded anyway.

"All right, get going. Wait, your wig is loose." Carefully, he straightened it and looked her over critically. "You'll do," he whispered. "Good luck!" All the way back through the office rooms she tried to think of an opening line. Inspiration and a good memory came to her aid; she'd never forgotten Marilee Windom's entry.

Using her parasol as she'd seen the overdressed society women do whenever they stopped in the street to pose and chat with each other, she opened the door to Stuart's cottage, halted dramatically five feet inside, rested both hands on the curved handle of her parasol, swept her eyes haughtily around the room, and focused them on the angry face of Janet Talbot.

"Who," Marsh asked in frigid tones, "is this woman, and what is she doing in your home, Stuart?"

Her face unattractively mottled with shock, Janet spluttered in fury, her eyes reflecting her contempt for the brassy nature of Marsh's dress and makeup. "Where did you find this tramp, Stuart? And is she the reason I haven't seen you for weeks?"

The tip of Marsh's umbrella tapped Janet lightly on the shoulder. "My name is Blanche La Tour," she paused and repeated, "Blanche La Tour MacKenzie. And the next time you refer to me with the word tramp, you'll be lucky to leave with—" She didn't need to finish her threat. Janet was screaming at Stuart, using words Marsh had never heard before, and she'd thought her vocabulary fairly complete.

Twice, Hiram Creighton tried unsuccessfully to break into his client's tirade, but she screamed on. He settled back to study the new Mrs. MacKenzie, who kept her eyes rigidly on Janet to avoid making contact with the fat man's. When Janet finally subsided into angry tears, Creighton demanded of Stuart, "Is this woman your wife, MacKenzie?"

As angry at Marsh as he was disgusted with Janet, Stuart nodded grimly.

"You have documents to prove your claim, MacKenzie?" At Stuart's second nod, the lawyer continued, "Then you can expect to be sued for breach of promise, since your relationship with my client will be construed as a promise of marriage in the advent of her husband's death. I think, my dear," he said to Janet, "that we should leave now and allow this despoiler of women"—his nod indicated Stuart—"the opportunity to think in terms of a financial settlement." Rising with the agility that had startled Marsh before, Hiram stood up and helped Janet to her feet.

Not wanting to be left alone with an angry husband, Marsh picked up her carpetbag from the pile of luggage in the center of the floor and threw one last verbal bolt into the charged atmosphere. "Don't forget to have the place fumigated,

Stuart," she taunted before she left the cottage. Just outside the door, the anger she had been half pretending turned into authentic fury when she heard Stuart's voice.

"I'm sorry, Janet, I didn't mean for you to learn about it like this. I—"

Marsh didn't wait to hear anymore. Forgetting all about the role she was playing, she ran without dignity to the office cottage, slammed the door shut, and locked it. Pausing only long enough to rummage through the drawer where Angus had stored his usquebaugh and grab the half-empty bottle she found there, she fled into the rear of the house and into her old bedroom. After locking that door, too, she sat down breathlessly on the bed and glared at nothing. As ironic as they were, she almost felt that the fat man's words describing Stuart as a "despoiler of women" were accurate. A soft knock on the rear door interrupted her stormy thoughts. Like a shadow, Seth Hanford eased through the door and closed it silently.

"Did he recognize you?"

"He all but swallowed his leering eyes to keep me from knowing," she blurted.

"Then I think you'd better get into your working clothes. Do you have them with you?" At her nod, he locked the rear door. "I'll stand guard while you change. We don't want a surprise attack until we get set."

Marsh was just starting to change when an angry pounding sounded at the front door. She heard the detective move to admit her husband, and her husband's angry shouts gradually change to milder speech. Let him wallow in his own emotional gutter, she fumed as she yanked the hated La Tour dress and wig off for the last time. After pulling on her breeches and boots, she carefully checked both pistols and put the leather jacket on and started toward the door. She paused and cursed the lack of a mirror in the room. Grabbing a comb from her reticule, she pulled it through her tangled hair, cursing again at every wayward knot. Angrily, she dampened the edge of a discarded petticoat with the usquebaugh and scrubbed the makeup from her face. When she finally left her old room, carrying the bottle in one hand, she looked and sounded like the Marsh of four years earlier.

"Did y'all get that lil' ol' cat all sugared up again? My goodness, I thought she was goin' to scratch your eyes out. Just think, honey, if I hadn't come along today, y'all just might have your second shotgun weddin' in two weeks."

"Shut up, Marsh," Stuart bellowed, "you were going to mind your own business and let me handle mine. But you couldn't resist using that big mouth of yours, could you?"

Seth Hanford made a futile effort to interrupt this acrimonious exchange, "I think we have more import—" He never finished, Stuart had just noticed Marsh's clothes.

"Well, look at you! All you need are a pair of pistols to look like a two-bit cowboy from Arizona. I see you already have your bottle of rotgut."

"I've got the pistols and, right now, I could use some of this rotgut to get rid of the nasty taste in my mouth," she taunted him.

Hanford had heard all he wanted to. He took the bottle from Marsh's hand, pulled three glasses from the cabinet, and poured a liberal portion in each. "You two can finish this domestic quarrel later—much later. MacKenzie, your wife interrupted your reunion scene with your—with Mrs. Talbot because I ordered her to. You can't really be fool enough to think that she wanted to see that slimy lawyer again or that woman. I also ordered her to change into her working clothes because, like it or not, she has some very dangerous work to do. And yes, she does have pistols, which I hope to God she knows how to use. Drink up, Marsh, you and I have unfinished business to attend to. I'm sure your husband will excuse us."

Stuart's anger and bluster had disappeared. "Just what kind of danger, Hanford, is my wife facing?"

"She's going to play stalking horse to a murderer."

Chapter
15

Stuart's voice was calm, but his eyes were not as he moved over and tried to put a protective arm around his wife. She jerked sharply away, leaving only one arm vulnerable to his strong, grasping fingers. "I think you'd better explain yourself, Hanford."

"Your wife was in danger even before she married your father, but nothing like she's faced ever since. As I started to tell you earlier, MacKenzie, Marsh and your father hired me three years ago to watch Alice Nelson, but that woman was smart enough to know she was being watched. So she hired Creighton to do her dirty work for her. Creighton and others just as bad. While Marsh was in Wyoming last year, I followed the Nelson woman to another detective agency in Baltimore where she hired three men. It's an ugly group who work there. Two of the men she hired have been suspected of complicity in a dozen violent crimes, but they've never been convicted. My operators traced all three of these men to Cheyenne, but according to authorities, only one tried to reach the ranch. His body was found on the trail. The other two were bottled up in town during the winter.

"Just by luck Marsh changed her appearance while she was in Cheyenne, and that disguise may have saved her life. But it wouldn't have for long. There's too much money at stake for this game to end so easily. Only by trapping Blake Creighton at attempted murder can we get rid of the threat he poses. Since he's been cleared of your father's murder, he's hungry for more money so he'll try again. And we just can't kill him. Then we'd be charged. That's what your father wanted to do, Marsh, but he'd have been convicted. Technically, he deserted you and your mother while Creighton raised you. Public sympathy would have been badly split.

"But Creighton isn't the real threat, MacKenzie, Alice Nelson is. This new marriage makes Marsh's death doubly necessary if Alice is to get hold of what she considers the Ryder fortune."

"That's no longer true," Stuart interrupted. "I now control the bulk of my father's estate so I'd be the target."

Hanford looked at him in contempt. "The only thing you'd be the target for would be marriage to the Talbot woman or a paternity suit." Marsh moved sharply away from her husband as the detective continued.

"They know Talbot isn't dead as well as I do. But by having him declared dead, they've forced him to return to Virginia. John Mosby, whom Marsh's father hired to help out, has sent three of his men to Georgia to bring Talbot back; even so, his life will be in danger. As I told Marsh once, poisoners are a hard lot of killers to trap. And the Nelson woman is a damned clever one. She is determined to get the money into her brother's hands and to get you, MacKenzie, married to Janet."

"May I ask why you never mentioned any of this to me, Hanford? You seemed to have talked to every one else," Stuart demanded.

"Why should I? My client did not see fit to tell me about

her interest in you. Had she done so, I'd have told her father about you and the Talbot woman." Hanford's eyes were cold and hard as he continued his blunt, brutal attack. "Right now, I'm not one damned bit convinced that you didn't marry Marsh just for the money and that you don't really care what happens to her."

Marsh had a sudden, sharp memory of Stuart by the side of her bed after Jamie's murder. "That's not true, Seth. Stuart has always helped me."

At her words, the hot anger faded from her husband's eyes. "Now that we have decided I'm on my wife's side, what's the plan to protect her?"

"We wait. No one except the two of you know that I'm here or that I have operators already on the farm. Creighton will have to lure your wife away to some remote area just as he did your father. It's my guess he'll use his rifle again. And, undoubtedly, he's got his alibi all prepared. Quite simply, if he shoots, we plan to return fire."

Stuart turned to his wife. "Do you know how to use those guns?"

"Yes."

"A pistol against a rifle is not very fair odds, Hanford."

"We'll handle the rifles. If your wife were to show up with one, Creighton would know it's a trap. Right now, I want Marsh to go with me down to the paddock area and be seen by the workers as if she's returned to work like any other owner."

"All right, let's go."

"MacKenzie, I don't think it'll be necessary for you to accompany her."

"To hell with what you think, Hanford. My wife is not going to take one step on this farm without me." As Stuart grabbed Marsh's arm again and propelled her through the front door, he didn't see the smile on the detective's face; and no one saw Hanford as he moved silently through the wooded area toward the main barns.

Marsh was silent as Stuart led her up the steps of his own cottage and into his bedroom, where he removed his army revolver from a chest of drawers. While he was checking it, she tried to pull away from him, but he jerked her back, pressed her against the dresser, and worked around her. Putting the gun into his pocket, he pulled her out of the house and onto the main road. Only then did he break their tense silence.

"Since you've decided you can't stay in my house, we'll use one of the worker's cabins and eat at their mess. I'll send for our luggage." Minutes more passed before he spoke again, this time defensively. "Marsh, why all this sudden shock? You said that you've known about Janet for years."

"Because you treated me like the unwanted woman in there today."

"You made threats like some cheap harlot and I was ashamed of you. I didn't know you were just acting."

She looked at him in disgust. "Why hadn't you told them about me?"

"I was trying to hear what they were saying about Talbot."

"Tell me, Stuart, if I hadn't married you, would you have let them suck you into a marriage with that slut?"

Stuart stiffened. "As you recall, I'm not very easy to 'suck' into marriage. No, I wouldn't have married Janet. I don't love her and never have. I didn't even ask her to move in with me. She just did. And since we're down to basics, she was available and you were not."

"Good old MacKenzie stud farm." She felt his fingers dig into her arm.

"Are you trying to convince me that you've been a celibate for fourteen months? With your talents in bed?"

Marsh sucked in her breath and let it out slowly. "You won't have to worry about those talents ever again." Abruptly, she changed the subject. "I want to see my stallion."

"You can't. He's in a rear pasture."

"Like some old discard? He's a good horse."

"And his colts are good horses. But the Shires and Clydesdales support this farm."

"Then I'll take him back with me to Wyoming."

"Aren't you forgetting something, Marsh? The little fact that you're married to me whether you like it or not? You're not going anyplace."

Tightening her jaw, she refrained from blurting out her intentions. "Did you hear what I said?" he persisted.

"Your voice is loud enough, it's what you say that—"

"Well then, lady, we stop talking right now." Marsh stumbled as he dragged her to the side of the road and into a clump of screening shrubs. There, he kissed her and his fingers dug into her buttocks with a steely strength as he moved her at will across his hips.

"We have," he muttered thickly, "some unfinished business." Picking her up roughly, he carried her a hundred feet to an empty row of stalls and dumped her down into a pile of hay. As she tried to squirm away, he was on top of her, with his body pushing her down into the resilient, fragrant straw. Imprisoning her head with one arm, he began to kiss her with the violence she remembered from years earlier. Instinctively, her one free hand reached out for a weapon, but he quickly imprisoned both arms. "Not this time you don't," he mumbled as he withdrew briefly from her lips and then returned to his savage attack. She responded, but against her will and with a sense of outrage; she tried to halt the warmth that flowed through her in automatic reaction to his grinding hips. As soon as she moved with him, he released her arms and began to fumble with her clothing.

"Take those damned things off if you want to keep them." His eyes never left her as she obeyed his demand, and in turn she watched him as he undressed. He shuddered as he bent to kiss her breasts and groaned as she caressed him. He didn't hesitate because he couldn't, but plunged into her with a power that would have hurt if she were not as ready. There was no waiting this time, there was only the rolling wave of ecstasy, and even before the sensation had subsided, he was building again with an equal strength of desire. They were sweaty and covered with bits of hay by the time he finally left her, only to reach out again and pull her close.

"If we'd done this years ago, I'd never have let you get away. Why do you drive me to violence, Marsh? You know I want you and always have."

Laughing a little shakily, she pushed him away. "I don't think either of us is very civilized yet. And look at the mess we've made of ourselves. I feel like a pincushion." Stuart's hands were gentle as he reached over to brush her off; even after they'd dressed, he continued to pick the bits of straw from her tousled hair.

"You look more like my wife now," he pronounced with satisfaction.

"I look like a farm girl who just got rolled in the hay."

"That too," he grinned.

Hanford was waiting for them inside the great barn, smiling laconically. His words of greeting brought a bright flush to Marsh's cheeks.

"I'm glad you two have kissed and made up. Neither of you would have been worth a tinker's damn if you hadn't. Let's go to dinner and get the rest of our talking done."

Stuart's brief grin of acknowledgement at Hanford's remarks faded quickly into a frown as he noticed a pair of shabbily dressed workers rolling dice in a corner of the barn. Remembering Hanford's warning about the men Alice Nelson had hired, Stuart's hand was on his gun as he strode over to the men and demanded, "Where'd you men come from and who hired you?"

"Anudder boss man, boss," one smiled vaguely.

"Yassa, boss, we 'uz told to sweep up, but there ain't nothin' left to sweep," the second man drawled impudently.

Stuart looked at them sharply and snapped, "All right, let's go around once more. Who hired you?"

Hanford's lazy voice sounded from the rear, "They're my

men, MacKenzie, I wanted to find out if you'd recognize any strangers on your place. I figured if you didn't notice my men, there could be other people sneaked in. All right, gentlemen, that will be all." As if ramrods had been shoved down their throats, the two blacks straightened and saluted with military precision before they strode off.

"Those two have been with me for seven years, four of them working for Union intelligence in the South." Both Hanford's and Stuart's attention was drawn to the sight of Marsh intercepting the two operators and talking to them. When she approached her husband, she was smiling.

"Those are your men, aren't they, Seth? One was in the hotel lobby in Cheyenne and the other posed as a porter on the train."

"You're a sharp observer, Marsh," Hanford commented. "If you ever need a job, Pinkerton can use you."

"She's already got one," Stuart smiled, "running the home we're going to build. Let's go to dinner." Smiling in return, the detective was amused; somehow he couldn't picture Marsh MacKenzie in the role of homemaker. He'd learned too much about her other abilities. However, in the two tense weeks that followed, he did lose his distrust of Stuart MacKenzie. He had expected this son of a rich father to be a playboy. Instead, Stuart ran a precision farm and maintained excellent morale among his employees. Furthermore, he proved a first-class bodyguard for Marsh; she couldn't go anywhere without him. On the fourth day, when he finally consented to take her to see the stallion, Stuart insisted that two of Hanford's men go with them.

For Marsh that day was her homecoming. Armed with a sack of carrots, she approached the fence and whistled. At first the stallion only raised his head and sniffed the air; it wasn't until she called out to him that he moved cautiously toward her. Soon, he was munching carrots and allowing her to rub his nose in the old established manner of their long friendship. In three days, he was waiting for her by the fence, and in five, she was on his back with only a halter as guiding equipment. During those rides, Stuart sat nervously on the fence and worried, as much about her reckless nature as any danger from this particular horse. Far more than she, he felt the oppressive tension of waiting.

"I'd rather face a rebel cavalry charge than wait around," he grumbled.

"That's because you know what to expect from brave men," Marsh reminded him, "this white trash killer is a coward. But," she added cheerfully, "it's easier to shoot a coward because you don't have to worry about whether it's right or wrong." Marsh was remembering Shannon's advice; Stuart was worried about the terror she would feel her first time under fire.

On the twelfth day, the operator watching the big house reported that the five principals there had taken the ferry to Washington. Marsh was dismayed about the possibility of an interminable delay; Stuart was almost convinced that the "plot" had been the product of Hanford's imagination; only the detective was imperturbable.

"Creighton will make his move now. He couldn't very well act while he was a guest at the home; he'd have been the prime suspect then. It's my guess he'll get his alibi set, then return to the farm from some remote point. But you can bet your boots he's got the trap planned, so we'll have to increase our vigilance. Marsh has to stay right here where we can watch her until we get the signal."

The following day, the operator at the big house reported that Clinton and Sophia had returned to their home, that Alice Nelson had taken a train bound for New York City, and that Janet Talbot was staying with friends in the capital. There was no news on the whereabouts of Blake Creighton. The mystery of the location of the missing man was solved two days later when one of the farm guards reported hearing rifle shots in a heavily wooded area near the riverbank where there was no levee road. Hanford left one agent with Marsh and

Stuart and took off with the other three. Two hours later he returned, alone, dirty, and tired looking.

"We've spotted the carcass of a horse. That's the trap he's set for you. We think he's there waiting for you and your husband to ride up. He knows that two workers have seen the horse, and he'll expect them to notify you."

Marsh felt a chill premonition. "Seth, did you see the horse?"

"From a distance, it's a large animal."

"My stallion," she whispered, "he's killed my stallion." The tears ran down her face as she fought to control them.

Stuart put his arms around her. "Honey, you can't be sure." But Stuart himself was sure, Creighton would have known that stallion was the only horse Marsh cared about on the farm. He explained to Hanford about Marsh's ownership.

"Where was it pastured?" Hanford snapped. "Show me on this map." When Stuart pointed to the rear area, Hanford drew a line to the house. "Direct line of sight. He could have watched you through a field glass. I'm sorry, Marsh, but you're probably right. Can you still go through with it?"

She nodded and her jaw tightened into a grim line as she listened as Hanford mapped out the final instructions. "My three men are already in position and I'm going to be at this spot. Now comes the hard part, MacKenzie. You and Marsh will ride to the end of the trail, dismount, and continue on foot. There's good cover all the way to the clearing. The carcass is lying roughly in the middle. We figure the shots came from this dense tangle of shrubs and trees, and we think Creighton's hiding there now. The hard part is going to be that open ten feet between your cover and the carcass, but we do have an advantage. Creighton will expect you to stand over the animal, so Marsh'll crawl over and he'll have to re-aim. That way its body will provide her cover. Give me a half hour and then ride."

Just forty-five minutes later, Marsh's world almost stopped again. She and Stuart had followed instructions and arrived at the clearing still protected by shrub cover. Both of them had recognized the stallion at the same time. Stuart had hugged her briefly and then shielded her body with his own as he stepped out into view. Marsh heard the rifle shot and saw her husband drop to the ground. Screaming with terror, she dragged Stuart back into the dense shrubbery. She was still screaming when he spoke sharply.

"Shut up, Marsh, it's only my leg. For God's sake, don't you go out there." As soon as she knew he was all right, she looked across the clearing and her eyes were grim. Taking out both pistols, she dropped to the ground and crawled belly-style as Shannon had taught her to do. Using the great body of her stallion as a shield, she positioned herself until she could see over its neck. Then she held still. "Don't move your head," Shannon had told her, "just your eyes. You can see a lot out of the sides of your eyes. Lie as still as death for as long as it takes to make the enemy nervous, and watch until you spot him."

Minutes passed as she lay there motionless, her guns resting on the stallion, her eyes moving slowly from side to side. She ignored Stuart in back of her, blotted out the knowledge that four armed men also waited, and continued her vigil with every sense concentrated on one end: to kill the man she'd hated all of her life.

And then she saw them, the toes of a pair of boots—boots like the ones she'd worn for six years. Imperceptibly, she raised the barrel of one gun. "Don't rush!" Shannon's command sounded again. "You'll only get one chance. Brace that gun so it doesn't deflect when you fire. And aim for the man's middle. Remember his height and then estimate where his chest is." Four feet, she thought, four feet from the soles of those boots. Slowly, she took aim and squeezed the trigger once and then five more times; automatically, at the count of six, she laid the used pistol down and picked up the fresh one. Slowly, she aimed again but it wasn't necessary to pull the trigger. She watched without emotion as the boots changed position and a man's body crumpled on top of them. Still, she remained where she was until she saw Hanford's men break from cover and go to the fallen man. Then she petted the still head of her horse for the last time, crawled back to her husband, and put her arms around him as he lay propped against a tree. They were sitting there minutes later when three horses were ridden off, and Hanford walked over to them.

Gently, he pushed Marsh away from her husband, and with methodical efficiency, examined Stuart's leg. "It didn't hit an artery so we don't need a tourniquet. But that close to your knee, it's probably painful. Major, you undoubtedly know as much about morphine as I do, but I've got some tablets here which I want you to take. I've sent for Dr. Damon and for a wagon to take you back to the cottage. I've also sent to Alexandria for the sheriff. Marsh, are you all right?"

"Is he dead?" she asked.

"He's dead. That was a smart thing you did. Indian tactic, wasn't it?" She didn't reply; now that the tension was gone, she felt drained. Seth talked on. "He missed you with four shots." She looked up in surprise, she hadn't heard any shots, only the one that hit Stuart.

"Did you fire any shots, Seth?"

He looked at her strangely. "We all did. Marsh, where did you learn to concentrate so completely that you blotted out as many as twenty rifle shots?"

She shrugged indifferently. "Horse racing, I guess."

Sensing her mood of withdrawal, Hanford left her with her husband. She remained where she was, staring at nothing. She didn't see the odd look on Stuart's face or the grim set of his jaw. The first help to arrive were the workers with the litter. Automatically, Marsh rose to accompany her husband as he was being carried off, but he stopped her with his hand. "Stay here, Marsh," he mumbled, "they'll probably want to talk to you. I'll be all right."

She nodded without much emotion and sat down again,

slipping back in memory to another shooting and another man who hadn't been as lucky as this one. She was, she reflected leadenly, a dangerous person to know. Disturbed by her immobile posture, Hanford came over and sat by her.

"Marsh, you don't have to wait here. I'll take you back so you can be with your husband."

She shrugged. "He doesn't want me."

"I imagine he was terrified all the time you were out there. I think you must have been, too."

Her eyes were cold and calm. "No, I wasn't. I wanted him dead. He killed Jamie and he killed my stallion. And he tried to kill Stuart."

"No, he didn't. He just wanted to wound Stuart so that he could reach you."

When the sheriff and his men arrived, she and Hanford were still sitting there. Without much interest, she saw that it was Dan Rumford who was in charge. She paid little attention as Seth Hanford described the shooting, and none at all as the sheriff ordered the bloody body tied on the back of a horse. Rumford was equally indifferent about the slain man; his sympathies were all with the girl who'd been victimized by the villain whom Rumford was convinced had killed her husband. He really didn't care whose bullets had done the job. Lawman though he was, Dan Rumford was a realist: he knew that, with lawyers like Hiram Creighton in the world, guilty men could be set free—unless they were dead. He left the grisly scene without even speaking to the main witness. It was Hanford who pulled her to her feet and half-carried her to the waiting horses. "I'll send someone back to bury your stallion, Marsh." Only then did he notice the glint of tears in her eyes.

Nothing of that homeward trip penetrated her consciousness, and only the glass of brandy Hanford ordered her to drink back in Stuart's cottage returned any color to her pale cheeks. When Damon and Carina emerged from the bedroom, she didn't ask how Stuart was. Wisely, Damon pretended she had.

"Stuart will be fine, Marsh. Both bones were injured, but they'll mend. I've set his leg, but he'll be in bed for weeks and on crutches for still more. How are you feeling?"

She smiled faintly. "I'm fine. I'm always fine. It's my husbands who get hurt—or killed." Carina looked closely at her young friend.

"Damon, I'm going to stay here with Marsh. I think she and I should be alone for awhile." Trained by years of marriage to Carina, Damon only nodded and left this patient to his wife. Deep shock was more in her line of medicine, anyway.

However, there wasn't anything medical about Carina's first treatment. She ordered Marsh to accompany her into the bedroom where Stuart lay in a drugged sleep.

"I just wanted you to see that he's all right before we go to work. Marsh, bring me a box from the kitchen or storeroom—a big one. We're going to get rid of everything that woman left here."

"Won't he wake up?"

"No, he's out for the rest of the afternoon, and I'll see that he's under for the night before I leave." As she talked, Carina was busily gathering up perfume bottles, brushes, combs, rouge jars and hairpins. Marsh ran to the kitchen and dragged in the large basket normally used for laundry. It was filled even before three drawers were emptied. Next, a large box was packed with the ruffled dressing gowns of pink and purple and with pieces of scattered undergarments. A third box held the three dresses which had hung in the closet and the two critical garments Carina found stuffed into a corner of the mahogany wardrobe, heavily boned corsets. The sight of those two revealing garments broke the tension of both Marsh and Carina. While Stuart slept on, they dissolved into a laughter which continued all the time they dragged the boxes onto the back porch and told one of the guards to locate a couple of workers. Only when the last of Janet's things were being carried to the big house did their laughter subside enough for them to clean the bedroom.

"Now we talk, Marsh," Carina said crisply. "I want to know everything you've done this last year." Marsh felt the months roll back as she talked about her child and her home, her uncomplicated life in Wyoming, her adventure with Crazy Horse, and her career as Blanche La Tour. Only when she reached the Stuart part did her fluency falter.

"He tried to protect me today, but afterward he didn't even want to talk to me."

"Stuart's still an angry adolescent in many ways, Marsh. He's as good a businessman as Jamie was, but his personal life has always been a shambles. He's too immature for a wife like you, but maybe he'll grow up. Meanwhile, Stuart or no Stuart, you have to finish the job you started today. With that one I'll help you." Marsh started to shake her head, but Carina just nodded. "Oh, yes, I owe Alice Nelson, not just for Jamie and you, but for the years of her nasty-nice insults to Damon and me. A good Indian never forgets an insult."

"Seth insists that she has to confess because there's no evidence against her."

"That's why he asked me for advice. I will help you make her talk." At Marsh's questioning look, Carina laughed. "Not with torture or threatened scalping—much as I'd enjoy it—but with a little tasteless powder in her tea, she'll talk for hours. Even so, it won't be easy."

"How do I get the powder into her tea and not my own?"

"In the sugar, cream, and lemon. Your detective friend is very thorough. During this past year he has had his helpers observe her at twenty different restaurants. She always uses sugar and cream in her tea, but she might try the lemon anyway. She'd expect the tarts and sandwiches to be poisoned because that's what she did, but we don't think she'll suspect the other things."

"When does this tea party take place? And will you be there?"

"I'd love to be, but it wouldn't work with me in attendance. In the first place, Alice Nelson wouldn't stoop to having tea with me."

"She probably won't with me, either."

"For your sake, I wish she wouldn't. But that's just wishful thinking. She'll be there. Now, let's go join your detective and Damon for dinner. Stuart will be fine until we get back."

That pleasant, relaxed dinner was the last one Marsh would enjoy for twenty long, miserable days. Not only were Seth and his operators in a jovial mood, Damon presented Marsh with the gift of three weeks of service by his most accomplished assistant, a six-foot, three-inch Bermudan who outweighed the doctor by a hundred pounds. Like Damon, Beau Jonas was a mixture of races; unlike his aristocratic, educated employer, his medical training consisted of twenty years in the British navy as a surgeon's assistant. He had a pair of hands powerful enough to wrestle the most reluctant sailor onto the operating table or to subdue a terrified mare about to foal. He was also a cheerful, non-respecter of any other man's color or position.

"Beau will keep Stuart company while you run the farm, Marsh," was Damon's dry comment. "Stuart tends to be a difficult patient."

Stuart was an impossible patient, and Marsh was to bless Beau Jonas a hundred times each day. Awakening in a mood of cantankerous obstinacy, the patient demanded that his wife wear nothing but dresses, take all her meals with him, follow his instructions about farm management to the letter, and perform her services to him with ladylike servility. Beau winked at Marsh from across the room, approached the bed, lifted Stuart up as easily as he would have a child, and chided the bedridden man good-naturedly. "Blimey, mate, you're a bloody tyrant. Mum's got work to do, so it's you and me what's going to get that leg healed.''

That day and the next were bearable enough because Damon came over from Maryland to make sure Stuart's leg was immobile and that he was sedated. On the third day, though, life became a chaotic whirl for Marsh. Three hours each morning were spent going over the books with her husband. Then she would change from the required dress into her riding clothes for a four-hour stint carrying out the orders he'd given her. Once again in a dress, she reported to his bedside and spent another three hours dining with him and going over the house plans he was drawing for their Virginia home. During those six hours, Marsh fretted silently about the shortness of time left to accomplish her most important goal and about her need for hypocritical secrecy. Stuart was in no mood to tolerate even the mention of Wyoming. She was also chaffing under the oppressive estrangement of their relationship; he had made no attempt to explain his changed attitude toward her.

Only on two occasions did she have any relief from the domination he exerted. Ten days after Blake Creighton's death, Seth Hanford escorted her to the legal hearing in Alexandria. In the hot courtroom, she spent two hours answering terse questions about her relation with the dead man and about Jamie's murder. Seth Hanford's testimony was accompanied by a complete record of his investigation into Creighton's actions, but he made no mention of Marsh's part in the killing other than to say that she was the intended victim. Yet it was Dan Rumford's testimony that decided the justice of the peace. Largely on the basis of the sheriff's eyewitness account of Creighton's attempt to shoot Marsh four years earlier, the justice announced two verdicts: ''justifiably killed during the commission of a violent crime'' and ''a necessary investigation into the circumstances surrounding the earlier alibi provided by Hiram Creighton.''

After the hearing, Marsh spent another two hours with Seth

while he described all the recent developments in the case. Wayne Talbot had returned to Virginia two weeks earlier and had been successfully "resurrected" by John Mosby in a Richmond courtroom.

"Where was Alice?" Marsh asked sharply.

Hanford frowned. "We don't know. She did board the train for New York as her aunt claimed, but we don't know anything else about her actions. According to the operator assigned to watch her, she did not show up in the courtroom."

"Where's Wayne now?"

"Still with Mosby. He'll return to Georgia only when Mosby thinks it's safe enough." The rest of the afternoon, Hanford discussed his plans for the confrontation with Alice, if and when the suspect returned to Baltimore. Marsh arrived home too late for her evening ordeal with Stuart and went to bed with a pleasant sense of relief.

Her second respite from a convalescing husband came with a two-day visit by Craig and Phyllis, when eighteen-month-old Pamela crawled all over an indulgent uncle's bed and romped about his room. Marsh stared at Stuart in amazement; not only was he indulgent, he loved the little girl, and Pamela adored her playful uncle. However, Marsh was concerned about the speculative gleam in her husband's eyes whenever he looked in her direction. She learned the reason for that gleam after the Craig MacKenzies' departure. Stuart demanded that she return to his bed. Since she'd never been in that particular bed with him and had no desire to take Janet Talbot's place there, Marsh tried evasion.

"Not until Damon says it's all right."

"To hell with Damon. You're sleeping with me tonight if I have to beat you with one of my crutches.

"What you need, Marsh, are a dozen children," he told her once she was lying awkwardly by his side, "to keep you out of trouble and at home." She thought longingly about Carina's powders and failed to respond during their first uncomfortable union. Relieved because Stuart made no comment about her lack of passion, Marsh rolled over and went to sleep. Sometime before dawn, she was awakened by his insistent hands and by her own body chemistry. Awkward splints and all, the reunion was fiery and complete; she could see his grin of triumph in the pale light as he held on to her. "I liked you better with straw in your hair, but welcome home, honey." The separation was over and Stuart kept her close beside him during the following days, even to the extent of hobbling around after her on crutches. Surrendering to the playful tenderness he now lavished on her, Marsh returned to her pretend game of contentment. She was not enthralled, however, on the day he interrupted her hurried conference with Seth Hanford with an autocratic demand.

"When you have a minute, Hanford, I want to talk to you." Since Stuart did not move from the room, Seth knew that the minute referred to meant right now. Making no effort to signal Marsh, the laconic detective followed Stuart into the other room. Fuming with anger at the high-handed tactics, Marsh remained where she was, determined to finish her necessary talk with Seth. But ten minutes later, Stuart called her into his bedroom. Reaching out his hand to her, he pulled her down to sit in her usual spot beside him.

"I've just told Mr. Hanford that you will take no further active part in his investigation. He is fully empowered to handle the Alice Nelson situation himself in whatever way he feels is most effective. But there will be no repetition of the danger you faced the last time, or of your subsequent actions. I told him that I did not approve of his encouraging you to act like a savage Indian on the warpath." Stuart smiled at her with the insultingly superior smirk of a schoolmaster about to administer a well-earned punishment. "That day, Marsh, was a lesson to me. When I told you to keep out of the line of fire, you ignored me completely. Even Mr. Hanford agrees that it was a very dangerous thing you did."

Marsh glared over at the impassive detective, who merely shrugged. "Your husband has a point, Marsh. I'll handle it from now on and report any news I have to both of you." As he turned to leave, Marsh tried to pull her hand free from Stuart's restraining grip and gave up only when his fingers tightened painfully.

"Just relax, hothead," he taunted her, "you're not going anyplace. You're going to learn that you're just a woman and not one of Mosby's marauders." He laughed down into her stormy face. "If I could manage, I'd throw you into the river right now until you cooled off. But if you'll act like an obedient wife for a change, I'll share a glass of brandy with you or even something stronger. You go get us a couple of glasses."

Whatever it was she intended to do at that moment, Marsh never really determined, because she found Seth's note tacked unto the cork of the usquebaugh bottle in the kitchen. "He's worse than your first husband. Everything's all set. Just wait for my signal." She was laughing when she returned to her husband and poured two full glasses. Later, when he got out his house plans, Marsh helped by drawing a crude picture of her Wyoming home.

"Where did you ever see anything like that?" Stuart asked. "It's too barbaric for a plantation estate."

"So am I," she grinned at him.

Three days later, a racy two-horse buggy stopped in front of the cottage and a debonair Bradford Marshall stepped down and knocked on the door. "Stuart," he announced as soon as his son-in-law opened the door and stood awkwardly aside on his crutches, "I've come to borrow my daughter for a week or so. Her grandmother's ill and wants to see her. Where is she?"

"I sent her down to the paddock on an errand, but she should be back in a few minutes." Stuart spoke stiffly to his father-in-law; had he dared, he would have denied the request. However, a Major MacKenzie, aged thirty, was no match for a Colonel Marshall, aged forty-three, in either authority, charm, or arrogance. By the time Marsh arrived, the two men had finished packing her luggage. With just one simple request, Brad had won his son-in-law's complete confidence, "Just don't pack those damn britches of hers. I'll see what I can do about her unbecoming independence this time, Stuart. I know that she's a worry to you."

Had Marsh heard her father's words or her husband's enthusiastic agreement with them, she might not have accompanied Brad so willingly or kissed Stuart good-bye so warmly. However, her ignorance was a fortunate circumstance, since she faced a grueling, twenty-hour drive to Baltimore. Seth Hanford and Carina were waiting at the Maryland farm with a larger carriage; and halfway across the state, Captain John Mason met them with an official police wagon. It was the captain who described the details of the plan, stressing the "can do's" and the "cannot do's" with stern authority. Under police supervision, Jamie's old apartment had been altered to provide three places of concealment behind the wall of bookcases in the living room. Hanford, Mason, and Craig MacKenzie would be the hidden witnesses during Marsh's interview with Alice Nelson the next afternoon at four o'clock. Mason had insisted on the exclusion of Bradford Marshall from the official scene.

"You'd place the whole plan in jeopardy, sir, because you'd be too worried about your own daughter. The only reason we included the suspect's brother is that his testimony will help our case. So far he has proved extremely cooperative and has already given us several damning pieces of evidence. Not enough for a conviction, but enough to justify this means of apprehension."

"How do you know Alice Nelson will even show up?" Marsh asked nervously.

The policeman cleared his throat noisily. "I'm afraid we may have resorted to an illegality there, Mrs. MacKenzie. We forged your name to a note of invitation she can't afford to ignore. In it you claimed that your late stepfather implicated her minutes before he died. If she's guilty, she will feel even more strongly about your elimination, especially in light of a recent development which I will reveal to you as soon as we receive confirmation.''

It was a nervous and exhausted quintet of people who dismounted stiffly from the uncomfortable wagon in the service alley behind the expensive, elegant apartment house. Quietly, they were admitted through the rear door by one of the two black agents Seth had called his finest. His disguise this time was that of a white-coated janitor. Silently, he unlocked the door to the apartment which had last been used by Phyllis and Craig as their first home. Not having been there since she helped Phyllis move eighteen months earlier, Marsh could detect no difference in the arrangements; the false wall which now masked the bookcases was exactly like the original, and the sliding panels which would allow the witnesses to break out quickly were indistinguishable from the rest of the wallpapered surface.

Carefully, Mason searched the entire apartment before he allowed anyone to sit down in the comfortable chairs. When he was satisfied that no one had been there, he invited the tired travelers into the living room and continued his instructions. ''Our dinner is being prepared in the next apartment where Mr. Hanford and Mr. Marshall will sleep tonight while you two ladies occupy this one. Both Mr. Hanford and I will post guards in the hall tonight and all day tomorrow, just in case, but all food will be prepared next door.''

When a discreet knock sounded at the front door, Mason rose to admit three policemen—one handed the captain a folded note and the other two distributed hearty box dinners containing slices of cold, baked ham, bread rolls, bananas, oranges, and a slab of cake. No one thought to complain about the absence of cutlery as they dug in and ate inelegantly with their fingers. Over the large cups of steaming hot coffee brought in to them twenty minutes later, John Mason revealed the ''recent'' development.

''Two months ago, when Mr. Hanford first proposed this

maneuver to the Baltimore police, he was reprimanded and refused permission. When he returned a month later with the news that Blake Creighton's bank account showed a five thousand dollar increase days before his death, we reconsidered. Ten days ago we agreed. In the company of three of his lawyer's agents, Wayne Talbot arrived in Savannah, Georgia, by steamboat and registered at a hotel while awaiting rail transportation to Atlanta. On their second night at the hotel, two of those four men were poisoned, one fatally. A Mr. Ronson and Mr. Talbot escaped because they had not touched the water served them. Because Mr. Ronson and Mr. Talbot also pretended to be poisoned, all four men were rushed to a hospital. At Mr. Ronson's insistence, the hospital announced that all four had died. Savannah authorities began looking for a gray-haired, plump waitress who had reported that night at the hotel as a replacement for her sick daughter. The 'daughter' waitress admitted to police that the middle-aged woman had paid for the uniform and for the one-night job. If that woman proves to be Miss Alice Nelson, the Baltimore police want her convicted.''

Marsh and Seth looked at each other. Alice had not been in New York, and Marsh wasn't the only one to realize the advantages of wigs and makeup.

Chapter
16

Marsh would never forget the precision of the police organization she experienced the next day. Exhausted by twenty hours of travel, she had slept for twelve hours and awakened at noon on the fateful day. She breakfasted with Carina and her father and then dressed. At two o'clock, Captain Mason rechecked the apartment and went over the questions he expected her to ask the suspect. At three o'clock, Carina prepared the cream, sugar, and lemon tray, well out of sight of the Captain. At three thirty, Craig arrived with Mrs. Tucker, who had been asked to serve the tea, but had not been told anything about the reason. She brought a sealed box of tea cookies and tarts with her, polished the silver tea service, and put the water on to boil. Marsh talked briefly to a nervous Craig in an attempt to lend him the courage to face the ordeal. At three forty-five, Brad Marshall kissed his tense daughter and escorted Carina to the apartment next door, leaving the four main conspirators waiting in a limbo of apprehension. When the doorbell rang five minutes before the hour, the three men slid into their compartments and a terrified Marsh walked to the door and admitted a smiling Alice Nelson.

The epitome of an innocent woman eager to clear up a slight misunderstanding, Alice bounced into the entry with the ruffles on her dress and cape in vigorous motion. Warily, Marsh hung the cape up on the entry stand, but Alice insisted on keeping her reticule and knitting bag with her. Marsh tried to remember whether or not Alice knitted, but gave up to follow her bouncy guest on a tour of the apartment as Alice checked into the bedroom, the bath, and the small guest room.

"I've never been here before," she gushed, "Phyllis was always too busy to entertain."

In the kitchen, Alice scolded Mrs. Tucker for not heating the teapot before brewing the tea and insisted that a fresh pot be made correctly. When a frustrated Marsh finally had her guest seated in the carefully placed winged chair with the wide footstool in front, she took her own place on the straight-backed chair about six feet away while Mrs. Tucker spread out the tea service on the table between the two adversaries.

"Mind if I leave now, Marsh?" Mrs. Tucker asked. "The missus is entertaining tonight and I'll be needed there." Marsh smiled stiffly and nodded, waited until the front door clicked shut, and then reached for the teapot. Willing her hand not to shake, she filled the two cups. Following the instructions laid out, Marsh reached for a pink-frosted tart and ate it, choking down the sugary concoction. Alice ate an identical one. Marsh sipped her plain tea and held her breath. Alice smiled and reached for the cream and sugar.

"They never use lemon in England," she commented, "they use only cream and sugar." Alice sipped her tea and waited for Marsh to take another tea cake, then she ate an identical one. Marsh could feel the cold drops of perspiration on her back as she counted the minutes. "Seven to ten minutes," Carina had warned her, "don't start asking the important questions until then."

"I didn't know you knitted, Alice," she said desperately.

"You don't know anything about me, Pamela," her guest responded.

"What are you knitting? Something for the new baby?"

"How could I do that? I don't know whether it'll be a boy or girl. This is a scarf for Aunt Sophia. Would you like me to show you how to knit, Pamela?"

"No," Marsh answered sharply, "I wouldn't have the time. That wasn't why I asked you here today. As you may know, I was present when my stepfather was killed."

"When he was murdered, yes, I know." Alice didn't look at Marsh as she fumbled around inside the open knitting bag and removed a half finished, gray-blue scarf and a pair of large steel knitting needles. "These belonged to my great-grandmother," she boasted, "aren't they interesting?"

"I wouldn't know," Marsh said, desperately aware that Alice was controlling the dialogue. "My stepfather said that you had paid him to murder Jamie and me," she blurted.

"He was a liar," Alice snapped. "I didn't ask him to kill Jamie."

"Did you pay him to kill me?"

Alice's eyes darted around the room, once again checking the corners. The smile on her face had grown more reckless and she leaned forward in excitement. "Now you, Pamela Creighton, are a different matter entirely."

"Did you pay my stepfather to kill me?"

The smile broadened and the pale blue eyes gleamed. "Of course I did. And I've paid other people as well. Lots of them."

Marsh gripped her shaking hands on her lap and tried to control her voice. "If you didn't pay my stepfather to kill Jamie, why do you think he did it?"

The smirk became a simper, a terrible travesty of a flirtatious girl. "Blake loved me and he knew that, once you were dead, Jamie would marry me and then Blake would have no one. He was jealous, jealous of Jamie because Jamie would have me and he wouldn't. But the fool let you live." Her face twisted with hatred. "He let you live to go on ruining people's lives. Before Jamie married you, he and I were happy. I ran his house and I was his hostess."

"But Jamie never asked you to marry him. You're the one who told me about his mistress."

"Catherine? I didn't mind her. Jamie couldn't marry her."

"Why did you want to marry Jamie?"

"To have a son. Then the Ryder money would belong to a Ryder. I was going to name my son Joseph, after my grandfather."

"Did you love Jamie?"

"Of course I did. I always loved him and he loved me even when I was a girl."

"He was married to your mother then."

"He didn't love her. He loved me."

"Jamie married me, Alice."

"Only because he was sorry for you. But I knew he'd be glad if you were dead."

"Is that why you poisoned me at Craig's wedding?"

"Of course it was. And I would have succeeded if Stuart hadn't interfered."

"I can see why you wanted to kill me. But why did you try to kill Wayne?"

"Because he would be better off dead. And then Janet could marry Stuart and her children would inherit Ryder money, too." The sly smile shone again. "Just like she will now as soon as you are dead."

"How Alice? Don't you know that Wayne is still alive?"

"No, he's not," her voice was jubilant. "No, he's not, not since Savannah. He died in Savannah."

"Did you poison him there?"

"Of course I did. The fool didn't even recognize me."

"Why did you poison the men he was with?"

"Because they kept me from getting close to Wayne in Richmond."

"Alice, why haven't you ever knitted anything for your niece? She's a pretty little girl."

"I don't like her. If this next child is a boy, Craig won't need Pamela and I will get to raise his boy."

"How? Phyllis won't let you do that."

"Phyllis isn't the wife for Craig. She runs his life too much."

Marsh felt physically ill as she watched the oddly changed face opposite her with the smile that came and went as Alice stroked the gray-blue length of scarf in her lap and held the knitting needles as if she was planning to knit again. Marsh wanted to end this insane interview, but something Alice had said about Jamie loving her as a girl bothered her. Jamie could never have loved this twisted woman.

"Alice, you said Jamie loved you as a girl when he was married to your mother. Is that why your mother killed herself?"

The laughter was piercing and horrible. "My mother? You never knew my mother. She planned to live forever, just to spite me."

Marsh let her breath out slowly. "So you poisoned her?"

Instantly, the glaze disappeared from Alice's eyes, replaced by a feral look of a vicious animal. "Yes. Yes. Yes. She was like you. She didn't die the first time, but she did the second time. She died then." Alice was on her feet now, with the knitting needles in her hands.

Suddenly, a scream sounded from one of the concealed men, and Craig shoved his way out, his face a mask of horror. "The needles, Marsh, watch out for them," he shrieked. As he stumbled toward his sister, she swung the needles toward him. Ashen-faced, he backed away as Alice laughed and turned back toward Marsh, who was now on her feet shoving the tea table and chair in Alice's path. The murderess was still laughing shrilly as Hanford and Mason grabbed her arms, laughing and struggling as she stabbed the needles violently about, still trying to reach her target. Slowly exerting his strength, Hanford forced her arm to bend more sharply at the elbow until that needle was no longer pointing outward. In her frenzy to break free of his hold, she jabbed once more with a strong thrust. It was one of her own breasts the needle penetrated. Her pale eyes widened in an instant flash of understanding, then rolled up in sightless agony as she sagged. Only the men still holding her kept her from dropping, lifeless, to the floor.

Hypnotized by the horror, Marsh could see nothing but the terrible sight of the dead woman being lowered to the floor. But gradually, her other senses recovered and she could hear the sounds of violent retching coming from the bathroom. Slowly, she looked around the room; it must be Craig who was ill because the other men were still busy opposite her. Mason was wrapping the needles carefully into the knitting bag while Hanford had gone to the hall for Alice's cape and was now covering the body.

"Marsh," he ordered sharply as he noted the shock lingering on her face, "why don't you clear away those cups and things, and go next door for a pot of strong coffee? I think we could all use a cup."

Galvanized into action by the command, she gathered the tea things with shaking hands and carried the tray toward the dining and kitchen area. Mason held the door for her and then stepped to the front door and issued a series of commands to the man on guard. In the kitchen, Marsh sagged against the sink as she dumped the sugar and cream into the slop pail and buried the lemons deep in the garbage bin. More slowly, she washed the cups and tea service. Still pale but otherwise composed, Craig came into the kitchen and helped put fresh cups and saucers on the table. Marsh took time out to hug him briefly; he had saved her life today and she was deeply touched. Mason was carrying a steaming pot of coffee as he and Hanford entered the room.

John Mason drank a deep draught of the bitter brew before he broke the constrained silence. "We have all had a shattering experience, but under the circumstances, I think the ending was the most merciful. Mr. MacKenzie, how did you know about the knitting needles?"

"I didn't think about them until she lunged at Marsh. Then I remembered how she had frightened me with those same needles when I was a little boy."

"She claimed that they had belonged to your great-grandmother," Marsh insisted.

"I don't know, they may have. She valued everything that belonged to our great-grandmother as if it were solid gold. But she always used those needles."

Mason turned to Marsh, "Why didn't you use your gun to defend yourself when you saw her coming toward you?"

Marsh stared at him with a forming glint of anger. "I was too busy trying to dodge those needles to get the damn thing out of my pocket. Why didn't you shoot her?"

Mason smiled, both amused and relieved by the healthy anger. "You were directly in line of fire. Hanford, what's your guess about the poison she used?"

"Cyanide, judging by the speed of action. She'd applied it to the tips of those knitting needles."

"My God," Craig cried out in renewed horror, "she could have killed us all. And all the time she was talking, she looked so crazy."

"No," Marsh corrected him sharply, "she wasn't crazy. She was full of hate and she was evil, but she wasn't crazy." Marsh did not want Craig to live in the shadow of insanity; he was not strong enough. If she had to, she would tell him about the drug.

Mason had been watching Marsh oddly. "Whatever it was, she was different today. Whenever I questioned her in the past, she was cleverly evasive."

"You never saw her on the brink of committing a murder, Mason," Hanford inserted smoothly. "I think she was just boasting today. Now let's get the record written while we're all here to remember the sequence.''

Both Marsh and Craig were awed by the accurate memories of the professionals; the two detectives seemed to have memorized most of Alice's responses; Marsh could not even recall her own questions. As the others talked and Seth recorded the notes, she could hear the sounds of activity in the next room. When they ceased, Mason cleared his throat and requested that everyone sign the record. "It will be used as evidence at the inquest," he announced. "Between now and that time, I must ask all of you to remain in Baltimore." Marsh groaned, she didn't want to be reminded of this day.

Emerging from the kitchen, she found her father and Carina quietly waiting for her and Craig with the luggage all neatly packed. Wordlessly, Brad hurried them downstairs to a large carriage the police had supplied and ordered the driver to take them to Craig's home, where a nervous Phyllis was waiting. More affected by the grim horror than anyone else, Craig retired immediately to his room, and at his wife's insistence, Carina prepared a special cup of tea for him. In the library Marsh remembered so well, the others sipped the brandy Mrs. Tucker had given them and waited for Phyllis's questions. She had only one.

"Did she intend to kill my baby?" When Marsh nodded, Phyllis declared, "Then I'm glad Craig and I went to the police. About a month ago, Alice got into my home while Mrs. Tucker and I were both gone. The nurse found her standing over Pamela's crib with a pillow in her hand."

Marsh looked at Phyllis with a sudden understanding of the one part of the interview which had puzzled her. "Then that's why Captain Mason insisted I ask those questions about you and Pamela."

"She was crazy," Phyllis muttered, "all of the Ryders are."

Before Marsh could protest, Carina spoke sharply. "No, she was not. I'd given her a drug to make her talk, but she was not crazy. As for the rest of the Ryders, the two in Virginia are just spoiled women, but Craig's grandfather was a good man. And you are a wealthy woman because he was also a very bright man.'' Gracefully, Carina rose as she finished talking and walked toward Marsh. "Damon is waiting for me outside. Come see us before you leave.'' Marsh kissed her friend as she and Brad escorted her to the buggy where a smiling Damon greeted his wife, nodded to the others, and drove off.

That night in an unfamiliar guest room, Marsh tried to write a letter to Stuart, but the memories in this house belonged to Stuart's father, and she was unable, even unwilling, to push them aside. In the days that followed, her father became her focal point as she watched him reorganize Craig's shattered life. While Phyllis refused to attend Alice's funeral, Brad and Marsh flanked a trembling Craig as the only guests to hear the impersonal words uttered by a young minister over a grave far removed from her mother's. Later, Brad would not allow Craig to hide. Forcefully, he escorted the young banker to his place of business where the name Ryder was removed from the building. "If millions of Southerners can face reconstruction, you can face the disapproval of a few people in Baltimore,'' the Virginian admonished sternly.

He was equally insistent that Craig meet the public in other ways, too. Choosing one of the smaller, less pretentious hotels, Brad arranged a dinner party to greet John Mosby and Wayne Talbot upon their arrival with Mr. Ronson, Philip Addison and Wayne's sister. At Marsh's insistence, the Mac Lachlans, Angus Balfour, and the Covingtons were also invited. All four members of Phyllis's family came and brought the blond Mildred with them as well. Wearing the burnt orange dress her father had given her, Marsh arrived at the party to find another old friend there—Wilbur Brant, the *Baltimore Herald* reporter. What began as a quiet dinner party soon became a rollickingly informal ball as John Mosby whirled her onto the public dance floor. Quickly, Wilbur

Brant followed suit and claimed her for a second dance. Her third one was almost an exhibition as Philip Addison and she performed a flawless waltz together.

Worried about the reckless gaiety on his daughter's face, Brad insisted on dancing with her. "Marsh," he scolded, "you're a married woman now. You have to be careful around single men."

"Why? Because I danced with my single friends? You just danced with Mildred what's-her-name, and is she ever single! What's the difference in our marriages, Brad?"

Brad shook his head and smiled helplessly. Even after two husbands, his daughter was not broken to the halter. "Have you told Stuart yet?"

"No."

"When are you leaving to retrieve your baby?"

"The first day of October."

"When will you return?"

"I'll bring the baby back to see you next summer."

"What about Stuart?"

"I don't think Stuart approves of me, Brad. He wants me to be something I'm not."

"Will you come see your mother and me before you leave?"

"Yes, I will, and my grandmother, too."

Marsh spent the next half hour with Angus and Wayne and secured Angus's promise to meet her at Bruce Mac Lachlan's office the next day. Her quiet conversation with them was cut short at the insistence of Wilbur Brant, who claimed her again as a dance partner. Only after another hour of uninterrupted dancing with her three "single" men did Craig MacKenzie ask her to dance. Marsh was amused when his expression looked as disapproving as her father's.

"Marsh, Stuart isn't as tolerant as my father was."

"Your father, Craig, wasn't tolerant either for a long time."

"I don't want anything to happen to you and Stuart. I like having you in my family."

"Stuart or no Stuart, stepson, you've got me in your family for life. I happen to be the mother of your infant brother."

Craig stopped short and stared at her. "When? Where?"

"Last October and he's with Robbie."

"Does Stuart know?"

"No, Craig and I don't want you to tell him—not until—not for a couple of months yet. And don't tell anyone else, either."

"I'm glad Alice is dead, Marsh."

"So am I, Craig."

Early the next morning, Brad left quietly to go home, and life for everyone in the house was emptier. For Marsh the day seemed endless as she instructed Bruce Mac Lachlan to give her the releases she'd signed three months earlier. Silently, she handed Angus the one for Adah and Jake.

He shook his head. "They'll no' accept it as a gift, lass. They need the land but they'll want to buy it."

"You handle it, however you think best, Angus."

On the way to Craig's bank, Angus asked sharply, "What d' you want me to do wi' the money I'm holdin' for you?"

"I don't need it." As Angus had always done with her, he waited until she asked for his help. This time, though, she seemed reluctant to talk other than to ask him to deliver the release papers of her share in the remaining Baltimore properties to Craig.

"Aye, I will if you'll tell me what's botherin' you."

"I don't want to go to this inquest, Angus."

"It'll be a simple thing, lass, accordin' to Mr. Hanford, and it will no' last more than a day."

"I hope so. Will you go with me?"

"I've already been summoned to be there."

Angus underestimated the length of the inquest by three days, and its importance by many degrees. Although it began simply enough with an inquiry into the cause of Alice Nelson's death, Marsh was instantly aware that this was no simple coroner's inquest. In the first place, it was being conducted by one of the leading judges in Baltimore, and the people admitted into the courtroom were there out of necessity, not curiosity. Besides the four witnesses to the death, there were only police and courtroom officials. A police doctor described the cause of death as poisoning, administered by her own knitting needles. And John Mason and Seth Hanford described the circumstances. Marsh and Craig were asked only to corroborate their testimony. The judge pronounced an immediate verdict of "accidental death, self-inflicted by Alice Nelson."

Marsh heaved a sigh of relief and prepared to leave until the judge announced that the second phase of the inquest would resume in the afternoon. The number of witnesses was tripled by the addition of three groups of people: Wayne Talbot, Mr. Ronson, John Mosby, and the Savannah hotel waitress formed one group; Sophia and Clinton Randall, Janet, and Hiram Creighton made up the second; several doctors and additional police officials constituted the third. Just before the judge entered the courtroom, Angus and Bruce Mac Lachlan quietly joined Marsh and Craig. The judge's opening statement ended Marsh's earlier relief.

"This part of the inquest will determine the guilt or innocence of Alice Nelson in connection with the deaths of Helen Ryder Nelson MacKenzie, James MacKenzie, and Ralph Lomax and the attempted murders of Wayne Talbot, Henry Thornwall, and Pamela Marshall MacKenzie." Marsh listened in horror to the next three hours of testimony by police officials, handwriting experts, and one doctor, and she watched in fascination as fifteen bottles containing an assortment of poisons were introduced as evidence. Between the time of Alice's death and the inquest, the police had searched her home and found the concealed cupboard in her bedroom. All but one bottle of poison had been purchased in cities other than Baltimore; that one bottle contained the poison which had killed Helen MacKenzie. The pharmacy records held the recorded name of the mother, but the handwriting was identified as that of Alice Nelson, who had been only eighteen at the time. On the stand, Sophia and Janet denied all knowledge of Alice's action; they had both been living in Virginia. The judge ruled the verdict in the Helen MacKenzie case as murder on the basis of physical evidence and on Alice's confession. Court was dismissed until nine the following morning.

On the second day, Marsh relived four horrible periods of her life, and she was called upon to testify all four times. The proceedings began with testimony from the residents of the Randall home in Virginia during Wayne's bouts of illness from 1864 to 1865. All denied any knowledge of those poisonings. Despite the judge's caustic questions to Janet and her mother, both women maintained that they knew nothing and had suspected nothing. In the hours that followed, the judge withheld all verdicts until the final recounting of the scene enacted in the Baltimore apartment two weeks earlier. Only one witness from the Savannah murder contributed any real evidence to connect Alice with that case. The waitress stated that the woman who had bought her uniform was not the older woman she appeared to be. "When she put the uniform on, I could see that her body was padded with cotton and that the white makeup was only on her face," the waitress claimed and added, "and the gray thing was a wig. Her own hair was light brown."

"Weren't you suspicious?" the judge demanded.

"No, sir. She said she needed the job and wanted a chance to impress the manager. I believed her because half the people in the South need jobs."

After a brief recess, the judge declared Alice guilty of the murder of Ralph Lomax, John Mosby's assistant, and the attempted poisoning of the other three men. She was guilty of the poisoning of Wayne Talbot and Pamela Marshall MacKenzie and of paying Blake Creighton to murder Pamela Marshall MacKenzie on two separate occasions. Alice Nelson was absolved of murder of James MacKenzie and declared guilty of the fourth attempt on Pamela Mackenzie's life.

The third day of the inquest began with a partially changed cast of people: Clinton Randall, Janet, Wayne Talbot, John Mosby and Mr. Ronson were missing. In their stead were six impassive looking men whom Bruce Mac Lachlan identified as United States Treasury officials. Beginning with only a minimum amount of delay, the judge announced that the purpose of this third session was the redistribution of the late Joseph Ryder's estate. He held up a musty looking account book of the type used a century earlier.

"This document was found in the concealed cupboard of Alice Nelson's bedroom. Its author was Louise Ryder, the mother of Joseph Ryder. I shall read it in its entirety. The first entry is dated 1774 and is in the nature of a preamble.

"It begins: 'Two months ago a Gentleman entered my Father's Apothecary Shop in London. I started to serve the Gentleman but he insisted on speaking to my Father. I overheard him ask my Father for certain Chemicals which I knew to be Poisonous. When the Gentleman left the Shop with the Poisons, my Father said that they would be used to kill diseased Animals. Two weeks later, the Gentleman was accused of the Murder of his Wife, but in Court he and four Gentlemen like him claimed that my Father had assured them that the Poisons were harmless Medicines. The Gentleman was cleared and my Father was charged with the murder of the Gentleman's Wife and convicted in one Session of Court. My beloved Father was hanged a month later and his Estate confiscated. Being penniless, I was forced into domestic Service and my only Inheritance is the Box of Poisons I removed from the Shop before it was boarded up by Soldiers. I have sworn to avenge my beloved Father's murder.' "

The judge looked up from the ledger and surveyed the silent court. "This document was signed by Louise Penrose. The name Ryder was added in 1778. Now I will read the rest of the contents." Those contents proved to be an account of murder for profit and revenge, with detailed statistics which included the names of most of the victims, the dates, the places, the poisons and precise dosages used, and, most chilling of all, the exact amount of the profit. In all, thirty-eight people had died to create the original fortune of Louise and William Ryder, but only six of the victims were American. Some of the sums acquired had been small, those from the unnamed victims; but the amounts from the gentry and aristocrats had been substantial, the largest having been from Lord and Lady Wetherall.

"In the same concealed cupboard," the judge continued, "two other objects were found: this gold money box with an insignia on top which an expert assures me is the Wetherall coat of arms, and this box of pearls on which the same coat of arms was found on the original lining." Marsh gasped—the pearls Alice had coveted had not been Ryder pearls after all.

Concluding the brief session for the day, the judge requested an immediate conference in his chambers with Mr. MacKenzie, Mr. Balfour, and Mr. Mac Lachlan. Marsh waited in the courtroom in lonely silence for an hour until her three sober-faced friends rejoined her. After a brief luncheon, the three men entered the bank and Marsh was driven back to the Baltimore home, where an avidly curious, extremely pregnant Phyllis waited. In accordance with Craig's despondent request, Marsh told her sister-in-law nothing about the day's events.

The final day of the inquest was devoted to the judge's rulings on property restitution to the descendant heirs of the murdered victims of Louise Ryder. He began by requesting the removal of Hiram Creighton from the courtroom on the grounds that Virginia courts had disbarred him two days earlier and issued a warrant for his arrest on the charges of criminal perjury in aiding his cousin to escape earlier prosecution. After the perspiring fat man had been forcibly removed and remanded into custody, the judge accepted the four documents Bruce Mac Lachlan handed him and the one from John Mosby. With six subsequent rulings, the judge concluded the inquest, the first one of which was the confiscation of the entire estate of Alice Nelson, including the home which had once belonged to her great-grandmother. The second ruling concerned the estate of James MacKenzie; only four minor pieces of property would be confiscated and these were the four Baltimore ones which originally had belonged to the six murdered Americans. Since extensive improvements had been made on the sites, the four assets would be sold and the proceeds distributed to the American heirs.

"The present owner," the judge announced, "has voluntarily given the court both the original deeds signed by Louise Ryder and the current ones for the improved property. Since this gift constitutes one-third of his joint inheritance from his father and grandfather, the court has decided to demand a similar percentage from Mrs. Sophia Randall."

Sophia's outraged protest was summarily silenced by the judge. "It is your right to fight this decision. However, I warn you that this court has been severely displeased by your lack of cooperation in the Alice Nelson case. In any event, you will adress this court only through a reputable lawyer in the future.

"Next, I wish to clear the names of James MacKenzie and Joseph Ryder from any taint connected with the criminality of Louise Ryder and to state firmly that the MacKenzie Bank is an honorable institution. The court has retained the services of Mr. Angus Balfour and Mr. Bruce Mac Lachlan to make certain that these reputations are not injured.

"The last item is only remotely connected with the central

case, but because of the timing, I decided to rule on it, too. On the behalf of Mrs. Bradford Marshall, John Mosby has requested the return of personal items and art pieces which had belonged to her mother, Mrs. Pamela Randall, and which are now or should be in the Randall home. I have granted the request and hereby order the present Mrs. Randall and her husband to package and send the items on this list to the rightful owner. If said articles are not sent within two weeks, I will have Virginia bailiffs remove them and charge both Randalls with theft.

"One last word of caution, the same one I have issued every day of this hearing, do not discuss this case with members of the press or general public. I will issue an edited version to the press designed to minimize any resulting scandal."

In the MacKenzie parlor an hour later, Bruce Mac Lachlan proclaimed to the group of people assembled there, "We were lucky, it could have been far worse."

"I don't see how," raged Phyllis, "we lost half of our money, and our social reputation is ruined. The bank, too, probably."

Craig stared at his angry wife, but it was Mac Lachlan who rebuked her sharply. "Only a third. And the bank will not be harmed. Baltimore is too big now to be dictated to by a handful of social snobs. Your husband and Marsh have just undergone a shattering experience and—"

"Marsh didn't lose a cent of her money, nor did Stuart, nor Robbie, only we—"

Craig almost strangled over the words, but he got them out. "Shut up, Phyllis, or I'll give the bank away, too. To hell with your social ambitions. I'm just glad Marsh is still alive and that I've got enough left to support my family."

Smiling broadly for the first time in days, Angus boasted, "You'll no' find MacKenzie men so easy to handle once they take the bit in their teeth. The lad's came through this like his father's son and I'm proud of him. But right now I want to talk privately to my lass here about her MacKenzie man."

Having been worrying about Stuart for an hour already, Marsh was not in a very receptive mood for advice, even from her old friend. Reluctantly, she accompanied Angus to the drawing room; she could not have been comfortable in the memory-filled library. Once seated in a private corner, though, her spirit revived and she took over the conversation with a blunt announcement about her child.

For the second time that day, Angus's smile was seraphic with pride. "You had Jamie's son and you've made an old man happy. When do I get to see the new lad?"

"I'll bring him back here next summer."

"He's no' wi' Stuart?"

"He's with Robbie and I'm leaving in October to go there. Keep my secret for me for another few months, Angus, I don't feel like any more public appearances right now. And take care of Craig for me, he'll need your support. Angus, have we paid Seth yet?"

"Aye, and I've already asked him to drive you back to the farm tomorrow. You ha' no' answered my question yet, lass."

She grinned at him with some of her old impudence. "You haven't asked it yet and I don't want you to. I'll get it all straightened out with Stuart somehow."

Angus sighed. "Aye, I know you will, but I wish he was no' such a jealous man. He's got a temper I'm no' fond of."

"Jamie had one, too."

"Aye," Angus smiled, "that he did and you tamed him, lass. So I wish you well wi' Stuart."

This conversation bothered her all the next day as she and Seth Hanford drove across Maryland. Only a contrite and apologetic Phyllis had risen to bid her farewell, and Marsh knew that this practical sister-in-law would continue to fight for Craig's financial and social success despite a hundred setbacks.

Marsh was still basking in the post-crisis glow of relief as

Seth flicked the buggy into motion for what she fervently hoped would be her final dash across Maryland. By changing horses at the livery stables of Patuxent and Ardmore, the detective managed to reach the farm by nightfall. He departed at dawn the following morning, leaving his grateful client with a sheath of report papers and a stern warning that Wayne Talbot had started divorce proceedings against his unfaithful wife a month earlier. Marsh nodded in understanding. She had only thirty-eight days left to accomplish the miracle of saving her shaky marriage with a man who was as unsure of himself as he was of her.

With a sudden, overwhelming need to be with that man, Marsh whirled through the remnants of her life in Maryland. She ordered the boxes of her and Jamie's effects shipped directly to Cheyenne—sorting of memories could await a more peaceful time. Checking the records of her racehorses with a proudly efficient John Harding, she felt a sense of completion rather than challenge. With Rake-Star and now Marsh Wind already at stud, this farm would continue to be productive. During the quiet hour in Damon and Carina's small neat home, she gave them the release for her half of this property and secured their warm promise to sponsor her son during his school years on the east coast. As always, Carina intuitively articulated Marsh's own ambivalent emotions.

"The past never dies completely for anyone, it just blends with the future. We'll love your son."

Before she left to join Sam on the waiting tug, Marsh took one more lonely pilgrimage, one delayed for seventeen months. She visited Jamie's grave—not to weep or to pray, but to remember the happiness of their three brief years of marriage. Carina was right; Jamie would remain entrenched in Marsh's future through his sons—all of them, she realized with a conviction of destiny. Regardless of emotional upheavals and distances, she was forever tied to the MacKenzie family one way or another.

Even during the short trip across the Potomac, the past and

the future merged together as the doughty riverboat captain refused to use Stuart's efficient new docks. "Hate the durned noise," Sam grinned as he jockied the tug close to the mud bank and carried her luggage ashore. "You be waiting for me right here on October first and we'll get away without any caterwauling."

She waved to her old wartime friend and turned with quickened step to walk the quarter mile to the cottages, her heart beating with anticipation. She knew that Stuart would yell at her and glower before he would finally kiss her and mumble something original like, My God, Marsh, when are you ever going to learn that you're just a woman? Just what inspired her to enter the office cottage rather than Stuart's, she didn't know. But once inside, her heart stopped beating for the second it took her to realize that the pile of boxes on the floor contained all the clothing she'd left behind. Janet had exacted her revenge and reclaimed her lover of four years. Marsh had lost the gamble because Stuart had already ended their marriage.

Numbed by a helpless feeling of defeat, she sank down onto a kitchen chair and muttered, "I should have gelded him years ago when I had the chance."

Chapter
17

Trapped on a farm which was no longer her domain and lacking any escape route for the moment, Marsh studied her options. No one knew she was here, so she might be able to find at least one worker who'd still be loyal to her. But she doubted it. She might be able to steal one of those prized Clydesdales and ride off, but she knew Stuart's guard system was military in efficiency. Or she could wait until night and simply climb the paddock fence and take the public road to Alexandria. As her thoughts began to churn, so did her restless energies; automatically, she put her things away in the bedroom which had once been her home. By the time she had dusted the living area and recombed her hair, Marsh had made her decision. She'd be damned if she'd let a temperamental idiot of a man and his overaged, overblown mistress make a fool of her.

With the self-protective instinct which had kept her alive during recent months, she tucked the derringer into the pocket of her dress. Janet just might possess enough of the violent determination of her dead cousin to be dangerous. For good measure, she also armed herself with her steel-tipped parasol before she mounted her attack. Dressed in her prettiest green summer dress, she knew without consulting a mirror that her eyes would match her dress and be shining with the light of battle.

Striding, not walking, she opened the front door of Stuart's home and interrupted a cozy little scene which was even more than she'd hoped for. Both Janet and Stuart were drunk, and while Stuart was reasonably clothed, Janet was in sodden disarray. Her pink dress was opened in front to reveal the top of a very necessary corset and a perspiring cleavage between two ample breasts. The curls which had been so picture-perfect in the courtroom had given up the battle against the late August heat and hung in disordered masses around her shoulders, and the makeup liberally applied earlier now formed unpleasant little clots which competed with beads of sweat for facial space.

"It would seem," Marsh announced in a reasonably dispassionate voice, "that I arrived too late for the grand reunion." Tossing one of Janet's discarded petticoats from the chair it had littered, Marsh sat down and studied her husband's face. He looked much as she thought he would, except that his scowl was lopsided because he couldn't focus his eyes successfully. His dignity was further impaired by his inability to rise from his chair. Nothing inhibits even a sober man's mobility to react with good physical coordination better than a broken leg. Thus, it was Janet who shoved the newspaper Stuart was trying to reach into Marsh's hand.

Impassively, Marsh read the article on the sporting page of the *Baltimore Herald*. What began as a report about the retirement of the champion, Marsh Wind, to serve as stud on the MacKenzie Farm changed midway through to a story about the wealthy widow of James MacKenzie. Nowhere in the article was her new husband mentioned by the author, who described Marsh as she had looked at the celebration dinner party Brad had hosted: "like a soft flame from her hair to the hem of her shimmering dress." Other than Philip Addison and John Mosby, whose comments about her were quoted in the column, none of the other guests or her father were mentioned. Marsh grimaced faintly—either she or Wilbur Brant had had too much champagne that night.

"You lied to me," Stuart raged in a voice that slushed drunkenly around in his mouth. "You left me here all alone so you could be with your lover who didn't have a broken leg. And it didn't take you long to forget that you had a husband. The wealthy widow who—"

Marsh swung into attack position and cut him short. "Is this the only article from the *Baltimore Herald* your tabby cat brought you two days ago when she returned with her slimy little lies? Didn't she even mention her cousin Alice? She knows all about Alice. She should, she had to be in court for two days, just like the rest of us. And her mama was there the following two days squealing like a stuck pig."

As if ice water had been hurled at his face, Stuart began to regain a semblance of sobriety. "What happened to Alice, Marsh?"

"She stabbed herself with the poisoned knitting needle she was trying to jab into me and she died."

"Oh, my God," he mumbled helplessly.

"Stuart, I am going to be your next door neighbor for a few days until I can get word to my father. When you sober up, you come on over. I'll leave all the papers on the office desk for you to read. I won't be there, so you don't have to worry about another scene. But don't you dare bring this white trash with you."

Marsh stopped talking and leaped to her feet as the open-mouthed Janet lunged for her. Instantly, her parasol was raised to a rapier level of defense and she spat at the red-faced woman. "You touch me, Janet Talbot, and you'll be the oldest looking thirty-two-year-old slut on the water-front." Still holding her parasol at the alert position, Marsh backed carefully out the door and into the bright Virginia sunlight.

It took only a few minutes for her to arrange the papers on the desk: Seth Hanford's account of the apartment scene, Bruce Mac Lachlan's notes on the inquest, Angus Balfour's accounting of the division of Jamie's estate, and the official release of the property to Stuart. A nice, neat legal display that summed up her twenty-three years of life!

Locking the door securely behind her, she walked the quarter mile to the dining hall, hoping for lunch and a friendly face. She became aware of the smiles of greeting long before she reached the paddock compound. Inside the new mess hall, near the serving tables, one of the women cooks she'd known for years sidled up to her and whispered, "Lawsy, Miss Marsh, we 'uz glad to see you. Mister MacKenzie's been powerful upset." At the table itself, the two white foremen she'd met only a month ago sat down with her.

"Ma'am," one asked her, "what does Mr. MacKenzie want us to do with the two customers waiting in the barn? This is the second time one of them has been here."

"There's a third one coming at four o'clock," the other foreman reminded his partner.

"How long has this been going on?" she asked tartly.

"Your husband's been a mite peculiar for the last two weeks."

"He's been as snarling as a bobcat, Mrs. MacKenzie," corrected the larger of the two men, "but he hasn't even showed up for the last three days, not since that—"

"That female polecat arrived," Marsh finished bluntly. "All right, now let's eat lunch and then get back to work."

The first customer wanted a pair of matched Clydesdale geldings for carriage work, so Marsh sent him out with one foreman to select his own. For the next customer, the second foreman signalled two workers to bring the four, already chosen shires into the barn. While she was conducting this second sale, the third buyer arrived and stood looking at her with speculative eyes. Marsh's heart beat a little faster and her eyes regained a measure of their normal sparkle. As the first two customers left with their massive purchases, she turned to the last one and raised her eyebrow.

"My two Shires are already picked out." The man smiled, and Marsh recognized the smile. She'd seen it on the faces of many of the contemptuous males she'd sold to in the past. When the horses were brought in for inspection, he shook his head. "Ma'am, that one on the left ain't the one I ordered. The one in that stall over there is more like."

Marsh glanced over to the special stall the man indicated. Her eyes were sparking fire as she studied the buyer's hooded look of shrewd cupidity.

"The one in the stall over there," she drawled, "is a champion stud I brought from England three years ago. Now what about the pair here?"

The man nodded in defeat. "They'll do and I already paid your boss for them."

Marsh didn't need the frantic wig-wag signal from one of the foremen; she knew that no MacKenzie, drunk or sober, ever did business that casually. "Mister," she said sharply, "I don't know you from a Yankee carpetbagger, and either you pay up in hard cash or you get no horses." She smiled ever so faintly because she'd caught herself just in time to keep from demanding "hard Yankee cash."

But the slight humor was wasted on the man. As a Southerner who'd just received the deadly insult of being compared to a carpetbagger, he glared at her. "You've got a big mouth, lady. Someone ought to tell your boss that you don't know when to keep it closed."

"I wouldn't tell my boss that," she snapped, "that is, if you want to keep what teeth you have. He's my husband. You have your choice. Shut up and pay the money or get thrown off my farm!" Under her steady gaze, the man angrily dug into his pocket and dragged out a crumpled wad of bills.

Slowly, he counted out the amount of half the previous purchase price of four Shires.

"There you are, lady," he grumbled.

"Not quite," Marsh said icily. "You're forty dollars shy."

"What the hell, this is the same as you charged the last man for Shires."

"Yours are better horses," she claimed imperturbably, "so they cost twenty dollars more—each." She waited a moment; when the man didn't put any more money down on the feed box, she signalled the foreman to lead the patient animals away.

"I'll pay you twenty dollars more," shouted the man.

Marsh shrugged her shoulders eloquently. "Make it twenty-five and they're yours." She kept her face sober as the extra money was clapped onto the table and the man led the brutes to his wagon. Not until he was underway with his team of Shires did she return the grins of the two foremen.

"I sold MacKenzie horses for years," she told them airily, "and I've yet to meet the bully you can't bluff. Do you suppose we can get a cup of coffee in the mess hall?"

Marsh felt more useful than she had since England, when she'd helped pick out the horses that had created this success-ful farm, and her pleasant mood of accomplishment lasted all the way back to the cottage. She stopped short on the tiny front porch; the lamplight coming from inside warned her that she had company. Awkwardly, Stuart rose to his feet as she entered the office.

"Marsh," he began, "I'm not very good at apologies."

"You're not very bright in your judgment of people, either," she responded candidly.

"You mean because I married you in spite of your lies."

"You didn't marry me, Stuart. I married you with my father's help."

His eyes glittered. "Why the hell did you, since you hold me in such contempt?"

"I joined the MacKenzie family when I was thirteen years old. It was too strong a habit to break."

He wanted to destroy her arrogance. "Was that when you and my father—"

She looked at him with amused contempt. "Your father didn't come near my bed until after we'd been married for three months—and then I went to his."

"All pure and virginal, I suppose."

"Why shouldn't I have been? Do you really believe I'd have turned you down and accepted any of the scum who asked?"

"So you waited until you married me before you began this sort of thing? Did you read what your two admirers called you in this article? 'An exciting woman' and 'a lady who's not afraid to be herself.' Didn't you think to tell either of them you were married?"

"Would you believe that everyone at the party was more interested in something else? My father hosted that dinner as a celebration for the four of us there who had outlived Alice—Wayne, Mr. Ronson, Phyllis, and myself. It was also a party to cheer Craig up. Stuart, I can see how you might have misinterpreted this newspaper story, but one of your foremen said you were angry even before. Why?"

"Because your 'sick' grandmother and mother sent us an invitation to visit them while your father was on a business trip. So I knew you had lied to me again. Just as you had about dividing my father's estate. You let me make a fool of myself with Mac Lachlan right after our wedding night."

"You didn't need my help to do that. You were drunk on our wedding night, and you deserted me the next morning without a word. But the money's all evenly divided now, so take your possessions with you and get back to your mistress. You'll be glad to know that, as soon as you divorce me for desertion, you'll be able to marry her. Wayne's already started his divorce. Good-bye, Stuart."

Marsh rose and started to walk away from the desk, but

Stuart scrambled to his feet and stumbled toward her. "I'm not going anyplace, I've moved in with you," he shouted as he clutched her arm.

She turned to face him. "You may have moved into this cottage, but you haven't moved in with me. And if you try to rape me, Stuart MacKenzie, I'll break your damn leg again." Pulling her arm away from him with a jerk, she went to her bedroom and locked the door, cursing her own stupidity for not having left the farm when she had the chance this afternoon.

By noon the next day, everyone on the farm knew that the owner had sobered up and that Janet Talbot had returned to the big house. However, few of the workers were reassured by the stormy look on Stuart's face or by the unsmiling one on his wife's as he spoke with the foremen in the barn. He made no comment when they told him about yesterday's sales. Back in the office cottage, he worked briefly on the books while Marsh fidgeted in frustrated anger. "Stuart," she finally blurted, "this is ridiculous."

"I agree, but since you assured me last night and again this morning that you wouldn't share my bed, this is all the marriage we have left."

"I refuse to remain here as a prisoner."

"And I'm not fool enough to think that you'd remain any other way. So until we can settle our differences, things will continue as they are."

"Our differences, you hypocrite, have nothing to do with me. You're the one who forgot your wedding vows. I didn't."

"Well, I was convinced you had. If you had sent for me, I would have been there when you needed me. But you didn't even do me the courtesy of writing."

Since there was a grain of truth to his charge against her, Marsh endured the next six days without argument until the morning a heavy dray wagon traveled down the private MacKenzie road to the big house and stopped by the office cottage on its way back. When the driver knocked on the door, Stuart answered.

"We're delivering these things to a Mrs. Bradford Marshall," the man asserted, "and Mr. Randall asked me to stop by and give Mrs. Pamela MacKenzie this one package. He said this letter would explain."

Even before Stuart closed the door after accepting the package, Marsh entreated him urgently, "Let me go with that driver to my parents' home. I promised my father I would come to see him."

Stuart closed the door firmly and handed her the letter and the carved leather tube. When she made no move to open the letter, Stuart read its contents aloud:

"Granddaughter, since you are the only Randall left with any courage, I want you to have this reminder of your heritage. He was my father. I did not want the vultures to pay a dishonorable debt with it. Clinton Randall."

The reminder was a commendation of bravery in battle and of six years of meritorious service from 1776 to 1781 for Captain Charles Clinton Randall in the Continental American Army. The parchment was signed by General George Washington.

Stuart's lips pursed in a soundless whistle. "No wonder your grandfather wanted to get this out of Sophia's hands. She could have paid her debt with it."

"My mother should have it."

"No, your grandfather's right. You're the one with courage. Tomorrow, we're going to take this to an art dealer to see about preserving it. Our children should—" He stopped talking abruptly at her sharp intake of breath and concluded lamely, "I think it'd do us both good to get away from here for a day."

Automatically, she tried to deny the need, just as she had for every minute of the past miserable days. During the first ones, when Stuart had reached out to touch her, she had pulled haughtily away; but after he had begun to avoid her

equally, she'd felt shunned and forsaken. She had tried
reminding herself that she was being restrained against her
will, but she knew she could have escaped a dozen times and
hadn't. Feeling the double pressure of time and unwilling
remorse—at Brad's party in Baltimore she knew she had
deliberately ignored her marriage—Marsh was depressed about
her crushing commitments to visit with her parents and to
meet her fateful October first deadline. And now, with this
priceless Randall heirloom, she had one more obligation; her
grandfather had treasured it above all else in his life. Somehow, in spite of the unhappy past, she had to thank him.

Despite her general perturbation of spirit, she dressed the
next morning with the tingle of anticipation and experienced a
sharp thrill of pride at the sight of her handsome husband in a
pearl-gray suit that made his eyes look midnight blue.

"We may have to spend the night at a hotel," he announced tersely. "It'll probably take two days to get the
parchment mounted." Avoiding her eyes, he added, "Pack
your wedding dress. I'd like to see my wife looking like a
shimmering flame too." Just as his father had, Stuart possessed total recall about the reactions of other men to his
wife. Marsh tried unsuccessfully to still her speeded-up heart-
beat as she packed her suitcase and joined her husband on the
buggy seat for the hour-long trip into Washington. That he
knew the capital well was evident by the speed with which
he located an art dealer on a quiet back street and an
exclusive ladies' shop an hour later in the expensive, hotel
part of town.

He smiled sheepishly as he led her inside the dress shop.
"Don't look so suspicious, Marsh," he whispered, "this is
where your mother buys her clothing. She was the one who
told me about it." Marsh felt a little ashamed of the jealousy
that had flared seconds before, but she relaxed when she
remembered that Janet had never worn elegant clothes like
the ones in this shop. In compensation, she allowed Stuart to
choose the two dresses he bought for her, one an embroidered

silk the color of creamy honeysuckle and the other a dark persimmon velvet street suit.

As he helped her remount the buggy, he was almost playful. "Now you can sit with me at my tailor's and help me choose." Marsh jerked guiltily at his words. Rolled up inside her leather shopping bag were the stained pants she'd ruined the fateful day her stepfather died. She'd been worried about their replacement for days, and now Stuart had provided her the perfect opportunity. She felt doubly the betrayer, since riding clothes symbolized a life he would quite probably refuse to try. But necessity was still her driving taskmaster. Quietly, she left her husband with one tailor while she retired to the rear of the shop and spoke to the working partner.

"I want six pairs of these breeches finished before October first with matching overskirts for each. I also need a long sheepskin jacket and a leather hat," she ordered, and added needlessly, "it gets cold in Wyoming." Not only is it cold, she reflected, but it's on the other side of the world as far as Stuart is concerned. Hurriedly, she repressed the gloomy thought and returned to him in time to select a blue serge the dark color of his eyes. They smiled at each other then for the first time in months, and the remaining afternoon hours were the most lighthearted ones they'd ever spent together. Only as they were following the attendant down the corridor of the Clairmont Hotel did their self-consciousness return; especially when the smiling man put her suitcase into one of the adjoining rooms and Stuart's into the other.

Seated in front of her dressing table a half hour later, she was repairing the damage the wind had done to her pinned-up hair when Stuart walked up behind her and began buttoning her gown. "I remembered that you'd need help with your wedding dress," he mumbled. Marsh met his eyes in the mirror and her own dropped first, the raw desire in his matched the electric impulses which had been destroying her equilibrium for hours. As they entered the formal dining room, he bent down to her again. "Sorry we won't be able to do your dress justice tonight, but I don't trust my leg enough to dance yet.'' Marsh sighed in relief, she didn't think she'd have been able to manage a very dignified dance performance, anyway. They were silent throughout most of the meal; Marsh was remembering the dinner at the New George Inn when he had proposed a very different arrangement than marriage. For some reason she didn't want to analyze, she felt that tonight was probably more akin to an illicit rendezvous than it was to a legal marriage. The odd illusion persisted as Stuart unlocked the door to her room and put his arms around her. He didn't kiss her, he just held her and mumbled into her hair, ''I've thought about this for a month, but one broken leg is enough. Good night, honey.''

She stared at him in disbelief as he walked toward his own room. If there had been an object handy, she'd have hurled it at his retreating back; instead, she could only stand there with her hands clenched and let the disappointment and anger roll over her in waves. She's been sure that he had wanted her so intensely, he'd have torn the clothes off of her had she resisted him. Since she had virtually invited him and he'd still refused, she was left with the stunning realization that she was expected to sleep alone again. Not until she moved restlessly over to the dressing table did she remember. Smiling with a reckless relief, she dug into her suitcase and took out the bottle of usquebaugh and glasses she'd packed this morning. Stuart was in bed waiting for her.

''I was wondering when you'd remember that you couldn't get that dress off without me,'' he smiled. His hands, though, were stiff and awkward as he undid the row of tiny buttons and set the bottle aside. ''We don't need anything,'' he muttered, ''and if you don't hurry, I'll tear the rest of those things off you as you expected me to do a few minutes ago.''

''It would serve you right if I left right now,'' she murmured, well content with his impatience.

''You wouldn't get five feet away.'' He reached for her then and helped her push her frothy petticoats into a heap on the floor. Even before her stockings and shoes joined the pile, his hands began the ritual of seduction. This night, he vowed, he would remain the master and finally dominate this fiery woman who'd addled his brains since the day he'd met her. But how can a man caress a woman slowly and masterfully when her body is already searing his with its heat? He groaned when she kissed him and reached down with a caress of her own; helplessly, he settled for making love to her during, after, and later on. Nor were the few hours left for sleep any less disturbing for Stuart; he kept waking up to make sure she was still there, although how he could doubt the fact, he didn't know. Even as she slept, she exerted a power over him which kept him wanting her almost as soon as they had separated from their last throbbing union.

Awakening first in the morning, Stuart waited for his wife to open her eyes. Fervently, he hoped they'd be clear and green, without any regrets or lingering doubts. He'd never forgotten the words she'd spoken on their first morning together, "When I'm happy." That was the way he wanted her to greet him today. He didn't want to be reminded of the past. That she'd loved his father first still rankled, even though he knew that his father had deserved her love. But that he'd not yet proved his father's equal in her eyes had made him act the fool with jealousy and childish revenge. And now she'd never believe the truth, that he hadn't touched Janet, not since weeks before his wedding, that in a fit of rage over a newspaper article, he'd let his vicious ex-mistress remove Marsh's clothes and then he'd believed her lies. But he hadn't touched her. How could he when his every thought had been concentrated on recapturing this woman lying next to him now? However, his plans had not worked out the way he wanted. Marsh had not reacted with a jealous fury at all; she'd treated him with the contempt he'd deserved. But last night, when her passion had shaken him with its intensity, he'd vowed to win her love. God knows she had earned his! This slender woman, whose bloodlines made his own heritage seem ordinary, had the courage of a Phil Sheridan. He chuckled faintly, she also had the stubborn independence of a southern rebel. She'd be as hard to control as one of her own racehorses. Only with a firm, gentle hand could he make the promise of last night into a permanent reality.

Leaning down with an overpowering sense of possession, he brushed his lips lightly over her smooth forehead and prayed again that her eyes would be green and clear. He jerked sharply when she finally opened them, because they also held laughter.

"If you've finished taking inventory, Stuart MacKenzie, you can kiss me properly."

"You've been playing possum," he accused.

"And you've been bouncing all over the bed like a fish with a hook in its mouth."

He laughed at her comparison and sheepishly admitted, "I guess I have, because that's what I am. Do you still want me, Marsh?"

"Just try to get away!" As she moved against him, he chuckled again. She knew damn well that was the last thing he wanted.

All that day and the next, his pursuit of her love was a gallant courtship, the one he should have paid her years ago. He praised her graceful carriage as they walked along the street and her gracious manners as she thanked the art dealer for making a hidden scroll of parchment into a piece of art that would dignify the most prominent wall in their home. When a congressman he knew stopped by their hotel dinner table, Stuart introduced his wife with a pride that made the politician bend low in respect. In their hotel room at night, he unbuttoned her dress with reverent hands and promised that she'd have a skillful maid to help her in the future.

By the time they returned to the farm two days later, Marsh was nervously aware that she'd succeeded in rewinning this errant husband only to the extent that he was more determined than ever to make her into an aristocratic southern lady.

"We're starting our new home right away, and I want it big enough for children and for entertaining. Marsh, I want us to have the kind of life your parents have," he stated firmly as he helped her alight from the buggy.

She almost blurted out the truth then, that she had a home and a child and friends. But events had already made such a confession too late. When the public ferryboat deposited them at the dock, Clinton Randall was awaiting them with news that would make building a new home unnecessary. Sophia had decided to sell Randall Manor and move north! With a sinking heart, Marsh watched her husband's acceptance of the news. His blue eyes narrowed with the same shrewd speculation his father's had often displayed whenever Jamie was faced with a business opportunity. She groaned when Stuart took out the deeds to the New York properties and studied them intently. "Tell me about these places, Marsh," he ordered.

Resigned to the inevitable, she recounted the assets of the block of sixteen modest buildings with two flats each, the small garment factory fronted by six shops in a drab commercial district, and the reasonably attractive four-flat unit in a good downtown residential area. It was this third property that intrigued Stuart. "Let's talk to Sophia," he enthused, "this New York thing might prove exactly what she wants, and her present home would be ideal for us."

Marsh made another futile attempt to protest. "I hated living in that house, and Sophia would throw a conniption fit if she saw me anywhere near her property."

"You were an unhappy child when you lived there, but now it'd be our home. And it's everything I've ever wanted. You may be right about Sophia, though. She might be more spiteful to you than she'll be to me, but she'll listen because she won't get any other offers." Studying his wife's expressionless face more closely, Stuart added gently, "Janet's not there anymore. She left a week ago.'' Marsh shrugged lightly; she had not been thinking about the threat of Janet at the moment.

"While you're taking care of this, Stuart, I think I'll go visit my parents.''

He looked at her sharply. "We'll go visit them together. It'll take Sophia weeks to check over the New York property, so we have some free time.''

Desperately, she tried once more to blunt his enthusiasm. "I'd like you to see Wyoming before you buy that old house.''

"Next year, I promise, we'll go there for a visit and see about finishing that hull you and my father built. Meanwhile, I'll write to Robbie and tell him to take care of it.''

Forced by necessity to withdraw into her own thoughts, Marsh spent the week in an aimless round of activities while Stuart negotiated with Sophia. Twice, she drove her grandfather around the farm and studiously avoided any talk about the past. She served him a drink of brandy in the office cottage and showed him the newly-framed parchment. Through him rather than Stuart, she learned that Sophia had already left for New York; but she knew by her husband's irrepressible jubilation that he was certain of victory.

"All right, honey,'' Stuart told her one night, "tomorrow we go visit your folks for a week. Pack all your prettiest dresses, I imagine your mother will want to show us off.'' Marsh wondered sourly just how her husband understood her mother so well. But he did. Melissa loved to entertain, and Marsh Oaks was rapidly becoming the social center for rural northeastern Virginia. Marsh's only touchstone with her own reality during those seven days was her father's sardonic attitude. On the first day, Brad had urged his wayward daughter to tell her husband the truth; he'd given up when she refused point-blank to do so. Not only was she more convinced than ever that Stuart would not accept either a stepchild or a pioneer existence, she was alienated by the life he planned for her. As she watched her mother graciously host a roomful of women who adored this partial return to the good life of the old South, Marsh longed for the unpretentious hardships and people of the wilderness. She watched her husband adjust to these people as if his whole life had been antebellum, lived on a plantation and in a caste system society. Remembering Jamie's uncanny ability to adjust to aristocrats, she expected to hear Stuart's crisp Yankee accent become a slurred southern drawl.

Aware of his wife's withdrawal, Stuart redoubled his efforts to woo her. He was considerate, charming, and passionate. Both Claire and Melissa were delighted with him and with his plans to acquire the old home. "At last it'll become the showplace it was when I was a girl," Melissa commented quietly, "and it'll be a happy place with you and Stuart in it." Marsh felt like a traitor.

During their final week together back on the farm, Stuart's natural Scot's caution reasserted itself and he became more vigilant of his wife's comments and activities. The day their clothing was delivered from the tailor shop in Washington, Marsh attempted to conceal her riding habits; but Stuart immediately left off inspecting his own new suits to look at hers.

"Marsh, you can't wear things like these, not in civilized society. I know you loved them when you were a girl, but you've got a position to uphold now as my wife."

Gamely, she smiled at him and agreed. "You're right, Stuart, I'll put them away." Carefully, she packed all but one new outfit into the suitcases she would take with her. That night, in her old bed which Stuart now shared with her since she'd refused to move into his cottage next door, she lay awake and fought the tears which had become a daily part of her life. When she remembered her calculated pursuit of this husband, she bitterly regretted her lack of foresight and honesty. In a last minute surge of wishful thinking, Marsh decided to gamble; but his arousing words the next morning ended her last, faint hope.

"I'll be glad when you're pregnant," he grumbled, "and quit burrowing around at night like a restless chipmunk. Honey, your troubles are all over, and I mean to keep you safe. Speaking of pregnancy—" he mumbled, and reached for her. Fiercely, she responded to his caresses, silently echoing his wish for a child. Something permanent might yet be salvaged from this problem-torn marriage.

On the last night, Marsh moved the kitchen table into the large office room and polished the worn wood surface into the semblance of a shine. Rummaging around the kitchen shelves, she located candles and two bottles of wine. When Stuart returned from his final inspection of the day an hour before their evening meal was delivered from the mess hall, she was waiting for him in a candlelit room, gowned in her burnt orange wedding dress. She smiled at her husband's questioning look. "It's our anniversary, Stuart, we've been together for one month. I thought we needed a celebration."

It was the most successful party she'd ever hosted; Stuart was dazzled to the point of happy idiocy. When he finally stopped planning their idyllic future in a manor house with six children and carried her to bed, she was beyond logical thought. For her, this seemed almost as poignant a farewell as the one she'd bid his father nineteen months earlier. She kissed him good night and watched as his eyes closed in heavy slumber; she'd used a pinch of Carina's powder of forgetfulness to sweeten his last glass of wine and to ensure herself an uninterrupted departure. Moving rapidly now, she checked the contents of the three suitcases, counted her money, tucked it into her breast binder, and changed from the frothy dance dress into one of her new riding habits. With the derringer in the pocket of her sheepskin coat and the Indian feather tucked into the band of her new leather hat, Marsh was ready to face the life she'd chosen out of necessity. In a last, sentimental survey of her girlhood home, she held the candle up one more time to study the signature of George Washington and silently mouthed the words, Someday, Jamie, I'll show it to you.

Seated at the kitchen table, she wrote a letter, a painful forty-five words that stated her regret, but held little hope for a future: "I had no right to marry you without being honest or to change your life. I wanted so much to tell you the truth during our last happy weeks together, but I couldn't. My only excuse is that I love you. Be happy, Stuart. Marsh." Quietly, she placed the envelope on the empty pillow next to her husband's, looked at him one last time, and left the house.

On the way down to the dock she tried not to think of his anger; this time she knew she deserved it. But her commitments were too powerful. She had a debt of honor which must be paid to an Indian chief who held the power of life or death over the many people she loved. Had she told Stuart about Crazy Horse, his old allegiance to the army would have forced him to betray the Indian ravager. As for the debt of love she owed an infant son, it could only be paid with her loneliness. Had he known about a possible stepson, Stuart would have refused to marry her altogether. During the hours she waited on the lonely dock, she sorted out her memories and accomplishments. She had attained the goals she'd set for herself, and with one exception, she had secured her future. Unhappily, the question she tried to suppress kept recurring. How long would it take a suspicious, temperamental husband to forget her and to smother himself once more in Janet's overpowering perfume—this time in a beautiful old turn-of-the-century home?

Chapter
18

Not even Sam's cheerful greeting as he snugged his tugboat against the levee bank of the river or the cup of strong coffee he handed Marsh as she boarded did much to dispel her mood of guilty heartbreak. For once, her carefully forged determination to meet life's challenges almost succumbed to self-pity, and her lonely cab ride to the railroad station deepened her depression. Only her powerful sense of survival drove her to ignore the privacy of her compartment until after she'd checked on the shipment of horses. In the cattle pens in front of the four railroad cars she'd hired, she found a chaotic scene which instantly replaced her morbid unhappiness with a raging fury. The foreman the railroad had hired was a hard-bitten man who used the cruel prod indiscriminately and viciously. Already, two stallions were rearing in wild-eyed terror, and the other two-hundred-odd horses were milling around in a state of near panic. Knowing full well that the delivery of nervous mounts to a savagely angry Indian chief would be a disaster, Marsh used her parade-ground tone of voice for the first time in four years of superimposed gentility.

"Get the hell away from my horses," she barked at the foreman, "and report to the stationmaster for a day's wages. You're fired." Swiftly, she removed her overskirt and saddled the most nervous of the stallions. Soothing the tense animal with her hands, she mounted it and wheeled around to confront the eight cowboys who were watching her with a mixture of emotions. Summarily, she fired the two who were still holding prods in their hands and the one whose face was openly contemptuous before she addressed the remaining five.

"I'll double the wages you were promised if you'll take orders from me until we get these horses to Cheyenne. But don't be fool enough to expect an easy time on the job. Half of these horses will be delivered to a man who'll use every one of us as crow bait if his battle ponies are damaged. Since we're shorthanded, I'll work along with you, but I'll expect each of you who accepts my offer to work just as hard as I do. Any takers?"

"At double the wages, ma'am," sounded one man with the familiar twang of a Texan, "I'd work for the devil himself." The other four quickly seconded his sentiments, and Marsh grinned at the crew of men she'd live with until they reached the outskirts of Chicago.

"Gentlemen, I've been called worse things than a devil, so let's get these horses into the cars." Following her lead, the five men worked steadily for the next half hour until the discharged foreman returned with an officious stationmaster who made the mistake of addressing Marsh as "Miss La Tour" and of defending the man he'd employed for the job. Her answer was pithy to the point of rude pungency.

"My name isn't La Tour, it's MacKenzie, and I own and operate the three MacKenzie farms. If you're the jackass who hired this ex-army trash to transport my horses, you're as incompetent as he is. Now get out of my way or I'll turn my stallions loose on the lot of you." Since she was already mounted on the most powerful of the stallions, her threat proved effective enough to send the stationmaster fleeing to safety behind the fences. Reluctantly, the men Marsh had fired followed him; even they recognized the authority of the MacKenzie name in the world of horseflesh.

During the next four days, Marsh shared a cattle car with six stallions and five men, shoveled her share of manure out of the fenced gates, slept on a borrowed bedroll, and ate the plates of unappetizing food the train attendant brought in three times a day. Since each of the four cars had to be manned at all times, the work schedule was too demanding to allow for any relaxation except eating and sleeping. Only on the last night before reaching Chicago did Marsh even see her comfortable compartment. By tipping one of the porters to bring her buckets of hot water, she succeeded in scrubbing the fetid stench of manure from her hair and body. The dirty clothing she'd lived in for days was tossed out of the open window. By the time she finished washing, she was too tired to do anything but sleep. Not until the next morning did she realize that she'd been spared days of tortured regret, that hard work had kept her too busy for much introspective brooding over her personal problems. She smiled ruefully and wondered if the last few days were a prophetic forecast of the rest of her life.

Certainly they had been of the next few weeks at least. A grim and anxious trio of men awaited her in Chicago. As soon as Marsh saw Robbie's tense face, she knew that this unhappy trip had been more than urgent. It had become vital to the survival of the MacKenzie-Flynn ranches and to the safety of the hundred people on those three ranches, one of whom was her own year-old son. During the six months she had been in the East, the friction between the white settlers and the Indians had increased enormously. Crazy Horse had succeeded in stirring up even the peaceful villages of Sioux, and he now raided the countryside with a large band of skilled warriors and threatened even the railroad itself. Marsh knew without asking that the Indian chief had not forgotten her debt of fifty horses.

Even more distressing than Robbie's news about Crazy Horse was Devin's bitter denunciation of the whites' treatment of the Indians. Since the completion of the transcontinental railroad the year earlier, the herds of buffalo had been decimated by trainloads of white hunters who shot the animals from the open windows of the moving trains and left the carcasses to rot on the open plains. Villages of Indians all over the territory were facing starvation because of this cruel slaughter of their main source of food and warm clothing. Even more callous was the action of the United States government in the sale of Indian lands. Scores of legal and illegal land sale offices operated in every fortified town along the rail route, and white settlers were buying great chunks of Indian territory for a dollar an acre. Marsh felt the same helpless anger she had experienced in Georgia when she heard how the carpetbaggers and land speculators had destroyed any hope the majority of Southerners had for reconstruction. Her eyes were narrowed as she made a rapid calculation of her remaining cash. After she finished paying the five cowboys their wages, she had under eight thousand dollars—only enough to keep a few villages alive for the winter.

"What do they need, Devin?"

"Warm footwear and dried corn," he answered her question with the brevity she'd learned to expect from him.

"If we buy cured sheepskins, can the squaws make the footwear?" At his nod, Marsh turned to Robbie. "While Devin and I locate the sheepskins, you buy as much corn as you can find. How many hours before the train leaves?"

Colin consulted his watch. "About eight."

"Can we find spare wagons in Cheyenne?" she demanded.

Colin nodded. "The town is loaded with abandoned ones."

"Good." Suddenly, Marsh grinned at the three men; she'd just remembered where she carried the money. "Gentlemen, if you'll turn your backs for a minute, I'll retrieve my money." At their confused looks, she smiled again. "It's a trick I learned from a lady in Cheyenne last spring, and it was the only safe place I could think of." Not even the sharp memory of Philip Addison's disapproval dimmed her humor as she dug the bills out of their hiding place. She could always become a lady again when there were no longer any emergencies to be met. For the next eight hours, though, one crisis after another had to be faced. The only large shipment of sheepskins she and Devin located were already consigned to a coat manufacturer in Bangor, Maine. A valuable hour of time and a two-hundred dollar bribe were needed to convince a warehouse stock clerk to "lose" the shipment. Freight space also proved a problem until a railroad official finally consented to add another storage car to the Union Pacific train being formed for the westward trip. When the wagons loaded with sacks of corn began to arrive and Robbie took over the job of supervising the loading, Marsh realized that her impulsive generosity was resulting in additional hard work for her friends. An hour before the scheduled departure, the final and worst crisis occurred: two of the five cowboys demanded their pay and left the train. Upon hearing the news, Colin took off on a run and returned with six shabbily dressed men five minutes before train time.

"It's an old army trick," he explained, "free transportation in return for labor. These men are German immigrant farmers who want to buy farm land in Wyoming. They may not know horses, but they aren't afraid of work. I'll get them settled and join you three later."

As Marsh boarded the train, she felt alive and stimulated. The danger and adventure of an explosive frontier answered her need for a life beyond the dictated confines of a challenge-free Virginia farm. It was a land that was big enough to support the native Indians, immigrants from Europe, and a farm girl from Virginia. She wished that Stuart could have seen it just once before he settled for the staid social life of a worn-out South. Resolutely, she repressed the thought of

Stuart; she'd face the personal problem of missing him later. Right now there were other, more important decisions to be made. She turned her attention back toward her companions and watched as Colin rejoined the group. Silently, he passed around a sheet of newspaper advertising the sale of cheap land in six western territories.

"Indian land," he announced. "Our German workers were handed this as soon as they got off the ship. My God, there won't be an acre left in a few years."

Thoughtfully, Marsh voiced the idea which had been forming all day, ever since she'd heard about the government land offices. "If we want to keep any open spaces, we'll have to buy the land before it's all divided up into small parcels."

Devin glared at her. "Indians won't sell you any more. Why should we?"

Colin regarded his son with deep sympathy. "Indians are no longer being asked, the government has declared their land forfeit."

Alarmed by Devin's anger and outraged by the treachery of the government officials, Marsh thought about the money she'd put into the Cheyenne bank as her baby's share of his father's estate. One wealthy white child against thousands of victimized Indian children! Jamie could survive on far less, she decided. "Devin, how much land near us can you buy for twenty-five thousand dollars?"

He regarded her with the same antagonism she'd seen in the eyes of dispossessed Southerners. "Your government wouldn't sell me a square foot. I'm a breed."

"Then Colin and Robbie will have to do the actual buying. How many acres?"

Colin answered for his son, "About twenty-five thousand."

"How many more acres would we need to reach the mountains?"

"Perhaps ten or fifteen thousand."

"All right, you and Robbie buy the forty thousand. I'll give you the money once we reach Cheyenne."

Devin's voice was heavy with contempt. "So the redhead-ed squaw is as greedy as the others for Indian land."

"I don't want or need it for myself or my son, Devin Flynn, I want it held in trust for your people so that they'll have at least a part of their own land after they've been robbed of the rest."

"Why would a white woman do that for Indians?"

"Because if you weren't wallowing in self-pity right now like some old flea-bit hound dog, you'd realize that you weren't the only breed in the world. How about you, Robbie, do you also think I'm greedy?"

The sandy-haired man frowned slightly. "No, I don't. I'm worried about the reverse. My father wanted you and Jamie protected. I think you've already given away too much to my brothers and me. And now this. Will you have enough left?"

"Jamie would have been the first to admit that I can take care of myself, and there's plenty left for one little boy. Well, Devin, what do you say? I'd like your approval and your help. You're the only one who can convince the Indians that the land will be theirs in trust as long as they want it. No one will be able to steal it from them because not even a crooked land speculator would touch property protected by the MacKenzies and Flynns. Will you help me, Devin?"

"Marsh, the Indians don't intend losing this war, so you'd just be wasting your money." She heard Devin's use of her name and breathed easier.

"Then what's the harm? Any white people who survive, probably including us, will just have to leave. But I don't think the Indians can win. The South was beaten because there were more Yankees, and those same Yankees will keep on until they own every bit of land they can steal. You know I'm right, Devin."

Stubbornly, he hedged his answer. "What did you mean when you implied that you were a breed?"

She'd been thinking about her illegitimacy when she'd made the comparison, but she didn't want that old scandal to taint her son's life. She shrugged lightly and smiled. "You went to school back east. How do you think those snobs treated someone like me? A woman who races horses and has my sharp tongue?"

For the first time that day, Devin broke into laughter. "I imagine some of them wanted to tar and feather you."

Remembering Stuart and the fury he was capable of, she smiled ruefully, "I can think of one who'd like to use a whip on me right now."

Devin became serious again. "How did your personal problems work out, Marsh?"

"What problems?" Robbie wanted to know.

"The man who killed Jamie is dead and so is the woman who hired him," Marsh explained.

"Your stepfather and Alice? I thought you'd hired a detective to take care of them," Robbie persisted.

"I had and he did, but they weren't that easy to . . ." Her voice trailed off; she still shuddered when she remembered Alice.

"And you faced that kind of danger while you were there? Why didn't you tell me? I'd have gone with you."

"Stuart helped and Craig did, too. Even my father was there. I'll let you read the reports, Robbie. There was a lot more to the whole thing than anyone guessed."

Colin leaned toward her, a quizzical expression on his good-natured face. "Did you use the training Shannon and I gave you?"

She laughed. "The Pinkerton Agency offered me a job."

"You used it," he affirmed with satisfaction, smiling broadly at the forming scowl on Robbie's face. "We taught her to shoot and evidently she did it effectively."

"Then you actually took part in—"

"Yes, I did," she answered briefly, "and your brother Stuart was just as shocked as you are."

"Well, at least we'll be able to protect you once we get to the ranch, and we'll make the delivery to Crazy Horse."

Devin shook his head. "Tashunca would steal all the horses and supplies from us, but he'll accept the fifty from Marsh as payment for an honorable debt."

"I'm giving him a hundred."

Devin appraised her with a look of admiration. "You're a generous woman."

"Not really. Jamie and I got our land for a few horses. I figured I owed more than that. I'll just need the mares and four of the stallions to start a breeding farm. Robbie, did you have a chance to order six months of supplies for me?"

"I bought a year's supply for you. Everything's waiting for us in Cheyenne."

Far more than supply wagons awaited them in Cheyenne. The sprawling boom town was thronged with nervous, frightened people who jostled against one another's guns as they moved along the crowded streets. Anti-Indian sentiment was a palpable thing on the suspicious faces of the armed bands of men who watched the people dismounting from the train. Marsh shuddered at their look of hatred as she and Devin made their way quietly back to the cattle cars and supervised the unloading of the horses. At the way station they found only a tense Shannon and Lon waiting; all the Flynn and MacKenzie ranch Indians had been forced to flee from the townspeople. That afternoon, the six German immigrants increased their land-purchase money considerably by working tirelessly in unloading the hundred-pound sacks of corn and the great piles of sheepskins. As did everyone else, they too stood watch over the horses all night and most of the next day. Such was the ugly mood of the town, none of the newcomers knew what to expect.

Only the next morning, with Robbie and Colin, did Marsh learn the reasons behind the prevailing fear. At the bank they were told that Crazy Horse had been spotted by an army patrol within five hours riding time from Cheyenne. With him was a band of warriors much larger than his usual number. Leaving only a skeleton contingent to guard the town, the army troops had marched out hoping to entrap the marauder, while most townspeople expected Crazy Horse to attack the city itself. Knowing that the Indian chief had another reason to remain close to Cheyenne gave Marsh a thrill of anticipation, tinged by more than a little fear. At the land office, where they purchased the forty thousand acres, Robbie and Colin were warned not to attempt to reach their ranches. But it was at the telegraph office that Marsh heard what she considered the most alarming news; the telegraph lines had been severed two days earlier; the town was virtually isolated. She failed to note the odd expression on Robbie's face as he read a telegram which had arrived seven days earlier.

"After we deliver the horses, Devin and I will be returning to Cheyenne," he told her outside on the street.

"You can't," she protested, "Devin is the only protection we have."

"After today I imagine you'll be even better protection, Marsh." Then he asked her abruptly, "Why are you really moving to this wilderness?"

She stared at him. "It's my home, mine and Jamie's."

"What in the world are you going to do out there by yourself?"

"I'm going to raise my son and earn a living the same as you do."

"No plans to remarry?"

Damn, damn, damn, she thought grimly and wished this brother-in-law would quit reminding her of Stuart. Aloud, she admitted reluctantly, "I did have some plans when I went back east, but they didn't work out."

He was silent as he helped her mount for the ride back to the way station, but he was looking at her with far more than a casual interest. In his pocket was a telegram from a younger brother he'd not seen for eight years, and its contents were very provocative:

"The (blank) redhead has left me three times in four months of marriage. Stop. Take care of the (blank) woman until I get there and give her the beating she deserves before I drag her home. Stop. Don't tell her I'm on my way or the (blank) hothead will take off again. Stop. Stuart."

As Robbie watched her thread her way expertly among the restless horses, he smiled. Unless his younger brother had developed some unexpected strength of character, he'd have a hard time carrying out either threat with this particular redhead. She was, he remembered with humor, the only woman who had ever made his stubborn, egotistical father into an adoring husband. Stuart, he thought, was going to learn to bite a very hot bullet; winter at the ranch promised to hold more interesting entertainment than blizzard watching.

For her meeting with Crazy Horse, Marsh decided to ride one of the stallions, and without a qualm she chose the one that had sired Marsh Wind. If the arrogant Indian was quixotic enough to want another race, she planned to win. In a flush of bravado, she chose to ride at the head of the wagon train with Devin as her partner there. Deliberately, she refused Colin's suggestion that she wear her guns. Something of the remembered Indian chief reminded her of John Mosby, and she knew that a display of courage would be greater protection. She did jerk a little when, just three hours out of Cheyenne, the wagons were surrounded in a swift charge by a hundred armed and war-painted braves; and she faced a mounted Crazy Horse just fifty feet away on the trail. Signaling the wagon train to stop with her raised hand, she asked Devin to ride forward with her.

Eight feet away from the dark-visaged chief, she breathed slowly to control her pounding heart and spoke quietly. "I've come to pay my debt of honor." Quickly, Devin translated. "And to give you the additional gift of fifty more horses." Again her friend translated. "And to offer you a thousand sheep pelts for your people's moccasins and eight wagon loads of dried corn for their winter food."

When Crazy Horse made no reply, Marsh turned her stallion around and ordered the Indian horses and wagons separated from the rest of the train. As she watched her command carried out, she was aware that the chief had moved his stallion until he was abreast of hers. Out of the corner of a nervous eye, she watched him signal his warriors to surround the designated wagons and horses before he turned to her. Once again, he pulled a feather from his own headdress and placed it firmly in her hatband alongside the other one. Then he spoke some words in a gutteral voice and stroked her hair briefly before he wheeled abruptly away with the small army which followed him in instant obedience. From a hundred feet away he turned and saluted her with his spear as he had done six months earlier. She raised her arm in a return gesture of mutual respect, a little ashamed of the tears which sparkled in her eyes. She knew she would never see him again, but she would remember his war-hardened young face the rest of her life.

Not until camp that night did she learn what his words had meant. Even Devin sounded a little awed when Shannon asked their meaning. "An honored Sioux with red hair," Devin explained to Marsh, "the eagle feather he gave you today elevated you from squaw to shaman. You brought very strong medicine with you, and you will be welcomed by all Sioux people. Did you buy the land?"

She nodded, too emotional to speak.

"I was wrong, Marsh, when I judged you earlier. If you still want me to, I will help you make it into a home for our people. Whether you realize it or not, you're Sioux now as much as I am." Somehow, the thought made her feel humble. She'd met few men she admired as much as she did Crazy Horse and Devin, and the only woman beside Carina she respected without reservation was Winona.

The next morning, Robbie and Devin returned to Cheyenne, and the rest of the party moved toward the mountain trail which led to the great Laramie basin and home. Marsh worked steadily with the men in herding the remaining horses, but she felt so exhausted each night, she longed for an end to the grinding trail. Because the horses had to graze, the miles covered each day were reduced in number, and the time lengthened from two to three weeks and four days beyond. Eight days from home just after the Indian ranch hands had rejoined the train, she awoke with her stomach in upheaval and a half-dreaded, half-hoped-for pregnancy a reality. After only ten minutes up on her horse, she surrendered to the inevitable and climbed aboard one of the wagons. For six miserable days she struggled to maintain the appearance of relaxed comradery. During the final day and a half, sick stomach or not, she joined the others on horseback to keep the horses bunched together in hers and their first experience with a Wyoming snowstorm. When the visibility threatened to drop to zero, every one of the hundred and twenty horses were roped to the wagons and the reins of the wagon horses were allowed to slacken. Marsh learned at first hand the truth of a natural law she'd never had to test in the milder climates of Maryland and Virginia. A horse can always find its way home even when a man cannot. By the time the horses were secured in one of the barns at the ranch, she was too exhausted to do anything but climb wearily into the guest bed in Onawa's home.

The next morning, when Winona came into her room, Marsh had just finished being ill. She was certain the Indian woman guessed her problem, but all Winona talked about was the stupidity of men to allow a tenderfoot woman to do any work on a trail drive. "Now you will have to rest for two days before you can take care of your son, and you will need a tonic to feel better." By the afternoon, Marsh no longer felt nauseated, but she continued to submit to Winona's ministrations. "Better you wait to see your son until you are alone in your own home." Thus, not for two full days of anxious anticipation did she become reacquainted with her baby, who'd been just five months old when she saw him last. He was now thirteen months in age and an altogether different human being. Someone had taught him to say "Mama," but he didn't know this strange woman any better than she knew him. Like two aliens, they moved around each other all that first day, he on all fours crawling around the floor in front of the fire and she walking cautiously behind retrieving one toy or another.

At Jamie's first squall of hunger, Marsh picked her son up and carried him into the kitchen, where she found Nakana, the phlegmatic Indian woman who had been her servant all the preceding winter, already at work. Seated at the table was a plump young girl Marsh estimated to be fourteen.

"Wyeda," Nakana introduced the girl, "help baby. I cook and clean house." Marsh nodded in agreement, remembering that any two-way conversation with Nakana was not only unnecessary, it was useless, because Nakana rarely listened. However, the Indian woman's next observation reminded Marsh sharply of her own position in this isolated community. "No man. You work in barn." Not exactly a complimentary evaluation of her life, Marsh reflected, but it was the literal truth. She had a living to make, and she couldn't let the Flynns or Robbie do her work.

Determined to become reacquainted with her son before she tackled ranch life, Marsh waited until after she tucked him into bed with his leather horse before she donned her sheepskin jacket and walked through the foot-deep snow to the barn. Halfway there, she met Colin walking toward her back door with a coil of rope slung over his arm.

"Hey," he called out to her, "I thought you were supposed to play mama all this week."

"I plan to, but Jamie's asleep now so I thought I'd check on the horses. What's the rope for, Colin?"

"It's a lifeline from your house to the big barn. During a storm in this country you don't take a step outside without following one of these ropes. I've already fixed one between your house and Rob's." Marsh shuddered a little. Last winter she'd been too busy with her baby to leave the house except for brief walks during the days when the sky was clear, but

466

the next three winter months would be the only time she could do any heavy work. By early spring her pregnancy would be too far advanced for anything but book work, so she'd have to learn all the tricks of survival in a Wyoming blizzard during these final days of late fall.

As always when faced with specific goals, Marsh buckled down to meeting them in order of priority. She spent the morning with her independent baby, establishing a working relationship. She agreed that he should go to bed when he was sleepy and eat his food in whatever order he chose. Her only insistence during these morning sessions was that he limit his curiosity to safe areas of the house and pick himself up after a tumble with the minimum of tears. Each night after dinner, in place of the nursery stories she didn't know, she told him about Rake-Star and Marsh Wind, and twice during each story session, Jamie urged her to give him a vigorous horseback ride by crawling on all fours around the room while he screamed the gleeful word "horsie" in her ear. Occasionally during those first two weeks, she worried about her own lack of intellectual accomplishments—she couldn't hum a bit of music, she could identify only one or two of the bugs her son located in the woodpile, and she didn't remember a single Bible story. But on the whole, little Jamie seemed to be content with this strange woman whose low voice never shrilled at him and whose strong arms provided a safe haven. Impatiently, she reminded herself to stop wishing that Jamie was here to teach his son what she could not. "What is, is," she told herself fiercely, "Jamie is dead and Stuart—" Marsh paused as she thought about Stuart. She hadn't had time to learn his strengths; she could only wonder if he might have been able to control his temper enough to have been a good parent.

There was no doubt, though, that she missed both the MacKenzie men when it came to the four hours she spent with Shannon each afternoon learning about the ranch. Stuart and his father had been excellent administrators who seldom did the actual work, whereas she still had to learn not to try to do everything herself. Twice during the first session with Shannon, he reminded her humorously that there were men assigned to do the various jobs all over the twenty-thousand acres of combined MacKenzie-Flynn ranches.

"You don't have to shovel manure here, Marsh; we have a special crew who fertilize the fields in spring," he smiled. "And you don't have to herd the horses yourself. Just tell us how you want your mares assigned to your stallions. I imagine you want only the best for the one you're riding."

She patted the sleek head of the animal and admitted, "He is the finest one of the old MacKenzie line, but out here I want to breed him to the best of your western mares. With MacKenzie mares we'll only get good saddle horses. I want more than that, I want to breed a good cattle horse and maybe even a Wyoming racehorse."

"Like your Marsh Wind?"

"That was just a lucky chance, Shannon. But some of your wild mares might be faster than mine."

"I'll have the men round up the best candidates tomorrow and you can choose. Remember, though, that most horses here are sold as army remounts, and your MacKenzies will earn you good money."

"Earn us good money, Shannon," she corrected him. "I'm part of the whole ranch now. Robbie thought I'd be able to help keep the books. That way I could stay close to home and raise my son." In seven and a half months, she reminded herself sharply, she would have two children to support and an even greater need to work for financial success. Wyoming seemed a more formidable place to her than it had back in the controlled security of Maryland and Virginia.

During the next two weeks, this frontier territory became even more intimidating as winter storms increased in length and ferocity, and Marsh joined the others in a worried vigil for Robbie and Devin, who had not yet returned from Cheyenne. The first time she walked through a curtain of snow on her way to the barn, she clutched the lifeline tenaciously and remembered Jamie's hatred of Wyoming winters. For her the elements of danger only increased the enchantment and challenge of this wilderness and made her impatient to gain enough experience to become a useful partner to the Flynns and Robbie. She didn't enjoy the sensation of being taken care of and coddled. Last night she'd invited the Flynns over for dinner for the express purpose of cheering Onawa, only to find that they had accepted her invitation to do the same thing for her. The evening had been pleasant enough, mainly because Colin and Winona expressed confidence in Robbie's and Devin's ability to find their way home before the trails were closed for the winter.

"Besides, Tamca's with them," Colin declared, "and he's half-horse when it comes to direction."

Even Onawa seemed cheerfully unconcerned and far more eager to talk about politics than she was about her husband. Next month the first territorial legislators would meet in Cheyenne, and Esther Hobart Morris was confident that they would be forced to grant women political equality. Making up only twenty percent of the white population, Wyoming women had become a well-organized and articulate group since the spring of 1869. Although this equality had been one of Marsh's own goals two years earlier, it would prove of relatively little value in eliminating the one glaring lack in her life. She was the most pitiable of all social pariahs—a pregnant married woman without a visible husband—and, unless she wanted to be labeled a scarlet adventuress, she would be forced to reveal the circumstances of her marriage. She would have to tell Robbie at least. Equal rights might allow women to vote, but she was quite certain that the other games men played would not be tolerated on the part of women. Long after the Flynns had gone home, Marsh remained restlessly awake, deciding on her best course of action. By midnight, she had planned her strategy. She would become as indispensable to the operation of this ranch as she had been to the wartime Virginia farm. She hadn't been an object of pity there, and she was determined not to become one here.

Resolutely, the following afternoon, she plunged into the work piled up on the littered desk in the office room of the big barn and concentrated on untangling the haphazard records which had been only partially maintained during the busy months of expansion. The first indications she had of unusual activity were the thunder of horses racing for the barn at full gallop and, minutes later, the excited voice of Shannon Flynn.

"Lon and I rode out this morning to meet Devin and Robbie. They're waiting at your house now. Come on, I'll take you home."

"Thank heaven they're back, Shannon, but you stay here until you thaw out. I can find my own way."

"Rob would skin me alive if I let you go out in this muck alone. I thought we told you last night that nobody goes outside during a storm if they don't have to."

She was about to reply tartly when a blast of wind hurled her back against the barn door as she stepped outside into a world darkened and almost obliterated by whirling snow. It took their combined strengths to struggle the distance to her brightly lit home. Inside the kitchen, they found Nakana warming blankets in front of the stove while Wyeda held Jamie in her arms. Alarmed by the sight of the blankets and the expression on Wyeda's face, Marsh kissed her son briefly and handed Shannon a bottle of brandy to open as she arranged glasses on a tray. In spite of her resolve not to be intimidated by the violent weather, the scene which awaited her in the living room filled her with grim apprehension. Three ghost-like, snow-dusted men were huddled around the inert form of a fourth man stretched out on the divan in front of the fire. Robbie was the first to look up and greet her.

"We found this tenderfoot along the trail, Marsh; we thought he might belong to you."

Underneath the blue skin and frosted eyebrows of the

prostrate man, she recognized her husband. Fortunately for the sensibilities of the three other men present, Marsh was not a woman to scream or panic in an emergency. Ignoring her own pounding heart, she managed to ask one question and give three orders in her parade-ground voice before she reached Stuart's side.

"What's the matter with him, Robbie?"

"He's frostbitten and asleep on his feet. We've been traveling steadily for the last day and night."

"Nakana, get those blankets in here. Shannon, pour everyone some brandy, and Lon, help me get the rest of his clothes off."

By the time the blankets arrived, the sodden clothes were heaped on the floor and she was busy massaging Stuart's icy legs while Lon was forcing brandy past his blue lips. Gratefully, she smiled briefly at Robbie and Devin as they set their empty glasses down and quietly left for their own homes and families. By the time Shannon and Lon left an hour later, Stuart had swallowed two glasses of brandy and his arms and legs had been pounded and slapped into some semblance of normal circulation before the soundly sleeping man had been wrapped in blankets and tucked into bed. Only then did Marsh allow her emotions to surface. Picking her son up from his infant chair in the kitchen, she clutched him to her and whirled joyfully around the room.

"He's come. Oh, Jamie, he's come and, if we're lucky, oh, baby, if we're lucky, maybe he'll stay. But just for tonight, sweetheart, we have to be very quiet. We don't want him to wake up until—" Reality crashed down on her jubilant mood like a ton of snow sliding from a rooftop, and she finished the sentence silently, "Until he finds out about you and Crazy Horse and the money and this ranch." The list of her omissions suddenly seemed endless and unforgivable, especially to a proud, tinder tempered man like Stuart.

Disturbed throughout the night by her own guilty conscience and by the unaccustomed mutterings and heavy muscular jerks coming from her bedfellow, Marsh's own temper was defensively frayed by morning. And, as luck would have it—she was convinced that hers had been ruled by a heartlessly capricious fate lately—Jamie awoke with an outraged howl seconds before she could clamber out of bed, pick up his leather horse and shove it back into his hand. He went peacefully back to sleep with the unaware innocence of infancy while she tiptoed around the room, pulling on her fur-lined robe and sheepskin boots and praying that Stuart hadn't been awakened. As quickly as she could, she lit the bedroom fire and fled to the living room to start the one there and to locate Stuart's luggage. There wasn't any—not a suitcase, bedroll or carpetbag. She dreaded taking him the clothes that Jamie had left here two years earlier, but there was nothing else to do. Stuart's own clothing was still dripping wet in the kitchen. Rummaging through the boxes and luggage stored in an unused bedroom, she located a pair of wool pants, worn sheepskin boots, a sweater, and a set of heavy winter underwear. Her hands were stiff with cold when she finally gave up the search for stockings and returned to her own bedroom where a blanket-clad Stuart was standing over Jamie's bed, his face a thundercloud of repressed fury.

"Who the hell is this?" he rasped in what he thought was a whisper.

Her temper flaring at his slighting reference to her son, she snapped, "He's my son, who else would he be?" Momentarily, the anger in his eyes turned to questioning surprise until his half awake mind calculated the months. Marsh's voice hardened as she watched his blue eyes regain their anger. "No, he's not your son, Stuart, yours won't be here for another seven months. That one is your brother. But if you want to argue about him, get these clothes on and come to the living room. I'd just as soon he doesn't hear us scream at each other." Without waiting for a reply, she grabbed her brush from the dresser and ran from the room. She had a pot of hot coffee waiting for him on the dining room table when he joined her a few minutes later. Seating himself stiffly opposite her, he finished two cups of coffee and the platter of ham and eggs a silent Nakana served him before he deigned to speak to his wife.

"It would serve you right," he began in the measured, reasonable tones Marsh hated, "if I walked out of here now and left you alone to finish ruining your life."

Her lip curled in contempt. "You wouldn't live long enough to walk past the first Indian village."

Calmly ignoring her jibe, he continued his castigating evaluation of her character. "You have lied to me and tricked me since the first time we met. We'll forget about the ancient history, it's what you've done to me since our marriage that I resent. You lied about wanting to marry me, you manipulated the money to suit yourself, and you left me three times without an explanation. This last time you walked out without telling me anything about some damned Indian you owed horses to or anything about that child in there. Now, I want to know why."

"I couldn't tell you about Jamie until he was safe."

"Is that his name?"

"Of course it is."

"It would be. Why didn't you tell me about him?"

"If I had, you'd have beat the record for running the country mile to avoid marrying me, and I couldn't trust you not to tell Janet about him."

"What did you plan to do with him? Pretend he was mine at some future date or just dump him on me as another of your unpleasant surprises?"

Marsh was tempted to fling the pot of coffee at him. "I'm not dumping a damn thing on you. I can and will support my own children, and you can get back to your nice little life in Virginia. If you'll excuse me, Stuart," she rose abruptly and started to leave the table, "I'll get on with my life and let you get on with yours."

Both his voice and his scowl were menacing. "You'll sit

down and finish this discussion or I'll tie you down. I've put up with your arrogant disobedience for the last time."

More out of curiosity than fear, she studied her husband's face and wondered if he really had the courage to try physically restraining her. Her response as she resumed her seat was a flippant piece of impudence, "My, my, that sounds like a threat, Stuart. Did you also plan to put a gag over my mouth, or am I going to be allowed to take part in your 'discussion'?"

"You're going to take a big part in it, Marsh. Right now, you're going to tell me just how you got mixed up with an Indian."

"He beat me in a horse race and I lost the bet."

"Rob said he was of some importance around here."

"You might say that. His name is Chief Tashunca-Uitco. He's known as Crazy Horse to all the settlers. Had I not delivered those horses, both of your brothers could have been killed."

"Why didn't you ask me to help you?"

"Because you would have told your army friends all about it. And those ninnies would have tried to set a trap. There's no way they could have ambushed that Indian on his own home ground."

"So you bribed him by giving him double the number of horses."

"I gave him the horses because I believe he's right and that the settlers and soldiers are wrong. I just paid my debt in my own way."

"Your ways have gotten you into nothing but trouble all your life, and now I'm stuck with getting you out."

"The only thing you're stuck with, Stuart MacKenzie, is getting yourself out of here. If you're finished with your breakfast, I'll take you over to your brother's house and you can spend the winter with him. If Devin doesn't hate you by spring, he can take you to Cheyenne. If it hadn't been for him, neither you nor Robbie would have made it safely to the

ranch this time. But if Devin refuses to take you out, you'll
just have to wait until I can."

"Just how could you get me out?"

"Thanks to Crazy Horse, I'm under Sioux protection. It's
too bad you made this trip for nothing but a long, cold
winter."

"Your baby's crying."

"I hear him."

"Aren't you going to see what he wants?"

"I know what he wants. He dropped his horse again."

"Horse?"

"His animal sign. He sleeps with it." She moved restlessly;
Jamie's screams of frustration were making her nervous.
Ordinarily, she'd have rushed in to take care of her son, but
she was too angry at her husband to give him the satisfaction
of seeing her act like a doting mother.

When she didn't stir, Stuart exploded, "My God, woman,
don't you have any human feelings at all? If you won't help
him, I will." Like some medieval knight on an errand of
mercy, he stood up, knocking the chair over with his abruptness,
and strode toward the bedroom. With some trepidation, Marsh
remained seated and listened to the mantle clock tick the
minutes off until her husband returned, carrying an obviously wet
infant nappy.

"Where do I put this?"

"I'll take it."

"Just tell me where."

"The back porch."

After completing his self-assigned task, he came back to
the table, picked up his chair, and poured himself another cup
of coffee.

"He's a good-looking boy."

"I imagine you looked the same when you were a baby."

"Were you planning on raising him alone?"

"I am now."

"What were you going to use for money? I checked your

bank account in Cheyenne. Didn't you think that my father would have wanted him to share equally with the rest of us?''

"He'll have enough and this ranch will support us. You needn't worry about sending us money.''

"What about my child?''

"I'll support him, too. As soon as you get back to Virginia, you can divorce me for desertion and marry some woman who'll bear you a houseful of little Stuart MacKenzies. This one is mine.''

"Is that a fact? What makes you think you can handle a Stuart MacKenzie, young or old?''

"Maybe I'll get lucky. Maybe he'll have a sense of humor like his Uncle Robbie.''

"More likely he'll inherit your temper. I thought you told me that this place was just a shell. It looks finished to me.''

"It is. I hired someone to finish the interior two summers ago.''

"You moved back here to have your child alone in an unfinished house?''

"I wasn't alone. I have friends.''

"Then why did you leave here?''

"I went back east to make sure that my son's life would be safe. And I don't care what you think about my methods, Stuart, I did what I had to. You do what you like. Right now, I have to take care of Jamie. But you'd better not try going to Robbie's without me. It's easy to get lost in a blizzard.'' With this parting advice, she returned to her bedroom, dressed herself in her working clothes, and Jamie in his warm sheepskin coveralls. Stuart was waiting for her just outside the door.

"I thought you'd try to do something crazy again, like escaping through the window.''

She glared at him as he took Jamie from her arms and guided her back into the living room. "You get his breakfast,'' he told her, "I'll take care of him. That way I can be sure that you won't leave again.''

Her jaws were clamped shut as she strode into the kitchen to find Nakana stirring the oatmeal mush, and she held her temper at the Indian woman's words. "Man good for boy. Other one, too." Her pregnancy, Marsh reflected bitterly, had been about as secret as a town crier's broadcast. Telling Wyeda to take the baby his breakfast, Marsh grabbed her heavy jacket and was four steps along the lifeline to the barn when the amused voice of Robbie stopped her.

"I was afraid you and Stu might be having an argument, so I came over to referee. How is the big bairn this morning?"

"I've seen wild boars with better tempers."

"He was sporting a foul mood all along the trail. What in the world did you do to make him that angry?"

Marsh grinned at her brother-in-law as he helped her through the back door. "I neglected to tell him about Crazy Horse and Jamie. And I've just informed him that he's to become a father himself next spring."

Robbie burst into laughter. "So you just picked up and left him without any explanation. I think maybe you've earned a few of those spankings he was threatening to administer."

"You won't be laughing when he moves in with you for the winter."

"You're sure right. I'd sooner bed down with a wounded grizzly. Stu's disposition never was his greatest charm. Let's go in and give him these clothes I brought over. Maybe a little brotherly chat will soothe the big booby."

But the first brotherly chat was not with Stuart, it was a joyous reunion between the oldest and youngest of the MacKenzie brothers.

"Rob—bie," screamed Jamie and reached his chubby arms up with a happy squeal as the sandy-haired man picked him up and swung him into the air.

"Marsh, Onawa and I will take any foals you drop beginning with this one. Our house seems empty without him. Good morning, Stu, you look like you survived with all your toes intact. That's the worst of getting caught in a blizzard like the one that almost swamped us.''

"We'd never have been caught in that damned storm if what's-his-name hadn't insisted on visiting those damned Indian villages along the way.''

Robbie looked at his younger brother in amusement. "Stu, I'll never understand how you got to be a major in the army. You can't even remember peoples' names—you and our father.''

Stuart was sourly defensive. "I can remember the names of the important ones.''

Outraged by the implication that Devin was not important, Marsh exploded, "Devin Flynn is the most essential man on this ranch and in Wyoming right now. He keeps more people alive than anyone else.''

"Marsh is right, Stu. Devin's been our goodwill ambassador with all the Sioux tribes around here. We couldn't have survived without him. Now, of course, we have our own special shaman in residence.''

"You've got some dirty Indian witch doctor living on the ranch?''

His whole body shaking with laughter, Rob warned his brother, "I don't think I'd call this particular shaman either a dirty Indian or a witch.''

"I have no intention of even speaking to him. You were about to tell me why what's-his-name Flynn chose this particular time to visit his friends.''

Rob hesitated and looked toward Marsh. She shrugged. "Tell him, Robbie, he might as well hear everything.''

"In addition to the horses and food Marsh gave the Indians, she also bought a huge tract of land for them. It's their native land, but our government won't admit that Indians own anything. So the politicians are busy selling off the land to any white man with the dollars to pay for it. Wyoming land sales weren't supposed to begin until next year, but our territorial leaders jumped the gun. Because Indians can't buy land, this particular piece is in the Flynn-MacKenzie names, and Devin had to explain that circumstance to the tribes. But now, thanks to Marsh, some of the Sioux will be spared the indignity of being shoved into a barren reservation when this bloody war is over."

Stuart's eyes were speculative as he looked at his wife. "I take it our resident shaman has red hair."

"Don't let that red hair fool you, brother; she's an honored Sioux, and none of us will take it lightly if you treat her with anything less than respect."

Uncomfortable about Robbie's implied threat, Marsh changed the subject hastily. "Stuart, I've been wondering why you didn't bring any luggage with you. Didn't you check the distances you'd have to travel?"

Rob was the one who answered her question. "The pack animal carrying Stu's luggage was carried over the cliff in a snow slide, and the heroic major was almost trapped himself trying to rescue the animal."

"That accounts for all the bruises," Marsh nodded in understanding. "I didn't think they looked like freeze burns. I'm sorry that you had such a rough trip for nothing."

Stuart's eyes flashed with an angry blue fire. "Oh, I wouldn't say it was for nothing. I've learned that you deceived me in every way you could and that you're as reckless as an idiot and a spendthrift to boot. On an impulsive whim you've squandered half of your son's inheritance, and it'll take years to earn it back in this desolate wilderness."

"That's enough, Stu," Rob slashed across his brother's tirade, "what Marsh did, she did for all of us. And you're dead wrong about Jamie's inheritance; we'll take care of him and we'll take care of his mother, too. She has enough troubles without listening to your insults. I think we'd better go."

"I'm not going anyplace."

"Yes, you are. You're spending the winter with Onawa and me."

"I'm spending the winter right here with my wife. She's going to have my child, and I mean to keep her from killing herself by racing some damned Indian or other. When the baby's old enough to travel, we're going home to Virginia."

Smothered by the idea of having her life arranged without being consulted, Marsh sputtered in fury, "This is my home and this is where I stay, Stuart MacKenzie."

"This is one of our homes, Marsh MacKenzie," her husband yelled back. "If I can spend this winter here in a climate I hate, you can spend the next one in Virginia. After that we'll divide our time between the two. I've already hired a manager for the Virginia property and next summer we'll hire one for this place."

"I suppose you bought the big house."

"Yes, I did."

"I hate that house."

"I'm not exactly enthralled with this one."

By clearing his throat noisily several times, Rob finally succeeded in interrupting. "You two can compare your homes some other time. What I want to know now, Stu, are your plans for our little brother, the baby who's already here. Remember?"

"Jamie doesn't need grown men for brothers. What he needs is a father; and since his mother is my wife, I'm going to be that father."

"Aren't you forgetting, brother, that I have as much claim on him as you do? And somehow, I can't see you in the role of a benevolent stepfather to an offspring of James MacKenzie. You always claimed you hated our father."

"I didn't hate him, I just knew him better than you and Craig did. But whether I like the idea or not, it looks like his son is another part of my inheritance from him."

Marsh sucked in her breath with a resentment that almost strangled her. Removing her disputed son from Robbie's arms, she turned toward the two men and sputtered, "Jamie is not a part of anyone's inheritance, and he doesn't need an unwilling stepfather any more than I did. Nor, Stuart MacKenzie, am I a part of your father's leavings that you have to be burdened with. Thanks for trying, Robbie, but it's no use. If you're headed for the barn, I'd like to go with you and get to work. Wyeda can take care of my son."

"If you'd learn to listen, Marsh," Stuart snapped back at her, "instead of jumping to the wrong conclusions about me, you'd have heard that I used the word father, not stepfather. My experience with a stepparent was as bad as yours because Helen Ryder was as rotten as her daughter. As for work, you're not going to do one damn piece of heavy labor for the next year. I want our second son to be as healthy as this first one is. And you, Rob, can love Jamie just as much as your nephew. Right now, I'd appreciate it if you'd get the hell back to your nice, domesticated wife while I concentrate on taming this independent hellion I married."

Rob was laughing as he turned to leave. "Onawa would kill you for those unkind words, Stu. For two years my wife has been as much a social rebel as yours. Wait until you read the letter those two sent to every white woman in the Wyoming territory. Thanks to them and some fire-eating suffragette, we're going to be the only men in the union voted down by our own women. Marsh, I'll send Shannon over tomorrow with all the company records, and you and Stu can fight over who's going to keep the books." Just before he opened the door, he turned for one last attempt at peacemaking. "I almost forgot. Winona sent you a message. She said to remind both of you that eagles mate for life and that both of them defend the nest. Come to think of it, she's right. I hope you two can settle your differences and get on with the business of being happy."

The house was eerily silent for the hour after Rob's departure. In the kitchen where she fled, Marsh found Nakana and Wyeda wrapping themselves in hooded leather capes, about to leave through the rear door. "We go home three, four days," the older Indian informed her mistress, "you no spoil food. We come back maybe."

Nonplussed by the prospect of being alone with a disapproving husband, Marsh checked the hind quarter of venison roasting aromatically in the huge stone fireplace and the pot of thick soup simmering on the iron range. She tucked Jamie into his chair and sat down disconsolately opposite him. It depressed her that the primitive people of the wilderness were acting in a more civilized fashion than she and her husband. Shrugging off an unaccustomed sense of failure, she checked the progress of the soup and set the kitchen table before returning to the living room to summon Stuart. He was not there nor in her bedroom. Her heart sank; he'd gone with Robbie after all. She went back to the kitchen with a dull ache of futility and stopped abruptly inside the door. In the middle of the room stood her missing, unpredictable husband, his coat dusted with snow and his arms loaded with wood.

"I moved Jamie's bed into the room next to ours, and I just went outside to see if his stove was drawing properly."

"You shouldn't have gone outside without a lifeline."

"I just strung one from our front porch to the rear one. I sure didn't want to freeze to death in case a snow drift blocked one entrance. You finish getting lunch while I bring in enough wood to last for two or three days. Don't just stand there, woman. I'm hungry and I'm sure Jamie is, too."

He was, she reflected, being annoyingly efficient, conciliatory, and reasonable, just as if he didn't owe her a dozen apologies for three hours of insults. She felt the same frustration she'd often experienced with his father. As soon as she became angry enough to finish the battles they began, MacKenzie men settled down to a peaceful coexistence as if they hadn't just threatened to commit mayhem on her delicate person. But very peaceful coexistence was exactly what Stuart had in mind. During lunch, he good-naturedly forced her to drink her milk and cheerfully fed Jamie, restraining the lively little boy from indulging in his favorite game of throwing food. After he helped clear the table, he picked Jamie up and announced, "Nap time" as if he'd been doing it for months. "You too, mama," he added, "we'll do the dishes later."

"I'm not sleepy," she muttered.

"Neither am I," he responded promptly.

She felt a dull flush mount her cheek and fumed silently, He's accused me of being a liar which I wasn't really, a trickster when he's been a worse one, and a spendthrift because I was generous. He hasn't even kissed me, yet he expects me to go to bed with him willingly. I'll be damned if I will.

As if in answer to her mute defiance, his arm tightened around her as he propelled her toward the bedroom. "We can have that fight you're spoiling for later. Right now, we're going to have our last reunion. If you ever try to leave me again, you won't be able to sit a horse for a month. Kiss your son and I'll put him to bed while you get those damned britches and boots off."

Stubbornly, she remained motionless on the edge of the bed, glaring at him through the open door of the adjoining room. Her anger slipped a notch or two as she watched him change another wet diaper and heard him say, "That'll be enough of that, son. There's a better way to do it; I'll show you after your nap."

In spite of her resolve not to obey him like a mindless ninny, she giggled and noted that Jamie made no objection to having this strange man put him to bed in a strange room. He actually seemed to respond to Stuart's next words. "And there'll be no more dropping your horsey. He's tethered to your bed now."

She was starting to remove her boots when Stuart closed the door firmly and sat down alongside her to remove his own. "I'm glad my father hated the cold as much as I do and insisted on stoves in every room," he said, and then added casually, "Do you have any sentimental objections to my wearing his clothes? They fit me better than Rob's."

She shook her head, wondering what had happened to the stiff-necked man she'd married. His next words startled her still further.

"In the note you left on the pillow, you said you loved me. Is that the truth or just an easy way to let me down?"

"Do you really think I'd have put up with you for the last five months if I didn't?"

"I've put up with a thing or two myself, Mrs. MacKenzie, while you kept me dangling."

"You've done a bit of dangling yourself."

He grinned at her. "How else was I going to make a red-haired whirlwind notice a mere Yankee major when she had a southern general dancing attendance on her?" Not exactly an apology, but Marsh knew it was the only one forthcoming; and even it was weakened by the addition of still another complaint. "For a woman supposedly in love, that was a very lukewarm reception you gave me last night. I was mad as hell and half frozen, but when you touched me, I wanted you. And you just ignored me."

She laughed helplessly. "I didn't ignore you and I was perfectly aware of that moment when your circulation returned to normal. But by that time you'd had so much brandy, you'd forgotten that Lon and Shannon were helping me pound you back to life. As it was, I hope Robbie remembered to tell them we were married."

"Well, you sure didn't act very married later on when I woke up and tried to kiss you. All you did was mutter something about having to leave me."

"I had some pretty bad dreams last night."

"Not very flattering dreams to have about a husband who'd just risked his life to find you."

"I was afraid you'd be furious when you found out about Jamie."

"I wasn't furious about him, just about your lack of trust.

And now I find you didn't even trust me enough to say that you loved me."

"Well, at least I had the courage to tell you in a letter. So far, you've never told me how you felt."

He stared at her in amazement. "You can't possibly have any doubts about my loving you. Good lord, woman, what do you think has been wrong with me when I made a fool of myself every time I got close to you during the past five years? I'll admit that I didn't want to fall in love with a sharp-tongued, arrogant redhead who still has no intention of obeying a thing I tell her to do. But I did fall in love with you, so you're stuck with me."

It was a ridiculous declaration of love, she thought happily, and completely typical of the sensitive, thin-skinned, argumentative man who, in the course of one day, had forgiven her, adopted her son, and survived the shock of learning about his own impending fatherhood. Her body chemistry was rioting as she shrugged off the robe she'd just donned, climbed impudently into bed, and extended him an impish invitation. "Since you've finally admitted that I mean more to you than a roll in the hay, would you consider a snow country substitute?"

Grinning as he watched his jaybird naked wife, Stuart peeled off his long underwear and joined her in bed, enfolding her warm body tightly in his arms. "This is how I dreamed of finding you," he muttered thickly as he settled down to the business of adjusting her sinuously moving hips to his own throbbing body.

Sure of her hold over this man for the first time, Marsh nibbled at his ear and murmured huskily, "Obviously, I've had a few dreams about you, too." It was the longest nap Jamie MacKenzie ever took, and both grateful parents made sure that he was forever included in the growing love that would unite this turbulent family.

27 million Americans can't read a bedtime story to a child.

It's because 27 million adults in this country simply can't read.

Functional illiteracy has reached one out of five Americans. It robs them of even the simplest of human pleasures, like reading a fairy tale to a child.

You can change all this by joining the fight against illiteracy.

Call the Coalition for Literacy at toll-free **1-800-228-8813** and volunteer.

Volunteer Against Illiteracy. The only degree you need is a degree of caring.

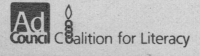

Ad Council   Coalition for Literacy

Warner Books is proud to be an active supporter of the Coalition for Literacy.